SELECTED AMAZON READER REVIEWS
FOR EARLIER FICTIONAL WORKS:

"Reading Tom Corbett's work will have you impressed and awed by his superb literary skills . . . the book is so engaging and captivating that one can only wish to read more from this author. *Ordinary Obsessions* will have you engrossed . . . as the plot is perfectly executed, and the story line flows well."

Aaron

"The author honestly does a wonderful job of making the reader relate to each character and fall absolutely head over heals for each one and their journey through the book! With politics, power, religion, family drama, romance, and cultural struggle, this book exceeds expectations. I look forward to more by this author and cannot wait for the next gem he writes."

Veronica White

"Fast moving political drama that will keep you turning the pages. I do not read a lot of political drama novels, but I could not put this one down. Ordinary Obsessions by Tom Corbett is engaging . . . it pulls you in with the emotions of the characters."

Karen A.

"The author's writing style flows naturally and . . . the story develops with perfect pace. There is not one thing I would change about it."

M.C.

“This book is inspirational as it relates to knowing ourselves better, understanding the world we want, and more so the things that most of us would love to do in life. Corbett’s polished writing style alone will get you hooked but his sense of humor and passion for writing will keep you reading.”

Trizah Kelvin

“The author’s writing style is so unique that I love to read his works. I get lost among the pages so easily.”

Carleen Makivich

“I . . . have always been impressed with his talents . . . and found myself drawn into each character’s struggles and triumphs.”

Stacy E. Vance

“An awesome read! Five out of five stars!”

J. Lantin

“An utterly compelling narrative of two disparate families separated by culture and experiences who come together by circumstances and serendipity.”

Amazon Customer

“It is easy to understand why this book comes so highly acclaimed. And the author’s background as a professor of social sciences really comes into play . . . he has masterly shared the plight of two families who could not look more different.”

Erin P

"Tom Corbett's *Palpable Passions* is the perfect combination of fact and fiction as it educates its readers about current events in our world today."

Lillie S

"The rhythm of the words attracted my attention and pulled me to the end. When I was done reading, I felt I had learned something new. Once you start reading, it is very hard to put down."

Jengel 106

"*Palpable Passions* is truly a great read that will leave you feeling empowered and determined to make a difference in the world in your own way. *Highly recommend* everyone pick this up."

Kimmy 4077

Five stars because of the twists and turns and shocking moments that left me speechless. I was really thrilled with the constant fast pace that left me engaged for several nights.

Ivana S.

Can Tom Corbett tell a story? You bet!

Florence Chavez

OTHER BOOKS BY THE AUTHOR

Evidence-Based Policymaking: Envisioning a New Era of Theory, Research and Practice (2nd Ed.) with Karen Bogenschneider (Taylor and Francis Publishing, 2021)

It Seemed Like a Good Idea at the Time (Hancock Press, 2020)

Ordinary Obsessions (Papertown Press, 2019)

Casual Choices (Hancock Press, 2019)

Confessions of an Accidental Scholar (Hancock Press, 2018)

Confessions of a Clueless Rebel (Hancock Press, 2018)

Confessions of a Wayward Academic (Hancock Press, 2018)

Palpable Passions (Papertown Press, 2017)

Return to the Other Side of the World with Mary Jo Clark, Michael Simmonds, Katherine Sohn, and Hayward Turrentine (Strategic Press, 2013)

The Other Side of the World with Mary Jo Cark, Michael Simonds, and Hayward Turrentine (Strategic Press, 2011)

Policy into Action with Mary Clare Lennon (Urban Institute Press, 2003)

FELICITOUS FATES

by:TOM CORBETT

Felicitous Fates

Published in the United States of America

ISBN *hardcover: 9781948000789*
ISBN *softcover: 9781948000796*

"You can't say civilization isn't advancing.
In every war, they kill you in a new way."

—Will Rogers

"The world as we know it . . . yields but one ending:
death, disintegration, dismemberment,
and the crucifixion of our heart.
With the passing of the forms that we have loved."

—Joseph Campbell

"One child, one teacher, one pen,
and one book can change the world."

—Mahala Yousafzai

"You use a glass mirror to see your face,
you use works of art to see your soul."

—George Bernard Shaw

"We die. That may be the meaning of life. But we do language.
That may be the measure of our lives."

—Toni Morrison

CONTENTS

PREFACE

Felicitous Fates is the third volume of a trilogy about Masoud and the Crawford families. The patriarch of the Masoud family, Pamir, was a physician who trained in England before returning to Afghanistan to aid his homeland and raise his children. Pamir's wife, Madeena, was a mathematician who taught at university level in the pre-Taliban era. We tend to forget that this beleaguered country once had a substantial secular population.

The Masouds had three children: a son, Majeed, and two daughters, Deena and Azita. The youngest, Azita, was passionate about following in her father's footsteps despite the obstacles imposed by a totalitarian religious regime. In the first volume, we picked up the Masoud's story during the height of Taliban rule, but prior to Osama Bin Laden's 9/11 attack on the United States. The Masouds were determined to escape Kabul and the oppressive rule under which they felt captive. The family's goal was to flee to the area still held by the Northern Alliance or *Shura Nazar*, a group of tribal clans who bravely fought the Soviet invaders in the 1980s, and who are now fiercely opposed to Taliban rule. This northern area in Afghanistan is where Pamir was born and raised. It is home to him, a place where he hopes to find comfort and safety in troubled times, and where his children might pursue their dreams.

The Crawford clan is headed by Charles Crawford, Sr., who was born in Poland just as Europe spiraled into World War II. Charles was spirited to the United States after his father, a leader in the anti-communist and exiled Polish government, was killed by Stalin at the end of the war when he returned to establish a new government. The fatherless boy grew up determined to accrue personal power and great wealth, part of which he obtained through a calculated marriage to Mary Kelly, a rich Catholic socialite from Philadelphia. Charles and Mary have four children: Charles Junior (Chuck), the oldest (and married to Beverly), followed by twins, Christopher (Chris) and Kristen (Kay), and their youngest daughter, Katerina (Kat). The Crawford family members know extraordinary comfort and privilege in Chicago but are gripped by serious internal divisions that eventually mushroomed into outright rebellion.

Other prominent characters include Abdul Zubair, an old family friend who helps the Masouds escape from the control of the Taliban, and Abdul's son, Ahmad who had fallen in love with Azita at an early age. Richard (Ricky) and his sister Juliana (Jules) Jackson are unlikely childhood friends of Chris. Ricky and Jules are black and from very modest means, growing up in a tough Chicago neighborhood just west of the Loop. Chris and Ricky bonded at a high school summer basketball camp and remained the best of friends throughout adulthood. The Jackson home provided a milieu of love he never experienced with his own family. Chris and Jules enjoyed a long on and off romantic relationship over the years.

Karen Fisher is Chris's assistant in his international service organization. From a working-class British family, Karen is a tough, yet perceptive, professional partner who also happens to be a lesbian. Amar Singh is an Indian-born doctor whose struggle to become a physician was made more difficult by her conservative family who wished little more than a good marriage for her.

Chris's twin sister, Kay, is a talented trauma surgeon who earned her medical expertise by attaching herself to the emergency room of a Chicago public hospital, partly out of dedication and partly to spite her father by working for the public good, something she knew her father would never understand. Kay married James (Jamie) Whitehead, a British Military doctor whom she met in Afghanistan.

The narrative of *Palpable Passions* traces challenges and struggles in both the Masoud and Crawford families. With the help of her biological parents, Azita violated the strict rules governing the proper behavior of Muslim girls. She stubbornly insisted on being educated at home by her mother and on helping her father with his medical work, sins that will no longer be tolerated by the Taliban as she approaches puberty. Azita will then be expected to become a servile and obedient woman as Taliban orthodoxy dictates. After Azita is almost killed by the religious (or morals) police while she is under Majeed's protection, Majeed is determined to fight these oppressors. The Masouds decide to escape Kabul and the Taliban when Majeeb is about to be forced into military service for a system he abhors. Under false pretenses, the Masoud family makes a dangerous escape to the Northern Alliance.

Following the sudden and tragic suicide of Chuck Crawford, who had been the forced heir apparent to the Crawford dynasty, much reflection takes place among the remaining Crawford offspring who come to reject their father's obsession with right-wing causes. Christopher, a Rhodes scholar with a doctorate from Oxford, uses his wealth and connections to develop an international service organization.

Chris is devoted to helping the world's most vulnerable people and is most gratified that his father dismisses these ambitions as soft and ridiculous. Chris makes his home in London and Oxford, England.

Kay has also rejected her father's ideals by her choice of medical specialties. She decides to escape the family in Chicago by joining Chris's international organization and manipulates her initial assignment in Pakistan to relocate to Afghanistan, an extremely dangerous site at that time. There, she becomes friends with Dr. Amar Singh and the two risk all to help those desperately holding out against the Taliban. Chris is outraged when he discovers that his sister defied him and joined Amar Singh in the conflict torn and dangerous country. Frantic, he travels to Afghanistan to remove Kay from harm's way.

The Masoud and Crawford families connect in this desperate and conflicted part of the world. Representing radically different backgrounds, they find much in common. However, fate, as it so often does, intrudes in the most disturbing ways. Majeeb Masoud dies fighting for the Northern Alliance. Pamir and Madeena Masoud are murdered by the Taliban in the tumultuous days following 9/11. Kay stays in Afghanistan with Jamie Whitehead, and Chris finally loses his heart to Amar Singh.

Moved by the intelligence and drive of young Azita, Chris and Amar bring her to England where she can receive the education about which she has always dreamed but did not think possible. After some time, Deena (now living with Karen as loving partners, joins Azita, Chris and Amar in their international work. Palpable Passions ends with Azita Masoud finishing her premedicine studies at Oxford University and giving a University-wide talk about the obstacles she overcame to pursue her passion.

In the second volume, *Ordinary Obsessions*, the timeline moves forward to the run-up to the 2016 presidential election. By this time, the roles and situations of the main characters have changed. Azita Masoud is well into her medical studies at Oxford and is thinking hard about her future as her medical degree approaches. Her relationship with Benjamin Kaplan floundered given his family's reservations about her religious and cultural background. Moreover, she feels increasing reluctance to being swept into a medical research and academic career that might keep her from her homeland and thus following closely in her deceased father's footsteps. Deena had advanced her education but remains working on education opportunities related to Afghan girls. Strains begin to develop in her relationship with Karen.

Charles Crawford Senior has been removed as head of the family financial empire. At first bitter, he soon turns his energies and resources toward advancing his long-espoused hard-right political agenda, including supporting, though with some reluctance, the candidacy of Donald Trump. As this hard- right agenda appears to gain further traction, Kat Crawford, now titular head of the Crawford empire, lures her brother back to the States, where Azita will do her medical internship in Madison Wisconsin at the University's Children's Hospital. By this time, he is mainly ensconced in the academy at Oxford University, writing books and still consulting with the ISO. Reluctantly returning to the States, Chris heads up a team whose mission is to tease out the reach of suspicious political activities designed to manipulate the election. His wife, Amar, reluctantly agrees to what is supposed to be a temporary exile back to America.

Karen Fisher has assumed day-to-day responsibility for running ISO, the service organization Chris founded. Ricky Jackson, who had left the financial world in Chicago to help her, returns to help Kat run the Crawford empire after the two of them marry. Karen, meanwhile, is gradually building up the management staff of ISO with an international team of talented people including Carlotta Ciganda from Spain and Atle Bergstrom from Norway.

Throughout *Ordinary Obsessions,* the characters struggle with issues related to their professional roles, personal relationships, and their futures. Chris and Amar are concerned that Azita will return permanently to Afghanistan, particularly after she meets a boyhood friend, Ahmad (Abdul's son), as her relationship with Ben ended very badly, with his suicide. Kay finds that domestic life and wife and mother leave her unsatisfied and she takes up with Karen after she and Deena had grown apart. Not surprisingly, Deena gets more involved in educational issues for girls, while her bond with her sister, never totally smooth, finally begins to strengthen. Azita and Deena form connections with Bahiri and Ferhana Gupta, two doctors who have picked up the practice once run by Pamir and with Archie and Agnes Singletary, who are managing the Panjshir Valley site. The pull to remain connected with their homeland is strong.

Yet, danger is real and ever present. Kat fears she narrowly escaped an attempt on her life. Deena is shot by an assassin and nearly killed during a visit by her and Azita to Pamir's historic family village. And Beverly, who apparently remained close to her father-in-law, Charles Senior, used her feigned relationship with her father-in-law as an opportunity to spy on him for Kat and Chris. Beverly was found dead after Christmas 2016, having fallen from her penthouse balcony. No one can tell if it was an accident, suicide, or homicide. Tensions come to a boil at her memorial service when the Patriarch, who finally realizes that his son will never join him, baits Chris into attacking him in this public venue. Charles Senior has Julianna Jackson, Chris's former lover and long-time friend who is now a network star reporter, banned from the memorial. She has been reporting unfavorably on the Patriarch's activities and those of his uber-wealthy allies. Then, in front of Amar, the father taunts his son that Jules has remained Chris's lover. Chris attack's his father, leading Ricky to break his best friend's nose as a security guard for Charles Senior drew a weapon to strike Chris down, thus averting a greater tragedy.

Trump's surprise election changes everything. Kat and Chris realize that the right-wing insurgency in America is on the verge of an ultimate triumph. They feel compelled to initiate a longer-term oppositional initiative to the decades-long effort to redefine American politics in a conservative direction including, as demographics threaten Republican political hegemony, subverting American democracy. Chris and his family return to England, but he will remain involved with his younger sister to thwart a growing international agenda to impose oligarchic control over the major countries around the world. The Putin-Trump conspiracy has ever widening implications.

At the same time, Chris works out a deal with his colleagues at Oxford, particularly Sir Charles Howard and Professor Shahed Ali-Hussein, to establish an international initiative to advance the cause of Muslim women. He anticipates that this will induce Azita and Deena to remain connected to England and ISO, which will partner with this initiative. He and Amar know that this will not keep these two young women whom they dearly love out of harm's way completely, but it will help to do so, or so they hope. The volume ends with Azita completing her internship and becoming engaged to Ahmad.

The Crawford clan prepares to return to England though realizing that this will not be a return to domestic serenity. Politics both in the US and in the UK continue to deteriorate and Trump and Brexit weave their evil potions around the souls of these two nations. In a unique narrative twist, several of the main characters from Casual Choices are woven into this story line. Retired Professor Jeremiah Joshua (Josh) Connelly, his sister, Rachel, along with her daughter, Cate, and Cate's partner, Meena Muhaisin find their way into the domestic and international intrigues explored in this third volume. It is a seamless interjection that brings a third major family theme into this political and personal drama.

This third volume takes us to the present day and peers into the future. Dark shadows loom. Dangers lurk. Existential questions must be addressed. The question is, as it always is, how will the human spirit respond to our ultimate challenges? Are final ends predestined or do we shape the arc of our lives? What about us is chosen, and what dimensions of our lives are based on chance as opposed to fate?

PART I

SHADOWS AND CONNECTIONS 2019

CHAPTER 1

VANCOUVER

Ellison Howard, now Dean of the Liberal Arts College at the University of British Columbia, was in twitter. He usually was when overseeing events that involved important guests. Apparently, the speaker today was a catch for the school. He must be, even though Ellison had been unaware of his international renown until so informed by the University Provost. That, along with the fact that the speaker held a faculty position at Baliol College at Oxford University sealed the deal for Ellison. He would be in the presence of academic royalty on this day. That was key for a Dean so taken with academic reputation and public image. No matter the quality of intellectual content, it was all performance theater in his mind. The school's PR resources would capture the event and, he was informed, local media might be present. It could not get better than this.

The *coup de grace* was learning that the honored guest had just flown up from Redmond, Washington, where he had just consulted with no less a personage than Bill Gates on international refugee health needs. Gates and today's guest, it turned out, shared a passion for saving the globe. Undoubtedly, they discussed the prospects of an apocalyptic pandemic, a specter that Gates seemed to obsess about. Inwardly, the Dean scoffed. Why worry about something that would never happen. When did the last of these occur, a century ago? There were enough real problems all about them. Still, the guest was important enough to move the publicity needle. That always kicked Ellison, relatively new to this post, into officious high gear.

As the speaker finished up, Ellison jumped to join him on the dais. "That was wonderful, just marvelous." Then he turned to the audience as if to encourage further expression of appreciation, but that gesture proved unneeded. The speaker had the look and presence of a Fortune 500 CEO and a speaking style that had been honed to perfection before too many prior audiences to count. The clapping was excessive by academic standards and seemed destined to continue beyond any reasonable duration. The content was sufficiently academic in nature to satisfy the eggheads in the audience and sufficiently applicable to current events to interest an eclectic crowd. "Now a few questions are in order for our distinguished scholar, writer, and humanitarian," Ellison offered to bring things back under his control.

Christopher Crawford, eldest surviving son of the Crawford financial empire, had made his mark first as a social entrepreneur, then a humanitarian, and finally as a scholar. He responded to several queries from the floor as numerous hands were raised to capture his attention. He loved this part of his public performances, the free-flowing exchange that enabled him to connect more intimately with his audience. Chris mused about the inevitable uncertainties associated with public displays of his expertise. You would look out over the faces of any academic or policy audience, a view that seldom changed from venue to venue. By this time in his career, he was reasonably certain he could detect the mood of the crowd along with their likely comprehension and acceptance, or the reverse when the magic failed. It did not happen often, but there were moments when his pitch fell short by his own standards, especially when addressing the money interests and outright begging for resources that had been a necessity, an onerous task he once did repeatedly to support his international service work. Now he was spared the schlepping about for funding for the most part, a freedom further guaranteed by the most recent commitment from the Gates Foundation.

Yes, there still were moments of doubt for Chris Crawford during his public and academic appearances. In the middle of a sentence, he might discover that he had no idea how he was coming across. The tells from the audience were too oblique, hidden behind unreadable faces or muted by some required courtesy. Were they with you, merely being polite, waiting for an opportunity to pounce, or desperately counting the seconds until this torture might be at an end? A frisson of anxiety, perhaps fear would then grip him, a lapse that he had long learned how to isolate and control. Doubts and fears inevitably evaporated during the Q and A sessions. Then, all was transparent and known. The back and forth enabled him to connect more easily with his audience, most any audience. He was quick on his feet, able to respond effortlessly to skeptical or even hostile queries.

This, he fully understood, is what he did best—connect with people. Perhaps in the future, he would insist on giving his Q and A before the formal talk.

A half hour later, as the mingling crowd dispersed and the brief TV interviews were concluded, Ellison accompanied a distinguished-looking man whose age intimated Emeritus status toward Professor Crawford. The move had been choreographed at the request of the visitor with the timing set to permit two scholars with similar interests some private time to exchange whatever they might want to share with one another. Apparently, it had been agreed at the highest levels that these two men of letters would, in fact, have much to discuss. In fact, Chris accepted the invitation to speak at this University based on the hope of spending time with the very man being led toward him by a pompous university official whose demeanor screamed obsequious deference.

The older man being maneuvered in his direction at first looked only vaguely familiar to Chris. Then came full recognition. Yes, this was the man he had been hoping to meet, known to him only by academic reputation and his writings. Now, looking at his approaching face, he was certain that they had not met before, the face only familiar from the man's book jackets. The very notion that they had not crossed paths at some prior venue had seemed improbable, given how closely aligned their mutual interests were. *That was more than a bit odd,* Chris mused silently. The academy was not that large when broken down into specific areas of substantive interest. Then again, neither of them had fully embraced that esoteric culture, what they both saw as an insular and often suffocating world. Members of the academy could treat each other as devotees of a cult—clannish and adhering to their own language and symbols. At the same time, they often were judgmental and dismissive of outsiders.

As they would soon discover, Christopher Crawford and Joshua Connelly were refugees from an incestuous world of committed do-gooders. They instinctively knew that. Perhaps that was the attraction. This introduction, then, was to be purposeful and meaningful to each of them. It was not to be a predictable and perfunctory interaction designed mostly to guarantee that each might later claim that he had, indeed, engaged a famous speaker in a substantive discussion which, of course, he had not. In academia, as in politics, name dropping was an unavoidable necessity.

"Professor Crawford, I want to introduce you to one of our most distinguished emeritus scholars, Professor Jeremiah Joshua Connelly."

"Josh, call me Josh. The last person who called me Jeremiah, or even Joshua, wound up with a black eye on a playground in Boston."

"I assume when you were a young lad." Chris smiled broadly.

"Just last month, in fact." Josh smiled even more broadly to indicate his jest.

Chris laughed heartily. "Yes, of course. I now realize why you seemed familiar out there in the audience. You look just like your book jacket picture. That's not always the case you know. Too often, authors put pics of themselves on their books taken a generation earlier, often the last photo in which they had a full head of hair. Even then, they photoshop the hell out of them. For sure, that's what I'll do in my dotage."

Now it was Josh's turn to laugh. "Probably past dotage time for me at this point, at least my wife tells me so. Besides, photoshop can only do so much."

"Damn, classic case of foot-in-mouth disease. I don't typically insult people I want to meet for at least two minutes, or until I've gotten a donation from them."

Ellison realized he was already redundant and made his apologies. These two obviously wanted to connect, and without him.

Josh looked relieved at the Dean's departure as he pulled out his wallet and looked inside. "Hope you have other fish on the line, spent all my money on a 90-foot yacht which my favorite charity, Yachts for Retired Academics, got for me."

"Yup, just like your memoir, funny and irreverent when it wasn't sad and insightful. But no, my international work runs pretty much on automatic these days with stable funding and a great staff. I am, as they say, redundant, or is the word obsolete. A great place to be by the way."

"I know." Josh smiled even wider. "I've been there all my life."

Chris segued slightly toward a serious tone. "In any case, thank you for making time to see me. It wasn't clear from our email exchange that you would be in town."

"True, my dear wife, Connie Chen, is always eager to send me away, but I changed my plans when I realized you would be visiting. My long-suffering spouse is finally on the cusp of retirement herself, from the bio-chemistry department, and frantic to finish up projects though I have no idea what the rush is. It is not as if academics stop working when they retire. In any case, she constantly complains that I am under foot these days." Then the older man smiled more broadly. "I must admit, in confidence of course, that getting married, really married that is, was one of my better moves. Being a stubborn Irishman, I waited way too long."

Already, Chris was glad he had taken the effort to arrange this meeting. The side trip to Vancouver had been a whim. He loved the city, that was a draw. But the man before him intrigued him, just from his biography and the words to be found in his recent books. As he finished Josh's memoir, he recalled sentiments that Toni Morrison had long-ago expressed. *We die. That may be the meaning of life. But we do language. That may be the measure of our lives.* "Like I said, I read your memoir, *Casual Choices,* though the cover was a bit disingenuous. The picture of a soldier when it was not about combat at all."

"I beg to differ." Josh Connelly effected a look of mock hurt. "It is all about battle and conflict, just not the kind fought with bullets and bombs. Besides, the point of a cover is to sell the book. If a little bait and switch is demanded, what the hell."

Chris bowed slightly. "Points well taken! In any case, a gripping story, full of insights but also many personal revelations. You were honest on a brash level. Perhaps that is the reason it grabbed me so. Well, that and how much I could relate to your struggle. After that, I read some of your other works, your more substantive efforts. I totally love your attempt to reach out to audiences beyond the academy. Most of our peers are fixed on impressing others just like themselves. So bloody myopic, incestuous in a way."

The two men now shook hands, taking the measure of the other in that instantaneous manner through which lasting impressions are forged. Chris assessed a man who, by dint of age, easily could be his father. What he saw impressed him, drew him in, and confirmed his prior instincts. Josh Connelly still had the bearing and grace of movement that had made him an athletic star in his youth. His face now was creased with the lines that a man in his seventies would be expected to bear. Somehow, they did not make him look old but distinguished in the manner one might anticipate in a senior scholar. An aura of innate wisdom was accentuated by a full head of hair, thinning a bit at the top, yet borne in a casual style that fell over the top of his ears suggesting a conscious lack of interest in appearance. The overall effect carried him well on his way toward that sense of eminence often attributed to an elder statesman.

Josh looked a bit puzzled. "My story grabbed you on a personal level, really? That strikes me as odd since we are so different. I was issued from common, working-class folk while you were of the manor born. I worked my ass off to get through college while you floated through Princeton and then on to a Rhodes scholarship, never having to worry about your next meal. I used to envy guys like you. I cannot imagine less similar beginnings, other than the Irish thing. Even there, you were lace-curtain Irish, and we were from the wrong side of the tracks."

Chris cocked his head, as if suggesting that the similarities were obvious to him. "Well, let's start with the fact that we are both half-Irish, lace curtain or no. That fact mutually curses us right there. We both had contentious relationships with our fathers, mine continues right to this day. We both broke away from our cultural roots, and neither escape was easy. I can attest to that in my case. From your memoir, I am most certain that the pain of escaping your roots remains the case for you."

"True enough," Josh agreed, "but the differences are also stark. I checked on your background though I eagerly await your own memoir."

"Mine is yet swirling around inside a crowded head, I fear, though one of these days who knows. But when you do read it, any envy you harbor regarding my so-called advantages will evaporate."

Josh laughed quietly. "I am a patient man, but don't put it off too long. Let's face it, I'm not getting any younger."

Chris paused as if deciding where to go next before starting in. "Well then, here is the preview version, just in case you don't want to wait for the nine-part mini-series. As you know, I grew up in Chicago to a wealthy family. After my older brother passed, I remained the one surviving son of a wealthy financier and devoted robber baron who discounted my two sisters since he saw them as inferior females of no intrinsic worth. My father fancied himself as that self-made man triumphing against great odds in a cruel world. And he did accomplish much by his own efforts. That, I will grant him. However, he was helped mightily by marrying the only daughter, only child for that matter, of a wealthy Catholic family from Philadelphia. Charles Senior, my father, saw himself as both a survivor and as an example of superman, one of those destined to lead because of superior genes and unsurpassed intelligence. Unfortunately, he read Ayn Rand's books and saw himself as the heroic protagonist, a Howard Roark character. I will admit, some of his Horatio Alger pretenses do have merit. His earliest family history involved real traumas around the Second World War, the Nazi invasion of Poland, and the loss of many family members, including his father, during a Stalin purge that wiped out most of the Polish government in exile at the end of the war, as well as the intelligentsia. He was brought to America by distant relatives with little except some good contacts. He had been born to privilege and it was suddenly snatched away. That loss seemed to further scar his soul with the lesson that only the toughest SOB's survive in this world. He made it his mission in life to be the biggest SOB of them all."

"That point rings true of my dad as well." Josh interjected. "His holy grail was not personal wealth, though, but the unification of Ireland."

"Yet, you call him Dad. I would never call mine that. He is Father, the Patriarch, the SOB who . . ." Then he stopped himself, looking about to see if there were anyone within earshot. Satisfied that the others had dispersed, he spoke in a soft tome. "To continue, my father is the very definition of a first-class narcissistic sociopath."

"Rather harsh?" Josh looked at the other man quizzically. "Besides, I thought Trump had that honor sewed up."

"Good point but no." But Chris had lost his usual smile. "That label is not harsh enough. He murdered my older brother, Chuck, or Charles Junior. Not directly, of course, but by pushing him mercilessly to take on the role of heir to the throne. Father knew, we all knew, that Chuck was too sweet for such a role. He was an artist by temperament. But he was also weak enough to try to do Father's bidding. My sisters and I tried to save the poor wretch but that was hopeless. Funny, he was older than me, but I always thought of him as a kid, the younger brother needing protection." Chris paused a second to reflect on that point. "Ever watch a family tragedy unfold in slow motion. You just know what is coming but are hopeless to stop it. Chuck slowly buckled under the pressure until his only escape was somewhere beyond this mortal coil."

"I had no idea. The suicide is in the public bio but not the backstory."

"Of course not, Father controls the public face of the family. In the end, his plans to dominate the family unraveled as his offspring struck out on their own. I had run off to Oxford, using the Rhodes scholarship as cover. I never returned, in part to keep out of his orbit and partly to pursue my interests in international aid and development. He tried, more than once, to slide me into the role of heir to the financial empire, a role he sees falling to the male issue since females are only useful for limited purposes. He yet rages at my refusal. My twin sister, Kristen or Kay as everyone calls her, escaped him by taking on one of the worst medical jobs in Chicago, an ER doc, in a public institution where the detritus of society get dumped night after night given our national fascination with guns and violence. But after Chuck's death, she joined me overseas, probably to get even further away from the bastard that raped her as a teen."

"What?" Josh stammered and was instantly embarrassed at his display of innocence.

"Also not in the official biography. It was then that my youngest sister, Katerina or Kat, spread her wings. She had been the one who appeared the most docile and the least likely to rebel. She had been the quiet one, hovering in the background unobserved. When she did emerge from her cocoon, she proved amazing as she engineered a family coup by ousting Father from atop the family financial empire."

"That, on the other hand, is in the official bio-material."

"What isn't there is the fact that what appeared like a victory turned out to be pyrrhic in the end. Freeing Father from his daily responsibilities simply gave him more time to focus on his primary passions—his insatiable desire to engineer a right-wing coup to take over the US and then the world."

"Surely, a fantasy for an old man," Josh said.

Chris stared coldly into some distant place. His usual smile absent. "I desperately wish that were the case but his dream, as you know, is shared by many others among the elite. And now, we have Trump in the White House, a Republican Senate protecting him, a court system leaning further right every day, and a hidden pseudo-government that has been systematically undermining our political institutions for years. Trump and McConnell are appointing federal justices as fast as they can. They are not working alone. The Federalist Society has been grooming right-wing zealots for various courts for about three decades now. Just in the last three years, Leonard Leo admitted that they raised some $250 million for the cause. And that is just one of their initiatives."

"Yes," Josh mused in a low voice, "I also have been looking hard at the hidden campaign to undermine democracy by the hard right. When your agenda is to protect the financial interests of a small elite, the last thing you can permit is a robust democracy. Gerrymandering, Reagan ending the Fairness Doctrine, the Citizen United decision that has flooded politics with unregulated dollars, sinister back deal bargains with former enemies, and non-stop political hit jobs through Fox and other propaganda outlets. Such antics have convinced millions to vote against their self-interests. I watched this unfold with decidedly mixed feelings."

"How so?" Chris was curious.

"I was so thankful that I had escaped, though not by choice, to live in a civilized country. At the same time, my overwhelming regret is that I and my friends focused on an easy target way back then—the Vietnam War. We missed the bigger threat, the rise of the hard-core right determined to bend democracy toward their own narrow interests."

"Don't be hard on yourself. We all missed it for way too long," Chris responded.

Both men looked at one another. They knew that much more needed to be shared. Josh broke the short silence. "You busy now?"

"No, nothing until the morning. I kept this time free." Chris wondered if he should reveal that sizing up the man before him was the very purpose of his side trip to Vancouver, other than the fact that he loved the city.

"Great. Let's walk to my place. It's not far. We can take the way back along the shore, I find it relaxing." Josh loved showing off Vancouver, the place he fell in love with as an exile almost four decades ago. "The sun will now be at our backs. I just love the way the end of the day bathes the mountains to the north and the city to the east with the setting sun. The red and amber hues seem . . . peaceful, quite seductive. I was smitten my first day in this city. I had arrived for a job interview without much enthusiasm and immediately realized I never wanted to leave. Fortunately, I was able to fool the University into hiring me."

In a bit, they were ambling casually along the rocky shore that bordered the peninsula on which the University of British Columbia is located. After casual comments on the beauty of the natural surroundings, Chris brought the conversation toward Josh's past and how he ended up in this marvelous setting. "I recall the details from your memoir, your flight to Canada in the '60s when the pressures of the draft and the war protests, in which you were caught up, became overwhelming. Still, you can never get inside a person's head. I mean, that must have seemed to be an irrevocable choice or no choice at all. What goes on inside our heads in those moments?"

Josh walked silently for a few moments. Chris thought that he might have stumbled into a taboo area, something that ought not to be dragged into the open after so many years. It was apparent to Chris that time does not fully heal all psychic wounds, and that he might have been intrusive. He was about to back away when Josh spoke up in low, measured terms. "You know, even after all this time, I cannot put myself fully into that moment. It has always been like this out-of-body experience where I am looking at this other person who must decide what his life will be like. Do I stay and increasingly get caught up in greater violence to try and stop an insane war, knowing it was a futile gesture, and that I would likely end up in jail or dead? Or do I flee and let down my friends and especially my sister whom I loved dearly. And there was Eleni from college in the States whom I also loved back then with a passion that, I must admit, has never been duplicated. Then again, perhaps first loves cannot be replicated. My parents were lost to me in any case. Fleeing the country would paint me as a coward, staying and continuing along my path of resistance would make me a traitor. I was the classic experimental rat caught in a maze with no escape."

When Josh lapsed into silence, Chris felt this need to push his companion along on his confessional path. He searched for some loose end to pull as a way of letting even more escape of the detritus being held within. "I missed out on the '60s, both the good and the bad of it, being so much younger than you. I came of age in its aftermath, close enough to feel many of the raw passions it had unleashed but not the experience of them. How odd it is that what we face in the moment typically seems of such consequences, as if our personal choices are monumental. How many have sacrificed body and soul on something utterly dramatic at the time, yet no one can recall what the fuss was all about afterward. Stopping the killing seemed so imperative in the moment back then. Now, kids can't even identify in which part of the world Vietnam lies, which continent even. Why did we care so passionately, so desperately? After all, America continues to wage unceasing war, spending almost $6 trillion on the profitable business of killing others just since 9/11."

Josh responded as if he were talking to himself. His words seemed cautious, wistful. "Some of us, I fear, are cursed. We are born with a conscience, that sense of purpose that pushes each of us to think beyond our own sorry lives. For me, personally, I was not aware of it until college, when I rebelled against my Catholic, working class culture and carved out my own understanding of right and wrong. That broke my father's heart, and mine as well. It took decades to put it back together again, the sense of who I was as a total person. Who am I kidding? We never put those things behind us, the sense of betraying family . . . the ones we love the most . . . and most of all the culture that defines each of us."

"I suppose not, though when your father is a total sociopath, the task is easier."

"Really?" Josh looked unconvinced.

Chris decided to evade the other man's skeptical retort. "The decision to leave your country, to emigrate to Canada. Did you ever come to terms with that? I mean, any lingering regrets?"

"I suppose that, in the end, I saw no other choice. If I stayed, I would have slid into greater violence as a protest to what I saw as institutionalized evil at the time. Can you ever regret the necessity imposed by youthful certitude? This path toward irretrievable acts of violence seemed unavoidable given my sense of righteous passion. Once you start down that road, with others pushing you on, it's hard to apply the brakes and impossible to reverse course. You must remember, I was still a kid. We can never quite calculate the full consequences of our actions at that age. And yet, after all this time, with all the presumed benefits of maturity and experience, I doubt I would have done anything differently. One thing I did come to terms with over time—becoming a kind of proto-revolutionary pursuing justice through violence was not me, no matter the righteousness of the cause. I could not let myself become what I saw in those I despised. And so, in the end, I ran away. The guilt I felt for my companions nearly killed me. Yet, in the end, after hating myself for four decades, I found that they never hated me. Wow. Does any of this make any sense?"

"More than you can imagine," Chris whispered. "Don't forget. I read your book."

Then Josh went on more eagerly, as if Chris had not spoken. "I can still remember the morning I was to leave. Even then, after debating inside my head for weeks, I was not sure I could do it. I would be leaving an entire life behind. Was anything worth that? As you know, since you read the book, I flipped a coin. That was how casual the final decision seemed. I flipped a damn coin in the early hours of a frigid November morn. I think my goddamn brain must have been frozen."

"You really did that then? You left your fate to be decided by a coin flip? I wondered if parts of your story involved using literary license for emotional effect."

"I tried for complete honesty, but memory plays tricks of course. I did flip a coin. Of that I am sure. What I did when it landed is a bit hazy. I was so torn between staying and fleeing that I recall thinking that a coin toss somehow would reflect divine will, even though I had long given up believing in such things. My memory, though, is that the darn quarter ended up in some snow that was accumulating. I couldn't quite see which side was up. Then it hit me, I knew what I really wanted to see, no need for divine guidance. So, I picked up the coin without looking, got in my car, and headed for Canada. Maybe I peeked, can't be sure now. Here was the seminal moment of my young life and I still can't quite pull that memory back, likely too emotional. I suppose that, in the moment, I never really considered it would be the rest of my life. Surely, America would come to its senses. Then I could return and make amends."

"But that never happened. Why?"

"Good question," Josh murmured. "You know, in our delusional young minds, we thought that America would get things right. As my generation matured, we would assume positions of power and lead the country in a different direction. Well, we were spot on in one way. It did go in a different direction . . . things got much worse. But that's not the only reason I stayed up here. I fell in love with this place, at least after I got through a dark period at the start. I knew nothing about Canada when I headed north that day other than it might provide some refuge and it was cold. Then I found this wonderful place filled with civilized and polite people. What a shock. In the end, I stayed because I wanted to stay and, for many years, I thought they might throw my ass in jail if I went back to the States."

Chris immediately sensed a warmth toward his companion. His instinct that this man might be a kindred spirit was proving correct. Such a man could be the much older brother he had wished for all his life. For a private man, this was an impetuous feeling but was it real? Then a question he harbored and did not want to forget forced its way into his head. "Before I forget, tell me what's with the title *Casual Choices*. Just a cute alliteration. You kind of explain it in the narrative but now that I have the horse's mouth in front of me . . ."

Josh laughed quietly. "I am never sure from which end of the horse my book titles emerge. I couldn't decide between *Tenuous Tendrils* and *Casual Choices*. The first focused on relationships while the second tapped into the decisions made without great consideration, those that shape our lives. Both themes are important to the book."

"I can see that." Chris looked thoughtful. "How did you decide?"

"Easy, for *Tendrils,* the cover would have been a picture of a vine, a metaphor for the familial ties that bind. For *Choices,* I stumbled over the dark outline of a soldier which seemed more appropriate for the ominous choices we all make in life. Of course, the text was not about war, so the military pic was not kosher; the story line was more anti-war really, but I love the dramatic feel of a brooding soldier. Lure them in with a false promise of an action story and then try to make them think."

"Hey, as long as people pick up the damn thing."

"Exactly!" Josh agreed. "In the end, though, I think I was fascinated with decisions that frame our lives. We make so many with such imperfect knowledge, so little real consideration. Should that shock us, is there something we can pass on to the next generation. I have no idea."

Chris smiled. "I have thought on this topic many times, in fact. This is silly but I sometimes wonder if, despite our limitations and faulty decision-making, we are supposed to be where we are. Perhaps all is foreordained. Maybe predestination is a reality after all, and we are where Providence has assigned our sorry asses. Alas, all is fate in the end." Chris seemed to consider his reflection and issued a dry chuckle. "You know, in the end, we are not so different. You ran off to Canada, I to England. Both were supposed to be temporary escapes yet have become permanent exiles. As with you, I grew very fond of my place of exile. It strikes me that we really have much in common."

Both men stopped to face one another. It was a moment in which decisions would be made. Josh spoke quietly. "I look around and see much that dismays me, and not just in the States. The hard-right BJP party led by that Hindu nationalist, Modi, is poised to affirm control of India. Conservatives are on the rise in Brazil, Hungary, Poland, the Ukraine, and so many other places. Britain wants to reverse course on unity with Europe. It is like old passions and self-destructive behaviors are bubbling to the surface everywhere. The liberal impulses toward inclusiveness and participatory democracy are in retreat again. People are falling back on their primitive tribal instincts. I really thought I could spend my golden years enjoying this magical place and writing the books stored inside me. But I cannot escape this thing inside that keeps screaming at me not to give up. The battle for the future of humanity is never over unless we permit it to be."

Chris chuckled as he put one hand on the other man's shoulder. "You ever feel like Don Quixote, charging illusory windmills. Unlike the poor sap from La Mancha, you know absolutely that the quest is futile, but you still cannot stop."

"Every damn day of my life," Josh replied. "You know, I find I am way too much like my father. We hated one another at the end, he hated me at least. I think . . . I think I mostly felt sad for him. Whatever, we butted heads constantly because we were so much alike—stubborn Irishmen too full up with conviction with large doses of excess passion. That is a terrible disease, conviction. But once infected, you cannot get rid of it."

"Absolutely! It is like a congenital condition. You got it, or you don't." Chris said with a surprising bit of excitement. "I look about and am driven mad by this emerging tribalism we both see. In America, we have seen tribal hates dominate over time. Hell, Henry Clay formed an American Colonization Society not long after the War of 1812 with come half-assed plan to recolonize Blacks back to Africa since southern whites feared they were becoming outnumbered and endangered. That concept lingered for decades though only several thousands of the millions of Blacks ever returned to Liberia."

Josh smiled. "Yeah, with the rise of cotton on world markets, the plantation owners needed free labor, no matter the risks."

Chris nodded to him and continued. "We had the Know Nothings in the 1850s that saw further threats from the Irish and other immigrants from the wrong countries like Italy and China . . . *those* people coming here whom everyone knew were idiots, diseased, and criminals waiting to pounce on good Americans. This was ethnic hate on steroids, the core belief that some nationalities were known, without doubt, to be inferior became part of our national consciousness. This naturally led to the Chinese exclusion laws and later the punitive immigration laws of 1924, never mind the genocide of American Natives and the apartheid that African Americans were forced to endure. Where did Hitler get much of his racial hatred, from the Nativist writings in America? All the rhetoric aside, we have been a boiling pot of tribal anger, unfounded fears, and mutual suspicions since our foundation."

Josh easily picked up on this theme. "It is impossible to overlook the outright genocide practiced against the original inhabitants of this land, so hideous, nor the concentration camps we erected for American citizens of Japanese descent in World War II. But who needs to go back that far? We had the so-called Federation of American Immigration Reform started by John Tanton as recently as 1979. That was nothing more than an ill-disguised attempt to preserve a white race dominance in the US. Now we are building walls on our borders with children being thrown into contemporary camps while so-called patriots armed to the teeth take it upon themselves to hunt down asylum seekers. Are we great yet, or should I say pure enough yet?"

Chris suddenly shifted toward a somewhat more upbeat tone. "Despite that, I do have my moments of optimism, though. Without them, I couldn't go on. So, think about this. This whole new socialist movement in the States is encouraging. I mean, socialist Eugene Debs only got 6 percent of the vote in 1912 in a day when labor had an identity. Back then, socialists held 1,200 offices around the country including 79 mayoral seats. Hell, the mayor of Milwaukee was a socialist until 1960. After the Bolsheviks came to power, though, the very word socialist got caught up in the red scare. It slid from a term focusing on community, sharing, and equality to state control and authoritarian oppression. Principles succumbed to the thirst for power. Millennials see the things differently. They look at the Scandinavian countries that Fox News labels as Socialist and think that those people got it right. Their people are not riven with anxiety and fears for the future, not starting out with debt and panicked that one medical emergency can bankrupt them for life. Socialism, democratic socialism that is, may not be so bad after all."

Josh stopped his companion and pointed across the bay. The mountains rose in the distance while the center of Vancouver bustled with life across the water to the right. "Yet, when I get vexed at the utter stupidity of my species, I come to a place like this. Water and mountains always calm me. The first time I saw this view on my recruitment trip, I fell in love."

"I can see why, which makes my reason for tracking you down a bit more complicated," Chris murmured as Josh turned to him with a quizzical expression. "Do you think you could leave it for a while?"

Josh sensed the importance behind the question and did not respond right away. He slowly began to speak. "I think we make up our minds about others very quickly. Hell, I remember reading Obama's first book about his early years and thinking that this is a guy who is just like me. I became an instant devotee. Of course, there always are differences but at some deeper level you recognize those that see the world as you do. You can sense those others who employ the same filters in life, those who integrate the world about them in similar ways to you. What do you see across the waters?"

"Hmm," Chris responded, looking at the scene before him more closely. "For me, I see permanence and vitality. The mountains and the city are opposite sides of the same coin, they complement one another."

"Exactly," Josh responded. "Our struggles arise out of the complex way we see the world. We are sensitive to the failures all about us as well as the promise that remains. If we had been captured by the bad, which is undeniable, both of us would have simply enjoyed our lives. You would have spent your life in indolent luxury, simply basking in the limitless benefits of winning the birth lottery. But that was not you."

"And you."

"My lot would have been less attractive, I suppose, but I would have remained content to live the life of a pampered academic. I would have stayed cloistered, writing paper after paper for elite journals that would be read by a few colleagues. How provincial is that. What a waste! No, I was compelled to get out and tackle real-world problems. That did not sit well with my colleagues but I, for one, could do no other. Trying to straddle the academy and the real world is a hectic life, as you well know, but not without considerable rewards. The problem for folk like you and I is that we can see hope in all the bleakness. We know that, in some ways, life has improved for so many. People like you have been responsible for that progress."

Chris reached out and put a hand on the other man's shoulder. "That is what Bill Gates and I were talking about just yesterday. We have built in negative biases. We see the bad around us, it is the way we filter the world. If we looked closely enough, we would see something different. Many things around the world, in fact, are improving. Extreme poverty has been halved in just a few decades. So many metrics of well-being are on the rise."

"Yes," Josh affirmed. "I also have read Rosling's book."

"Then you know where I am going with all this. I am wondering if you will join our effort. To be clear, I divide my time between fighting my Father and his allies for the soul of America and doing my best to help those in the worst hellholes around the world."

"I assume you want me for the American fight."

"Well, your medical skills seem a bit less developed than I would prefer for the other. However, you think clearly and write very persuasively. This American battle is about ideas and which form of those shall prevail. I think we have a shot at recapturing the souls of the young, the next generation. Ready for that?"

"Truth is," Josh smiled, "I am getting a bit bored. Time to stir up the pot a bit while I still can. But I may have more to offer. In fact, I am such a persuasive cuss, I might be able to persuade other members of the family to join your international work. I am, perhaps, the least talented member of the clan."

"I had no doubt about that." Chris smiled.

Josh laughed heartily. "Come on, the house is just a block away. We can have a drink and talk things over. If we are lucky, Connie will have some food for us. I gave her a heads up that I might drag you back if it were possible."

CHAPTER 2

MILWAUKEE

Charles Ashley Crawford Sr. settled into the back of what was, for him, an ordinary looking sedan. He grimaced as he looked about, preferring the limo which conveyed luxury and a certain status to others. Now, of course, there were too many stretch limousines wandering about the city of Chicago. There were fewer when he first started using one, how long ago was that now? No matter, it said to him, and more importantly to others, that he had arrived. He had made it to the top of the heap. He was where he belonged. Today, though, he wanted to downplay any displays of his public eminence even as he privately reveled in his presumed superiority. Of that elevated position in society, he had no doubt nor sense of shame. Tactically, however, flaunting his station might not be wise on this day. No, he had decided, it would be wiser to fly under the radar, as his head of security had put it. He glanced at the vehicle ahead of him. His team of protectors were there.

He decided to leave early that morning, telling his driver that he wanted to take the longer route north. *Go past North-*

western, the Botanical gardens, through Winnetka, then over to Highway 94. He gave no reason for the more circuitous route. He did not need to. His staff always nodded and obeyed. Inside, he wanted some time to muse on things as they wove through affluent neighborhoods lined with the houses of those who also had grabbed some measure of the American dream. The residents of these modest mansions were behind him in the race for power and treasure, of course. Most were far behind him, but a few, very few indeed, were close enough to be considered one of his tribe. Permitting his mind to wander would better be done in the limo, of course. But he had seen the wisdom of the cautionary advice from those charged with keeping him safe.

It had been a long climb from humble roots, at least in his remembering of history. He had been born Karol Chrezsinski not that long before Poland would be swallowed up by the Nazi menace whose fury had been edging outward but would burst all sense of proportion in September of 1939. He could never remember those earliest days, of course, the frantic flight to England as the Polish army collapsed. They fought valiantly but how could men on horseback stop men in tanks. How could 19th century military tactics stand against the 20th century blitzkrieg. The slaughter was preordained. He and his family escaped the slaughter given his father's mission to establish a Polish government in exile.

No, his earliest memories were of an estate somewhere north of London, a place populated by other Polish dignitaries and aristocrats who also had escaped or had the good sense to avoid the inevitable beforehand. He only became aware of his situation in retrospect, through stories that served to imprint life's lessons on him. Still, he had some shadowy images that he could not shake, like meeting Winston Churchill whose cigar smoke nauseated him and whose bonhomie he somehow found disingenuous even at that early age. But his father had always been excited by such meetings and, as the war was ending, was brimming with optimism and expectation. They would create a new Poland and the Chrezsinski family would return to where they belonged, back in Warsaw and in a position of authority and surely eminence.

Then, as his memories became crisper, the good feelings seemed to evaporate. Soviet tanks commanded Poland. For all his promises, Churchill did nothing. He was thrown out of office in the hour of victory. How could that happen? Surely, people could not be trusted. How could such unconscious rabble know what was best for them? He yet remembered his mother begging his father not to return to Poland, not to believe Stalin's promises of an independent Poland and free elections. His mother knew that such a man could not be trusted, just as Hitler had assured that Czechoslovakia would be his last territorial claim in Europe. Such evil knew no bounds, retained no shred of human decency, recognized no law above their own grasping and narcissistic ambitions.

His father—simply a insubstantial image in the mind of Charles—still went on his mission. He could do no other. Surely, such a public assurance could not be utterly disingenuous. After all, the world was watching. His father, of course, had to believe since the stakes were too high. His country, his religion, and his national pride were at stake. Free Polish soldiers had fought bravely for the allies, especially at Monte Cassino Abbey, the last line across the Italian peninsula before Rome. The allies could not soon forget such sacrifice. So, his father kissed him on the lips that day, promised to return for his mother and he, and boarded a plane. He would never return. In the end, Stalin had lied. His father, and other brave nationalists of the Polish government in exile, simply disappeared. They were irritating threats to be erased by the Communist dictator.

Charles leaned back in his seat. He noticed signs for Northwestern University as his reverie continued. His mother, now penniless but still having contacts, made her way to America with her son. There, they scratched out a living, not dirt poor, but far from the pampered life they had endured as part of the Catholic aristocracy in pre-war Poland. So many nights, she told them of what they had lost, what she felt had been denied them as a right. Her bitterness became part of his own existence. Eventually, he lied about his age to get a job at Northwestern, there to scratch out a living in his youth and, when he could, sneak into larger business classes where he might escape notice. He should have been there as a birthright, not as a sneak thief, keeping silent so that a detectable Polish accent might not betray his sins.

Later, he had hoped one of his sons would attend this place that spurned him, at least in his eyes. But his eldest failed him, scraping through Loyola while dreaming of becoming an artist, while his gifted younger male offspring ran off to the East Coast, first to Princeton and then even further east to Oxford.

No matter how much he tried, he never could bring Chris back home—to him and to the family destiny. To his dream and to his destiny. Charles let out a small gasp, which caught the attention of his driver. "It was nothing, just a sneeze," he lied. It was more than that, more a groan of despair. Who had gone to Northwestern but his younger son's best friend, the colored boy? What was his name . . . Richard or Ricky? It mattered not, Charles grimaced, they were all the same, just another west-side nigger who fortunately was good at basketball. Chris would bring this Ricky and his sister into their home, their sanctuary from the evils of the world and his own wife, Mary, let him do that. She was always soft, always.

Scenes from those days danced through his head in a random, dreamlike fashion when he noticed the Wisconsin welcome sign. They were on I-94 now. It would not be long now before that would leave the interstate and wind their way through what had been, and still was, a working class, Polish stronghold. Aside from a mutual ancestry, perhaps the fumes of a common religious attachment, he had no affinity with these people. They scratched out a meaningless existence with their labors, held onto pedestrian dreams and limited ambitions. How did they survive, get up each day? Their lives were so finite, irrelevant.

No, Charles mused. He had been born to lead. He had absorbed the stories of what had been lost from his mother. At first, he had been confused. His warm sentiments for a father figure he barely knew had clouded his judgment. What mostly raged in his heart was a blind fury at both Hitler and Stalin. The first for crushing his homeland and his family dreams, and the second for picking clean the carcass of a dead government and society, including the assassination of his father in some unknown Soviet hellhole.

One day, though, he had an epiphany. He recalled watching privileged students amble across the pristine campus as he labored to keep the campus looking attractive for these spoiled shits, not that they ever noticed. What did they have that he didn't? The answer was nothing, not a thing. He was superior in every sense. He had been forged in fire and desperation, with all ripped from him by persons and forces stronger than himself at the time. The college students about him merely eased their way through life without effort. His epiphany encompassed a resolution to his burning hate for the historical figures whose callous cruelty had taken so much from him.

At the end of the day, hate was silly. The despots of his childhood were not simulacra of despotism or evil. If anything, they were inspirations. They faced odds perhaps greater than he did. Hitler was an outcast, a homeless drifter who rose to lead a nation. Stalin started off as a reject from an Orthodox Christian Seminary who used crime and cunning wiles to rise to leadership of the Communist world. Mussolini had been a common journalist before strong arming his way to the top. Early on, no one would have suggested anything but failure and obscurity for such nobodies. But now the world knew their names while so many others with far more promise fell into utter obscurity.

He looked about him that day, staring at the passing faces. He was invisible to them. No, he would crawl out from the shadows and master their world, dominate them. It was among the strongest, the survivors of society, that those able to will their way to the top could be found. He was going to be a winner in that universal and desperate competition for control, even domination. The ones to be hated were those who now stood between what he was and what he needed to be.

He recalled sneaking into a class one day, sitting in the back of the lecture hall hoping not to be noticed. It was introductory economics as he recalled. He preferred the smaller, graduate business courses but they held too great a risk of discovery. That day, the professor talked about the application of Darwin's theory of natural selection to society coupled with Weber's thoughts on the Protestant ethic. He sat enraptured as the man at the podium outlined his thoughts on what drove Western progress. Business acumen was not merely a matter of financial expertise, not a command of balance sheets or a command of investment tactics. It was an expression of will and aspiration. Some were blessed with superior attributes, others were not. Society, if it were to continue forward, needed to sort out that wheat from the chaff. Only the blessed of god were positioned to propel the species forward. They were not only useful for the common good, people like him were utterly essential.

He had been electrified that day, running from the classroom to the library. He had been using a discarded or lost student library card for months at that point. At first, he worried that his deception would be uncovered. Now, he was known to the staff and they barely looked at his proffered and false identification. He spent hours devouring Herbert Spencer and William Graham Sumner as they applied Darwin's biological concepts to sociological phenomena. He knew it was nonsense in a way. Darwin's notions were limited. Small mutations that occur from generation to generation resulted in some adaptive features that favored some over others. These were random rolls of the genetic dice that, over time, resulted in lines of offspring winning life's struggle . . . and then passing their advantages on to the future.

That wasn't the point, though, he thought. The mechanics were not important, the vision was. Eagerly, he went back further in time to devour Thomas Malthus who laid out a vision where the struggle for scarce resources was the crucible in which existence was determined. Then, he leapt forward to immerse himself in the works of Francis Galton, a half cousin to Darwin, who developed the theory of genetics. It was less a theory, he realized, and more of a worldview. Everything suddenly fell into place for him. All now made sense. The rise of social Darwinism in the 1880s, the survival of the fittest, and later to the racial ideas of Madison Grant in the 1910s. Any distribution of wealth, no matter how unequal, was the hand of God in action. If you were at the bottom of the hill, accept it. It was God's design, a natural law. The universe operated according to a given hierarchy.

But what struck him at the time was the insight that this was more than a struggle among individuals. That was true enough, of course. But we also had a titanic struggle among groups, tribes, aggregates of people destined by nature and god to advance humankind. This was not all that different from the sea creatures that slowly developed proto organs such as primitive lungs that enabled their escape from the waters for increasing periods of time. They proved to be the pioneers who, after eons of generations, permitted a few of them to thrive on the land with real lungs.

What if they had thought about what they were doing? What if they had said to themselves, "We shouldn't leave our weaker brethren behind. That is unfair to them. We'll stay in the seas and not take advantage of our good fortune." He leaned back in his seat, lost in his thoughts. There was no doubt in his mind. Compassion, if there is such a thing, was to be found in leaving the less fit or fortunate behind. Otherwise, no one would have left the soupy swamps that cradled early airborne life. There would have been no mammals, no consciousness, no society, no real future.

"How much longer?" He barked to the driver.

"No more than thirty minutes, sir."

He glanced at his watch. Not a problem, he will arrive no more than 5 or 10 minutes late. The longer route was worth it, gave him a chance to ruminate. He was doing more of that these days, a luxury he did not permit himself in his youth. Perhaps that was to be expected. As one becomes an octogenarian, it is natural to look back. These years are a time for summing up, taking stock, settling scores, and leaving a legacy. It hit him with renewed clarity. His path probably had been set on that long-ago morning, in that lecture and the literature it led him to devour in the following weeks.

And yet, perhaps the trajectory of his existence had already been set, in the stories shared by his bitter mother and the other

Polish exiles who frequented his home in those early Chicago years in the Pulaski Park section of Chicago. For a while, he had been taken by the rites he found in Holy Trinity Polish Catholic church, and the respect the priests had among the parishioners, especially the women who yet conversed in their native tongue and held desperately to the old ways. That did not last long, however. As a young boy, he had wondered why some of these men who visited his home, often former associates of his now lost father, spent so much time with his mother. The sad epiphany, when it came in reluctant bursts of shame, explained how they managed to live comfortably on his mother's sales position in a department store. Even then, he felt conflicted, thrashing between waves of rage and respect. He hated them for what they did to his mother but admired their ability to take what they wanted. And all the time he listened to their stories of what Poland had been before the war, before the Nazis and then the Communists, when they had been at the top of society. Any God that could permit such atrocities would never benefit from his loyalty or fealty.

Of course, that was the big lesson, wasn't it? No one lamented the species that remained stuck in the primordial waters as those with greater adaptive abilities sought new possibilities. Even if you could never appreciate the end of the journey, it was moral and right to push forward. The weak fell behind. The future would be shaped by the strong and the adaptive. He had never paid that much interest to history, it was past after all, but he never forgot the figure of Charles the Hammer. He loved that name, adopted it when he Anglicized his own in his late teens.

So, the story of this historical figure stuck with him. In barely over a century, the Muslims had swept across North Africa and up into the Iberian Peninsula. Their march continued north into modern-day France until Charles rallied various tribes to stop them at Tours. See, he told himself, Charles was no saint, more like a savage warlord. But he saved Europe from being overrun by Islam. He wondered why we have no monuments to this hero. After all, he saved the Western world and transformed the course of civilization. Strength and will conquered all.

He shook his head to escape that historical tangent. The point of all he had absorbed in life was simple. There were the strong and the weak, the winners and the losers. In the end, no one long cried over those who worried about silly matters like compassion and civility. It was strength and survival that mattered. Pure will conquered all else. Even the spiritual icons like Christ and Muhammed supported his worldview. Who remembered the messages of love and understanding they tried to spread around? No, it was their followers who cherry-picked what they wanted to hear and then slaughtered those who did not believe who determined remembered history and created religious hegemony. No one was more savage and unforgiving than those motivated by religious conviction. Blind faith excused all manner of infamy.

In the distance, he could now see the twin towers of St. Stanislaus Catholic Church, the center of Polish culture in South Milwaukee. The building abutted I-94 and was visible from a distance, surrounded, as it was, by modest working-class homes and small retail shops. Of course, there were a surfeit of neighborhood bars to be found. They were not as plentiful as they had once been, but many remained as centers of social life for those who mostly labored with their hands. They pulled off the interstate, drove past St. Anthony's School that was part of the parish's mission, before passing a Planned Parenthood office located only a stone's throw from the citadel of Catholic orthodoxy. The driver then slowed to check his GPS before pulling into an alley adjacent to one of those ubiquitous bars.

"We are here, Sir. Really, this is where you want to go?"

"I have my reasons, Rogers." Charles responded crisply, slightly annoyed at the impertinence of the hired help. "You stay with the car. It's not a nigger neighborhood but it's not civilized either."

Upon exiting the vehicle, he waited for his security team to get into position and for one of them to enter a nondescript establishment through a back door. A moment later he looked outside and waived in the small group. The transition from bright sunlight to semi-darkness made it hard to see for a moment. Charles quickly realized they were in a backroom of one of these ubiquitous family-owned bars popular on the southside. Cases of beers and various spirits lined the walls along with other essentials to keep a tavern going. The place smelled of stale beer, decay, and a hint of something more nauseating, perhaps dried vomit. Charles fought to keep from betraying any outward signs of surprise or disgust.

It took only moments for him to focus on the three men seated at a table. They clearly were the principles with the others sitting on beer cases or lounging casually against the walls.

All were sporting weapons of various sorts. If things went south his men were clearly out armed. They were veterans, either of the military, SWAT teams, or Eric Prince's militia that served as mercenaries in various Mideast and African hot spots. But it was like they had brought water pistols to the O.K. Corral. He dismissed his momentary concerns. They were on the same side, after all.

He took a seat and looked at the men across the table. All seemed to have faces scarred by life, features mostly obscured by scraggly facial hair, and expressions centered about dead eyes. For a moment, Charles imagined how he might describe these men to the authorities. Caucasian, for sure. Hair color, not sure since each was wearing a bandana or helmet. Eye color, hard to say since he could not get past the hate and suspicion they contained. Clothes, something straight out of a bad Sylvester Stallone movie. But their guns were large and menacing . . . exceptionally menacing. And these weapons were all too real.

Charles caught himself, realizing it was time to end the ominous silence in the room. "Gentlemen, thank you for taking the time to meet with me." When he received no reply, he continued in the same even manner that he might employ while addressing a company Board of Directors. He had been in rooms with some of the biggest SOBs in the business and financial worlds. These men looked tough but were probably easier to handle than some of his former business associates. Then he broke the silence once more. "You can easily see that we are vastly different on the outside. However," he paused for effect, "I can assure you that we are cut from the same cloth on the inside."

"Really?" Came from the one seated in the middle. "How do you figure?"

"For starters, you are white, as I am. You are of Aryan stock. You cannot get more Aryan than I am. But, more important than that, we all realize what that means. You know, as do I, that the future depends on us. Every advance since the dawn of time has been made by a group that, for whatever reason, has been superior to all those around them. You may not have heard of natural selection, but it is everything. Out of many, some are blessed, and rightly challenged, to push the envelope of evolution and progress into the future." Charles paused at this moment. It struck him as odd that this ragtag team of cartoon characters would be the vanguard of anything. But he might need them, and so he continued. "Some are destined to bear the weight of history on their backs. While a number are given that opportunity, only a few have the guts to take up that challenge."

The middle one grunted, Charles could not quite tell if in approval or boredom. "Nice history lesson, but what the fuck has this to do with us?"

"You want the bottom line," Charles smiled absent mirth. "Good. You would make wonderful businessmen."

"We are businessmen," one of the others chuckled. "Though I doubt you've ever sampled our product."

"I'm sure you are." Charles knew they survived, even prospered, in the drug trade. "But you have another product I'm interested in, and I'm willing to pay for it."

"That's why we're here." The middle one barked without any change in expression.

"Okay, you might well represent different organizations . . . the Atomwaffen, the Boogaloos, the Aryan Nation, the Proud Boys, too many other groups to mention. No matter, I do not need to know which. You all are about the same thing, defending the kind of America we all want, that President Trump wants. In the end, we all want a great America again, a country that is pure, and powerful. Am I right?"

"Fuck, yeah, you're right." Someone along the wall almost shouted.

"Go on." The one seated in the middle said, seemingly annoyed at the interruption from his back.

"Well, here's the thing. Trump is our hope, the only leader in my lifetime that's really understood things." Charles fought against the urge to add that it was too bad the man was totally incompetent and a bit crazy. "But he may be in trouble. There won't be an easy opponent this time, like Hillary."

"Bitch." Someone sputtered.

"The left will be more organized this time, and they won't succumb to overconfidence. We are going to need a cadre ready and willing to take chances. Now, let me be clear. I'm looking into my crystal ball. I see the left organizing mass protests against the very things we know are good for this country."

"You want us to beat their asses?"

"Perhaps, but not necessarily. Frankly, I'm not sure you have the numbers. You have the balls, just not the numbers. No, I'm thinking you can blend in with them. Here's the thing. If they remain peaceful, that's not good. But if a few of you loot and burn things down, incite violence, that's all Trump will need to respond with force—be the protector of America and real Americans."

Charles paused. There was silence as Charles began to worry. But the middle one finally spoke. "I like it. You're making sense."

The tension broken, they got down to some earnest planning. Ideas were thrown on the table with Charles discarding most as silly or preposterous, wondering if these men were consuming too many of the drugs they peddled to fund their dreams. But he responded favorably to enough of their input to keep them engaged. After about an hour, he sensed they were coming to an end.

"Nixon," he said as he looked at one of his own men. A man in a suit wearing dark glasses despite the low light, stepped forward and put three track phones on the table. "We'll keep in touch through these track phones. Unless it is critical, you won't hear from me directly. Nixon, here, will be in touch, not his real name by the way. And don't underestimate him. He may look like a businessman, but he's been in the kind of hellholes around the world that you could only imagine in your nightmares."

"What would be something critical?" Their leader was curious.

Charles sighed, looked at his hands as he decided how to respond. "There are a few people in my life that bother me very much. Well, they have disappointed me very much. A few are family who have joined the other side and opposed me at every turn."

"That sucks."

"You have no idea," Charles murmured.

"Sounds like you want us to . . ." One of them started but was cut off by the leader.

"Whatever you need, when you need it, if the price is right of course. That includes making problems disappear," the leader uttered, then added, "I mean, we're after the same things. That's clear. But we've got expenses. You understand."

"I understand and thank you. You would get any instructions about my family directly from me. Regarding action requests for broader political purposes, Nixon here will be in touch." Charles looked directly at the man he presumed to be the leader. "And you will be rewarded for your . . . contributions. In cash, nothing traceable."

The middle one smiled. "It's what you suit-types call a win-win-win partnership. You get power, we get money, and we both get the world we want."

Charles thought that this man was smarter than his appearance suggested. Yes, he could do business with this one. "One last thing. When the election comes around in November, there is no guarantee we will have the votes. No, probably not since we didn't have them last time. But there is no way we, I mean Trump, is leaving the White House. I have ideas about how you can help; indeed, I do."

Later, in the car heading south to Chicago, he pondered why he had crossed a line in the sand. What would provoke him to attack his own offspring? He had been on the edge for a long time, but so far had not attacked his own flesh and blood. There was Beverly but she was only related through marriage.

Of course, there was that time he saw his youngest daughter and her nigger husband crossing the street at night. He told his driver to scare her, make it look like an assassination attempt. It had not been planned, just an impulse really. Normally, he was not an impetuous man.

No, he was not above killing others. He had proved that to himself already. Before taking that step he had pondered how it might feel. Did he have any residual softness, any human sentiments that would render him cautious, introduce doubt? He thought about that in the car as it retraced the path on the interstate back toward Chicago. He scoured his insides as he brought up images of his estranged wife and each offspring. There was nothing left inside, merely revulsion. No one had stood by him. What had Trump done right, and he done wrong? The President's family had remained loyal, spouting the family line to advance a common front while his had turned on him, fought him tooth and nail on all matters where right was on his side. Why weren't they with him? Why?"

He had his theories, of course. He didn't pay enough attention. He let Mary, his spouse, handle the child-rearing. He didn't keep control of the money, letting his wife create those damn trusts for them. And worst of all, he never saw the plot to take over his empire coming, certainly not from his youngest daughter, the quiet one. She had stayed out of sight, just biding her time until she was ready to strike. Trust, he never should have trusted anyone. Nietzsche and Machiavelli were right. The race goes to those unburdened by sentiment, by caring, by the detritus of useless human emotions. No matter how strong and directed he presumed himself to be, it had not been enough.

How many times had he tried to coax Christopher, his heir apparent after the eldest, named after him for God's sake, had committed suicide . . . too weak and too much like his mother to be of any use. That yet hurt, not the suicide, perhaps that was convenient in the end, but that he had sired someone so useless, so soft. How could he have not passed his genes on to the next generation? That was all to him, the strong passed on that which gave them advantages in the future. The weak would fall by the wayside, sometimes with considerable help, and the species would advance in the end.

As he sat back in the comfort of his luxury sedan, that troubling thought intruded again. It always did when he permitted himself to consider these things. Perhaps he was not the real father after all, that would explain a lot. Mary seemed the quiet and submissive Catholic girl but maybe she had a secret life, unknown lovers. That would explain all, or at least a lot.

His dark reverie was broken by something moist on his cheek. Momentary confusion turned to shame. It was a tear, more than one. Furious, he brushed them aside. This was no time for weakness or sentimentality. That was for others, those without the right stuff. His blue eyes blinked away the residual moisture. Then they hardened. This was no time for regret or second thoughts. Not now. That idiot Trump would surely screw up all the work that he and others had done to turn America around. Buffoon that he was, he was yet their best chance to create a state run by better people, populated by the better people of society. It was destiny. Too bad they were relying on someone so weak and self-absorbed. Then again, so was Hitler, he also was a lazy incompetent. Sometimes you went with the cards you were dealt. And sometimes it meant doing unthinkable things. If he had to eliminate those who had been most close to him, his family, so be it. At all costs, you had to keep your eyes on the prize.

CHAPTER 3

LANGARA AVENUE, VANCOUVER

Josh Connelly and Chris Crawford arrived at a comfortable bungalow on Langara Avenue, where Josh had resided for several decades. Professor Corinthia "Connie" Chen, his spouse for about ten years now, was working on a laptop as they entered. "As I suggested might happen, I have dragged the famous Christopher Crawford home with me. Hope that still is okay?"

"More than okay. I get to enjoy some interesting dinner conversation for a change." The slim Asian rose to greet the guest. Taller than most of her peers, she remained very comely with black hair only beginning to be streaked with grey and eyes that danced with humor.

Josh laughed. "My dear spouse is such a jokester. In truth, she worships every word out of my mouth."

"Of course I do, dear," Connie said with exaggerated deference. "You know us Asian wives, so deferential."

"I fear, Professor Chen, that the conversation will not be much elevated tonight. Your husband and I share many similar interests, remarkably so. You are likely to hear the same dribble from me as you do from him."

Connie cocked her head. "Somehow, I suspect the dribble will sound profound when you say it."

Chris laughed aloud. "I am now certain I will feel very much at home here. My own spouse treats me just as badly as you do your lesser half. Have you two traded notes?"

Connie burst out with her own infectious laugh. "Not yet but give me her email address. I am sure we have much in common. I insist on Connie, by the way. And to put you at ease, there is little fear that you will bore me with any political conversation. I have perfected the art of appearing to listen even when I am not. Another Oriental skill which has saved our marriage."

"Unbelievable." Chris broke into a broader smile. "My spouse, Amar, has that exact same skill set. If you were not from hugely different parts of Asia, I would swear you two are sisters. You know, all the marriage counselors push for greater communication. How silly of them. Really, who in the world came up with that stupid idea? Experience has taught me that ignoring one another is the key to happiness in marriage."

"Now, if I had said that I'd be cooking my own repast." Josh winked at his spouse who stuck out her tongue at him.

Chris realized that he could press on without offending anyone. "Oh yes, and I have support from the medical establishment for my position."

"Do tell." Connie cocked her head in a way that suggested she was not convinced.

"Oh yes. A few years ago, I noticed that my good spouse never heard anything I said. Her response was always *what* no matter what I said. I might ask her to pass the salt or be telling her that I was running off with Angelina Jolie. She would look at me blankly and say *what*. So, one day, I pulled her aside and told her, 'My dear, I really think you are developing a hearing problem. Why don't you get it checked out?' For once, she listened to me and went off to an audiologist. They soon figured out the problem."

"Which was?" Josh asked when Chris hesitated.

"Oh yeah. Well, when all the tests were in, they asked her what brought her in for these tests. What did she think her problem was? At that, she relayed my initial concerns and asserted that was the reason she had sought expert advice. I had suggested she had this problem. The specialist immediately laughed. 'Oh yes, you have a common affliction found exclusively among married couples. You hear perfectly except when your husband says anything. The condition is called selective spousal hearing.' True story by the way."

"Now that explains a lot." Connie glared mockingly at Josh, then returned her gaze to Chris. "You, sir, have earned yourself a dinner. And to think, when Josh mentioned this visit from an Oxford scholar, I envisioned a crusty old Don."

"A stereotype mostly found in old English movies but there still are a few of those fossils poking around."

Connie smiled more broadly. "Just glad you are not one. By the way, I hope to meet your wife someday. She sounds like a wise woman indeed."

"I am hoping you will as well," Chris said with an unusual measure of seriousness. "And she is . . . a remarkable woman that is. I still have no idea why she agreed to marry me."

There was a pause where Connie considered a witty retort that she decided against. Instead, she said, "Hope you like lasagna, which is in the oven as we speak."

"Perfect," Chris responded, "my mouth is watering already."

Suddenly Connie became serious. "Before we continue, I want you to know I don't ignore everything Josh says to me. Before heading over to hear your talk, he mentioned your international work and your adopted Afghan daughters . . ."

"Why, yes. I adopted one when she lost her parents as a teen and her sister is like a daughter to me. We did get guardianship of the older one just so immigration would not become a problem, but she had reached the age of majority before adoption was feasible. Why the interest?"

"They still spend time in Afghanistan?"

"Yes, they are there now."

Suddenly Connie seemed hesitant but pushed ahead. "Well, just a coincidence I'm sure, but I was half listening to the news as I prepared the food and there was a story from Kabul . . . a well-known female activist being killed by terrorists. So tragic . . ."

"Shit." Chris spouted. He reached for his phone and began hitting buttons. "Damn. I turned this thing off. The girls are in Kabul right now."

"I didn't know, I would have listened more closely." Connie stopped, desperately trying to recall more about the story.

Chris was frantically looking through his phone. "The Taliban has tried to kill them before. Shit, shit, shit. Did you catch a name?" His face was creased with fear as he flipped through messages and emails.

"It was Mena something . . . Mangal, I think. She was a journalist. I didn't listen all that carefully. So sorry."

Chris exhaled. "Okay, I found the messages. My girls are fine. Just give me a moment to send some texts back, and get my heart beating again."

"Let me get you that drink," Josh said. "Sit down."

Chris sat and pecked away at his phone for a few moments. Then he looked up at Josh and Connie who looked on with apprehension. "I will probably bore you with stories of my fears tonight. My Afghan children, now adults of course, along with my wife, Amar, and my sister, Kay, put themselves in danger all the time. They insist on returning to the world's cesspools to help . . . why did I use that word, cesspools?"

"Understandable in the moment." Josh gave a tiny smile of understanding.

"When I started my international work, the dangers were abstract, they didn't involve people I . . . love so. Every moment they are in harm's way I suffer like you cannot imagine. When they are there, every message gives me cardiac arrest until I can open it."

"I can believe that," Connie said with feeling.

"I am not a religious man. Still, I have prayed for them on many occasions. Azita Masoud is now a physician. I met her when she was a child prodigy helping her father, a great doctor as I came to learn. As an eleven-year old, she became part of my medical team in the Panjshir Valley when the Taliban was at its peak. Azita and her family had escaped Kabul and headed north to join the forces of the *Shura Nazar,* what we knew as the Northern Alliance, which was headed by Ahmad Shah Masood. It seems like ancient history now, but it was front-page news then when the Taliban was sheltering Osama Bin Laden as he prepared his US attack."

Connie wrinkled her face. "I vaguely recall that name, Masood. He was known as the Lion of something or other…"

"Oh yes, that man was a legend who fought both the Soviets and the Taliban until a suicide bomber got him just before 9/11, the day before if I recall correctly. Anyways, Azita thirsted to become a healer in a land where even going to school was hazardous for girls. Her older sister, Deena, took a bit longer to find her way but followed in her mother's footsteps. She became an educator of girls, as her mother had been before the country . . . descended into insanity." Chris sat down while looking at his phone. "I met Mena Mangal. Deena had worked closely with her. Such a sad country, always bleeding . . . always."

"They now live in Afghanistan, Azita and Deena?" Connie asked, taking a seat herself.

"No, no," Chris said quickly. "We've set up a program at Oxford, sort of a hybrid academic-real world effort to reach out to Muslim girls and pull them away from the shackles that keeps them down. My original international work, focusing on health and community organization, is in good hands now and runs itself. I focus more on this new project of uplifting Muslim girls, my writing, and certain political issues. I would prefer they never went back but that is my selfish side talking. I love them so. Still, I must let them be who they are. I cannot rip them away from their purpose. That would be worse than physical death."

"Do you really think so?" Connie asked as she pondered the question. "Physical death has a certain finality to it."

"But tearing someone away from their fate results in a spiritual death. That is what Chris and I were chatting about on the way over, how those of us burdened with a moral compass must suffer so from our personal follies."

Connie suddenly stood and gave Chris a warm hug. "Welcome to our home. All this time I thought men only talked about sex and sports when they were by themselves."

Josh smiled. "You think that because you listen to me talk to myself all the time."

Chris emitted an involuntary chuckle before deciding to get back on topic. "It is the same with my sister and my wife. My twin, Kay, a doc who cut her teeth in a Chicago ER, now spends a lot of time working in Syria and other Mideast hot spots. Even my wife, Amar, goes back into harm's way too often for my liking. That's where we met, by the way, in Afghanistan, when things there were really in the crapper."

"So, what do you think about Trump pulling out?" Josh asked.

Chris grimaced. "Mostly, I hate war. But sometimes, I'm conflicted. These religious bigots are so bad, it would be like letting the Evangelicals run things in the States."

"Like they do now, you mean," Connie said with a twinkle.

"Good point." Chris admitted. "Besides, Trump is cutting and running for the wrong reasons. He can't see any economic payoff. There's no money to be made there and everything is a transactional analysis to him. How can I make a buck?"

"No shit." Josh shook his head sadly.

"Back to my family." Chris shifted to a topic that interested him. "They all keep putting themselves in harm's way, drives me nuts. Azita, Deena, Amar, and Kay keep returning to Afghanistan. Hell, even my youngest sister, Kat, lives in danger and she is the one with a normal life . . . running the family financial empire in Chicago. I suppose that is not quite normal, the windy city can be more dangerous than Kabul. Still, it is not a declared war zone."

"Why is she in such danger," Josh asked, "beyond living in such a dangerous city which looks like a damn war zone to me?"

Chris breathed heavily. "Long story, the short version of which is that Kat stayed home and bucked our Father in his mania for right wing causes. He is up there with the Koch brothers and the Mercers and Adelson and all the other robber barons who seek total control of the country and its wealth. You cannot believe the money they throw around to assert some hegemony over our political system. Such people spent a half billion dollars just in recent years convincing Americans that climate change was bunk. They merely want to maintain their profits from extractive energy sources, hold on to their stranded assets. So, what if the earth burns to a crisp, they'll be gone by then."

"Yes, the obsessive self-centeredness stuns me," Josh muttered with some venom.

"And that is just the tip of the iceberg, no pun intended. Have you heard of Charles Crawford Senior?" He directed this question to Josh's spouse.

"No, I don't think so." Connie was shaking her head.

"Most people haven't. My dear Father is a player behind the scenes, less visible than some but even more lethal." Chris looked at his two hosts with an intensity he seldom displayed. "If you ever have had an interest in meeting the anti-Christ, I'll introduce you to him one day. My sisters and I are convinced he killed my sister-in-law but have no proof. Our take is that he figured out that she was spying on him for us. And there is reason to believe he may have similar designs on Kat, who has challenged him most directly and in his own arena, high finance. The man doesn't lose, and she bested him by engineering a hostile takeover with the help of the rest of us. That puts a target on her back, and maybe mine as well. She is convinced that he tried to run her down on a Chicago street."

"His own child?" Connie sounded uncertain.

"Listen," Chris said with total conviction, "there are certain people who simply do not function according to the rules of civilization. They don't operate with sentiments such as empathy or compassion or anything resembling what we associate with human sensitivity. My two siblings and I watched as our Father drove my elder brother to suicide. While the patriarch didn't kill him with his own hands, the guilt is all over him in virtual blood. I tried to help my brother escape but . . ." Chris's voice caught.

"Everything is relative," Josh murmured so quietly that it took Chris a moment to understand what he said. "My father was just a run-of-the-mill son of a bitch who could be so charming when so moved."

"Here's the thing. Kat, my kid sister though she's no kid anymore, is getting even more worried. Of the family, she and I, along with her husband who was my best friend growing up, have most directly opposed Father's political agenda. You need to understand this. He has some sinister amalgam of racism, nativism, and authoritarian set of beliefs that match perfectly with the ascendant Trump regime. I mean, he knows that Trump is a deranged moron but that doesn't matter. So was Hitler in his mind. My Father, and too many filthy rich autocrats like him, would back Satan himself if that would advance their economic agenda. They are amazingly shortsighted. Right now, a year or so before the election, it is hard to say what will happen. Anyone with half a brain can see the harm he is doing to the country and the world, but America is burdened with a disproportionate number of total idiots. If something goes wrong for Donald, and he sees danger ahead, there is no telling what he will do to keep power. He would tear the country apart in a nanosecond. That is what being a megalomaniac is all about."

Connie stood up. "Listen, on that positive note, dinner is ready. Let's continue this delightful conversation over some food."

An hour later, they were still at the table drinking coffee. Chris had talked at length about efforts to counter the shift rightward in American politics and the rise of anti-science and fantastical thinking that dominated the new Republican Party. He also recounted the continuing efforts of his father to recruit him to his side, an exercise in fantastical thinking if there ever was one.

Josh sighed loudly during a pause in the conversation. "You know what I find so devastating about all this. When I emigrated from the States to avoid the Vietnam War, I yet thought that America's insanity was temporary. When my generation came to power, I thought a new America would dawn, one I could take pride in. Perhaps then, I could return home. Guess what! A new America was born but it sucked even worse."

Connie reached out to touch her husband's arm. "Well, we all fall back on small and unscientific samples when we want proof of our priors."

"Spoken like a true scientist," Chris added, "and now that Father might have finally given up on recruiting me to his side, if in fact he has tossed in the towel, I'm sure to be on his hit list. Good thing I hang out in England. The man is the definition of evil, I think his picture is next to the text for that word in the dictionary."

Connie sat down. "I will make a promise right now. I will listen carefully to everything you say tonight. Josh recently has talked about you and your work quite a bit, but I had no idea . . ." She hesitated for a moment before resuming in a clear voice. "I hate to admit this but I do listen to Josh and while I give my good husband a hard time about his causes and tilting at impossible windmills, that is precisely why I fell in love with him. He cares and cares deeply. I like to think my scientific work has led to breakthroughs that help people, but the connection is not always direct. I can see the good he has done in the policy arena. He seldom does but I do. This lug has been such a good spouse these years as I worked my way toward retirement. I know in my heart he wants to get back to fighting the good fight. So, let us discuss just how he, we, can do that. Professor Crawford, Chris I mean, you may have sought out my husband as an ally on this trip, but you may walk away with an entire family on your side."

"An entire family? I'm not sure I understand," Chris asked.

Connie continued. "I am sure I am speaking out of turn but here goes. Josh has a sister who is a fine doctor and looking for new opportunities as she reached retirement age. Her partner is an expert in international law. Her one daughter has a background in linguistics and considerable service overseas, including the Middle East while her partner—we have a lot of nontraditional arrangements in the family—is a Jordanian who has done considerable work with refugees."

Chris looked at Connie in amazement. "Damn, it would take me six months to find that kind of talent and only if I were lucky. This is a bonanza."

Connie smiled. "Well, this is only in theory at present, but I think it is possible to get them interested. The timing is good. Besides, they listen to me, not so much to Josh. I have an advantage with them since they are so thankful that I bit the bullet and married this guy whom we all agreed was hapless."

"Yes," Chris stammered, "I can see where that would be a great sacrifice."

Josh reached out and took his wife's hand. "Have I ever told you how much I love you."

"Not nearly enough. It's a good thing I can read between the lines."

"Josh," Chris found his smile again, "you and I may be total screwups, but I think we both managed to marry way above our station in life."

"No shit, Sherlock." Josh arose. "Now, let's drink to hopeless screw-ups marrying well.."

CHAPTER 4

AFGHANISTAN

"I finally got a text from Dad," Azita said, her eyes still red from weeping. "He finally has heard about Mena Mangal. He was on the other side of the world, in Western Canada when he heard about a high-profile assassination in Kabul. That was before seeing our messages. Of course, he feared it was us and was frantic for a bit. The poor dear, we do put him through hell."

"Can you blame him?" Deena replied. "This was a direct attack aimed at what we do, what I do at least."

"It's not like we make his life a living hell on purpose. He must understand that, at least I hope he does. After all, he wants us to live normal lives, he says that all the time." Azita's words were directed more to herself than to her sister, as if to assuage nagging doubts in her own head.

The two sisters were yet glued to coverage of the assassination of the well-known Muslim journalist and TV personality who had been outspoken in her advocacy of women's rights. Deena had met with her many times, discussing their common interests and visions. Mangal had even mentioned the work of the Masoud sisters though in vague terms, so as not to make the young women obvious targets. That was always a delicate balance for the young journalist. On the one hand, she wanted to advertise the work and thus praise women she felt were playing historic roles in the cause of change. On the other, she was deathly afraid of putting these advocates in harm's way. Her assassination, right in broad daylight on the streets of Kabul served as a visible reminder of the vulnerability of any woman who spoke out on behalf of their gender.

"We will never be safe," Deena murmured to no one in particular, "perhaps not even in England." Azita and Deena looked at one another. The forces of fanaticism waxed and waned but recently seemed to be making a comeback. While the central government seemed a bit more stable now, America clearly was reconsidering its commitment to maintaining peace and restoring the nation to some semblance of civility. This most recent trip felt particularly ominous.

Karen Fisher, now head of the international program that Christopher Crawford had started over two decades ago, came to sit beside the two Afghan women. She had met them as teens, as they had fled their war-torn country with the help of Chris Crawford and his new wife, Dr. Amar Singh. Now they were adult players on the world stage, noted for their own professional contributions. "I feel just awful for you. I had met her, of course, but the two of you knew her so well."

"She was like a sister," Deena managed to utter as the tears flowed again.

"Probably better than the one you've been stuck with," Azita murmured.

"Don't go there. None of your humor right now." Deena whispered and slid closer to her sibling, putting a head on her shoulder.

Karen paused a moment, recognizing the emotions that were spilling forth. "Listen, why don't you two grieve. The others have gathered but I can meet with them."

"No," Deena said forcefully. "If we back away, the terrorists win. Mena would be ashamed of me if I let that happen."

"Are you sure?" Azita said as she took her older sister's face in her hands, looking deeply into her eyes. "Perhaps she is looking down from heaven pleading with us to give up our crazy dreams. She could be shouting at us to stop being children, stop just assuming that, unlike her, we will survive. In a way, that's what we are, just selfish children who are doing what we want to do." Tears suddenly flowed from the young doctor's eyes. She hated when emotions got the better of her.

Deena grabbed her younger sibling and shook her. "Listen to me, dear sister. I would continue my work even if the fates took you away from me, but Allah will never permit that to happen."

"Oh, sweet sister, you cannot know that."

Deena forced a smile. "Then, no matter. I would continue until they kill me as well. So, you see, we will still be together. I will plague you even beyond this life, you can count on that."

Azita suddenly found that she couldn't go there, to humor. She had always been able to find refuge in that gift which her father bequeathed on her, along with his prodigious medical skills. But not in his moment. Her heart was too heavy. "No, I won't let you be taken from me. I'd give all this up . . ."

She never finished. Deena's hand shot out and slapped her sister's cheek with considerable force. "Listen to me. Just you listen to me. We cannot give up. What would Mama say, what would Papa say? What would we say to our own hearts?"

"I . . ." Azita started but lost her way.

"Damn you, girl." Deena now shouted. "When we were young, you let nothing stand in your way. I hated you for that, always feeling like that useless older sister who would never match up to the brilliant prodigy who had followed her into the family as an afterthought. I should have been the anointed one. You have no idea how often I sat in my room crying because I thought you were getting all the attention while I would be bartered on the marriage market to some suitable man. And I didn't even like men."

At that, Azita managed a tiny smile of recognition. "Yes, it must have been difficult."

"Difficult, difficult you say, it was hell. Good thing you could not see into my heart back then the many ways I plotted to do you in. Funny, that was my fantasy then, thinking of ways I might dispatch you into paradise and now . . ." The two sisters embraced, their tears intermingling. "You promise me one thing. If I die, you will continue on."

Azita pulled away so she could look into her sister's eyes. "And you do the same . . . if they kill me first."

"Well, I would take a couple of days off to see you planted properly in the ground. After all, we must observe Islamic law."

Azita smiled. "And when did you become the sarcastic shit in this family? That was my role." Her expression then turned quizzical. "And when did you become the big sister? That's what you are now."

"Is that a problem?" Deena asked.

"Not at all, not at all." Azita cocked her head. "I rather like it."

Karen Fisher, who had been watching the interchange from across the room, joined the sisters. Hard boiled, yet efficient in her role as CEO of the International Services Organization (ISO), she felt tears welling inside her as she looked upon the exchange. These were telltale signs of feelings she desperately sought to suppress. After all, she had a reputation to defend.

A moment from almost two decades ago flashed through her head. As his then executive assistant, she had accompanied her boss, Christopher Crawford, to the Panjshir Valley. He flew there in a panic after he found out that his sister had joined a small mission there to provide medical help to the Northern Alliance, a group desperately holding out against the Taliban.

This rather tiny medical outpost consisted of Amar Singh, a member of Chris's organization who had volunteered to relocate to this most vulnerable spot, and an Afghan physician named Pamir Masoud who was assisted by his daughter who was on the cusp of her teens but already versed in basic medical procedures. They had recently been joined by British medical personnel. Typically, his missions were larger in scope and based on the premise that integrated efforts were more effective than siloed programs. This small outpost was in an extremely dangerous site and dominated by a refugee camp. Bin Laden had just attacked America and the West was responding but it was in those early chaotic days. Chris had made his way to this place at great risk merely to yank his sister out of harm's way, if she would listen to him which was highly uncertain. Within days, Chris had fallen in love with the place, with his wife-to-be, who headed medical operations at the site, and with a fetching young medical prodigy who would become his adopted daughter. On that trip, Karen realized her life's work was with this man and his program.

Karen now stared at these two accomplished adults. Azita had her medical degree from Oxford, while Deena had earned an advanced degree in education from the same institution. What they had become was amazing. Yet, it was all such a tenuous start in those beginning days. The Taliban had struck back as their situation deteriorated considering the Western military response to 9/11. They murdered the Masoud parents one early morning as the girls escaped into the hills. Chris and some Northern Alliance Mujahideen warriors searched for them. Karen was frantic as the day went on and convinced the first contingent of British troops to send a search helicopter. They arrived just after Chris and his party found the girls but ran into a group of Taliban warriors. The rescue was successful though Karen was seriously wounded in a hail of gunfire. For years after, she joked about being so stupid for putting her life on the line for Chris, whom she shredded with light-hearted sarcasm at every turn. She knew that not to be the case, though. She loved him more than her own siblings and adored the Masoud sisters as if they were her own nieces. Still, it was important to her to maintain her tough-woman persona, a hard shell that had helped her escape a difficult childhood.

She came out of her reverie as the two siblings rose. “We’re ready to join the others.”

It was a meeting of several of the England based staff from ISO with those leading efforts in Kabul and the Panjshir Valley. It was being held in a western hotel in the Embassy section of town, usually safe from the terror that often broke out. But, given the day’s events, was anyplace safe? Karen started. “I am throwing the agenda out the window. I think we need to start with a security review, but let’s go around the table first. I am not sure we all know one another. I am Karen Fisher, the CEO of the International Service Organization or ISO program. Now the Afghan staff.”

“Let’s see. I am Doctor Ferhana Gupta and this is my husband, Bahiri, also a physician.”

“But not as talented as my dear wife.” The man next to her beamed.

Ferhana smiled back at him. “He thinks this will get him out of cleaning up after dinner, but it will not. We were working at a clinic in Kabul when Azita and Deena walked in one day. It had been their father’s clinic in the past, a man and doctor most revered by all. I had grown up nearby and knew their sainted father. I recalled them from when they were young girls. That was before I left the country for medical school in India. Even then, it was hard for women here, and it soon would get worse. In any case, we chatted that day. One thing led to another, and we are now part of the program."

"See," Karen said, "it was fate." Then she nodded to an older man.

"I guess I am next. I am Doctor Archie Singletary, retired from a practice in Australia and now heading the Panjshir Valley site, the site where Karen almost lost her life and whose name is yet spoken of with reverence for saving the Masoud girls, as they are called. Agnes here is my spouse and competent nurse. She and I decided one day we wanted to make a real contribution. This mission gave us that opportunity. We are grateful."

"Thanks." Karen interjected. "Now the British contingent."

"Well, I am Professor Shahed Al-Hussein, but call me Ali, everyone does. This is my first trip to Kabul which, in retrospect, I find odd. I have been to most other countries in this region of the world. I am Jordanian by birth but now located at Oxford University. There, I am heading a joint project with ISO to do what we can to cultivate the next generation of female leaders in the Muslim world. We have several things going but one of my favorite initiatives is to identify hidden gems like Azita and Deena and give them an opportunity to shine. We need female leaders, role models, so many that the fanatics cannot kill them all. The Taliban came so close to burying their dreams. We cannot permit that to continue."

"I am Deena Masoud, daughter of Pamir and Madeena Masoud. This is my younger sister, Azita. We like to think that she is our father's daughter and I am our mother's daughter."

She now tried to smile but signs of the recent emotions remained. "The great miracle of our lives, thanks to Allah, is that we made it through our childhood without killing one another. That is a good thing since I discovered that she was not nearly so foolish as I originally thought while I am no longer as foolish as I had been. Azita is hoping to find young girls who might pursue medicine and science while I am into the overall education of Muslim girls. You all know how desperate the need is."

"And I am Doctor Kay Crawford. Yes, Chris is my twin brother and, to be honest, I was tempted to cave in his skull on numerous occasions when we were young. But, under my guidance, he turned out quite well in the end though much disagreement remains on that score." She chuckled at her own aside. "Anyways, I oversee the medical operations in most of the international sites at present."

"Last but not least, I am Carlotta Ciganda. This also is my first visit to Kabul though I have been with ISO for quite a while now. I am a social worker and community organizer by training and oversee the general human services side of things."

With that, the door burst open as a handsome young man apologized while finding a seat next to Azita. She smiled at him. "This tardy young man is my husband, Ahmad Zubair. I will punish him later in private." The expression on her face betrayed a deep affection.

"So sorry. I was getting updates from my government contacts on what happened today. What have I missed?"

Azita grabbed his hand. "Just the introductions. Besides being a devoted spouse, Ahmad has degrees from Oxford and

Kings College-London. He is an expert in international community development though he has failed to explain to me exactly what that is. I think it is something that those who would faint at the sight of blood might study. I am glad I chose medicine as a vocation, at least I know what I am supposed to be doing." She smiled for the first time that day.

"You would understand what I do if you were trainable. I just need a better student, one who listens to me." His face broke into a broad smile.

"What have you heard, Ahmad?" Karen asked him, getting serious.

"Of course, information is sketchy, but the sense is that our own work is not a target yet. Mena was such a public figure. Moreover, she went out of her way to antagonize the fundamentalists, and not just the Taliban. She had been getting death threats for weeks, very explicit threats. She ignored them, kept upping her taunts on television. She had been working and making statements on Tolo TV which, for those who don't know, is the largest private network in the country. And she was constantly on social media. Just a few days ago she reported getting death threats that worried even her. They struck her as more legitimate but never said why. She didn't stop in any case. It was as if she hoped to invite martyrdom by taunting the extremists publicly."

"Do you really believe that?" Shahed asked.

"I have no idea." Ahmad protested. "That is what my contacts were saying. They tell me that if we keep a low profile, we should be all right."

"What bothers me," Shahed spoke up, "is that the security forces knew she was a target. This was no secret. And yet, she was gunned down on her way to work in the middle of Kabul. Is anyone safe? All of us, especially the women, are prepared to take risks for what we believe but I promised . . ." Then she suddenly stopped.

Azita laughed without mirth. "Deena and I can guess. You promised my dad that you would somehow keep me safe. I read his frantic messages when news of her death went out over the international press."

"And your mother, I promised her as well."

"That was a foolish promise," Deena said with a touch of harshness. She looked directly at Professor Shahed Al-Hussein with unflinching eyes. This was a woman she admired, respected, and even felt things she did not want to admit to herself. Shahed was a strikingly attractive woman in her early forties, loosely tied to the Jordanian Royal Family and already a full professor at Baliol College at Oxford. She had made her academic reputation in the study of the condition of Muslim women in their struggle for an independent voice. Her life was comfortable until Chris Crawford came along and convinced her to step outside the cloistered life of an academic and get more involved in those issues about which she already had cared about so deeply but had no vehicle through which to pursue them. "You have lived in the Middle East enough to know we will always be in harm's way, particularly in this tortured land."

Shahed looked back at Deena. At times, she had difficulty keeping a steady gaze on this woman. Deena had always been thought of as the beauty of the Masoud family. Her sister, Azita, had been the feisty, stubborn medical prodigy. Back then, they were oil and water, so different. Now, as full adults, they seemed more like siblings. Both were accomplished and focused. She had made that promise and, damn it, she was dedicated to keeping it. She had grown to love both but, in her quiet moments, she admitted that Deena tugged at her heart in a special manner. It was not a physical attraction, though she was uncertain about that. More likely, it was born out of a similar journey in life and a common passion to educate oppressed members of her gender. "True enough, but I still intend to do my best. This is personal now." Her gaze never strayed from Deena who looked away.

In the ensuing silence, Ahmad suddenly felt himself flush. He spoke up. "The government is embarrassed by this. Ms. Mangal had recently been appointed a cultural consultant to the National Assembly, so she had quasi-official status. The warnings were clear. They now believe they should have done more. Your program is in this country at the behest of the government, such as it is. They want to provide more protection but there is a dilemma."

Karen interjected. "Yes, the tradeoff is one we face in numerous sites. Sometimes inviting very visible official protection simply makes the target more inviting. Oh, they care about these people so they must be important. Let's go after them. Knowing what to do is all so . . . difficult."

Archie Singletary had been listening carefully. "You know, Agnes and I knew when we came here that we might face, what shall we say, some unfortunate realities. We are prepared. The rewards to our work are so precious, irreplaceable. At the same time, we are far removed from Kabul, up in a corner of this country. A lot of the conflict and turmoil seems distant, as if in another land. I fear, even after being here for a number of years now, I have so little understanding."

Deena let out a sigh that brought attention to her. "Sorry, I was thinking how little I knew about my own country until I became an adult and started paying attention. We forget that what is now has not always been so. I see how even educated colleagues back at Oxford react to any discussion of Afghanistan. Their eyes roll and they say something about the place being hopeless. But that is not true. I've taken the time now to understand our past, read some of our history."

"Really?" Azita interjected.

"Yes, dear sister. I stopped reading trashy romance novels a long time ago as you well know. After all, they were always about men who are not worth the bother. Do you want my history lesson or not?"

"Of course." Her sister had a mischievous smile but inside wanted her sibling to shine in the moment.

Deena hesitated, wondering if she had offended the males in the room but everyone seemed to be waiting for her to continue. "For so long we had no real identity of our own. We were a buffer between the great powers of Russia and Britain, both vying for control. But neither succeeded, we dealt the British some humiliating defeats. Don't fear, I won't go on forever. Eventually, a central monarchy got strong enough to stabilize things. Our mother, as a girl growing up in the final years of King Zahia Shah's reign saw a totally different world . . . in Kabul at least. There was a sense of diversity here and freedom, with a rather large secular population. Women wore western clothes, became educated, went to work. They danced and smoked cigarettes and even dated boys of their own choosing. Not all, of course, but such behaviors were not seen as mortal sins."

"I never knew that" Archie said. "What happened?"

"Well, almost five decades ago, the King was forced into exile by his cousin, Mohammed Daoud. This unleashed an era of instability that has never ended, not really. First, the struggle for control was between the Communists and the religious extremists. Well, both sides were extremists but with different gods. By the late '70s, two Communist factions emerged from the power struggle, the Parchan and the Khalq. Russia saw its long-frustrated dream of controlling Afghanistan ripe for the taking but were frustrated by the infighting. They intervened on behalf of the Parchan faction and were invited to shore up a shaky regime. Wait, is this boring?" Deena looked about her self-consciously.

"Not at all." Ferhana's husband Bahiri responded. "I've been working here for some time now and still know so little about the place. My wife tries to keep me ignorant."

"Which is not difficult," Ferhana added facetiously. "Please, Deena, go on."

"Alright then, the Soviets were able to impose hegemony over our country. Initially, they put Barkak Karmel of the Parchan party in power. But he proved ineffective and such an overt secular government never set well with the religious fanatics. Adherence to older Muslim traditions and beliefs became fashionable as a way of resisting Communist rule. Russia saw their prize slipping away so they deposed Karmel and put strongman Mohammed Najibullah in power. He tried the tough approach, but things were slipping away from the Communists. The Soviets invaded to shore up their crumbling satellite country."

"Now, this part I recall," Kay interjected.

Deena continued. "It was a bad bet by the Soviets since the abstractions of Communism were no match for the emotional appeal of religious fundamentalism. By the mid-1980s, the Mujahideen were now being supplied with American rockets. They were particularly strong in the north, the only land route from Soviet territory into our country. Over time, the Soviet air power advantage evaporated, as American supplied surface-to-air missiles gave the Mujahideen a fighting chance against a modern military force. The people rallied around older religious beliefs and customs and against the hated Russians. The secularism of a prior generation was disappearing fast, now associated with these foreign oppressors."

"Oh Pagwam!" Bahiri exclaimed. "I was living right next door, well two doors over in Bombay and paid so little attention to all this. It might have well been happening on the moon."

"So, I am not boring you," Deena murmured with an apologetic tone.

"Heavens, no, this is fascinating," Archie chimed in. "I should have read up on this myself. Please continue."

"All right, as most know the Soviets pulled out in 1989. The costs of keeping an invasion force in the country were becoming too much."

"Yes," Kay added, "I recall Chris and I talking about this being Russia's Vietnam. Well, in truth, I listened as Chris waxed eloquently on the subject. Amazingly, some of it stuck. Like you, Bahiri, I was too busy with my education to keep on top of this stuff."

Deena pondered that for a moment. "I know little about that Vietnam War but our fight against the Soviets surely helped weaken the Soviet Union. They could no longer hold it together. In Afghanistan, Communist control contracted gradually until Kabul fell in 1992. Then, the question arose. Who would move into the power vacuum? Various warlords fought for ultimate power. Masood, the lion of the Panjshir Valley, initially took Kabul, but the fighting continued, a warlord named Hekmatyar had considerable strength. The violence and bloodshed continued with no end in sight."

"This is where the Taliban emerged?" Ferhana's comment fell somewhere between a statement and a question.

"Exactly. They seemed to offer stability. They also took advantage of the reaction to the religious persecution under the Communists. The Mullahs had lost influence and power for a while and they wanted a comeback in the worst way. Talib means defender and they posed as protectors of the ancient religious and cultural virtues. As my British friends say, it seemed like a good idea at the time. More to the point, they were ready. They had been preparing a cohort of zealots in the Madrassas or holy schools both in this country and especially in Pakistan. This gave the religious extremists an edge. By 1996, Mullah Omar led the Taliban to effective control of Kabul and beyond."

"Huh!" Carlotta interjected. "They did a lot of damage in a short time."

"Yes," Deena affirmed. "One of the first things he did was to invite Osama Bin Laden, who had been ejected from Sudan under American pressure. The Taliban would stake out an extreme fundamentalist position. This is the environment in which my sister and I came of age. Our mother had been ejected from her University position, originally by the Communists since she opposed them and then by the Taliban since all women were now second-class citizens. Azita and I had no hope for a future, none really, except that my stubborn sister refused to give up. She would follow our saint of a father around like a puppy dog until he had no choice but to begin teaching her his skills, a brave act at the time. Her refusal to give in to reality eventually rubbed on to me. I had resigned myself to being the compliant Muslim girl until my silly sister almost got herself killed by the morals police one day. Funny, I had daydreamed of doing the very same thing to her myself. I had been quite jealous of her, until that day." Then Deena stopped, reaching out to take the hand of her sister.

"What happened that day?" Kay asked quietly.

"I only know what I think happened in the moment. I am not sure we ever really can get to the truth when emotions run so high." Deena's voice became quieter, so soft that several around the conference table leaned forward to hear. "What stays in my mind's eye, whether true or not I cannot tell, is that I got angry.

These people who almost killed my sister for no greater sin than reading a poster in a public square should not be permitted to define whom we were. No, their view of God, Allah, was false. Who were they to say we girls were worthless? I hate to admit this now, but I saw Azita as a kind of hero in that moment. Really, she was just a silly girl with a dream but if she could dream then so could I. That is when I gave over my silly girlish ways of that time and asked my mother to begin tutoring me."

"Such an inspiring story." Agnes, Archie's matronly-looking wife and his assisting nurse added. "It gives us hope that our work is worth the effort and the risks."

Azita's expression evolved into a mischievous smile and both Karen and Kay guessed what was coming next. "Yes, modesty prevents me from taking too much credit, but my poor sister was destined for an indolent life of eating chocolates and reading romance novels all day until I rescued her."

"Oh," Deena exhaled sharply, "you really are an incorrigible shit."

"Enough squabbling, children" Kay jumped in with a smile. "In their absence, Chris and Amar have given me power of *in loco parentis.* That means I'm in charge of you two."

As the group around the table chuckled with nervous release, Archie spoke up. "I think this sense of sacrifice and risk-taking is infectious. Karen and Kay know but this may be news to some for you. My son and his wife, both physicians, joined us at our site a couple of months ago. I suspect they were worried about us and suspecting that the work here was getting a bit taxing for two old farts. I was thrilled by this and desperately fearful. I now believe they have decided to stay. I am not sure how I feel about that." Agnes reached out to take her husband's hand. "It is one thing to place yourself in danger, but your loved ones, that is different I fear."

Karen wondered if Archie would continue. When he did not, she decided to bring the discussion around to where she wanted it to be. It was not the original agenda. This was supposed to be a fact-finding session to get a sense of the dominant issues faced by those in the field before setting out to visit each site in person and meet those doing work on the ground. The events of the day had pushed conventional plans aside, as they often did. "Listen all, before we do anything else, I need to say something. I never thought I would end up running this organization on a day-to-day basis. Some of you may not know that Chris originally hired me as a personal assistant, not because I knew what I was doing but because I had no qualms about giving him grief. That is still my special skill but over time I found I was pretty damn good at running things." She paused to look around the table. "However, there is one thing I have never gotten used to doing . . . that is dealing with the risks to people I know. Over the years, we've lost a few of our people to accidents or disease or worse. Every aid organization working where we do experiences this, it is an inescapable part of the landscape. For some reason, though, I never knew any of them on a personal level. Each loss was tragic but part of the costs of doing business I suppose. I shudder even saying that, but it is true."

"Everyone who does this work knows the risks." Ferhana interrupted Karen, anticipating where she was going.

"But you see, that does not always make it easier for me." Karen paused to look at Kay, the woman who knew her best, her partner in life and the sister of the man she had adored as a loved mentor. "Kay, and maybe Deena, know me the best. I guess most people see this hard driving, funny, cynical woman who grew up in a tough, working-class Birmingham family. No lacy curtains for us, no frills or emotional niceties. It wasn't only the upper class that was supposed to have a stiff upper lip. Hell, we Fishers were never going to display the posh pretenses of the elite nor were we going to let ordinary emotions get to us. Nothing but gritty responses to hard-bitten reality for working-class blokes like us. So, in the end I am a Fisher, at least to the world. What I display to others is my own brand of brittle cynicism with little emotion and a huge amount of surface bravado. Any of you who have seen me around Chris know my take-no-prisoner's charm."

"That's what we, I, love about you," Kay offered tentatively.

Karen smiled at her. "Thanks. The thing is, though, that under the crusty shell I am not so strong. Often, when Kay is in the field I wake up in the middle of the night, wander around the house. I think of those out in the field, facing god knows what daily. But the faces in front of me are those that I know the best. What if I somehow sent Deena or Azita into a place from which they never returned. How could I face Chris, or Amar, or myself?"

"Surely, no one would blame you." Carlotta spoke up, thinking hard on what might pass as an appropriate response from a social worker.

"Don't you see. I would blame myself." Then Karen paused, perhaps realizing that she was sliding toward a place from which a retreat would be difficult. "Okay, maybe enough of the honesty. But I need to hear from each of you that this is where you want to be, where you need to be." She first looked at Archie and Agnes.

It was Agnes who spoke up. "Dear Archie and I have talked about this many a night, especially since our children have joined us. Putting yourself in danger is one thing, but those you love so dearly? Well, that is a different matter. But it all came clear to us. We always tried to teach our children through example. Oh, we would sit them down from time to time to reprimand or instruct, but we always found the indirect lessons to be the most effective. And they got our lessons even when we were not sure what they were. You know, money is not important, nor notoriety, nor power. No, that stuff matters little. At the end of the day, how have you used your gifts to help others."

Archie then added on. "I asked my boy why he had uprooted his practice and joined us. Did he worry that we were too old, over the hill? He just laughed. Then he told me that while it was true that I was older than dirt, that had nothing to do with it. He merely wanted to make half the mark on the world I had done." Archie's lip quivered slightly. "I am not the brightest guy around, but I am smart enough not to argue with my son. His problem is that he takes after his mother."

"What?" Agnes sputtered.

"Thing is, you aren't getting rid of the Singletary family, no way. It is not that we want to be here, it is more that we need to be here." Then Archie simply smiled.

Bahiri spoke up next. "My decision is simple. Ferhana told me we were staying, nothing for me to decide." Then he sighed with exaggeration. "I recall fondly when Hindu men were the masters of their households . . . now ancient history."

Ahmad broke out in a guffaw. "I get you, my brother. I still remember when I thought Muslim women were obedient. Who spread that nonsense around?"

"Excuse me?" Azita smiled broadly for the first time. "You quickly are becoming the man in this room who is in big trouble." She poked him in the ribs. "My good husband may joke but, Karen, please understand that we have talked this through many times." Azita reached out to touch her sister's hand. "All of us have faced the reality of our choices."

Karen smiled at the woman and turned to sweep her gaze to include Deena and Azita. "You are not in this part of the world as much, but you are bigger targets when you are. I need to hear from you as well, even as I know the answer."

Azita and Deena looked at one another as if deciding which would affirm the obvious. It was Kay, the beloved aunt who spoke instead. "We know what these two would say. They have already been assaulted for their convictions, almost dying. The persons you must deal with are Chris and Amar. I never, ever thought my brother capable of such love, but he is beside himself with anxiety over these two. Me? He would sacrifice me for a six pack but these two . . ."

Karen nodded in agreement. "And you, Shahed, or should I say Ali?"

The Jordanian national smiled, which made her face more attractive if that were possible. "I still recall Chris hailing me from across the college green one day. He asked me to tea, said he had an idea he wanted to run past me. Ah, I should have told him I was too busy as a scholar, but I didn't. And he is such a charming, persuasive man. Plus, he promised money for this hair-brained scheme, and we academics are always on the look-out for research money."

"Yeah," Karen half groaned, "always disappoints me to find out that scholars are no better than us mere mortals."

"Good one. Chris was inspired by you two, he told me that day." She nodded toward Azita and Deena. "It had occurred to him that he had thought that you two were not unique, that there must be others. Yes, that is what he said, but I am sure he was fibbing. His point was that there were other Azita's and Deena's who needed to be identified and nurtured. Then he went on about your new initiative to expose isolated families and girls to the broader world through technology. I remember him saying that you girls had your parents as role models, and that I grew up with all the advantages, but that millions of girls have so little chance. We had to do something about this, and that he had already recruited the college Don to his scheme. By the third cup of tea, I was surrendering. As I said, he is so damn charming. More than that, he was right. What was I doing, merely carving out a cloistered academic career? What would I say at the end? What would I point out as my accomplishments, a bunch of dated journal articles? He was right, again. I knew it."

Kay cocked her head with a whimsical smile. "That is the hell of it. He is often right. Any regrets falling for his charms?"

Professor Ali-Hussein smiled broadly. "Not a damn one. This may slow up my conventional academic career, but I feel useful again. Besides, Sir Howard, who heads the college, is fully supportive. He reminded me that only four Oxford colleges accepted women when he started. He wanted to change all that, as I did. I am . . . what is it, connected to what I am within my heart and can never go back. And if there is danger on occasion, I want to share it. That is the least I can do."

Karen looked around the table slowly. "I can only say one thing. You people are a bunch of blithering idiots. Well, I love you all. I came to sort you out and you've done it to me." A smile crossed her face. "You know, growing up in the tough part of Birmingham, in the culture I did, I get a sense about what liberating young girls with few opportunities means. I do get it. So then, seeing that you have more convictions than brains, let's see what we can do to save the next generation of Muslim girls."

CHAPTER 5

PATER ET FILIUS AGONISTES

On his return trip from Vancouver to Oxford, Chris Crawford stopped in Chicago to see his sister and friends. He had spent that Saturday night with his youngest sibling, Kat, who now headed the family financial empire. Ricky, her husband and his lifelong friend, was again away on business, but he would get a chance to see him when he got back to Oxford. He would enjoy an evening alone with Kat. He could not recall the last time it had just been the two of them. There was much personal catching up, renewing painful family memories. But they also spent much time touching on the business challenges Kat faced. Chris had never taken to money matters, but his younger sister highly valued his perspective on things. She was wise enough to recognize that she lived in a business world bubble, daily interacting with those who thought and believed as she did. Real world contacts were precious to her though it amused her that she considered her brother to be in the real world.

As was her custom, the next morning she had already sequestered herself in her office before the sun had appeared even though it was a Sunday. Managing a significant financial empire was a taxing undertaking. She had mentioned the night before that she would be gone when he awoke the next day but would return by late morning. Just a few foreign market issues to deal with, people in Europe and Asia to contact. They did not rest on Sunday either. It struck Chris that her life now was always full of just a few more issues to wrap up.

He had often wondered where her skills and fortitude came from. Had they always been there. He had not seen them when she was a young girl. Had she merely kept them hidden, perhaps fearing that any display of high-level aptitudes for financial artistry might elicit unwanted attention, particularly from the patriarch. No, she seemed so ordinary, timid even. Only Chuck—the eldest thrown into, for him at least, the hated role of family heir to the Crawford empire—had any inkling of her drive and talents. With that designation automatically came the mantle of family right-wing bulldog. As Kat tried to help her oldest sibling cope with his unwanted family obligations, he sensed her business genius early on. She silently assumed his burdens as he struggled with the challenges of a world of finance well beyond his capacities and his dispositions. Everyone could see he was an artist except the person who counted, Charles Senior. For the patriarch, the heir had to be a male. There was no question about that and his second son, Christopher, was running away as fast as he could from that familial role.

Chris felt the stop in Chicago would be a good opportunity to be updated on the latest regarding their father and his ongoing political shenanigans. Chris often referred to his father's ambitions as just that, shenanigans, but in truth they were far more sinister than that. They were a vision that twisted political perspectives into a form of virulent hatreds that disgusted his surviving son. Chris had joined Kat in the States during a combined effort to stymie their father's political agenda. First, they tried to defeat Trump's presidential bid, and then to diminish Conservative thought as the default position of American politics. When that failed, and Azita finished up her medical internship at the University of Wisconsin hospital, Chris and the family returned to Oxford but continued to spend some time assessing and resisting America's slide to the ideological right.

So much had been anticipated from Robert Mueller's investigation of the Russian affair. That would bring Trump and his insane regime down. How could this narcissistic, misogynist, nativist, hateful conman enjoy the support of 40 percent or more of the American public? Trump had boasted that he could shoot someone in the middle of 5th Avenue and his base would still love him. He was correct. In the past, other politicians running for president quickly became yesterday's news for the smallest of transgressions. Liberal Republican Nelson Rockefeller faded when he divorced his first wife. Ed Muskie was toast after seeming to weep in public. John Dean tanked as a candidate simply for letting out an excessive whoop of celebration after an early primary victory. The reality, or even rumor, of an affair was death to most candidates if the press found out.

Trump, on the other hand, had a string of women alleging sordid affairs, had paid out hush money in six figure amounts, bankrupted numerous businesses, stiffed thousands of vendors, lied on an hourly basis regarding things easily fact-checked, started ill-conceived trade wars, and consorted with historic enemies and international thugs while aggravating traditional allies. If such a plot had been written for Hollywood, it would be relegated to the science fiction category of story lines too unbelievable for the screen. The hate message he pedaled yet struck a responsive chord in a nation still ravaged by unresolved racial and tribal animosities.

Chris's conversation with Kat the night of his arrival left him restless. Mueller had left it all up to Congress. He had not exonerated Trump of wrongdoing. Neither had he produced any unambiguous smoking gun, especially regarding obstruction of justice, just a mountain of circumstantial evidence. Now, however, she was convinced that Congress could not remove him from office. The House could certainly impeach but the Senate would never convict. To even start the process would fail before the next election. The thought of him parading around heralding his innocence of all wrongdoing was too much to bear. Worse, both Chris and his sister shared several scenarios where he might be reelected. Then, the future was forfeit, climate disaster could not afford four more years of neglect. No matter how they dissected their data, and made their arguments, his base remained unmoved. It would still come down to a handful of swing states. The Democrat would likely crush him in the popular vote but that did not matter. Foreign actors now knew how ignorant the American electorate was and just how easily they might be played.

Even if he mentally melted down in public, they agreed, that might not be enough to bring him down. He had given his base of supporters the gift they most desired, permission to hate those they feared — people of different color, ethnicity, religion, culture, and language. They now could give vent to their primal fears as they looked adoringly toward the strongman who might ease their anxieties. This is how even the cultured Germans had gone mad in the early 1930s. After a brief economic recovery in the late 1920s had pushed the extremists to the margins of the political arena, a world-wide depression gave the demagogues another shot. Hitler proved the most effective of the lot, making bold promises and, more importantly, telling the average folk whom to blame for their plight. It was the Jew. They alone had been responsible for the military collapse in 1918, the 'stab in the back' by agreeing to the despised Versailles Treaty, and by propping up a weak and ineffective Weimar Republic. Democracy didn't work. No, Germany needed purpose and obedience and, most of all, a leader.

Chris soon was restless and made his way from his sister's penthouse apartment on the Gold Coast across the street to Oak Beach where he found a bench facing east to Lake Michigan. This was a special place to him. He had always loved it when, as a child, he had stolen away to this spot at this same time of day. He would be scolded upon his return, but it was always worth it, to find refuge in the city to witness a new day unfold and permit his mind and thoughts to wander. Those were the moments when his mind would wander through imaginary conversations with others or himself, with his dialogues striking him as insightful, bordering on the brilliant. Back then, he would kick himself for not bringing something to make notes. Often, he would go over his frenetic thoughts, hoping what seemed so breathtaking in the moment might remain so upon further consideration if, in fact, he might retrieve them in the harsh reality of day.

The morning sky was just lighting up. A few clouds could be seen to give the emerging morning some texture and even a bit of substance. It calmed him, permitted his breathing and heartbeat to slow just a fraction. Responding to the newfound sense of peace, he tried to push the American political malaise out of his head but could not. He could never fully escape the sense of impending disaster that dominated his thoughts most days.

Thank God he had fled this stricken land now rent apart by unbridgeable divides. For a while he mused over the fact that those most loudly proclaiming their love of Christ were the least likely to understand or follow the message of the very being they considered divine. They elevated the most corrupt public man in America to the status of a demigod, a man who never stepped in a church nor could recall a single Biblical passage when pushed. How do the Evangelicals twist reality to accommodate such contradictions? Would not their brains explode at the mere effort? Then again, the prophecies of the end days, and the revelations that spoke of the anti-Christ now struck Chris as relevant. Was not one sign of the Anti-Christ that he would persuade the multitude with a silver tongue before being revealed as Satan's minion? Wasn't that part of God's ultimate scenario? Surely, Donald fit that role perfectly, pretending to be divinely appointed while leading the flock toward division and perdition. Sometimes, Chris thought he was the only one who saw what was so obvious but pushed such thoughts aside as excess hubris.

As the sun peaked through the morning clouds, Chris let his mind continue to wander. There is nothing special about this sorry episode in American thought and political life. In fact, Trump and the Republican-Evangelical endorsed crusade of hate is deeply rooted in American history. It is American history. Most of the original colonies were founded on religious intolerance, a spiritual tribalism where fights over which God was the best became a daily sport. This was an age when absolutist monotheism was practiced on a healthy dose of steroids.

Perhaps, in reaction, the founding fathers went out of their way to ensure that religion would not have a role in public life. They tried at least. The Constitution not only does not mention God but goes out of its way to keep religion a private affair. No religious tests for public office, no state endorsed religions. They instinctively knew that an integrated body politic had to disassociate itself from the divisiveness of belief.

Those founding the ship of state in America were enlightened men, educated and thoughtful. They knew that the mass of folk out there were not. Thus, the architects of our republic desired the notion of democracy in principle but feared it in practice. They agonized over the checks and balances that might deter tyranny, both of authoritarian rule on the one hand and the passions of the mob on the other. In turn, they limited voting, erected an electoral college to serve as a buffer against the popular sentiments of the rabble, and appointed US Senators as another check on popular rule. For several decades, numerous states had no popular vote for the President.

Their precautions failed to secure their fondest hopes. A second awakening swept the eastern seaboard with irrational passions in the 1820s and a first populist revolution brought Andrew Jackson to power in the last year of that decade. His populism saw the further entrenchment of slavery at a time when the framers of the Constitution thought it might wither away. His ascension to power also saw the Indian Exclusion movement, a ramping up of systemic genocide of Native Americans. By the 1840s and 1850s, the ire of mainstream Americans had spread to the Irish, Italians, and other non-Northern Europeans who were not adherents to Protestant truths or American originalism. The hope for equality and equal opportunity and inclusiveness had lost its way.

Chris let the morning breezes sweep over him. It was a perfect time for simply thinking about things, letting his mind wander. The streets were still quiet, a few cars and fewer joggers were about but mostly he was alone in his thoughts. The last decades of the 19th century were dominated by a struggle between capital and the common folk, not unlike today. As the economic elite tightened their grip on the economy and political life, mass oppositional movements emerged. Western farmers organized into the Grange and other cooperatives while manual workers in factories and mines created the Knights of Labor and various other unions. They seemed powerful enough to counter the power of money and political corruption. But it never quite happened. The populists of the time, including Evangelical orator and Presidential candidate William Jennings Bryan, focused on white working men. Blacks, Latinos, Native Americans, and Chinese were specifically excluded. In the West, the Asian issue became particularly acute. An exclusion act was passed to end Chinese immigration and assign the yellow races to second class citizenship. Tribalism always trumped any broader understanding of self-interest.

In the election of 1876, Samuel Tilden won the popular vote, but the Republican Candidate Rutherford B. Hayes contested the election in the electoral college. Compared to today, that election was a disaster. The political parties often printed their own ballots, outright fraud was common, privacy at the voting places often nonexistent, and competing electors were put forward as legitimate. It was so hopeless that the election was thrown to Congress to sort out. There, a compromise gave the Presidency to Hayes if the Republicans would abandon protection for freed slaves, thus effectively endorsing the Democratic Party's traditional hope of reestablishing white hegemony over the South. Though six hundred thousand gave their lives, in no small measure, to end the national disgrace of human bondage, that victory was compromised away for a short-term political gain. Soon, Jim Crow laws replaced slavery with a legal form of apartheid.

By the end of that century, the major political parties were aligning themselves into their present positions. Republicans were now the party of business while the Democrats tried to cobble together a coalition of Northern workers, Western small farmers, and Southern whites. People of color were consciously excluded. In that election, William McKinley went head-to-head with Bryan whose big tent excluded all but white workers and farmers. It was the first election to be decided by money. Rockefeller himself contributed almost as much as the Democrats raised in total. The Republicans used their twenty-fold advantage in money to blitz voters with fear-based propaganda about what a Bryan election would mean. McKinley won easily and the modern era of American politics was born. He who commands the gold shall rule.

What had changed since then? Sure, Chris thought to himself. Events permitted a brief period of reform early in the 20th century and the depression allowed an era of liberalism that reduced inequality and increased opportunity after World War II. But the underlying dynamics had not changed, Chris ruminated as the sun rose in front of him. The same racial and ethnic divisions keep the center-left divided. Money is yet dominant in elections. Inequality and disappearing opportunity define American life. Chris recalled that the top 1 percent held half of all the wealth in the early 1890s, the golden age of rampant capitalism before there was even a tax on income. *It won't be long before we are back there,* he mused to himself. The few are leading lives of unimagined luxury while the many struggle. And yet, unlike then when the losers, at least the Caucasians, tried to organize and fight back, the losers are now joining with those who oppress them with irrational devotion, merely for the benefit of being permitted to feel superior to someone who isn't of their tribe. What a pathetic bargain.

As Chris mulled that thought, he became aware of someone approaching, a man coming toward him. He glanced to his left as an elderly distinguished-looking man sat next to him on the bench. For a moment, the image did not compute. It looked like his father but how could that be. His mind fought his perception, and ultimately perception won out when the man spoke.

"Perhaps I should apologize for startling you," Charles Senior said smoothly. "I was on my way to my favorite Polish bakery, a Sunday morning ritual, when I thought I might find you here."

"More than startling me, something like shocking the crap out of me." Chris looked around. He could see three well-built men lurking nearby. Each wore a jacket that he assumed concealed a weapon of some sort.

"And if I had called to arrange a meeting, what would have been the outcome?" His father gave Chris a patronizing smile.

"I can see your point. But how the hell did you even know I was in town? This was a rather last-minute stop on my way back home."

"Ah yes, home!" The elderly man apparently decided to evade the question. "This used to be your home. This was one of your favorite places of escape when you wanted to be alone. I have not forgotten. I have forgotten little about you."

"And I, dear Father, have forgotten nothing about you, despite how hard I have tried. And again, I ask, how did you know I was here?"

"On Oak Beach, on a Sunday. That was not hard. Old habits die hard."

Chris exhaled sharply. "Not that. In Chicago, how did you know I was in town."

"Oh, my boy, you continuously underestimate me. I have my methods."

Chris stared at the lake ahead, his mind furiously racing over several possibilities. Then he decided to consider that mystery later and focus on what was sitting next to him. "All right, to what do I owe the pleasure of your company? Perhaps you are ready to confess to killing your daughter-in-law. Confession, as you know, is good for the soul. You are still a Catholic, are you not? You must be remarkably familiar with that sacrament."

"It pains me to think you would even entertain that notion, my son. I loved Beverly. I had doubts at first, but she turned out to be a fine wife for Junior."

Chris looked deeply into the pale blue eyes of his father. They did not flinch. There was not a scintilla of evidence that he was being deceitful. Then again, is that not the peculiar strength of a sociopath? They can lie without guilt, or at least any evidence of a conscience. "You are so fucking good at this." Then Chris moved on before the other man could respond. "No matter. I will give you the benefit of the doubt for the moment. However, Kat is fully convinced you are guilty as hell. Perhaps that is because she is convinced you tried to run her down on the streets of Chicago. That would be a nice touch, killing one of your own children, I mean directly as opposed to hounding one to his own suicide."

"Oh really, now you are sinking into the absurd."

"Oh, Father, I cannot envision you giving out a contract to one of your henchmen. No, that would be too film noir. What I see is you pulling a Henry II with Beverly. You would be surrounded by your lackeys one night and, perhaps in a fit of pique, merely say something oblique . . . who will rid me of this nettlesome sister-in-law. For Henry, his knights tracked down Thomas Beckett in his role of Archbishop of Canterbury and struck him down on his alter. Your minions were more prosaic, and less dramatic. Just a push off the balcony."

"This is all very amusing. Christopher. I must say you have always had this amazing imagination, so clever and inventive. Taken to the extreme, I fear, it borders on the delusional. I doubt you want that. So, let me close that subject with one observation. I knew that Beverly was, how shall we put it, betraying my trust. That is such a distasteful thought but what else is there to say. She hurt me in a very personal way. Still, I would never hurt her. That suspicion has been sitting between us for too long. So, listen carefully, I would never hurt her, or my own daughter. I am not the monster you have made me out to be."

Chris looked hard at the man next to him. Again, his eyes were steady. How did he do it? Chris was certain that if he lied in such a way, everyone would know. "All right, then, why would she kill herself? She was not depressed or unhappy. She had much to live for."

"I am not a student of the mind," Charles said as he leaned back on the bench. "She did realize that I had found out about her little game. Perhaps it was shame or a sense of failure, or some unjustified sense of the consequences to come. I suspect we will never know. And people hide what is inside all the time. The outside of a person, what we see, can be so deceiving."

Chris had been wavering for a moment. But he sensed his father went too far and snapped back into focus. He wanted to dismiss this theory as pathetic but decided that would go nowhere. "You might be right. We can never know what is inside a person. I suspect my psychology courses were a bit of a waste."

His father laughed, causing Chris to startle a fraction. "Yes, son, you were all over the map in your studies, such an eclectic mind. I worried that you would ever learn anything useful. In truth, I fear you never did, given how you have wandered through life dabbling in this and that. What would you have done without my money to support your hobbies?"

"Hardly hobbies. At Oxford, they don't give professorships to random blokes sitting in the local pub."

"Apparently I hit a nerve. I apologize. I merely wish to find out how my remaining son is doing. Surely that is not a crime. So, tell me what you are about these days? My interest is genuine, of that I assure you."

Chris looked at the man seated next to him. Was he serious? Did he care or was this one of his occasional efforts to snare his surviving son into his own nefarious world? Why him and not Kat or Kay? Kay's interests seemed orthogonal to his, that was true. And Kat clearly led the family revolution against him. That was unforgivable. But in the end, he concluded that this was mostly sexism. Chris was the male issue and the patriarch's world held little truck with smart, strong women. Chris considered the possibility this was a serious conversation but then dismissed the notion. "Well, I thought you would know all about my plans. I still have not figured out how you knew I was in town. I will be open. As I flit about my everchanging interests, perhaps I will focus on stopping the reelection of Trump. The American experiment cannot endure another four years of that maniac. You know us wealthy, indolent children of the rich, just worthless dilettantes who never fix on anything worthy. But really, I could not decide what ought to be next. Then it hit me, saving the world seemed like a way to pass the time. I woke the other day and said to myself, doesn't the world deserve saving, or at least this country. I cannot think of a more worthy ambition."

"I know whom you want to save it from, me and my kind. But from what dire fate or circumstance? What imagined sin of mine, or my compatriots, captures your concern?"

"Well," Chris said slowly as he considered the possibilities, "there are several excellent candidates but this Sunday morning, as the sun rises higher in the sky, I'll pick hyper-economic inequality. I could pick climate change, that is a species killer. But no, I am not a climate scientist. Besides, money is power and if the current maldistribution of appropriated wealth can be altered, then so many other changes are possible . . . even erecting a government that serves all and not the few. Yes, I still have a dream."

Charles Senior stared resolutely out over the water. "That equality shibboleth, how droll and mundane."

"Dear Father, that is hardly an argument to get me to abandon my lifelong quest."

"The real reason it is so silly," his father said quite sharply, "is that the evils you believe exist are, in fact, the natural order of things. Efforts to change what is natural will always fail in the end, they go against what must be. You cannot escape fate, my boy, what we, who see things clearly, call the natural law."

"Fate? Surely you are not serious." Chris tried to reek of sarcasm.

"Yes, fate. Some have always argued that government ought to interfere with the market to raise up those who cannot compete. That seems compassionate to the unenlightened, but it is not. You don't see packs of animals hovering about the weaker members to keep them alive. No, they recognize the immutable laws of nature, shoring up the weak reduces the prospects that the pack will survive. You have to cut your losses."

"Many packs of mammals protect their weakest members as well as they can. You cannot cherry-pick your examples."

"In the end, it really is a matter of fairness."

"Fair? My god, over the past couple of generations we have regressed back in the gilded age of the late 19th century where 10 percent of the population controlled 75 percent of the wealth, where 4,000 families had gathered as much as almost the remainder of the country. And this elite controlled everything, not because of fate but rather primitive public policies. There was no income tax, no inheritance tax, no corporate tax, and governments were merely extensions of corporate interests. When the steel mills workers rose against Carnegie at the Homestead plant outside Pittsburgh, the Governor sent in the national guard to crush the workers after the private army of Pinkerton men had failed. What in god's name is fair about eight-year-old children working twelve hours a day and families starving while a few live lives of unimaginable luxury. Fair? Only a sociopath would consider that Dickensian horror show fair. What's next, shall we bring back debtor's prisons?"

The elder man smiled grimly. "If god or the fates wanted them to have a better life, perhaps they would have been born with more talents . . . or drive . . . or some semblance of a brain."

"Oh, for Christ's sake . . . sod off."

Charles Senior smiled at his son's use of British slang. "I will, soon enough, but in the meantime I hope to keep our conversation reasonable. Let us focus on fairness for a moment. I look at what government appropriates from us in taxes in the following way. They have always tried to take more from me, and those like me, than from the rest of society. Think about that. We all get the same benefits from government. Why should I pay more simply because I have been more successful? Do you consider that fair? No, we should all pay the same amount. Equal benefits, equal contributions. Now, that strikes me as fair. I would even go as far as saying that I would be willing to pay the same tax rate as the least fortunate even though that would result in a much higher absolute contribution."

"Your generosity almost moves me to tears." Chris tried not to let his sarcasm become too obvious. "But it strikes me that you profit disproportionately from our vast military apparatus, the price tag for which exceeds that of the next several countries combined. You pretty much have the courts doing your bidding, and treasury, and most other executive agencies, which has permitted your kind to accrue such vast sums as to pretty much control everything in sight. Personally, I think you are getting one helluva return on your investment, or should we stick with the less inflammatory term of contribution."

"Ah, it does pain me, you know."

"And what exactly is that?" Chris asked.

"That I lost you somewhere along the line. You were the brightest."

"Hardly," Chris scoffed. "Kay was always a much better student and Kat is a business genius. Perhaps if you hadn't beaten me so when Kay brought home better report cards?"

"That was for your own good, damn it. You had all the potential in the world, you could have inherited everything but . . ." The elderly man stopped. "I blame your mother. She spoiled you. I suppose you will be seeing her."

"Of course, I love her dearly."

"Please give her my regards."

"I really doubt she will accept them."

"Perhaps, but try in any case. And your siblings. As you can imagine, I never hear from them. As one ages, the pain of absence hurts at a deeper level, as you might imagine."

Chris turned to face the other man for the first time. "I'm sorry. Yet, I am somewhat confused. Don't you have to be human to feel pain?"

"That was cruel, coming from someone who has pretense to such compassion and so much caring."

For a moment, Chris was caught off guard. He had let his anger put him at a disadvantage. Then he recovered. "Okay, enough of the chitchat. Why did you track me down? I cannot believe it was to be a conduit to your lost family members. Surely, this is not another attempt to recruit me to the dark side I hope?"

"No, even I can see when a cause is lost." But his father went no further.

"I thought you never gave up. Are you dying or something?"

"I am afraid your wish in that regard is not coming true."

"Damn." Chris interjected.

Then his father continued with some hesitation, as if he wished not to misspeak. "It is just that we are entering some very uncharted waters. You and I both agree that we have a loose cannon in the White House. Trump shares much of my, our, worldview but, it is sad to admit, he is too stupid to lead effectively. We have a man who commands such loyalty but risks destroying everything we have been working for."

"Okay, now you're losing me. Why admit all this to me? Are you afraid Trump will be impeached? Not going to happen! The professionals in the Democratic Party know full well that bringing up impeachment will fail in the Senate. They won't risk his acquittal if it helps him get reelected."

"It really has little to do with Trump, though you are wrong on the Democrats. In the end, they will try to impeach him. No, it is all about larger events and changes. My people see things slipping away. Demographics are evolving, the millennials are consumed with crazy notions like socialism really is a good thing. A good thing? They should have witnessed what I did as a boy, heard the stories I heard first-hand. When you see the work of a generation, no two generations, on the cusp of being lost and options becoming limited, desperation erupts. Yes, every cornered animal strikes back. You do everything and anything on one last roll of the dice. Do you understand?"

Chris wanted to end what he saw as a futile debate, but something inside would not permit him to let go. "Perhaps. The need to go for it and control everything was delusional from the get-go. Your group would end democracy and seize control of the levers of power. You cannot trust people to see it your way, can you? Don't feel alone. The founding fathers were wary of real democracy, the tyranny of numbers, the mob, as they saw it. The election of 1892 and especially 1896 was a portent of today, almost identical in many ways. Both parties were seen by desperate farmers and factory workers as being controlled by an economic elite. Like today, corporations wrote the laws their paid hacks passed for their personal advantage. Desperate workers and farmers flocked to prophets of hope such as Henry George and Mary Lease, and to third parties such as the Land Party and the Workers Party. Despairing of working on the outside, the disenfranchised threw their lot in with the Democrats when William Jennings Bryan was nominated. He would have been the first to represent average folk, at least the white ones, assuming you discount Jackson who was little more than a backwoods barbarian. The now familiar architecture of modern politics was created with Republicans completely representing money and Democrats the mob."

"And how do you explain Teddy Roosevelt? Not exactly a friend of corporate interests," Charles Senior asked.

Chris waved an arm. "Merely a mistake of history, an aberration. McKinley was gunned down; the party bosses hadn't seen that coming. Taft eventually got things back on track."

"See, you are the smart one, a worthy opponent. You, Kat, and your allies are feeling buoyed by events. Mueller was a disappointment to you, I am sure, but you took back the House. Now, you see a Senate victory in 2020, and you wait daily for Trump to implode. Even the Republican professionals are looking on with despair. I am afraid what you, Kat, and that colored girl Jules will do if you sense optimism."

"Wait, afraid we might be successful? We are not even the major oppositional players. We do what we can, but . . ."

"Stop!" His father blurted out, losing his control for the first time that Chris could recall. "Listen, my people have invested billions over the years working to get control of things. It is just about in our grasp, but they see it untangling. They will not let that happen. Do you understand me? Too much is at stake. You and I know that Trump is merely a side show. The main arena is about who will take the world forward, not some vague notion of inclusive participation. The mob cannot lead us anywhere. We are the ones who really know how things work and how to get things done."

"Wait, if your people are so omniscient, explain their positions on the climate, their fascination about fossil fuels, or the benefits of a few controlling all the wealth. Really, how will the economy function when there are no consumers left? Sounds more like we are on the verge of a kakistocracy than any kind of utopia. You are nothing more than a bunch of selfish bastards.

You want it all and justify your greed after the fact. That is it . . . end of story."

Charles Senior winced. "Son, I don't have the time or the patience to debate the philosophical niceties with you. Just listen and listen carefully. They know what you and the others with you are doing. Of course, you are not alone in the opposition to us but that does not make you any less . . . vulnerable." He paused as Chris stared at him coldly, trying to fathom all the meaning in his words. "We may not agree on things, perhaps not on anything. But, in my way, I still love you and don't want to see you hurt, or Kat, or even that colored girl. And surely, that family of yours, so precious."

"Is this a fucking threat? For god's sake!" Chris hated that his face had flushed with emotion. "And who is they? You mean you!"

"No, silly boy. I am trying to help you. Can't you see that? For Christ's sake, listen to me. Just this once, listen. Don't stand in the way of what is inevitable. It's not worth it." Then Charles suddenly rose and walked away. The men who had stood out of earshot effortlessly moved about him as they walked toward the street where a limousine appeared as if by magic.

Chris stood and watched until his father and his entourage disappeared. Then he sat down heavily as his mind raced. What was that all about? How did his father even know he was in town? What were this shadowy corporate oligarchy worried about? His own pathetic attempts to turn history around. Not likely. The democrats would probably shoot themselves in the foot with infighting and pave the way for another Republican triumph. How much of democracy would remain by 2024, he wondered. For a moment, his cynicism ebbed a bit. Trump had his resolute base but was quite unpopular. The left was mobilized and fired up. Women, minorities, the educated, and the young could well sweep in a political era. It was very feasible, just what his father so feared. And yet, Chris could not forget the election of 1896. Bryan had enormous crowds wherever he went. But McKinley had the money. Republicans introduced the first modern campaign where messaging was key, vote for Bryan and you could kiss your job goodbye. The Democrats could only capture the deep South and plain states, not enough. Look today, and the pattern of support is identical, except the party names have changed. So much has transpired in a little over 120 years and yet, so little.

Chris pulled out his phone and dialed. A moment later he spoke. "Jules, its Chris. I see you are not in church. Okay, stop laughing. Can we meet . . . at Kat's? Good."

CHAPTER 6

KAT'S PLACE

An hour later, Chris looked out from his sister's penthouse suite on to the same waters that had witnessed his recent paternal conversation. As was often the case with Midwest weather, a cold front was moving swiftly across the city bringing wind and heavy showers. The inviting morning was an instant memory. The water had turned steel grey as sheets of water danced their way across the lake's surface. The weather matched his lugubrious spirit. Chris pondered what he was looking at. We think of rain as merely descending liquid. However, each burst of moisture has a certain character if you look closely with unique patterns revealed as the drops seek out the earth. What played out before him on this day struck him as severe, even tormented. Perhaps this was a portent of turmoil and conflict waiting over the horizon of his own life but, with effort, he shook off such a thought as silly.

The doorbell rang. He immediately rose to answer it when he recalled there was someone there who would carry out such a pedestrian task. His sister Katerina, or Kat, had given into one temptation of the super wealthy. She had a staff to take care of those tasks that burden ordinary people. Kat hated pretense. She accepted that luxury with reluctance but eventually realized that her attention and energy were needed on more important tasks. Chris took one final look at Lake Michigan. He loved water, the ways in which it reflected various moods through movement and color. Only the sky was as similarly responsive to human emotion and what was any body of water other than a reflection of what lies above.

His reverie was aborted by a familiar voice. "Hey, you've seen that view a hundred times."

Chris turned and walked over to the attractive ebony-skinned woman who had been his friend and lover for so many years, until he had accepted the fact that she loved him but would not marry him. He embraced her and gave a quick kiss on the lips. "So good to see you. Amazingly, the network still hasn't figured out you are a fraud. See how easy it is to fool people."

"And I see that those so-called smart people at Oxford haven't discovered that you passed your courses using Cliff Notes. They still let you have access to students. Really, is that true?"

"Jules, admit it. In your heart, you know that I'm a rock star among the next generation of scholars and world leaders."

"Oh my, then I have lost all faith in the future at long last." Jules laughed aloud and gave Chris another hug. "Oh, how I miss trading insults with you."

"Same here." He wanted to add that he missed other things as well but caught himself. He never fully put aside his physical attraction to this woman, or his deep affection for her. He mused for a moment that what had been lust was now a deeper appreciation, almost filial in character, but not quite. But she knew that, or he thought she did, so no need to go down that road.

Instead, Jules spoke, "I am totally flummoxed that your father tracked you down on Oak Beach of all places."

"Well," Chris reflected, "it was a favorite haunt of mine as a kid."

"But how did he even know you were in town?"

"Not a clue. Believe me, I asked."

"Shit," Jules exclaimed distractedly, "this worries the *bejesus* out of me. I didn't think he paid that much attention to you when you were a kid, too busy making money. Now, he seems tuned in to everything you do. Maybe we all should be worried. How much does he know about my life and what I am doing? I hate to say this about that man, your father, but he is the only one I fear, really fear. I've done some risky investigative reporting on some powerful dudes, guys that you would not want to run into in any alley, dark or not. But he is the scariest SOB I've run across. There is something about his smile, always has been, even when we were kids."

"You mean like he always was fantasizing about how he would torture you."

"Yes, exactly." Jules nearly shouted.

"Well," Chris said slowly, "your name came up more than once. Okay, not your name but references were made to that colored girl."

"You are freaking kidding. Not even the racists use that term anymore."

"See, now you know where my charm comes from." Chris smiled. "I worry about how much he knows about what Kat is doing, and about the people she has working on our political stuff. Who knows how far his thirst for revenge might reach? I'm insisting she has everything swept for bugs immediately."

Jules sat next to her former lover and took his hand in hers. When he imperceptibly pulled back, she smiled. "Don't worry, I'm not going to jump your bones, not that the thought does not tempt me. I blew my chance with you and now I like your wife too much. Damn, why couldn't you have married a shrew. Then we could have gotten down with a torrid affair."

"As if you could ever have handled me." Chris kept it light, wondering if the regrets were serious or the woman was just playing nice.

"Yup, should have snapped you up when I had the chance. That, alas, is a lament I've made too many times, about you, not in general."

"Jules, I've concluded that you would have been as bored with me as with that poor schmuck you tried marriage with."

"You're wrong," she said decisively.

"Convince me," Chris shot back.

"You ended a sentence with a preposition. And for an Oxford man . . ." she laughed at her own cleverness, "that is unforgivable and simply wrong. However, on the other matter, you may be right. Guys hit on me though not as often as you might think. Most are intimidated by my independence and success, but some give it a try."

"And?" Chris prompted her when she stopped.

"Nothing, or not enough. My dear, when you've been to the mountain top, everything else pales by comparison." Jules then squeezed his hand. "Did I ever tell you that scumbag Trump put the moves on me?"

"No freaking way." Chris looked dubious.

"He did, after an interview I did with him early in my career. He was all over me, but I shut him down immediately. He just shrugged and moved on. I was just another piece of meat to him, dark meat."

Chris was about to respond when a voice caused him to jump a bit.

"Oh, for heaven's sake, don't make me get a hose." Kat used a favorite joke of hers as she swept into the room. "Jules, I didn't know you would be here. Delighted to see you as always. Unfortunately, your brother is off on the continent again, or is it Asia now. But he insists he will stop in Oxford to see this clown next week. It still amazes me."

"Why do I sense a cut coming?" Chris tried to look offended.

"No, really, my husband is such a dashing, smart, and successful man. Why in god's name did he befriend my hapless brother. And that was not a cut, merely an observation."

Chris responded with exaggerated sarcasm. "Oh, he was merely reaching out to the wretched, and I was rather a basket case back then, unlike now. Still, breaking my nose the day we met was hardly the expected first step to a lifelong friendship."

"And then he did it again when you attacked your father to defend my honor." Jules smiled at the thought.

"Your honor..."

"Don't even try." Jules cut him off.

"Fair enough," Chris laughed. "In any case, I'll get my revenge on him someday. I'll make him listen to one of my lectures. Perhaps I'll tie him to a chair and replay one of my talks repeatedly." Chris tried to chuckle in a sinister manner but soon gave up the attempt. "Speaking of Father, I have news for you, Kat."

"Shit. I'm already tensing up, unless he died. Now, that would make my day." Kat's face turned serious.

"He tracked me down."

"What?" Kat exclaimed. "Did he come here? He knows he is not welcome."

"Nope, not here silly. On a bench at the beach across the street. He knows I loved that place as a kid."

"How did he know to find you there, that you were even in town?" Kat was now on total alert.

"A bug, maybe? Do you sweep this place and your offices downstairs?"

"All the time," She said distractedly. "Just last week, in fact. I don't think that's it. He might have a plant, someone in the office or . . ." She looked around. "Perhaps even someone who works for me here. I hate this. I hate him. I'm afraid we have to just assume that we need to keep some information extremely close to the vest." She exhaled deeply. "Goddamn, this is like running some CIA covert action, one of those black-ops thingies."

"As if any of us would know what those things are." Jules tried to lighten the mood. "In any case, what did the great man want? Is he still trying to recruit you to the dark side?"

Chris issued a cynical chuckle. "Hardly, though he still wastes time lamenting my poor choices in life, one of which is you, my dear." He nodded toward Jules.

"Hell, I was the best thing that ever happened to you." Then she paused. "Second best after Amar . . . okay third best after Amar and Azita and Deena and then your babies. Okay, okay, but I'm still in the top ten. So, why in god's name did he track you down?"

Chris took a deep breath. "I think he wanted to warn me."

"Warn you?" It was Kat who spoke up.

"Yeah, warn me, and all of us probably."

"About what? Why?" Kat continued. "I mean why now. It has been some time since that car tried to run me down. I no longer even have Ricky try my food first before I eat."

Chris guffawed involuntarily. He wasn't sure why that struck him as so funny, perhaps a release of tension. "Listen, he was his usual obtuse self. But here is what I think. His side sees victory in their grasp and, at the same time, that they are losing control of things. Trump is a two-edge sword. He has enormous appeal among the hard-right base but is so stupid and unbalanced that he risks bringing down the economy at a most inconvenient time. If anything goes awry between now and election day next year, do you think the Donald could manage his way through a crisis? He can barely read and is now surrounded by sycophants and incompetence. And that is the rub for guys like Father. They see the brass ring, what they have worked for all these decades. One more election and they probably can dismantle the remainder of our democratic institutions. Hell, not even the founding fathers were all that excited about a real democracy and clearly the right wing is not a fan. The thought that they can get so close to total control and then lose it all is unacceptable." Chris paused to consider his next words.

"And so . . ." Jules murmured.

"I think he threatened me, or us, with physical harm at the least, or something worse."

"What's worse?" Jules looked skeptical.

"Death, I suppose. I mean, he wasn't open about it, but I came away with the sense that we are to back off or else. I was so shocked to even see him that I'm not sure I heard him correctly. It was more like he was giving me, us, a friendly warning. This was our last chance, as if he was saying that he might not be in control of what could happen, so we better damn well be nice."

The three looked at one another absorbing Chris's words. For what seemed like an eternity, no one spoke. Each looked inward. Then Kat stood and began pacing. "They're looking ahead to impeachment, indictment, the election, all the things that can bring an end to the rule of the hard-right. Trump wasn't what they had in mind. Still, they'll ride him as far as they can get."

"Hmm," Jules murmured. "I've almost gotten to the point of not checking under my car before getting in. That's how paranoid I got after the incident with Beverly. I guess it's back to full-time, full-out paranoid thinking. I hate this stuff. Maybe I should just expose corrupt Illinois politicians. They're a dime-a-dozen."

Kat had walked to the large window looking out over Lake Michigan. She loved Chicago's gold coast, probably much as Bostonians loved Beacon Hill and the Freedom Trail or San Franciscans were enchanted with cable cars and the Golden Gate Bridge. Some sights and sounds and even smells became part of you, clinging tenaciously despite the years, the familiarity, and the competing claims on one's interests. Like relationships, the earliest images of youth remain the most enduring. She looked out over the water now broken with white caps from a stiff breeze. She didn't spend enough time enjoying this. There never seemed the time. "You know what bothers me?" She finally said.

"What?" her brother responded.

"It all seems so futile." Kat turned and walked back to the group. "The staff interviewed a visitor the other day who spent time in one of the Russian Troll factories. She told them how they had operated. They functioned 24/7 in rotating shifts. They had these different sections. I won't remember them all, but there was a news division, of course, but it should be thought of as the fake news division. Then there was a section devoted to spreading discord through social media, they were called *seeders* since their mission was to spread discord. Then there was a group that created memes in the hope that some would go viral. All of this was designed to spread division in the western world, bring Trump and Trump clones to power and destroy the European Union through ultra-nationalism. It is the contemporary version of war except you don't kill the enemy. You merely scare the crap out of them, confuse the hell out of them, and then blame the easiest scapegoat."

Jules exhaled. "You guys think you feel impotent? Hah! I supposedly have a large following out there among the unwashed masses. Lots of good that does. Pretty much, I preach to the choir, the same people who read the *New York Times* or *Washington Post* and *The Economist.* All I do is confirm their priors, what they already know. The ones I need to reach are watching Fox News or paying attention to Breitbart and Info Wars to get the latest hate-filled crazy talk. Really, what's the fucking use? Maybe I should start a freaking cooking show."

With that, Chris guffawed loudly. "I've eaten your cooking, dear, try a home repair show. But thanks for lightening things up."

"Oh, bite me. The trouble with not sleeping with you any longer is that I can't threaten to withhold sex anymore. That always gave me a lift."

Chris opened his mouth with a retort but thought better of it. Rather, he finished a thought on his mind. "I know the feeling of hopelessness. I was chatting with Bill the other day, Gates that is. By election day, the climate deniers will have spent almost a billion dollars denying the most critical threat to our future. And who is on the other side, Greta Thunberg, a Scandinavian teenager. Seems like an unfair fight."

"Come on, Chris, she is not alone."

"Oh, I know that. It just makes me angry. These billionaires just want to protect the stranded assets that make them so rich while the planet be damned. They fund over 90 so-called think tanks and advocacy groups just going about raising doubts about what every freaking serious scientist knows. Humans are destroying the climate that sustains life . . . our freaking future. We only have a few years to turn things around and they will spend any amount to bring on doomsday. It's like a mass delusional death wish but at least the next quarterly fiscal report will look good and the stock price will stay inflated. Yippee! My year-end bonus will be boffo. That's exactly what I was thinking about when Father interrupted my depression this morning. I remember when I sat there looking out for half-naked women's bodies. Where did it all go wrong?"

Kat looked at the two of them. "So, what are you thinking? Are we wasting our time? We all have other dreams that we can pursue, possibilities that are not utterly ridiculous. Give all this up?"

Chris leaned back in his chair, looking up at the ceiling with an expression that suggested deep, internal anguish. Kat and Jules looked at him expectantly. But nothing came out. His face remained poised on the edge of agony, apparently ready to explode but unable to do so. Finally, he let out a deep breath. No explosion, just quiet words. "No way." The others were not quite sure what he had said.

"What?"

He spoke more forcefully. "No fucking way are we giving up. If we did, it would be like deciding to have a fun time playing whist on the Titanic as the ship filled up with water. In the end, it does not matter if you win or not. You must try. Hell, Alexander the Great and Genghis Khan conquered the known world in their days but it all soon fell apart. Should they have stayed home and enjoyed their concubines?"

"What the hell are you babbling about?" Kat rolled her eyes at her brother.

"Sorry, I'm going to use these historical characters in an upcoming lecture back at Oxford. They are on my mind. But there is a point. In the end, we do what we do because we can do no other. Whether the effort is futile or not is irrelevant. We must act according to our destiny, or is it fate. I am not going to live my life in any way that I'll be ashamed of later. If I am asked what I did when things were on the line, I want to have a good response. I mean, someone has to oppose Father and his jackal-like associates."

"Where's this coming from?"

"Listen! I met a guy in Vancouver when I gave a talk at the Uni there. He is emeritus and came of age in the states during the '60s, the Vietnam conflict. He had to make a choice—fight in a war he thought immoral or go to jail or Canada. He chose the latter and it altered the course of his life. It's all in his memoir, *Casual Choices*. But the thing is that he was faced with that ultimate scenario that bugs us all. What will we say to the generation down the road when they asked what you did when all was on the line? In the end, he did what he had to do, he could do no other. Neither can we."

"Even if it puts us in harm's way?" Jules asked.

Kat breathed hard. "I'm glad I have Ricky at my side. If he were not there I'm not sure if I could keep going. I mean, I like to think I'm strong but . . . sometimes we need someone."

Chris looked at her. It was a small admission from a woman he knew to be much stronger than he ever would be. Perhaps we are all vulnerable at times. "Well, I have concluded there are three lessons about life we must never forget."

"Oh no, I fear what is coming next," Kat said but managed a tiny, if forced, smile.

"You cannot put in what god has left out of a person, you cannot take out what god has put in, and you cannot avoid what god intends for you. The three of us know what we must do. It is just fate, really." No one said anything so Chris spoke again. "I see my brilliance silences you, no mean feat. By the way, this guy, Jeremiah Joshua Connelly, will join me in Oxford soon along with members of his family . . . a talented group as I understand it. We have some ideas for things we need to publish. I can't back down now."

"Of course not." Kat smiled at her sibling. "Was there any real doubt about that, you stubborn Mick."

CHAPTER 7

BALIOL COLLEGE

Chris led Ricky Jackson, his friend since their basketball high school days in Chicago and his younger sibling's husband, down one of the long ornate corridors that make up the skeletal form of Baliol College which constituted one of the many centers of learning that make up Oxford University. With them was Josh Connelly, the man he recently befriended in Vancouver and who had agreed to join him for a visit in Oxford on a whim.

"Are you familiar with my native habitat?" Chris asked.

"I've seen your native habitat many times before, even spoken here. It was the States where I felt unwelcome after I went into exile," Josh responded.

"I know you have, Josh. I was speaking to this lost soul here who grew up in a Chicago ghetto." He nodded to the black man on his right. "I know he's been to the town of Oxford, just not sure he made it to the university, being allergic to knowledge and all."

"Wait," Ricky replied, suppressing a smile. "I thought your native habitat here was the Hairy Hare, the worst pub in Oxford, if not all of England. I have been to that pig's trough way too often while listening to your tiresome political screeds. Tis true, though, I've never seen you put your students into a deep coma. This will be a first."

"Very funny. You are lucky they let you into the Hairy Hare, a superior hostelry well beyond your humble station in life. Hmm. We might try seeing if they would rent you a room above where they serve the fine food and drink that has made the Hare famous. If they refuse, it wouldn't have anything to do with your skin color and everything to do with your obvious lack of class and limited taste in discerning fine cuisine."

Ricky tried to look aggrieved. "Oh, I think not, dear brother-in-law. I speak the Queen's English, am a well-respected maven of the financial world, and married extremely well, or so your sister keeps reminding me. Now you, on the other hand, are beginning to look a little seedy. Is that a paunch I detect around your middle? And your chin?"

"What of it?" Chris instinctively reached up to touch his cheek.

"Did you shave this morning?" Ricky could no longer suppress a smile. "And just when did you sprout a second one?

"Second what, chin? Posh, my acolytes are here for my considerable intellect, not my looks. Now, I can't speak for all the young women in that regard but still . . ."

"Well, all I am hoping is that you do not bore me with that political harangue I've heard a thousand times before."

Josh appreciated the banter. “I hate to admit this but I’m looking forward to the seminar. I’ve only listened to one of his talks. To be honest, he reminded me of a young me on that occasion, though with more insight of course.”

“That,” Chris said in triumph, “I take as a distinct compliment.”

“Really? I was claiming the greater insights for myself.” Josh laughed.

“Hysterical.” Chris laughed as they arrived at the tutorial room which was always packed for one of Chris’s sessions. There were always additional attendees beyond his registered students. His reputation for giving entertaining, even informative lectures was almost legendary. It was less the lecture itself than the vigorous intellectual exchanges that inevitably erupted. Besides, they loved pumping him about the political goings-on in the States, which became a fascination, an obsessional focus, ever since the election of Donald Trump and the subsequent rise to power of Boris Johnson.

“Morning, everyone.” Chris started immediately while pointing to Ricky. “I hope no one minds that I brought an old friend along, though we are now joined by marriage.” There was a titter across the room. “Not to each other, no need to feed that rumor mill. Rather, it turns out that my younger sister lacks judgment regarding men. She stooped to marrying a man from Northwestern University, not even an Ivy League school. In any case, this is Richard Jackson. We played high school basketball together, but he stayed in Chicago for school while I attended a real university, Princeton. He then played the game professionally for a bit before deciding that, given his modest skill level, there was more money to be made by becoming a robber baron in the financial world." This brought out real laughter. "Take notes, Ricky, this material will be on the final."

Ricky smiled broadly. "I've been asked by his sisters, everyone that knows him really, to determine whether he is as good a teacher as he claims to be. We all have serious doubts."

Chris ignored the humorous cut. "My other guest is emeritus Professor Joshua Connelly of the University of British Columbia. He will be spending some time in town and asked to join us today. I won't introduce him further since you are acquainted with some of his writings which I was smart enough to assign. I assume no one minds, not that it would make any difference if you did. *Mea cathedra, meae regulae.*" Then Chris turned to the class. "Another large crowd. I am going to have to start being more boring or figure out who really belongs here."

"Is that possible? That part about being more boring I mean." Ricky said to considerable hilarity from the assembled students.

"All joking aside, I will acknowledge that Ricky, as he is universally known, is a talented financial wizard of some repute. In addition, some of you may have seen his much more talented sister on the telly. Julianna, known to her friends as Jules, is an American network reporter and commentator on political news. If you have seen her, you know she inherited all the beauty in the Jackson clan as well as all the brains."

Christopher Connelly then eased himself onto the desk that sat at the head of the seminar room. It always signaled the moment when he was about to get serious, or what passed as serious for him. He was part Irish and that meant two things. He was a gifted storyteller and he had great difficulty in repressing his natural wit. Humor, he had found, was essential to keeping today's students engaged. Otherwise, he would lose them as they checked out their smart phones. He quickly had found that he loved the graduate seminars, the very challenge of keeping them engaged. The students were, for the most part, feisty and bright. He invited their own thoughts and perspectives, mostly treating them with respect. This proved an attitude not prevalent among some of his more encrusted colleagues. He had wondered if, perhaps, some were wary of any intellectual competition from their young charges.

Despite his accomplishments, he yet thought of himself as one of them. They would explore ideas and issues together. He remained firm in only two foundational principles regarding his intellectual world. First, he would always strive to learn more as he communicated his thoughts to others. And second, there was always more to learn, even from the students in front of him. That was the joy and frustration of life in the academy. The vast world of knowledge was beyond conquering but the quest to know as much as one could was insatiable.

This was less the norm among European citadels of higher learning where the divide between student and teacher was too often zealously guarded. American universities, one of the final arenas where the US yet excelled, had always been more egalitarian, even democratic. Perhaps institutions of higher learning had drifted too far in that direction. Students, often backed by anxious and fawning parents, were loath to accept that their demonstrably lackluster efforts and inferior output deserved anything less than an A. The whining and protests around grade issuance time now bordered on the grotesque, no matter how much grade creep had taken place.

This crowd of young scholars were among his favorites, serious about learning for the most part. They typically reveled in the class repartee and did not object to the extensive readings he assigned nor his strict, though fair, assessments of their performance. He was entertaining but not a pushover. Fortunately, he had been at this long enough for self-selection to work its magic, populating his class with some of the better and brighter of students interested both in the world of ideas and the world of policy. He fancied that he was looking out over future members of parliament or even a Prime Minister among the faces that awaited him to begin. Certainly, a number of those seated before him would populate the various ministries that kept the country running.

As usual, all was not perfect. He could ignore the occasional laggards and less promising types that found their way into his happy lot of scholars. A few brought challenge and reward at the same time. A couple of the males, sporting hair down to their shoulders, thought him a bit too conservative, usually trying to push him in a more radical direction. Chris had hoped they were not building explosives for the impending revolution in their spare time. Then there was the tallish gal with long, dark, straight hair that fell past her shoulders who caused him weekly grief of a different nature. Her large, inviting eyes would have been distracting enough. The total package she presented was virtually impossible to ignore. She always sat up front where her mere presence was a statement, sporting a short skirt and stylish boots that came halfway up her calves. While her blouses typically were loose fitting, a good thing, they plunged at the neckline and she somehow never remembered to fasten the top buttons. Every week, at some point in each class, she would lean forward to ask a question or make a point. The blouse would fall forward just enough to reveal her breasts, or most of them at least since she was always *sans* bra. He tried not to look but inevitably he snuck a quick peek, and he knew that she knew. Damn it. It would be easier to ignore her if her comments in class were not so pertinent, even insightful. That made the distraction even harder to ignore.

"I am confident you all devoured the assigned readings for the week. Of course, they probably were a bit disappointing since none of them were authored by me." Another titter ran through the students. "That is an omission I will try to avoid in the future. I am committed to making a point or two before we inevitably descend into a discussion of the comparative state of politics in the US, the UK, and the EU. That is probably inevitable given the presence of my guests who have kept abreast of the shenanigans across the pond, and the channel."

Ricky smiled. "Did you inform them that revealing anything I say in this room is punishable by the pain of enduring yet another of your classes? My wife, and the real financial wizard of the family, has informed me not to divulge any corporate secrets or else."

"Any business secrets you might divulge I am sure are easily available in any business 101 text." As the students expressed their amusement at Chris's retort, he started into his material. "Even those of you who mostly nap through these sessions realize that we have been juxtaposing and comparing big ideas that have resounded through history with some more contemporary events and trends. I focus on these contrasts since, I am sadly convinced, we are becoming an ahistorical society. We are not sufficiently appreciative of what has come before. It used to be, within these very hallowed halls, that truth was only found within the ancient classics. That clearly was a misguided view."

"I suspect Professor Muirford would disagree with your dismissal of his life's work." Came a voice from the back.

"No doubt but let us not forget that I also look back in time for insights into the present and the future. But my point is that we have gone too far to the other side. Many seem oblivious, if not disdainful, of what the past can teach us. I read on the internet just yesterday about an American Republican politician appearing with Trump somewhere who claimed that history was not worth studying since it was all in the past. True story. You can see why my homeland is swirling about in the crapper."

"Perhaps it is time for a good flush." The remark came from one of the long-haired proto revolutionary students.

"In any case, how many of you have thought about Genghis Khan this past week? Never mind, rhetorical question. Think about this. When Europe was just feeling its way out of the Dark Ages, a band of nomads from the Asian Steppes conquered more lands and people in one generation than the Romans did in four hundred years. And they did it while being led by a man who arose from the lowest depths of his society and from the most abject degree of poverty. He was illiterate and without any family fortune or connections. He would have been considered lower than an untouchable in traditional India and less promising than a graduate of that faux pretender to scholarship . . . Cambridge University."

"Hear, hear," rang out among several students.

"This amazing man organized his own people, a motley array of small warrior tribes who managed to scratch out a marginal existence on the bleak steppes of Asia. From there, he went out to conquer everything in sight from China through northern India to the edges of Egypt and eastern Europe. How did he do it? Was it merely force of will and strength of arms? That is hard to imagine. The Mongols were barely one million strong with an army of one hundred thousand or so. Was it all about superior military tactics? More likely, since he did introduce tighter discipline and, having achieved some early success, did import technologies from those he had subdued such as gun powder from China, display rockets from Persia, and iron casting skills from Europe. His ingenuity and adaptability led to the command and primitive employment of early canons. Even with all this, the man purportedly sired between 1,000 and 2,000 children, perhaps the most in history. Where did he have the time to conquer the known world since he was always busy buying presents for the kids? By the way, it is highly likely that some of you have a bit of his blood in your ancestry. What is more remarkable, even more astounding than his admirable sex life, is that he managed to find time to embrace and introduce a number of world-changing ideas." Chris paused to silence. "What, no one is going to ask what they were?"

"And what were those ideas." Came in various forms from several as if on cue. It was part of the rhythm of his seminars. "Hey, I'm still wondering why one of his girlfriends didn't sort him out." Came from a female voice in the back to general laughter.

"There you go, and I also am amazed he survived all those women. I could barely handle two girlfriends at the same time as a young lad."

"Wait," Ricky piped up, unable to resist a soft opportunity, "you once had two girlfriends? At the same time? Amazing."

"Well," Chris resumed with emphasis, "it turns out that Genghis Khan was an early egalitarian. Coming from the lowest level of his society, he had a built-in enmity for privilege and entitlement. True, he was not a saint, starting out toward the top by killing his own brother. It, however, was another time, a different set of rules. Though absent any education, or the ability to read, he had vision and purpose. He destroyed the aristocracy and kinship system, erecting instead a primitive meritocracy built upon talent and effort. This was rather unique for the time, believe me. He went way beyond that, however. He fostered participation among his troops, a form of primitive bottoms-up democracy which engendered considerable buy-in for his military adventures. He let conquered peoples keep their own gods and cultural norms as long as they pledged fealty to him, created a set of near universal laws that everyone, including the former aristocrats, were bound by and established advanced trade and communications systems for that era. This was remarkable given that other tyrants usually slaughtered conquered folk or sold the losers into slavery. Long before the American West civilized, as Americans see it at least, he created a pony express system. The Khan also developed an early system of paper money backed by precious metal and instituted a primitive system of free trade. Perhaps even more than the Roman Empire, the Mongol Empire had developed an early form of the modern state. All from the mind of an illiterate peasant. What does this tell us?"

"Well . . ." someone started but never got any further.

"You don't have to attend Oxford to be smart," offered another.

"Nor take your class," came from another.

"And consider this," Chris continued, "even before the Roman Empire emerged, Alexander the Great mobilized an army from the hardscrabble land in the outskirts of what we now know as Greece to conquer a large majority of the known world at the time, including the mighty Persian Empire. How could this motley army from a backwater area of the world carry out such an incredible feat? It defies common sense. Or does it?"

"Discipline, tactics, and purpose." Someone offered to fill in the gap when Chris once again paused. This was a sign that they were beginning to focus on the questions he had proffered.

"These factors are surely critical," Chris responded, "but let us also consider an antecedent factor. Some argue that the secret of these particularly successful warriors was that they were able engender buy-in from their troops. In some ways, Genghis reflected principles that might be traced back to Ashoka who led the Mauryan Empire in the Hindu Valley two-plus centuries before the Common Era. Ashoka espoused a set of spiritual principles based on the teachings of Buddha. He might be thought of as the Constantine of that religious tradition. His precepts embraced pluralism and inclusion that were unique for the time and impacted leaders as far away as Emperor Wu of China. When Nehru searched for some symbol to put on the new flag of independent India, he chose Ashoka's wheel, something that reflected continuity and integration."

"But the Mauryan Empire did not last." A student from the rear threw out.

"True enough." Chris agreed. "They seldom do, but ideas are more resilient. The Khan was always outnumbered, or usually at least, often by large margins and by forces who were able to hide behind fortified cities. Earlier, Xerxes and the other Persian rulers were always able to bring to the battlefield many more troops than Alexander. But they were conscripts, lacking in any real understanding of why they were there and what they were fighting for. Alexander swept the opposing forces away, despite their superiority of numbers. The Greeks fought off the Persian Empire with even a smaller number of warriors than the Macedonians. There is something about believing in what you are a part of that makes a huge difference. The Romans were most successful when Romans themselves, or people accepted as citizens of Rome, fought the battles. Later, as the empire relied on hired mercenaries from the far reaches of an expanding empire, things did not go as well. Rot from the center did not help but the lack of integration and a common culture also weakened things from within."

"Isn't that Boris's pitch, don't let non-Anglos into our sacred island?" A student mused.

"Keep that thought for next week. Let us now fast forward to something your grandparents know full well—the Nazis running amok through Europe. France had its impregnable Maginot line. It fell immediately. In weeks, Germany accomplished what they could not do in four bloody years a generation earlier. Okay, you are the best and the brightest, what can we tease out from this seemingly hodgepodge of examples brought forth from the demented mind of your leader. That's me, in case there was any doubt. Are they all idiosyncratic and unrelated historical examples or can something common be taken away?"

"My takeaway is that the class leader is, in fact, demented," Ricky said to general laughter.

"While my unlearned friend is quite correct," Chris nodded to Ricky with a smile, "that's not exactly what I was looking for. Let us take another seemingly random event, one that your grandparents experienced in real time. The Allies invaded the Normandy coast on June 6, 1944. None of Hitler's top generals would wake him with the news. His Panzer divisions lie in wait off the beaches to be sure this was not a diversion since the attack was expected to the east, at the *Pas de Calais* site. Even when they were certain that Normandy was the main event, they hesitated until it was too late. Why?"

"It was a hierarchical system." Someone said tentatively.

"Exactly," Chris enthused. "The Wehrmacht was a top-down world, the Nazi edifice even more so. No one could take any initiative no matter how compelling the need. So, they waited for orders from above as the Brits, Canadiens, and Americans pushed off the beachheads, ending Germany's best chance for victory. That was the one thing Rommel had so feared. His preparations were all premised on an immediate response to push the invaders back into the sea. If that failed, it was all over but the fat lady singing."

"What?" Someone asked. "Excuse my ignorance of what I assume is an American colloquialism."

"Never mind, my bad. Military organizations are, by definition, top down but they differ remarkably on that score in real life. Had the local commanders taken any initiative, would world history have been any different? Could they have thrown the Allies back and would that have made any fundamental difference in the long run?" He paused just a moment but not long enough to invite a response. "Not bloody likely, the war was lost to the Nazis by this time. Hitler already had made his critical mistakes, but the cost of liberating France would have been greater and the Soviets would have controlled more of Europe at the end."

"I think you overstate the case for that." The fetching gal in the front leaned toward him as she spoke, it was show time for her.

Chris looked past her to the class as he responded to her doubts. "Perhaps, but let us think of it this way. If the western allies had been pushed into the sea, perhaps the next invasion attempt would have been delayed a year. Maybe that gives the Russians time to roll right past Berlin to take more of Europe, and without much help from their allies. That would not put them in a generous mood. Something to think about. And now, at long last, what do you make of all this." This time he really paused. The students knew, by virtue of experience, he was shifting the floor to them. This is what they came for, the give and take where even stupid comments were tolerated, not always the case in august halls of Oxford but not unheard of either.

A thin young man with an angular face topped with mop of black hair, unbent his body a fraction, singling that he was about to speak. "I sense a couple of seminal, or at least thematic points here. One theme running through these is the notion of a common culture that binds a group together. The Germans had that, as did the Mongols."

Then another voice rang out. "But the Wehrmacht had lost its common culture by 1944. The troops on the Atlantic seawall were mostly conscripts from conquered countries."

"But the Panzer divisions weren't. They were hardcore for the most part." Another voice threw in.

"True," a plump girl with Harry Potter glasses said, "but they were handcuffed by a rigid, hierarchical chain of command. Perhaps you need both, a common world view and a participatory culture. Perhaps that is where national strength comes from."

For another fifteen minutes or so, the debate raged on with students picking apart the comments of others as they tried to get to some core insight that might be embraced, if any existed. A turning point came when the attractive girl who always positioned herself in front of Chris leaned forward once again. On cue, her loose blouse fell open just enough to reveal most of her enticing breasts. "It strikes me," she said in a sweet voice, "that we are discussing such things because they apply to America today."

"Not everything does," Chris shot back.

"But this does." She did not back down. Chris hated that she was both attractive and stood her ground. "You have a president that is divisive, holding on to his base by pitting segments of society against one another. He thrives on division and conflict. And then, he despises inclusive politics, hates democracy. He praises dictators around the globe since that is exactly what he wants to be. Not just him, but the party and the people he represents."

"So," Chris said slowly as he looked out over the crowd to avoid staring at her revealed cleavage even though that sight was firmly entrenched in his brain now awash in unwanted hormones, "you are saying that an entire political party that goes back to the venerable Abraham Lincoln himself has set out to dismantle American democracy? Is that your position? The Republican Party would destroy the American experiment to retain power?"

To Chris's discomfort, she leaned further forward as she apparently considered what to say next. Finally, she spoke. "Yes, that is exactly my position."

"I see." Chris paused for effect as his mind briefly contemplated positions of a different and more sensual sort. "We have been assaying several core attributes of society and how they impact the success of a body politic. It would appear from the prior discussion that successful regimes evidence participatory governance, cultural inclusion, a shared cultural vision based on bottoms-up buy-in, and a willingness to try new things or, in other words, innovate. Going back to the empires we have discussed, the argument can be made that, on balance, they exhibited some of these attributes. The great Khan worked to break down the old Mongolian aristocracy, paid attention to his troops and even his wives, showed mercy to most conquered peoples and absorbed their cultural norms, and learned from the technologies and practices he saw as his world expanded. Now, Ashley here is arguing that not only the U.S. President but his whole party, one that which holds power over most levers of national government, along with a majority of the states, doesn't have as much sense as an 11th century barbarian from the cold and barren steppes of Asia. Seems rather harsh, what do you think Ricky, Professor Connelly?"

Ricky quickly responded with support for the assertion while Josh asked what the others thought. A babble of voices broke out, but the consensus was clear. America had lost its way. It was an empire on the precipice of decline. A consensus emerged that any moral authority it may have held, and that was always suspect given its record on race relations, was being forfeited by its more recent moves to embrace climate denial, rattle its militaristic muscle, facilitate untold deaths through its health and gun policies, redistribute further wealth to the super rich, turn women back into baby factories, and foster nativist and tribal hatreds. There was little dispute over the facts, with the dialogue ending with one student claiming that the Statue of Liberty now was a mockery that exposed American hypocrisy. The only remaining contention was regarding whether Britain offered the world a clearly better example of a more civilized body politic. The immediate response to that was no, given the Brexit vote and its confused aftermath.

Chris held up his hand, indicating that he was about to take control. "Hmm. This discussion has turned out to be rather disappointing."

"Why?" The seductive girl in the front said, straightening up to Chris's relief since he no longer had to stare down her cleavage when glancing in her direction.

"Because everyone agrees, at least on the perfidy of the United States, and most of you agree that Britain is not far behind. If it makes you feel any better, arch villains Steve Bannon and Stephen Miller, along with the right-wing financier Robert Mercer, played a big role in the run-up to your Brexit vote. They pounded the tired old nativist Trump card to great effect here as well as later in the 2016 US election. For a while, it was working throughout Europe. Hate and fear are powerful motivators, stronger than hope and love often."

"Bloody disappointing that we are no better than the Yanks." This came from an unkempt young man with a shock of red hair. "You set such a low bar."

"Yes, surely the Yanks, as you call them, set an extremely low bar. I suspect that while we on this side of the pond are not without sin, my two guests would agree that America is swirling about the toilet bowl with even greater speed than we are, the Brits that is."

"Having trouble figuring out whom you are?" The co-ed Ashley asked with her most fetching look.

Chris responded with an involuntary smile and quickly continued. "So, let us shift to a more interesting question. How did the US get to this sorry state? Warts and all, many others have looked to America with envy, or support, and even inspiration over time. Now we, oops, I mean they, are the joke of the international community, a pariah among civilized nations. Did this happen with Trump? Is this merely an accident of Russian interventionism and white angst, or are we seeing something more fundamental and longer-term at play here?"

"Oh no," Ricky said though not loudly enough for all to hear. "I sense a classic Crawford screed coming."

But Chris did not offer his opinion. In the ensuing silence, several students jumped in. Some argued that the decline started with Reagan, others picked Vietnam as the beginning of the end. One student went on at some length espousing a comparative analysis of several parallels between the Britain's Boer War in South Africa and America's incursion in Southeast Asia. Both sapped each empire's treasury and, more to the point, introduced grave doubts respecting the moral authority each nation presumed to possess. Doubt about one's sense of place in the world and whether one lives according to a code worth emulating precedes a general decline. That was the argument proffered. Several wanted Ricky's perspective as a black man who apparently succeeded in a hostile culture.

Then Joshua Connelly broke his silence in this latest debate. “This has been a stimulating discussion. It reminds me why I miss the classroom so much. I was going to remain silent but, since I am the elder statesman in the room, I have the comparative advantage afforded one by mere longevity, and perhaps by being an exile from the States. May I add my perspective?”

The class turned in his direction in anticipation. “Well then. America’s unique political environment surely goes back to the beginnings of the Republic but, to keep this manageable, I will make a few selective comments on events within my own life span. In short, American political rhetoric has always elevated its constitution as the shining beacon of democracy and freedom. Yet you, without a written constitution, embrace popular rule with far more ardor than we, my country of birth that is, ever did.”

“How so?” The seductive girl turned in his direction and leaned toward him in anticipation.

Josh looked first at her before glancing at Chris with a bemused look that asked how he managed to avoid staring at the nubile lass. “The great struggle in America, and elsewhere, is about core values between fundamentals like security and equality, liberty and opportunity. Strip aside all the momentary disputes over specific policies and this Is what it all comes down to in the end. What is your moral compass as a society? We must determine each of our own ethical centers. I sure did many decades ago, and that was not easy. Determining my core beliefs was the most challenging endeavor of my life. Then we must sort out the collective center, which is another way of saying that one must discover a common culture, if one exists. That becomes more difficult in a diverse or heterogeneous society like the US, as you well can imagine. Sadly, we, or they, have never pulled it off."

Ricky decided to play the Devil's advocate. "Wait, I thought the bloody States were the shining representation of free market capitalism. Do you dispute the holy gospel according to Adam Smith as being America's creed? Are you suggesting that economic freedom does not provide optimal opportunities for all or a just society?"

Josh did not miss a beat. "I doubt few in this room believe that all have equivalent chances in life when some win the birth lottery and others don't. I admit that Trump becoming President proves that literally anyone can rise to that high office in America. However, the notion that opportunity is freely distributed is purely delusional. You think an idiot like Donald Trump would own Mar-A-Lago if his father had not dumped several hundred million on him as a youth back when hundreds of millions meant something. And he still managed to squander most of that before turning to the Russian mob and other questionable sources. But the point is that most civilized countries decided that government did have responsibility to even out the playing field, at least to varying extents. Right after you created the National Health Service, our President Truman proposed a universal, mandatory insurance system for the States. The same conservative hit men that tanked a similar state scheme proposed by California Republican Governor, and future Supreme Court Chief Justice, for his state set about destroying Truman's plan. That governor was Earl Warren, by the way, head of the liberal Warren Court though a life-long Republican. The AMA raised $5 million, a decent sum in the late 1940s and spent three years convincing Americans that public financing of health care was a step toward Communism. One argument offered was that America could not afford to go down the Socialist road like Britain had. Conservatives in the US were so blinded by conviction they could barely distinguish England from Russia."

Chris picked up the discussion at this point. "Of course, these things don't happen in a vacuum. Oddly enough, the political differences between Republicans and Democrats at that point were negligible. If you looked at the party platforms, they were more alike than different. The intellectuals, people like Lionel Trilling and future Kennedy advisor Arthur Schlesinger, had concluded that liberal thought was on the ascendancy, that conservative ideas, perhaps excepting the rabid anticommunism of McCarthyism, was on the wane. But they were missing the big picture. One unsuccessful Presidential candidate managed to get the future right even back then. Thomas Dewey was the overwhelming favorite to defeat the Democrat Truman in 1948 and somehow lost. Later, in talks at Princeton, he predicted that the parties would go in extremely different directions, that Republican moderates like himself would be pushed out and the extremists that remained would join with the racist core of Southern voters. This new coalition would shift to the Republicans sharply to the right to create a new face of conservatism. He did not get it entirely right since he saw the democrats sliding sharply to the left though that may still happen as the millennials mature. We will just have to see. George Kennan, one of the so-called 'great men' of the post-war period also proved prescient, arguing that the success of the McCarthy paranoia suggested that Americans could easily be panicked. Participation in the American Communist Party was falling fast, with the entire membership able to fit into a small American football stadium. And yet, the public was convinced that they were omnipresent and omnipotent. Events proved Kennan right. Fear will always trump reason, no pun intended."

Josh now took over again. "Fear of Communism was a major theme of my childhood. People did see them behind every tree. I recall a teacher of mine making an off-hand remark about there being no income taxes in Russia. I was maybe thirteen at the time and this was toward the end of the McCarthy paranoia. I asked him if he were a Commie. I thought he would pass out in the fear that I might mention his remark to someone. If it got back to the school board, he could have been in big trouble. Sad, but the paranoia was palpable."

Chris jumped in. "By the way, read this man's memoir, *Casual Choices*. Sorry, please continue."

"What my generation did not see was that the foundational basis of an extreme conservative movement was being laid as the pain of the Great Depression was being forgotten in the post-war boom. The so-called GI Bill was paying for college for millions of returning soldiers, helping them buy homes, and giving them free health care. Taxes were still high from the war years and so poverty fell, the middle class grew, and opportunity was spread broadly. The price of fear in some unknown threat was that a new set of voices slowly began to gain traction. You all know of Ann Rand and Frederick Hayek who praised greed and spread hatred for collectivism. But other new intellectuals such as Richard Weaver at Chicago, Russell Kirk at Michigan who wrote *The Conservative Mind*, and William Buckley who wrote *God and Man at Yale* beat a different set of drums but with a similar melody. Taken together, their common themes focused on authority over participation, tribalism over inclusiveness, property over happiness, liberty over security, inherent truths over empirical facts, and opportunity over security. Now, if you look carefully, you will see how some of these themes contravene what we find in the great empires of the past, though you must look carefully in some cases."

"Surely, though, a few egghead books did not transform American thinking." It was Ricky joining the party.

Now it was Chris's turn. "Oh no, as we have touched on in past lectures, a whole campaign started in the 1950s to alter how we saw economic life. James Buchanan, Gordon Tullock, Ludwig Von Mises pushed back hard against the emerging power of Keynesianism. Public Choice theory was developed at Chicago under Milton Friedman. They were all members of a Mont Pelerin Society, financed by the Volker fund and others and founded right after the war. They were still reacting against what they saw as the scourge of collectivism. Then, pushed by the Brown versus Board of Education Supreme Court decision which desegregated public schools, the hard right saw a danger in any real democracy, something that the early founding fathers also feared—the tyranny of numbers. Broad based democracy would give voice to all those who wanted to lay claim to societies' benefits like health care. Politicians would be powerless to stop them. Giving too much voice to the unruly masses upset the natural order of things and tended to distort the outcomes that normally would be dictated by inherent advantage and the outcomes dictated by an unerring free market. They had to change both how people viewed government and to negate the excesses of democracy. That has been what the subsequent political fight over the intervening decades has been about."

It began to resemble a tennis match as Josh now took over. "What is fascinating to me is that this emerging right-wing cabal borrowed Bolshevik principles absent any reservations. For example, Murray Rothbard of the conservative Volker Fund admired the tactics of Vladimir Lenin. He thought the right needed a hard core of fanatics to bring the message of right thinking to the masses. The committed would advance this hard-core libertarian form of worldview to a public that needed to be led by the hand. So, Buchanan's Virginia School of Political Economy and the more famous Chicago School would churn out thinkers. The Virginia Commission of Constitutional Government would work to undermine the foundations on which growing public regulation of private activities and the power of unions were based. Not long after, the seemingly unlimited resources of the economic elite could be tapped to erect an infrastructure of think tanks and advocacy groups that might serve as an outlet for any oppositional thinking to the established consensus of the time pouring out of university-based settings. These would be the so-called 'second-hand traders in ideas' who would reach out to the average voter through outlets they trusted. Where they did not exist, they could be created. Fox News is a case in point. Goldwater was an early attempt to take over American politics by the hard right but that ended in disaster. Undeterred, the core of the committed hard-liners regrouped and continued to build their infrastructure. By the late 1970s, much of it was in place; by the 1980s, they were prepared to push their agenda full throttle with Reagan in the lead."

Back to Chris. "And what do we see, what we all know as the new conventional wisdom. If you want to know if things are changing, always follow the money. The top 1 percent of the population has 40 percent of wealth. Then look at the top 0.1 percent, 1/10 of 1 percent, a tiny slice of the pie. They alone possess over 20 of all the wealth in the US, some three times as much as they had in 1979. Regarding income, the top 1percent has seen share of the pie go from less than a tenth to almost a quarter of it all after 1980. This is a tectonic shift of historical proportions. Now, most countries have become increasingly unequal, but nothing like America."

Josh noticed that some of the students had slipped out of the room. He laughed. "I think we are having too much fun here. Perhaps the rest have lives beyond this seminar. Either that, or it was probably something I said."

"I'm sure that's it." Chris acknowledged with a smile. "But most likely we have slipped past our allotted time. Unlike those American schools where lives are run by schedules, we often fail to notice the end of session. Somebody always records the remaining discussion. I assume the rest of you are okay if we finish things up."

"Of course," came from several directions. "Besides, we even have someone who is making sense." Chris loved that the students were able to poke fun at him. Oxford had loosened up a great deal in recent times, but a patina of formality remained that Chris, with his irreverent wit, was determined to further erode.

"Good, since I want to add a notion or two." Josh jumped in with a slight sense of urgency. "I feel closer to the Commonwealth, having spent most of my life in Canada, even though I was born and raised in the States. I emigrated, if that's what we call it, in protest to the Vietnam War. It was only much later in life that I came to realize that I, and others who cared so deeply, had missed this largely invisible campaign to transform my homeland into a faux-democracy that would better be considered an oligarchy run by an economic elite. When we were young, we focused on the bright baubles on top of the Christmas tree, an immoral war, and missed the growing rot underneath, a creeping form of Fascism."

"Bright baubles on a Christmas tree? You're a freaking poet." Chris smiled broadly.

Josh chuckled but went on. "Just like the Russian interference in the American 2016 election, we became aware too late about what was going on. But let me warn all in this room that it is way too easy to pick on the States. Sure, they are a primitive lot where many yet cling to fantastical beliefs such as the world being 6,000 years old. Some of the things that come out of the mouths of elected officials are utterly childish, things you would not hear in this country, or any civilized nation. But you did have Brexit. You also were fooled by Russian trolls, not you personally most likely, but many of your peers. You have this nativist undercurrent that is sapping your common moral purpose and creating horrific divisions within the fabric of society. If you look across the advanced countries of the world, those that have the highest poverty and the most unequal economic outcomes are English speaking. America is the outlier, but the Brits are not far enough behind along with Australia and Canada. And never forget that your iconic leader of the last century, Winston Churchill, espoused some very suspect opinions. In the early 1920s, he favored gassing IRA strongholds in Ireland, a tactic that soon would be outlawed by the international community. He also entertained the thought of assassinating Gandhi and had racial views surprisingly close to Hitler's. None of us can escape our darker secrets and our repressed thoughts." He paused again. "Well, that screed should get me banned from Oxford."

"Hell no," said the seductive female. "Welcome to our stuffy old center of learning and please come back."

"Yes, welcome," Chris said with a big smile. "Stay as long as you like."

"Careful of what you ask for." Josh said with a smile. "This was fun. I do miss the students. My colleagues, not so much."

"Listen all." Josh said in a voice that indicated he was bringing this to an end. "Once again, we have run over and went way off course. But as I said at the beginning of this course, you can get all the information in your readings and off the web. No one, however, can teach you how to think. That demands that you stretch your minds, think about stuff in new ways, make interesting connections. There is a relatively new book out by Jeffrey Epstein titled *Range*. It is about who makes the biggest contributions to the world, hedgehogs or foxes. Hedgehogs are those that burrow deep into narrow topics to know everything about nothing. Foxes range the countryside to get the big picture. Both contribute, of course, but my bet is always on the fox to win a race." He raised his voice as students began shifting about, preparing to depart. "Despite the wandering nature of our discussions, there are common themes and central questions if you are clever enough to figure them out. Let me leave you with this conundrum. If you were building a new society, how would you create a common vision and culture? Let us say you were Genghis Khan. At the end of the day, how would you create a vision of society that could get all rowing in the same direction? But let us say you were not trying to do that with a common tribe like the Mongols. What if you were dealing with a heterogeneous society like the States or like Britain is becoming, just to make it interesting."

The room emptied out. He knew that some of the students would normally gather around with final questions, but the outside visitors today probably suggested that this was not the time for more idle chatter. Josh and Ricky approached Chris. "Fun time," Ricky said. "I have one question."

"Only one? I would have thought you would have many."

"Hah, hah. Here it is. Do they really pay you for this?"

"Well, dear friend." His voice slipped into his jesting mode. "I would not expect you to comprehend the finer points of intellectual discourse. You took those mundane and boring business courses at, what was it, Northwestern. Is that an accredited school?"

Ricky affectionately threw a fake punch at Chris's nose. "How long has it been since I broke this beak?"

Then Chris turned to Josh. "Wow, we make quite a team. It was almost as if we had prepared for this lecture."

"Team?" Ricky scoffed. "I would have guessed you two were twins except for the fact that Josh has a more mature presence and certainly is better looking than you."

"Bite me!" Chris shot at his brother-in-law with a smile.

"It was fun, more than fun." Josh decided to end the banter. "It was something I've missed for too long now."

"Josh, I am hoping it was more than fun. I am even more convinced that you should join our informal team here. I know you probably can't move to Oxford full-time, but I'm thinking of an intellectual partnership. We are both concerned about the same stuff. And I travel a lot, sometimes have trouble fitting in lectures. Perhaps you could fill in, guest lecture on occasion. That would help immensely as well. But it really helps with what we are doing back home, the fight for the soul of the home country so to speak, that I'm talking about."

Josh looked at him for a long time. "You know, it's as if we are two exiles who cannot quite kick a bad habit. We may have run away from home for different reasons, grew up in different realities, but we see the world in a remarkably similar way. How odd is that?"

Chris smiled. "Odd? No. I would say fate. Not that I believe in such things, but if I did, I would say this is fate working her magic."

"Fate or whatever, the important thing is that this clown needs all the help he can get." Ricky added, throwing an arm around Chris while smiling broadly.

Josh laughed. "If he needs my help, he's really screwed. Still, let's chat some more. Connie will be stuck part-time in Vancouver with her research but we both will have more freedom now. I am thinking it may be time to get involved again. I've stuck my damn head in the sand for five decades now, been way too long since I plotted any revolution. Perhaps the time has come again to mount the ramparts, perhaps it has at long last."

CHAPTER 8

CABALS

Ala hu Akbar. The boy in his late teens uttered the obligatory greeting as he entered a room already occupied by several older men. He wore the typical garb of a rural farmer, but his hands seemed too smooth, betraying a life spent doing things other than toiling on the harsh land. His face remained unlined and it was apparent he was struggling to grow a beard that would mark him as a man. It was the eyes, though, that would capture those who might cross paths with this youth. They had a hard edge to them, not often seen in one so young. Their expression oscillated between a brilliance suggesting some form of total absorption in a cause and the dead stare of one already devoid of life's spark.

After some small talk and the sharing of tea and sweet cakes, the tone turned serious. "You have come a long way on your quest. You are Tajik?"

"Yes, I am from the Panjshir Valley, or my people are. I have moved about the country as a fighter with God's warriors. Does it make any difference that I am Tajik?"

"No, my son. Whether Tajik, Hazara, Uzbeck, or Pashtun, we are all one when we fight the infidels. *Ala hu Akbar!* The expected phrase resounded through the room. "You are here on a personal mission, however. That is what we have been told. Please, tell us in your own words."

"I am most grateful for your willingness to hear me. This is a matter of great honor for me that has worn upon me for many years. The story is long, but I shall not waste much of your time."

When the boy hesitated, one of the elders coaxed him on. "Simply tell us what has brought you to us today."

"Yes, it is a simple request for help. Many years ago, my father was killed in a gun battle with the infidels."

"That is not unusual, quite common in fact."

"Yes, of course," the young man responded deferentially, "but there is more. He was searching for the Masoud girls. Pamir Masoud, their father, had lied to our Taliban leaders and then crossed over to those who fought against Allah's justice. My father and uncle were among those who tracked the Masoud family down when they visited their family village. They struck hard against these blasphemers. But the two girls escaped, the one who defied the will of Allah to practice the healing arts even as a child and her sister who has told girls that they should be educated. These surely are insults against the will of Allah."

Ala hu Akbar! Rang out around the room once more.

"It was when they tracked down the girls in the surrounding hills and were about to exact God's just vengeance that all went wrong. British fighters arrived in a helicopter. My uncle was wounded by their bullets." The young man then hesitated.

"And your father?"

"According to those who saw, he was shot by one of the sisters and died soon after." The young man's words caught in his throat.

"A martyr for sure, with Allah in paradise."

"Yes, he is." The youth did not seem excited by this prospect. "I was but a baby at the time. My mother raised my brother and myself with great hardship. Years passed before my family had a chance to restore our honor. We heard that these infidels, named Deena and Azita, had returned to the Panjshir Valley. It was difficult to get to them in their camp, but one day they visited their traditional family village where their parents had died. The reason was something about a school for girls." At that he spit on the ground. "It was our chance. I was still too young, but my brother slipped into the village to avenge our loss."

"Yes, yes," the elder murmured, "I do recall this. The blaspheming girls were British citizens by then, so it received much attention. It was like that infidel Malala all over again. Your brave brother wounded one of them, but she survived, am I correct?"

"Yes, and he died in the attempt . . . also a martyr to Allah. My mother never recovered from that. She also passed within a year. I stayed with relatives for a while, but I could not get these infidels out of my mind. Every night I burned inside for revenge. It was torture for me. I soon drifted off to do what I could do for those continuing to resist, those who continued to work with the enemies of Allah. I have killed three Americans."

The elder looked at him with a bit of skepticism but let his boast go. "And what do you want from us, my son?"

Now, the boy's eyes flashed with incandescent righteousness. "I must have my revenge, Allah demands it. Those blasphemers return to our country time and again to mock our faith and beliefs . . . to spit on the memory of the prophet. They are here right now. I simply want a chance to finish the job my father and brother started. Allah demands it."

The elder looked at the boy with kindness. He had once been as righteous and committed as the young man before him. And yet, he also knew the risks involved. Some targets were prized but fraught with difficulties. These girls were now protected by the British government, as well as the central government in Kabul. There would be consequences but no more than when they killed Americans. Of course, our warriors were paid for each American who died in battle, a profitable consequence of Russian national confidence as American authority declined under Trump. There would be no bounty for these killings. Still, honor was a powerful motivator in this part of the world. How could he deny this young man his chance? "Let me discuss this with the others and we will let you know our answer."

* * *

Charles Crawford Senior hit a number he had stored in the track phone. No one answered. He hadn't expected anyone to be waiting for his call. Two hours later, that same phone rang. He knew who would be on the other end. The device was only used to communicate with one other person.

The gruff voice on the other end was familiar to Charles. It was the person he was expecting, of that he was sure. Still, they had established a protocol. "To whom am I speaking?" Charles asked and immediately wondered why he bothered with using correct grammar.

"Aaah, Himmler," came back over the speaker. "And you are?"

"Mr. Goebbels." Charles winced at the lack of creativity in creating code names but that was a small sacrifice to keep his potentially useful jackals happy.

"We're good then . . . Mr. Goebbels. What's on your mind?"

"I simply wanted to let you know that you will be receiving a visit from Mr. Nixon soon. He will have detailed instructions for you including possible targets, addresses, identification pictures, background information, and so forth. At this point, no action is to be taken other than reconnaissance and getting familiar with the targets."

"One thing . . ."

"I can anticipate your concern. Mr. Nixon will have a bag of cash, merely a down payment and more than enough to cover all expenses. I want you to be ready for when I decide to launch the initiative. Mr. Nixon will provide clothes suitable for such an operation and instruction in tactics to use. If you have one glaring weakness, it is that you are so obvious. No subtlety."

"Fuck you. We're not trying to hide."

Charles grimaced at having to work with morons. "I understand that. This is just a matter of tactics. The whole point is to ensure that the leftist protestors get blamed for the violence.

You would be well advised to listen to Mr. Nixon. He has been, what shall we say, involved in actions across the globe."

"Fine . . . when are we likely to begin?"

Charles felt as if he were talking to children. "Events will dictate that. Tensions with the police are at a boiling point. One more shooting and passions will boil over. That will be our opportunity to manipulate events and paint all demonstrators as anarchists and Trump as the savior of our land."

"Which he is," the gruff voice said.

"Of course, you and I know that. We just have to convince others of that fact." Charles tried not to evidence any exasperation.

"The other matter. Your private agenda. What about that?" The gruff voice sounded eager.

"That will come, I'm sure of that now. It starts with surveillance . . . discuss that with Mr. Nixon. Get familiar with everyone on the list, their habits, their vulnerabilities. He will have details from me. As far as the real thing, patience my friend, patience. I will let you know when the time is right."

"How?"

"When you hear the code word . . . Barbarossa."

"Where do you come up with these fucking codes?"

"Never mind." Charles was getting irritated, time to end this. "Are we good?"

There was a pause and then. "We're good."

Charles had made the call many miles from his home and office. If, at some future time the authorities were investigating, he wanted the call to ping off a tower not easily traced to him. He looked about as the students of Northwestern walked by him, intent on pursuing knowledge or careers dominated by ordinary ambitions and limited visions. Clueless, he thought. Utterly clueless. But still better than the morons he was now relying upon. Had he erred? Too late now. The idiot on the other end of the call did not know what Barbarossa meant. It was Hitler's code name for the 1941 Nazi invasion of Russia, the largest single action in the history of warfare. Okay, he could understand that they might not know that the name was borrowed from a 12th century Holy Roman Emperor. But these guys loved Hitler, or so they pretended.

Charles suddenly had an image of his son, their meeting on Oak Beach. So disappointing. Crushing, really, though his pride prevented him from displaying any feelings suggesting failure. Should he try again, should he? No, what was the use. He had lost Chris, forever. The boy already was dead to him. As was Kat, his youngest and the one he thought might remain loyal. She, however, stabbed him in the back, remained innocuous as she plotted with the siblings to lead a family revolt and take control of the Crawford financial empire. Those two were at the top of his list. There were others, but they held a special position in that place where dreams of retribution are nurtured.

There were better times. Charles remembered them with biting clarity. Though he had little time for his children when they were young, he did recall evenings when the young Chris would listen to him with adulation, hanging on his every word. Now that he thought about it, his eldest son had never been that attentive. Charles had spent much more time with the designated heir apparent to no apparent effect. Charles Junior looked at him with vacant eyes, obedient but clueless, preferring to be with his mother or the nanny. Chris, on the other hand, had that sharp and inquisitive response to the world about him. He should have selected him as the heir right then, started grooming him early. That was his mistake, he chose poorly.

Still, he did include both sons in his efforts to bring them along, train them to embrace his worldview. But something went wrong with the second one. Where? What? Each time he posed that question to himself, the same answer came. It was Mary, his wife. Her money was a blessing to him, but she proved a curse. She never opposed him and his views outright, but she was always weak, looking at him with increasing wariness and disgust over time. He doubted she intentionally drove her children away from the truth. No, she did not have the backbone for that. She did it all by indirection, by filling their minds with poppycock from her spiritual digressions. She loved those parables where Christ was meek and served the poor and loved strangers. It was nonsense but she loved that and passed it on to the children. That is where Christopher went astray, he was certain. And Christopher eventually brought Kay with him, and Kay subsequently dragged Kat along. It was a chain reaction that all started with his spouse. Worse, she never provided any sexual satisfaction, being too wrapped up in her Catholic sense of purity to even recognize any carnal desires, never mind pursue them.

Odd, he thought, look at Trump's offspring. Each one loyal to a fault. How had he done it? Clearly, he had not been any better of a father than Charles. Yet, the President's children reflected the will of the father, totally supportive. That is all Charles ever wanted. He never sought affection, merely obedience to a shared vision. That is why he spent time directing them to read Ayn Rand and Hayek and all the other intellectual heavyweights of his own youth. And yet, it never took.

How odd, he mused, since that was the central thesis of his life . . . his worldview. We were all about passing on the best of ourselves to the next generation. That was the prime directive of life, found in all species at all levels of biological and social sophistication or complexity. We advanced, fought against the tide, or we merely succumbed to that thing the physicists claimed would be our ultimate end . . . entropy. And what would that be, nothing more than dissipation and death, a cold void of meaninglessness. But you could not fight against that horrific fate by letting the mindless masses procreate and try to govern their own lives. Any future of substance was beyond them. No, only those with strength and vision could turn things around.

From day one, that vision, his vision, was to be passed on to his own lineage, his own seed. They should have reflected him as a matter of course. That was the natural order of things, but it had all gone wrong, an abominable fate he had questioned a thousand times. For all their failures, this is where the Nazis had it right, starting with the Nuremberg Laws of 1935. The state would control marriage and, ultimately, procreation. Call it eugenics or racism, who cares. Worry about euthanasia, all such reservations were sentimental claptrap. One had to focus on the longer-term picture, what really counted. It was evolution that mattered, the teleological understanding of our common struggle. In his world, softness and compassion amounted to ultimate death.

They would educate the children from the cradle on. There would be no nonsense about a liberal education, about challenging the individual to think for themselves. Training would focus on useful skills. That was what was wrong with universities today, they had caved to this fantasy about preparing the young to think. Therein lies the essential weakness of America. You should never teach the young how to think, only what to think. Personal freedom is a shibboleth useful only as a mirage to sedate the masses. Obedience is the key to the future.

Where did the Nazi's get their insights? Did they look to the heart of darkness to find the inspirations they tried to bring to the world? No, they went to that place purporting to be the beacon of democracy and the hope of civilization, the United States of America. It was there that the harshest anti-miscegenation laws were on the books. Most US states prohibited both marriage and sexual relations between minorities and those of the white race. This was where the Nazi purists went for the legal precedent and the language that would start them down the path to their final solution. Hell, Charles thought, it was not until 1967 that the Supreme Court overturned such laws that yet remained throughout the Southern States, long after every other advanced nation had repudiated such abominable principles.

A tear formed in his eye. Damn, even his own youngest daughter married a nigger. His son had wedded some Asian bitch, and his older daughter spurned her husband to live in abomination with members of her own sex. Did they do such things to spite him? Did they stay up nights thinking of ways to make his existence a bloody misery?

Charles bolted up. Well, it was at an end. They were dead to him. For now, metaphorically, but soon . . . soon! He looked about him, somehow expecting onlookers to be staring at him with disgust or reproach. But no one seemed to care about his private thoughts. They went about their business without a thought or care about his internal agony.

CHAPTER 9

A GATHERING

Josh eventually was now thinking that his decision to visit England and spend time getting to know Chris and his associates was an excellent idea. He had been to Oxford in the past but always in a professional capacity. On those prior trips he would fly in, give his talk, or attend his conference or do his consulting and then leave. Now, he spent time walking around Oxford, imbibing the feel of the place and taking a few side trips to destinations like Bath and Stonehenge and the seaside places that were off the tourist track. He even trekked up to the midlands to see the village where Jane Austen lived and wrote as a reclusive child of a provincial minister. Most importantly, he reached out to his family members and told them what he was thinking. He managed to convince his niece, Cate, and her partner to join him for a few days in England. They were always delighted at the prospect of spending some time with him. With that, his wife, Connie, and sister, Rachel, agreed to come. The latter was drawn by the prospect of spending time with her daughter and new daughter-in-law. In turn, her partner, Usha, joined the growing group.

Josh found that his argument that a family reunion was past due proved surprisingly effective. Moreover, it would be easier to gather in England since Cate and Meena, her partner, were still working in the Mideast. Cate had remained in the US State Department and her partner for an organization working with refugees mostly in Jordon and Syria. If he detected a hint of resistance, the default excuse being that it would be difficult to get away, he fell back on the guilt ploy. Do this as a favor to him, he had asked so little of them in the past. Besides, he stressed that he had some thoughts about the future, for all of them. At the last minute, he called Peter Favulli, an old friend from his childhood who had spent his career as a distinguished agent in the Federal Bureau of Investigation. He was shocked when Peter readily agreed to jump on a plane, using the excuse that he had never visited England.

Chris also convinced Jules to wrangle an assignment that might bring her to London. He knew that getting Kat across the pond would be a challenge given her corporate responsibilities, but he pushed hard. He argued that it was time that they regrouped, their effort to counter the rightward swing of American politics had gone stale as the Trump era persisted. Kat and he were confounded by the general normalization that had attached itself to the Trump presidency. Behaviors that would have rocked the country or created a constitutional crisis in the past were now greeted by a huge yawn. They needed some time together simply to work out a future strategy. Ricky could run the corporate ship for a few days. Her husband, and his long-time and best male friend, spent at least a third of his life traveling the globe working financial details for the family corporation and probably needed to see what she put up with as he enjoyed himself in foreign capitals.

As this eclectic group of visitors surprisingly fell into place, he made sure that Karen Fisher, the woman who now ran his international organization, and other key officials would be available. Next, he turned to the two now adult women he considered his daughters, Azita and Deena Masoud, to ensure their availability, as he would his own sister, Kay. His sibling now headed the medical division for his ISO. The last piece of the puzzle was Professor Shahed Al-Hussein, commonly referred to as Ali, who headed a newer joint initiative between Oxford and his international program to nurture the next generation of Muslim female leaders, an effort yet in the conceptual stage for the most part. The only missing piece of the puzzle was Ahmad Zubair, Azita's husband, who had to remain in Afghanistan based on prior commitments.

Chris liked Ahmad a lot. He loved kidding him and Azita about how much pain his adopted daughter inflicted on her poor husband. Then he would compare his son-in-law's sorry plight to his own purgatory as a harassed husband. Even though Azita knew this was Chris being Chris, she often fell for his teasing, much to her subsequent embarrassment. Still, Chris was proud of himself, it was not easy to coordinate the schedules of busy people who flitted around the world on a seemingly continuous basis. He put his success to his own magnetism or just dumb luck.

For a while, he debated where to have the meeting. Should he have it in London or Oxford? Should he go for an ornate setting or something more casual? In the end he went with Oxford and the Hairy Hare. He would take grief for this choice, as usual, but that was the price he would pay for being himself. He needed these people to bond. That would more likely occur with the availability of good food and drink. Okay, he admitted to himself that the food was not great at his favorite pub, but good drink forgave most other sins. It was his favorite watering hole in his adopted home even if it were a fake establishment dedicated to fooling the innocent that they were enjoying an authentic English culinary experience and ambiance. In the end, he was attached to the place. He even went out of his way to secure a private room at the Hare, what he considered his room. Perhaps that would minimize the grief he was bound to elicit from Karen and his two sisters, particularly Kay.

The out-of-country guests had arrived already except for Jules and Kat who would be flying in that morning on Kat's corporate plane. After some mingling over coffee and some introductions, and before they would all congregate as one, they broke up into two groups, divided by gender and avocational interests. Kay and Amar took Rachel, Cate, and Meena on a tour of Oxford while Chris and Josh led Peter Favulli and Josh on a tour of the University, a place he had never been before. Chris took an immediate liking to Peter, who obviously had a strong bond with Josh that went back to their childhood. Though they hadn't seen one another often over the decades since Josh had fled to Canada as a college student amidst the Vietnam War protests of the 1960s, their ripostes were vigorous, unending, and extremely funny.

Josh started in almost immediately. "Peter, it must be amazing for you to be on the site of a world-class school. Remind me, where did you get your law degree again? It was through a correspondence school, wasn't it? Send in so many box tops and you get a diploma in the return mail?"

"Bite me, asshole," Peter replied. "It was Georgetown, Chris, which still could take Oxford on the basketball court. UBC probably doesn't even have a basketball team."

Josh loved getting under his old friend's skin. "Helluva cricket team though."

"Now, now, children. No squabbling." Chris intervened. "I might have to put the two of you to bed without your Guinness."

Peter scowled. "I can't believe I kept this guy's ass out of jail. Really, what was I thinking? Nothing but a pain in the butt. I should have brought my FBI file on him, to clue you in on what a dangerous character you've buddied up with. I can just imagine the nonsense about me he filled up your head with."

"See," Josh jumped in, "finishing a sentence with a preposition. Unschooled for sure."

"In truth," Chris cut Josh off before he could go further, "Josh couldn't say enough good things about you. He was quite insistent that the two of us should talk, get to know one another. In fact, after he praised your many virtues, I expected you might just walk across the Atlantic, except for your lack of athletic prowess of course. Were you really the slowest running back in Massachusetts High School history?"

"Few extra pounds today but it was all muscle then. I knocked this pansy on his ass more than once. Worst linebacker in New England."

Chris raised his hands in mock surrender. "Okay, enough of the glory days, my mistake. And by the way, I recall beating Georgetown on the roundball court when I played at Princeton. But I digress. Tell me, Peter, I read the memoir Josh wrote but what was it really like when the agency was after Josh and you were involved, from your perspective."

Peter looked reluctant to give up one more shot at his long-time rival, or to respond to Chris's deft slight of his alma mater. He recognized, however, that it was time to ease into more serious topics. The informal tour stopped, and they sat on some benches in one of the many quadrangles that dot this ancient citadel of learning. "I will admit, this is an impressive place. But so is Georgetown, and that is located right in the middle of one of the world's great cities. But let us not go there. You wanted to know about this clown and why I saved his sorry ass."

"If you're comfortable going into all that." Chris quickly encouraged him.

Peter looked thoughtful. "Well, it was a bit complicated. You know that he and his friends did some crazy shit, felony type stuff. The others went to jail except for the rich one who lawyered up with the best talent available. And then there was our prodigal son here, off in Canada and, as time passed, clearly not returning. His timing was good, the worst stuff was done after he left. Still, there was one Justice Department official who had it in for Josh, a personal grudge. He really wanted to nail Josh's ass."

"Why was it personal?" Chris asked.

"Josh had despoiled his innocent sister."

"I did not . . . she threw herself at me." Josh protested.

"Hey, you couldn't fight off a 115-pound female." Peter cut him off. "This is my story and you, in fact, did though, as it turned out, you were far from the only one to enjoy her virtues. Long story short, I was with the Bureau in the 1970s and, as luck would have it, working on tracking down these Vietnam era terrorists. It was not glamorous by this time, so they gave this kind of shit work to the newbies. I knew Josh wasn't dangerous. He just cared too much, a common ailment in those days. So, I did what I could do to protect him. God knows why. Fortunately, this gang of wannabee revolutionaries did not come to the attention of the authorities until after prince charming here had fled the country. Otherwise, he would surely have been tracked down and dragged back to the States. At the least, it would have been more difficult for me to protect his sorry ass."

Chris was fascinated. "Will you tell me why you took this chance? There must have been some risk to you, or should I ask god directly for that info?"

"I've asked myself that question a thousand times. But here's the thing. We were tight from the old days. Well, Josh and I shouldn't have been, he was a Mick and I a Wop, but sports brought us together and we bonded. The strongest bonds typically were within neighborhoods and tribes. If you followed the story of Whitey Bulger, the top Boston thug and head of the Winter Hill gang, he was protected for years by another Bureau agent who had grown up with him in the old hood, they were both Southies. You must remember, south Boston was for the Irish, the kids were known as Southies while those from the North End typically were Italians. Funny, the kids who grew up in the ethnic ghettoes back then flipped one way or the other. In Bulger's family, Whitey became a thug and murderer while his brother became the Speaker of the Massachusetts House and the most powerful politician in the state."

Josh chuckled. "Both were crooks, just different cons."

"Whatever," Peter continued. "It happened that this agent grew up just houses from Whitey, who was a few years older, and admired him as a demigod. We all picked some odd heroes. I was in awe of Rocky Marciano, the Italian heavyweight champ, when I was a toddler. In the end, this poor agent's loyalty to the local thug got him a long stretch in the slammer. Loyalty was one thing, and we all used some shady informants but there were boundaries. You couldn't overlook your snitch whacking people, that was *verboten*. Besides, Whitey played this poor schmuck, using him to neutralize the Wop wise guys so his gang could run things. It was like having a government agency running interference for you."

"Wait," Chris asked quickly, "let me get one thing straight. Could you have gone to prison for protecting Josh?"

"Oh, sorry, not similar at all. As I suggested, Whitey was killing people during the time he was being protected by this agent, who had to know. This clown here," Peter nodded in the direction of Josh, "was merely boring his students to near death in Vancouver, likely a felony in some courts, though he was on the edge of some pretty serious shit before he ran off to Canada."

Josh winced. "Ah, I'm afraid I was a lot closer to some very bad shit than *being on the edge*, though I appreciate the effort at delicacy."

Peter waived his hand dismissively. "So true, some things he was into are better forgotten and left hidden. Still, his shit was never of the same order as putting a bullet through someone's head and burying their body in a local swamp."

Chris instinctively liked Peter's rough, honest demeanor. "But still some professional risk to you I assume."

"Oh yeah," Peter quickly assented. "No question I put my ass on the line."

"So why did you do it?" Chris pushed.

"Hmm. Good question, one I asked myself many times." Peter paused as he put a hand on Josh's shoulder. "The thing is, I almost went the same route. A group of us were protesting the war. We thought it either misguided or, for a few of us, pure evil. I was more in the misguided camp, Josh in the evil camp. Then we edged toward tactics that were clearly illegal when no one seemed to be paying much attention to us, though that eventually was to change. Each of us had to decide. I walked away at that point. In the moment, I am not sure how I made the decision. But I chewed on it for the rest of my life. Had I been a coward, sold my soul for a nice job and comfortable life?"

Josh gave his childhood friend a gentle fake punch to the chin. "Hey, don't beat yourself over what we did as kids. It's my job to make you feel like shit."

"And you're just the asshole to do it," Peter responded.

"But we all spent the rest of our lives trying to make sense of those early years. Everything we did seemed so dramatic, the decisions made, and the issues confronted. Hell, our brains were just coming into adult form and we were trying to grapple with what seemed like momentous moral questions. Do we fight for our country or against our country? If against, how far should we be prepared to go? How do kids make those decisions, with limited information and confusing pressures from all angles? Shit, everything seemed so final at that age. Peter merely walked away one night when we had to decide which way to flip. I almost went with him but hung in for a while. It was a razor thin decision made in the heat of the moment. Was that from conviction or misplaced loyalty to some other kids I liked a lot. Still, I knew at some point along the way that violence was not me and that's where the movement was headed, inexorably and absent compromise. The decision to betray my friends was a decision that I don't regret in hindsight. It had to be made. However, I suffered for the remainder of my life."

"Why?" Chris asked in a whisper.

"Because I lost so much, my family and a girl I loved, and some friends that were like family to me. Those friends, it turned out, never stopped loving me, it was all my guilt speaking. But that's not really it. What really hurt was that I didn't stay and fight for what I thought to be right. Before you jump all over me, let me finish. I've done the calculus. I could have engaged in more futile resistance before being caught, as all my colleagues eventually were. Then I would have gone off to jail for some stretch of time. Most likely, no doctorate and no academic post and no work on critical social issues nor adding to our stock of knowledge nor consulting with so many public officials on the social issues of our times nor lighting up the imaginations of my students over the years. I can quickly balance out the scales and my calculations objectively result in a net good. Emotionally, it was never that simple. I remained dissatisfied. I was weak."

"Can I ask?" Chris asked slowly, as if reluctant to pursue a line of discussion he might not be able to control. "Is that why you are here? You surely don't need to be. You've earned your season in the sun."

"Bullshit!" Josh responded with more force than he felt inside. "This is not about guilt. I have unfinished business. Time to fight for a country that I can be proud of again which, by the way, has gotten harder over time. In the '60s, I felt guilt about not serving even as I hated the war. I still had faith in the country that things would get better."

"Sounds as if things have changed for you." Peter eyed his friend carefully.

"Today, as things stand. I would not fight for it, no way, not when it is run by an oligarchic elite. Why would anyone?" Josh looked away, almost embarrassed by his sentiments. "But now, I have a question for you, Peter. Why the hell did you agree to come here, drop everything and hop across the pond? I know it wasn't to see my pretty face again."

"Hardly, you ugly Mick. By the way, what happened to that bag I asked you to wear over your head." Peter smiled broadly. "It should be obvious. I'm here for the same reason you are . . . unfinished business. Don't forget, I ran too, before you did and in a much more acceptable way but run I did." He slapped Josh on the shoulder. "Hey, we are goddamn Catholics, or at least were raised as such. We invented guilt. I also have a lot to make up for."

"Holy shit." Chris said. "I thought I would have to use my considerable charms, of which all the women who surround me say I have little to none, to get you guys to commit. This was too easy. Welcome to the dream of a better world."

"Or our common delusion," Josh quickly added.

Josh looked away and then spoke as if to himself. "I remember once being at the home of Ricky Jackson when the two of us were teens. His father, a wise and gentle man already was crippled at the time. He heard Ricky and I bragging to one another about how we trashed talked an opponent on the basketball court, a form of infantile bullying really. His father was reading, we had no idea he was even listening, but he called us over. *Boys*, he said, *you have a decision to make in life. You can make things harder for others, especially those not as gifted as you. Or you can make life easier. Your choice. Choose wisely.* And he went back to his reading. I never forgot that moment."

The three men continued to talk.

* * *

Kay and Azita had gathered Rachel, Cate, and Meena for their own tour of Oxford. Less of the University and more of the town. The group had not consciously discussed a gender-based division into groups but soon realized that is exactly what happened. After a moment's consideration of this politically incorrect decision, they agreed this arrangement would be far more pleasant. For Rachel and Cate's sake, as well as Kay who was not all that familiar with the school, Azita gave an overview of the place as she led them through St. John's College where she had spent her time. "Quite a bit of history here, as you can imagine. Teaching on this site can be traced back to 1096, though it was a rocky start. Conflict between gown and town led to many students and faculty fleeing and founding Cambridge University a few years later. But the place survived, and now there are some 44 distinct schools within the University, some 38 colleges and 6 Permanent Private Halls. The Halls are religious institutions though none are for Muslims. Perhaps someday soon since Islam is the fastest growing religion in the country. All told, there are over 23,000 students roughly divided between undergraduate and postgraduates. Some of the colleges specialize and most, but not all, have undergraduate students. You are selected by a college or Hall. That is where you will take your tutorials and classes and possibly reside. Some things are reserved for the broader University, such as special lectures, examinations, central laboratories, and the library. Each college is somewhat self-contained with their own eating facilities, a bar, dorms, living quarters for some Dons, and a Porter who stands guard against the outside world. Of course, each one has its own history and sometimes a distinct culture."

"And which did you attend?" Cate asked.

"St. John's," Azita responded.

"Which is the best I feel," Meena added. "I read at Baliol, but Cate and I met in Jordon when she was with the State Department in the embassy."

"Meena, were you taught by my brother? He is at Baliol which, as he brags endlessly, was founded prior to St. John's," Kay inquired.

"No. I think he arrived after I had completed my studies and returned to Jordon. But I understand he is somewhat of a star, sorry I missed him." Meena sounded genuinely disappointed.

"Oh my," Kay added, trying to keep a straight face, "I see you've received his propaganda mailings." Meena and Azita laughed.

After leading them through Radcliffe Square and past St. Mary's Chapel, Azita's favorite places on campus other than the green spaces along the river, she led them to a place where they might rest and regroup. "Let's sit for a moment and figure out what you want to see. We could do the town or walk along the river which is most scenic."

Kay looked pensive and spoke tentatively as she looked at Rachel. "I probably should not go here but what the hell. I have not read your brother's memoir, but Chris has talked about it and has given me a copy. It's on my nightstand, and I'm sure to crack it open now that I've met him. In any case, Rachel, you and your brother had a rocky relationship I understand. Now, it's none of my business but I'm curious, sounds a lot like mine with Chris." Kay continued to look at Rachel hoping she had not stumbled into treacherous personal waters.

Rachel, however, threw her head back and laughed. "Rocky? That's an understatement. It sucked the big one for decades. We only connected again, in any real sense, when he retired from the University of British Columbia. And then, only because I beat him mercilessly over the head until he opened up."

"And the initial break," Kay pushed, "it was because he emigrated to Canada from college."

Rachel cocked her head as if thinking on a response. "It was because he ran away without a word and then cut himself off from me. Well, to be honest, not just me but everyone. I worshipped him as a young girl and he abandoned me, or so it felt at the time."

"Hmm," Kay murmured. "Instinct tells me that it was more complicated than that."

"Of course, but you cannot figure such things out when you're beginning high school. Emotionally, I thought he was rejecting me. For a long time, I despised him. But in the end, he was just alone, confused, and wracked with guilt. And he also was scared shitless that he would be dragged back to the States and chucked into jail. Perhaps I would not have hated him so if I knew how unhappy and frightened he was. We see things as if the world revolves around us. I never saw his agony, all those years of shame and guilt. It is true, you know."

"What?" Cate asked.

"We all create our own hell and are quite reluctant to give it up."

"But you guys are good now, you are here after all."

"Yup, things are better for sure. Besides, perhaps I owe him something for my stellar medical career. I was so mad at him when he abandoned the family that I needed to prove to our folks that he was not the only achiever in the family. So, I worked my tail off in my studies. Not many went from the Irish ghetto to top spot at Johns Hopkins Medical School."

"That brings up the other thing on my mind. Are you just here as a tourist or . . ." Kay paused, suddenly wondering if this was the correct moment to raise what was primarily on her mind?

Rachel cleared her throat and started, "Ah, now we get to the heart of the matter. I want to share something before we get back into the bigger group. Let me first say that all I know about what might be proposed for us Connellys comes from my brother, a disreputable source for sure. To make matters worse, he was vague about things. So, I'm in the dark here, but I understand that Chris will try to recruit us, or me at least. That might be complicated. I have a partner I love and need to coordinate everything with her. Still, from what I understand, you are always looking for professionals, medical people, that are willing to take risks. Well, here I am, at the end of a successful career and thinking . . . what's next? I could sail on for another ten years at least, or so I believe. But is that what I want to do?" Then Rachel looked directly at her daughter Cate. "Josh had his hell based on guilt. I had mine. First, I stayed with a husband who, except when you were too young to remember, was never a father to you, and certainly not a husband to me. Worse, when you needed me I was seldom there, always working or improving my skills or whatever. My drive to prove something to someone never abated. I did have good intentions, though."

Cate scowled. "Here we go again with the hair shirt and self-flagellation. Any more of that, Mom, and over my knee you go. I will flay your backside so hard that you won't be able to sit for a month. Understand me?"

Rachel looked at her daughter uncertainly for a moment before breaking into a laugh. "Yes, dear, got it. Life was easier when you were smaller than me. Let me say one thing, though, before the public beatings start that is. What I want more than anything is for us to do something together, at long last. Does that make sense? I have been thinking. I want to do something together, where we can be a real family. Perhaps that is the reason I am here and at least willing to listen."

"And Usha?" Cate asked her mother.

"Oh, we've chatted about this. She is looking to hang up her academic shingle soon as well. Thing is, she's been playing around with international law. Remember how she helped you and Meena with getting married. That sparked her interest. Almost without really planning it, we've been preparing for some kind of international work. It helps that Trump is in the White House. Escape is a fantasy we share."

"How so?" Kay tried to make the connection.

"Everyone with a brain wants to flee the country." Rachel exhaled.

"You can just imagine where morale in the State Department is." Cate sighed as she looked quickly at Meena and then back at her mother. "So, you are thinking about doing some international work, mom, I mean seriously?"

"Totally, to be closer to you dear.."

Suddenly, Cate's eyes filled with tears as she fought back visible emotions. "Damn. I hate losing my cool and it's all your fault, Mom."

Rachel went to her daughter and swept her into her arms. "Hey, kiddo. You can forget all that top doc stuff for me. Only two things in life count in the end. The first is having you as a daughter, and the second is reconciling with my useless brother, and he barely makes the list." She smiled at her witticism. "I mean that about you even if I didn't always . . ."

Cate cut her mother off. "You're once again creeping closer to that public whipping."

"Yup, sorry, damn Catholic guilt thing." Rachel's voice caught but she managed to bring it under control. "You know, what hit me one day, after a call from Josh, is that this thing, however it works out, could bring us back together as a family. Think about it. We had been just living our lives for so long, you in your foreign postings, Josh in his lonely exile, and me in my professional oasis. We weren't a family, not in the least. Even after reconciling with him, we still led separate lives, living in different countries. Then, when Josh called to get me here, and as I listened to him talk about Chris and you, Kay and Azita . . ." Rachel briefly turned her gaze at the two women standing off to the side. "I knew this was an opportunity to rectify things. I mean, I could tell from my brother's voice that he was ready to man the barricades again, save America from itself. And this other stuff, as much as I understand it, with Muslim girls and education, and the next generation and all the medical needs for women, sounds intriguing. What better way to cap off a career? We could be together and doing something together. How great would that be. Even if this doesn't pan out, we will find a way to be a family again. That I promise you." Rachel and Cate melted together, a moment later Meena joined them.

A few feet away, Kay turned to Azita. "Wow. I might lose it in a moment."

Azita turned to her aunt, eyes glistening with emotion. "Until you lose family, you can hardly appreciate what it means. I cannot even imagine what would have happened after my parents were assassinated if . . ." But she could not finish the sentence.

PART II

THE MORAE 2020

CHAPTER 10

THE HAIRY HARE

Chris and Josh arrived at the Hairy Hare first. Chris could never quite figure out why he loved this place, perhaps because it was the first he frequented upon arriving as a Rhodes scholar so many years ago. He came early to make sure that all was well plus he wanted to chat with Josh before the session started. The two men were apprehensive about the impending gathering. This struck them as odd. These were all family or close friends. Perhaps that was the reason. If relative strangers were disappointed in their ideas, who cared. They might never see them again in any case, or that is what Chris often told himself. But this was different. These two men had bonded over the past several days. Suddenly, they wanted their significant others to do the same. Would it happen, though. Nothing ventured, nothing gained, they told each other.

"I wonder how the distaff tour of Oxford is going?" Chris asked as they ordered ales and wandered into the private dining area that had been reserved.

"Normally," Josh replied with a chuckle, "as an unrepentant sexist, I would hypothesize that they are buying up all the tourist nonsense in town they can, but I know that's not true."

"Are you sure?"

"Yup," the older man continued confidently. "My sister and niece are two of the least materialistic females I know. Buying a bunch of crap isn't what worries me. Nope, it's what's going on in their heads."

"So, the fact that they are here is not proof that they are disposed to join our international crusade?" Chris looked a bit deflated. "I thought you told me you controlled your women."

"As much as you control yours."

"Touché!" Chris guffawed. "Then I'll have to be my most charming and witty self. Watch and learn how the master does it."

At that, the door opened, and Karen Fisher entered. Chris usually smiled broadly at the sight of the woman whom he had hired as an inexperienced college graduate to be a personal assistant and who, by pluck and innate skill, had risen to take over day-to-day management of his international service organization. Sometimes, instinct is far better than all the principles one learns in business courses. Here was the proof. With her was Carlotta Ciganda, a Spanish lass who had training in both social work and community development, and who now headed the services side of the organization. Her hiring had been less risky but still based more on instinct than accomplishment since initially she came across more as a rebel wannabe than a future executive. Others with more impressive resumes had applied but he sensed something in this woman who had spent a good part of her college days chasing revolutionary windmills as opposed to studying with diligence. Perhaps he saw a bit of his early self in this Iberian woman who still nurtured a passion to save the world. Caring was not a quality to be easily dismissed. Following them into the room a few moments later were Kay, Azita, Rachel, Cate, and Meena all still chatting about the tour of Oxford. A telltale bag or two indicated that some shopping took place amidst the review of this historic town's intellectual heritage.

As people sought out seats about a large conference type table, Chris addressed Carlotta while ignoring Karen. "This woman is one of our top management officials. She has immeasurably strengthened our services program components, which had lagged in the early going. And I see she has brought her secretary with her, not very competent but we try to hire those challenged in various ways. It's Karen, right? Now, in Karen's case, she lacks the proper interpersonal skills, has trouble relating to people, but we retain some hope for her."

"Oh, bite me, you degenerate sot." Karen broke into a broad smile on seeing Chris. She missed not having the opportunity to trade daily insults with him. She was not surprised that he would use their close relationship to set the kind of informal tone he hoped to achieve for a gathering where not everyone knew everyone else. As she became more comfortable running this complicated set of initiatives, there was less need for his hands-on involvement. That was a bittersweet reality for her. On the one hand, she reveled in her own success and now professional independence. On the other, this man she saw as a beloved brother was not readily available to her any longer.

"I have to ask," Karen started, "what is your fascination with this god-forsaken place. Really, with all your invited guests in town, I thought you might select a more appropriate meeting place than this hole."

"Now, Karen," Chris beamed, "I recall first bringing you here. They were reluctant to let you enter, something about not meeting their high standards."

"Oh my, your dementia is showing. See how easily you are confused." She shot back. "That was before you met Amar, back when you brought those so-called working gals here, the ones that you would employ for your 'personal' servicing."

"Oh, poor Karen. Do you really think you could compete . . .?"

"Stop right there," she cut him off. "I'm not totally sure where you are going, but it behooves you to stop right now. I am sure your friends here would not want to see what might happen if you were to complete your highly sexist thought."

"Behooves? Odd word for a working-class girl from Birmingham." Chris now laughed. "Peter, Josh, may I introduce Karen Fisher, the woman who really is responsible for keeping my institutional baby running smoothly. I hired her only because she had a wicked mouth and, I will admit, a quick mind. I thought I could curb the first and improve the second."

"How did that work out for you?" Josh smiled as he extended his hand to the new arrivals.

"Total failure," Chris uttered as he went about with the remaining introductions. "But I will admit, and I will not repeat this before a larger audience, that Karen has done a great job of molding my vision into something that works. Not sure I could have done that." When Karen responded to an unsolicited compliment with shocked silence, Chris filled in the void. "Oh my god, I finally found a way to render her mute, my fondest wish. Just give her a compliment . . . who knew?" They all laughed.

Slowly, the room began to fill. Next to arrive was Professor Al-Hussein and Deena Masoud. Peter and Josh did a double take. Though over a decade apart in age, they could have been sisters, looking more alike than Deena and Azita. Both women were unusually attractive, breathtaking was the word. Chris always laughed at how the males in any room would go slack jawed when they made an entrance. After some small talk and an order of drinks, Chris thought it was time to bring things to order. He clinked a water glass in front of him and most quieted. "I see that almost everyone is here, except for my younger sister and our guest celebrity and network diva, Julianna Jackson, or Jules as we call her. But I did get a text saying they will be here anon, they had to fly around some storm over the Atlantic. Odd, I thought my sister could just order the weather to change. She must be slipping." That aside brought an involuntary guffaw from his other sibling, Kay. Then Chris noticed that Azita and Professor Al-Hussein were engaged with something on their phones. Again, Chris used his commanding voice. "I see that my rude adopted daughter and my university colleague are totally ignoring me, as usual."

Azita's head popped up. "As usual for sure, but this time we have a good reason. Well, not a good reason but a compelling one."

Then Professor Al-Hussein took over. "Yes, I apologize but there is some distressing news here. First, for those who do not know me, I am Shahed Al-Hussein, a colleague of Chris's at the university. I am heading up an initiative that Chris inspired to reach out to Muslim girls and prepare the next generation of leaders, something we will discuss more later. And please call me Ali, by the way, that works better for Westerners. The thing is, a woman I work with in Pakistan has gone into hiding. Her name is Gulalai Ismail, she is a leader and activist among Pushtan women in the northwest part of that country where the Taliban remain strong. She spoke out about the kidnapping and rape of an eleven-year-old girl and has come under attack. With the recent assassination of Mena Mangal, another activist for women in Kabul, I am very frightened for her safety. Those women brave enough to fight back, well, we are a small community of sisters. We know and love one another." Ali looked as if she were fighting back her emotions.

There were several moments of silence before Chris spoke up in a different voice. "Everyone who knows me realizes that I joke a lot. I kid others mercilessly and I expect the same in return. I do that because it's me, I suppose, but also because what we do is so bloody serious. Deena here, and Karen, have already been wounded. My staff get death threats too often for my comfort. Sometimes, I need to laugh because, if I don't, I just might cry. I first met Azita here when she was ten or eleven years old, working with Kay, my wife Amar and her father in a facility holding out against the Taliban in the Panjshir Valley. She gave me a tour of the place set aside for refugees from those religious extremists. Funny how you can walk through life looking at stuff but not seeing. That was the first time I really saw my work. It rubbed me raw. I needed humor even more after that. I'm so sorry, Ali. Do you need to do anything?"

"No, there is nothing I can do. She is in hiding at this moment. Perhaps she is fine, but the uncertainty is worrying. I have contacted people to look for her, get her to safety if we can." Ali sucked in a half-sob. "Just when did compassion become a crime and human decency a vice? Don't answer, that was rhetorical."

Chris glanced at Azita and Deena, quickly embracing his fear that they routinely put themselves in harm's way. He had tried to keep them in England but soon understood the folly of this. You cannot separate a person from whom they are. That is one way of killing the person you love, a kind of slow death that cannot be forgiven. No, he knew his fate was to die a thousand deaths but that was something he could not yet quite accept in his heart. "Well, this touches on an issue we get into later, just how freaking dangerous what we do is. Let's start with something simple, we have a Deena and a Meena with us today. They are both smart women with similar names and who look alike so work hard on keeping them straight. I should have them wear name tags. In any case, let's go around and introduce ourselves."

When the introductions were complete, Chris looked around the table. "For me, this is a unique gathering. For over two decades now, I've been traveling around the world meeting with money people, government officials, service providers, and so forth. Much of that effort was devoted to getting my vision off the ground, financing it, and making all the connections with other service organizations. Most of you know that the original vision involved making connections with others so that comprehensive and seamless help could be provided that might make a real difference. It was a struggle at first, so much turf and encrusted attitudes to work through. But slowly things began to change. Perhaps the biggest factor was my turning operational control over to others and focusing on the big things—the vision and the money and the future directions. Karen really has done a marvelous job of running the program."

"Of course she has. Was there any doubt?" Kay piped up.

"Not on my part. Despite all my jokes at her expense, she is a gem." He looked at Karen who blushed, again not knowing how to take the compliment. "Of course, she has a marvelous executive team including Carlotta and my sister."

"We do little more than follow the vision of our founder," Carlotta said.

"What a suck-up." Kay smirked while poking the Spanish lass on the arm.

Chris cut in with a loud voice. "Okay, then, a number of things have changed. We have shifted our geographical focus over time to the Horn of Africa and Syria, for example. And some of us have been sidetracked by events in America which will be a topic of discussion later when Kat and Jules arrive. By way of anticipation, Joshua Connelly here is a man whose writings I have known for some time. Somehow, we never met until

I made a side trip to Vancouver where he had been hiding most of his academic life. He is like the older brother I needed to replace the one I lost, someone who sees the world as I do. But that will be a discussion for later. What I did not realize when we met was that he came as a package deal, at least I think it is a package deal. His sister, Rachel, as well as his niece, Cate, and her partner Meena Muhaisin, are treasures that we hope to bring into our efforts, at least that is what Josh has promised."

Josh looked at his sister with a bit of panic on his face. "No promises, really. I only told Chris I would get you here. The rest is up to you."

Rachel looked as if she might respond but Azita interrupted with excitement. "Oh, Deena and Ali, wait until you have a chance to befriend Cate and Meena, they can help you so much. Oops, sorry for interrupting."

"And Rachel is perfect for our medical efforts, talent like hers does not fall from trees." Kay enthused.

Chris suddenly realized that part of his agenda was on its way to being accomplished, until he saw the uncertain look on Rachel's face. Perhaps this was not a done deal. He had wondered if these new people, brought in as a gesture to the man he really wanted in his orbit, would need to be coaxed into cooperating. Worse, he had not vetted them at all, simply took Josh's word about their positive qualities. Perhaps, upon close inspection, they would not be a good fit, but instinct told him otherwise and instinct had served him well over the years. Seldom had he come across another person who struck him as a mirror of himself as he did with Josh Connelly. And if his instincts had not failed him in this instance, why should he not trust Josh when he claimed that his extended family would fit in with the future of his organization's labors. Perhaps there is a god looking over him.

"Listen," Chris assumed control of the conversation again, "I was going to engage in some shameless marketing about what we are doing for the benefit of our guests. Though I sense they arrived sympathetic to the nature of our meager efforts, I still am going to use the floor to chat about how things are evolving, and maybe a bit about why. More importantly, I want everyone to understand the risks involved."

"You know, you could have sent everyone the YouTube version beforehand." Kay said with an impish smile.

"You know, I've always regretted not smothering my twin in the crib when we were toddlers. I could have blamed it on SIDS."

"As if you could have taken me even then." Kay retorted to general laughter, with even the newcomers becoming familiar with the ease that existed among the veterans in the room.

"Continuing on," Chris intoned with a seriousness that it was time to get to business, "most of you know that I started IPO as I finished up my formal studies at Oxford. It was for a mix of reasons. I always had this impulse to do good, perhaps a residue of our mother's Catholicism. I felt this need to show my father that I could create something on my own, something of a nature that he would surely disapprove. Helping others, not exploiting them, was perfect for that purpose, and not to make money but merely to do good. That, our dear father would never understand. Even better, the others we sought to help were not of his tribe, but people he perceived as being genetically inferior. On a more selfish note, I needed an excuse to stay away from the States, I feared what I might do if I remained in proximity to my father's machinations. Some of you know that my brother-in-law saved me from doing him extreme harm one day when he drove me into a murderous rage, my father and not my brother-in-law. The latter saved me from committing homicide by breaking my nose . . . again. Though I suspect he enjoys breaking my beak, I'll admit Ricky just might have saved my life on that occasion."

"Harm Father you say? More than harm," Kay murmured. "You tried to kill the SOB, not that I wasn't cheering you on."

"Broken again?" Josh was puzzled. "Sounds like you have a more troubled family tree than mine. While saving your life, really? Is there a video?"

"Long story, but my father's thugs were pulling out their weapons when I started choking him," Chris said in a way that indicated it would not be shared in the moment. "I still think it was planned so I could be gunned down in public. In any case, I'll fill you in on the gruesome details when no one is around to correct the record. At the end of the day, there was one substantive reason for creating what we have, in those early days that is. I saw about me a host of programs that were highly specialized. Well-meaning people focused on whatever part of the human challenge they were most familiar and bore deeply into it. Not surprising, this is how we were trained in school, you chose a subject matter, or an avocational topic, early on. Then you drilled down into that specific and narrow silo. Our institutional world had become a beehive of specialized topical areas and skills. Then we would march out into the world to bring our shiny new vocational trinkets to an adoring public, mostly those who are buzzing around the very same isolated issue. And that's not all bad, the world needs specialists, needs them badly."

"I sense a but coming." Karen observed drily.

"And the but is that we need much more if we are to change the world. I guess that is what lies behind everything I did, this impulse to make a real difference and to improve the world even a little." He saw Kay open her mouth but then said nothing. It was as if she realized now was not the time for a witticism. "So, I focused much of my early work on building bridges across helping systems, stressing the need for collaboration and seamless cooperation. I won't go into the hellish difficulties involved in making something so simple a reality. The cultural impediments, turf and jealousy, and the competition for resources made even the simplest connections extraordinarily difficult. But over time, things came around. And yet . . ."

"Let me take a stab at it if I might," Josh Connelly interjected. "You got bored. Let me try if I might. We were reading each other's stuff back then. I almost got in touch more than once. I knew what you were up to. I also could have guessed where you might go. As you have pointed out, we have similar burdens and dreams. We get bored. Once something is off the ground, we need to search out the next mountain to climb. I know that compulsion. As a nominal academic, I should have focused on a narrow subject. I never could since I knew that would bore me to tears. I was always flitting from policy issue to policy issue, flying around to consult here and there, except for the States for obvious reasons. I suspect that Chris and I are both eagles."

"Eagles?" Karen snickered at an image that flashed by her. "I always saw Chris more as a weasel."

Chris jumped in, preventing Karen from continuing with her witticism. "I know exactly where Josh is going. He and I see the world from 30,000 feet. We look for the larger patterns among the mosaic of smaller issues that entrap most of us each day. Hard to explain but there is a new book by David Epstein. It is about how the world increasingly is full of specialists but what we need are generalists. We start pigeon-holing kids in the third grade to be left ear medical specialists and they become perfect at that one task. He starts out with a mundane sports metaphor, a comparison of Tiger Woods and Roger Federer, the tennis player."

"Who's Tiger Woods?" He heard Ali ask Azita. "Does he play for Manchester United?" Azita just shrugged.

"Tiger, for the uneducated among us, was the best golfer in the world for a while, by far. He started out swinging a club at age two and never put it down. Federer, on the other hand, played all kinds of sports and turned seriously to tennis later in his youth. Many so-called experts have argued that you cannot be great unless you focus early on, and then pursue your dream obsessively. But Federer became the best tennis player in the world despite taking a different, less specialized, path to greatness. Many who achieve much in a specific arena turn out to be limited as people. Bobby Fisher rose to the top of the chess world but proved to be extremely limited intellectually, and a virulent anti-Semite who knew little outside his one skill. He knew chess, period. The thing is that some of us, like Josh and I, are doomed to be restless guys who will be poking endlessly around the edges of our brains for new windmills to pursue, new puzzles to unravel."

"Okay," Kay said slowly, "I get that you, Chris, have an attention deficit disorder, a shortcoming you might share with Josh, but what does that have to do with our work?"

Chris laughed out loud. "Ah, my point exactly. You see, my dear sister focused her education on the mechanics of the human body. Now she is an expert in tissue and blood and gore. But, and this is a big but, she is limited outside her area of expertise . . . a mere bottom-line gal."

"How so?" Karen came to her partner's defense. "She strikes me as a renaissance woman."

"Well, she would to someone as limited as you. But isn't it clear? She cannot recognize pure genius even when she grew up with it. That would be me in case anyone is confused." That was greeted with general laughter. "But here's my real point. We cannot stand still. We've done great work developing these connections among providers, getting them to see collaboration as a strength and not a threat. But now the next frontier."

"Which is what you are about to lay out for us at long last, I desperately hope?" This from Carlotta Ciganda, the Spanish gal who had experienced a spectacular rise from low level staff to a high position in the London office.

Chris jokingly pointed at her as he thought how confident she had become. What a great staff he marveled, with few of the internal feuds that undermine most organizations. "I am there, almost." That brought a groan that even the first-time guests joined in. They were catching on quickly. "When we started, we focused on what I call horizontal integration, that is the blending of correlated service technologies into a matrix of co-ordinated assistance, or at least as close as we could get in some of these sites. Of course, that is an improvement over the usual siloed approach but not enough. We next needed to think about how we could move toward more preventative interventions, not just fix up existing wounds but focus on changing things to enhance prospects going forward. Even here, we, or I, saw something lacking. We needed at least one additional conceptual wrinkle." Then he paused for effect.

"You damn well better fess up to what it is very soon." His sister said as she launched a pretzel in his direction. Then she added, "the one reason I like this place is the pretzels. They always put out pretzels…great weapons."

Chris had ducked deftly, and Kay's missile harmlessly hit the wall behind him. "Simple enough, we need an intergenerational approach. Easy enough to say but what does that mean? We not only need to attend to the needs of people early in life, when we can make a difference, but we need to intervene in ways that will have an enduring effect. Basically, this means developing talent in troubled areas to change the local culture, especially how women are treated. Azita and Deena are prime examples of this. They came of age in the era of the Taliban and yet are champions of women's rights. How did this happen? It helped that they had parents who were saints. I know they were since I was fortunate enough to meet them. I will never, ever be half the persons they were." Now, no one was joking. They were down to business. "Unfortunately, saints are in short supply these days. So, Ali, Azita, and Deena have been working on some model sites in Kabul and the Panjshir Valley of North Afghanistan. It is focused on Muslim girls, designed to get them to think differently about themselves and their culture so that they can facilitate needed changes in the next generation. It is a crime to waste the talents of half the population. This is the long view."

"Wait." It was Rachel Connelly, Josh's sibling. "Wait a moment. If I get your drift, isn't this dangerous? This is not about just healing broken bodies. You would be challenging their worldviews. You would be going up against the existing culture in parts of the world, wouldn't you?"

"Damn dangerous," Chris responded with an unusually serious expression for him. "You may have heard about Mena Mangal, the journalist who was shot down on the streets of Kabul for advocating women's rights, and we just heard about a Ms. Ismail. Well, yet another story is breaking in the international press. I just read about Nasrin Sotoudeh, an Iranian woman who recently was sentenced to 38 years and 148 lashes for speaking out for women. I . . ."

"Chris, let me add something here," Professor Ali-Hussein or Ali interjected. "I knew Nasrin very well. She was a good friend and a lovely person." To her dismay her voice caught with emotion, but she continued. "She knew this day would come.

We talked about it many times. I tried to get her to be more circumspect, more cautious. She would have none of it, she would not back down."

Azita spoke up in a quiet voice, "You know, when Deena and I were young girls, we fought like cats and dogs. I wished her harm many times. But then, later, my worst nightmare came to pass. We were back in our family village when a young zealot shot her, though he may have been shooting at me. I saw my worst horror before my own eyes as blood flowed from her head wound. I have never been able to shake that image."

Deena reached out to find her sister's hand. "Nor I when my eleven-year-old sister was carried home from the public square by our brother after she was nearly beaten to death by the Taliban morals police, only for reading in public. No one needs to tell us about danger. But let me tell you a story. I was back in the Panjshir Valley, at a school we built to honor our parents whom the Taliban murdered. Azita was not with me. Word spread that Taliban supporters nearby would kill the female children who continued to come to school. I was paralyzed. How could I ask any parent to take such a risk?"

"My god, what did you do?" This was Cate. "I never ran across such backward beliefs working at the embassy in Jordon. My country is conservative but not reactionary."

"I talked to the teachers; all were female for the girl students. To a person, they insisted they would be there even if no students showed up. I think we all thought that maybe a handful of girls would show, if that many." Deena paused as moisture formed in her eyes. "It was amazing. The next morning, they started to arrive, and then more came, and soon the classes were filled. What we learned that day was something I could never imagine. The girls said they would walk across glass to get an education. This was their key to the world, to something . . ." Then she stopped. "You will never understand what I experienced in that moment. They can kill me, but they cannot take away that moment." Deena's eyes glistened with moisture.

Rachel leaned forward. "I came because my brother asked, and he seldom asks me for anything other than to stop bothering him. Frankly, I thought there would be little harm. I haven't been to England in a while. In any case, we talked earlier about this being a chance for me to do something with my daughter and her partner. Perhaps that would have been motivation enough, or perhaps we would have found another way. Now, I can see what this means. It is suddenly more real for me." Rachel caught her daughter's eye. "I'm willing to at least give this a try. Nothing ventured, nothing gained."

Cate smiled broadly. "Hey, for a long time I loved my work for the State Department. But with that lunatic in the White House, we have no foreign policy. I am ready for a change. And this is it." She looked to her partner next to her who nodded and grabbed her hand.

Josh looked at his new best friend and smiled. "Oh, you clueless son of a bitch. You are now stuck with the whole freaking Connelly family. You poor, poor bastard!"

Chris broke into a broad smile. "No, I fear that you are the loser here. You are stuck with the Crawford clan."

Josh looked about the room. "Not stuck, it was meant to be. Anyone know what the Morae are?"

"Oh my god," Kay murmured, "Josh is as bad as my brother, no wonder they connected."

Josh ignored her. "No reason you should except that I thought the classics were mandatory for anyone at Oxford. They are three Greek gods of sort, or maybe one god with three parts. But they are always depicted as three women in any case. One was named Clotho, the spinner. Another was Lachesis, the allotter. The final one was Atropos, the inflexible. I suspect they have different roles in various versions of the tale, but the gist is simple. They take each man, and woman, at birth and lay out their fate in life. They weave it into a fabric, an individual fabric, that one cannot escape. I know, we tend to laugh at mythology but think of it as an early form of religious determinism which has now found some legitimacy even in the cold mathematics of physicists, which makes as much sense to us mortals as mythology."

"So," Azita uttered as the meaning became clear to her, "we were meant to be here. It was written."

All raised their glasses in a toast as Josh shouted, "*Cave, adsum!*"

CHAPTER 11

PREPARATIONS

After another hour of bonding, mediocre food, and more drinks, Chris's younger sister and his former paramour burst into the room. "Sorry, we are late. Damn weather over the Atlantic, really slowed us up," Kat spit the words out as an apology. She hated being late.

"Not a problem," Chris said to minimize any guilt she might have felt. "We have been focusing on international work while saving the American revolution for your arrival. For the few of you who will not recognize our late arrivals, I present my sister, Katerina Crawford, universally known as Kat, and Julianna Jackson, network star and the sister of Kat's husband. She is universally known as Jules to her adoring public and various other things to me. Kat is a tigress of the financial world and robber baron par excellence while Jules is a diva in what passes as the news world these days."

Jules feigned disapproval. "I'm sure of one thing. The new people don't need to hear any of the other things you call me. And for the record, I've known this guy since we were teens when he befriended my brother at some basketball camp. I never forgave my brother for that. Word on the street is that they became acquainted when my dear sibling broke his nose." Jules smiled broadly.

"It was a sucker punch." Chris argued vainly.

"I don't know. He told me back then that you fought like a typical white boy," Jules responded.

"Okay," Chris said in a way that suggested he would beat a quick retreat, "now that we have all met, we need to reorganize now. Peter, Josh, Kat, Jules, and I will stay here to discuss plans to save America from the Fascists. I think Professor Ali-Hussein has made arrangements for the rest of you to continue your planning on campus."

"Yes, a more suitable place than a fake English pub." She smiled directly at Chris whom she loved sparring with. Then again, she knew that most people loved trading bon mots with him. His wit was quick and, more importantly, he never took offense at the slings directed at him.

"We will convene again as a group of the whole later, in a more social gathering," Chris added. "The real purpose of gathering here is to bring some new players into our family, in which I believe we have succeeded, and to help the old-timers reconnect. Lately, we have been too focused on our own worlds. I've been playing at being an academic. Kat has been focused on making us Crawford kids even more money. Karen and the ISO staff have been solidifying current programs in anticipation of launching something new. It seemed that we just needed a couple of days to reboot and get to know one another again . . . sort of like a retreat."

"Great," Kat said, "I didn't schlepp over the pond only to see your ugly face." She walked over and planted a kiss on the top of her brother's head. "I really wanted to spend some time with my sister and the girls, err women." She looked directly at Azita and Deena. "I've missed them terribly." With that, she circled the table to hug them.

"Fun time later. More planning work to be done now." Chris could sound businesslike when he wanted. "You know, I wanted to leave the ISO group with one final thought before you go off to save the world, or at least plan on how you are going to do it. I look at the evolution of this international work I've helped nurture, that we have all nurtured. Despite my initial theoretical rationale, the early efforts were focused on immediate needs, medical, and public health, and so forth. Then we became more multidimensional, by bringing in related services such as family planning, and community organization, and a big push in education for girls. That was a big leap toward realizing the original collaboration model. Now, I think we are on the cusp of the next generation." Then he paused until Karen realized what he wanted.

"And what is that next evolutionary step?" She asked with faked seriousness.

"I thought no one would ask. I will answer with an example. In the late 1920, after the Soviets abandoned the temporary economic liberalization in the New Economic Program or NEP, Stalin introduced classic Marxist collectivism with a vengeance.

Small family farms were to be steamrolled into large collectives and tied into the larger world. Economically and socially, it was a disaster, millions died from starvation or were killed off. But there were other effects, especially in pre-modern states such as Uzbekistan and Kyrgyzstan where things had not changed in centuries."

"Point, Chris, your point." Kat interjected with impatience.

"Almost there! A sharp psychologist, Alexander Luria, began investigating the mindsets on those who underwent these changes in sites that were at different places in the modernity scale. The more remote the area, the bigger the change in world perspective needed to adapt to the new world. Primitive families saw the world in very textual ways, based on direct experiences. They could not see things abstractly, or develop larger categories, or make connections between phenomenon that were dissimilar at first blush. In short, they were not capable of nuanced, subtle thinking—the mental operations essential to contemporary societies. Luria knew that this more advanced way of looking at things would be necessary for the future."

"Hey," Josh added, "you can see why Trump supporters cannot see the obvious. They are stuck in a pre-modern world." Giggles flowed about the table.

"Humorous, and not without considerable merit. My point, though, is that the next evolutionary step for us is to alter the way Muslim girls from extremely impoverished cultural areas consider the world about them. This is more than simply adding knowledge but enhancing the very way their brains operate. We know that young brains are very elastic. We can get to the youngest brains through better parenting and then the slightly older through the miracle of computers, and then through more and more innovative educational opportunities. This is the ultimate vision of change, not telling the next generation what to think necessarily but more about how to think."

"I'm with you," Deena asserted. "This will drive the Islamic fundamentalists crazy."

"As it would the American Republican party." Kat smiled broadly.

"Yes, keep that in mind as you go about making your battle plans for this campaign. You are, in effect, soldiers. Your weapons are knowledge and evidence while the battlefield remains contest of thoughts and perceptions. Nothing is more important to the future and nothing will bring you into greater danger. I often think of Victor Hugo's iconic quote that *'more powerful than armies is an idea whose time has come,'* but the resistance to those ideas will also be fierce. Let us never forget the harsh consequences being felt by Muslim women who advocate for change. You will be marked, never forget that. And never forget that I will die if anything happens to you, any of you. So, for Christ's sake, plan carefully." His eyes settled on Azita and Deena.

Kay opened her mouth then hesitated. She obviously replaced a snarky remark with what was in her heart. "You won't be the only one to die, dear brother." She also looked at the two women she considered her nieces.

* * *

Moments later, the smaller group settled around the table in the private dining area of the Hairy Hare. "Kat, Jules, are you hungry? Need some food?"

Kat guffawed. "Eat here? I had food brought on the plane before we left, shrimp and lobster. Good stuff. Do you even know what they put in the so-called shepherd's pie here? I would seriously check to see if any neighborhood dogs are missing. Come to think on it, any real shepherds gone missing lately?"

"Very funny. But seriously, it is nice to see both of you. I'm so glad you now have a chance to meet Peter and Josh. You will really enjoy Josh's extended family, Rachel and Cate and Meena, when we all socialize more later. He was blessed with a much nicer family than I."

"Not a surprise. I am sure he deserves a much nicer family than you." Then Kat turned to Josh. "I read your memoir, we glanced through it on the plane. My god, I can see why you bonded with my brother, you are so alike except, of course, that you are more distinguished-looking, undoubtedly wiser, and surely nicer."

"Why me, oh lord," Chris feigned being insulted.

"No, no." Josh put up a hand. "Your sister is on to something though my own sibling would dispute these points, obvious as they are. But as I've gotten to know Chris, I, too, see the similarities. We do see the world in the same way. We both are treated terribly by our siblings. And we both ran away from family conflict at the very least." Then his smile evaporated. "However, no more running for me. I still wonder why I gave up football, was it really because I hurt some kid during a game back in high school? Maybe, or maybe I wondered if I was good enough for Notre Dame, afraid of failing my dad. And why run off to Canada. I could have sucked it up and told my erstwhile fellow revolutionaries that they were going too far for me. Was it more about not looking them in the eyes and just being honest?" He paused. "Oh well, past tense, all of it. Let's get on with the work at hand."

The table was suddenly silent. Kat was ready to kick off the substantive discussion but that seemed suddenly inappropriate now. Instead, she added, "Sorry that Ricky has to be in the windy city. These days we both can't be away from our financial hub at the same time."

Finally, Chris took the lead as he looked directly toward his younger sibling. "Yeah, and this thing about who is the biggest coward in the room. I ran off to England to let my sisters fight my battles for me with our father."

"Yeah, but that made sense." Kat jumped in. "We have bigger balls than you."

That threw Chris off his game, but only for a moment. "Where in god's name did you come from? You were the silent, invisible one for so many years. When we got together for the family holidays, those ever so much fun times, I always had to ask Kay to remind me what your name was. And now, you are this feisty, take-no-prisoner's broad. Does my good friend Ricky still have intact balls?"

Jules guffawed. “My brother insists he still is in possession of them. Marriage agrees with him, he has never looked happier. However, if you look in Kat’s purse . . .”

“Stockholm syndrome!” Chris responded without missing a beat. “Still, there is one piece of guilt you cannot joke away. I should have come back to save Chuck.” Then turning in the direction of Josh and Peter. “He was the eldest, the one tapped by Father as his heir apparent. He was way too sensitive, and this overwhelming sense of failure forced on him by Father just killed him. By any legal definition, he took his own life but make no mistake . . . it was murder, pure and simple. I buried my fucking head up my ass until it was over.” Then, after an awkward pause. “Sorry about the language.”

“Damn it, Chris, we all bear some responsibility for that,” Kat said firmly.

“Yeah, but . . .”

“Enough of true confessions, enough! You hear me!” Kat now made it clear she was taking over. “First, I am taking Chris’s word that you two, Josh and Peter, can be trusted. Whatever we discuss here stays here, right?”

Josh just nodded while Peter decided he needed to be more upfront. “Absolutely. I was with the Bureau for thirty plus years, kept all kinds of secrets. But I will warn you of one thing. If you plan on taking anyone out, that may cross my line.”

Kat smiled. “Good. The only guy I’m interested in whacking is my brother here, and I doubt anyone objects to that.”

"Not me." Jules chimed in with a mischievous smile. "Just make sure the whacking is aimed at the correct part of his anatomy."

"Oh Christ." Kat pretended to be offended. "No flirting, please. Okay, let's start. Here's my take on where we are then. We had a robust group of technical folks working around the last election, gathering intelligence on voter preferences and what was going on in cyberspace, and so forth, which we still are doing at a lower level of intensity. Because of this, we saw what was coming and why. But we got started too late to do much about it. That effort was on steroids when Chris was in the States for that year. Then, after the election, and a continuing post-disaster autopsy of the American political corpse, we waited to see what might happen. Surely, this maniac Trump would self-implode. People would see the narcissism, the mental issues, the dictatorial ambitions, his dismantling of Western liberalism, and a rise in righteous but potentially destructive anger. In fact, there are a bunch of pissed off people out there. But no rising up. Yes, the Dems did take back the House but not the Senate. Then we put a lot of faith in the Mueller investigation, on which so many misplaced hopes were pinned. For reasons not totally clear to me, that has fizzled to an inconclusive end. Worse, the GOP has circled the wagons around this maniac, and his base remains solid. In fact, they worship him with greater devotion than ever. Trump is now so brazen that he now openly courts further intrusions by Russia and others in the next election. He just may win again unless one of two things happen—his dementia becomes undeniable or the economy tanks. They may keep the former hidden until it is too late and the collapse, though widely predicted, never quite materializes, though my closest business peers and I feel it is not far off now. We are all prepared to sell short. Fear not, we of the elite will always do well as main street suffers. Bottom line, I remain very worried, and so are my sensible wealthy friends. Look at the damage he has already done, what will four more years mean. We thought it unthinkable that he could win in '16, but he did. I've chatted with Hillary; she now gets that she was hoisted by her own hubris. All she had to do, she thought, was point out what an utter fool Trump was. But we all live in our bubbles. We don't have a freaking idea what Joe Six-Pack thinks, or if he can think at all. My God, just consider the climate challenge. Six years from now and it may be all over."

Peter let out a low whistle. "I'll tell you what pisses me off . . . Putin, Xi, and Un working as a loose coalition, with or without direct collusion. What if they all agree to sweet talk Trump and play the little man like the cheap harmonica that he is. They will give the idiot just enough worthless, quickly revocable, unverified agreements while they undermine the Western alliance built with such care after World War II. What my favorite spy character George Smiley terms a few glinting flecks of fool's gold in with the chicken feed, which that yellow belly crap slinger can then loudly brag about to his slavish devotees, all the while eyeing the possibility that these worthless foreign policy baubles will get the bastard reelected. Then, all three dictators will have their useful idiot in place, a phrase Lenin often used, for another four years. I need not belabor the consequences of controlling their former number one foe on the cheap. No tanks or bombs or nukes, domination over America because Americans are too stupid to find their own assholes even with the help of GPS. My god, the Donald, that ignorant fool and saffron-hued traitor that he is, has whetted that set of dictators sharpest instincts for weakness and duplicity by handing them this unbelievable gift from the gods . . . a spineless turncoat who can be, or has been, compromised into a bankable asset. And all that delusional, preening clown hears are the huzzahs of his own slavish acolytes, and sees only the sparkle and glitter infused in the sycophantic praise coming from Fox and a moribund Republican Party, but never the dull glint of the knife aimed squarely at the heart of our democratic republic."

It was Josh's turn to whistle. "'Saffron-hued traitor' and what was that other one?"

"Well, I liked 'yellow-belly crap slinger' myself. Writing that one down to use if I can without getting canned." Jules frantically pecked away at her laptop in in front of her.

"Yeah," Chris added, "a man this eloquent belongs on our team. Peter, you don't seem to be suffering from any *mal du pays*."

"What?"

"Home sickness for your country," Josh whispered to his friend.

"Damn eggheads! Can't speak plain English. I'm really pissed," Peter spit.

"At us?" Chris looked apologetic.

"No, no, probably with my life. Since hooking up with Josh again, I've thought about why I bailed on our college group of erstwhile revolutionaries. It came down to this . . . I hated the war but still loved this country."

"And I was more likely to let my dislike for my country's sins erode any remaining sentiments of loyalty." Josh looked at Peter with intensity.

"What really drove me over the edge with Trump was his attacks on the agency. I gave my life to the FBI. Sure, we made a lot of mistakes but most of us had the best interests of the country at heart. Then this pissant comes along and trashes us. Though we are of a different generation, I knew Comey and some of the others that his eminence threw under the bus." Peter took a deep breath.

Kat smiled. "I will admit. I had some trepidation as to how open to be in front of strangers before coming here. No more. I feel like I'm among friends. Let's get started. Despite everything he says and does, it looks like he will survive until the next election. Mueller gave a legalistic report which, while damning if viewed dispassionately, left any follow up to Congress. This is not 1974 when the Republicans had some principles left, and some balls. The Senate will never convict, and Pelosi apparently does not want a futile gesture in the House, but we'll see."

"From Canada," Josh offered thoughtfully, "Pelosi seems a tad cautious. I wondered why abandon your constitutional responsibility to impeach a traitor. Is her thinking all about timing? Perhaps she wanted to time any impeachment procedure to the election. Don't start anything until campaigning is in full swing but when Senate action will be too late to give him even the appearance of exoneration. See how he crowed about the

Mueller report finding him innocent, which it did not. But if the public only sees the House hammering away at him, then the press coverage will put Trump on the defensive just as the average Joe is starting to pay attention to the election. She is, after all, a crafty pol."

"My government colleagues and I have read the tea leaves as well, but nothing definitive," Peter noted.

"Unfortunately," Jules added, "she is a playing her cards close to the vest. Believe me, I and my media colleagues have tried to wrest inside info from her people, but the discipline is tight. Drives me to distraction. I've even used my feminine wiles to get them to open up, no luck."

"Well gorgeous," Chris purred, "you are getting a bit long in the tooth for that ploy to work."

"Kat, do I have permission to kick your brother in the nuts." Jules mockingly shook a fist at him.

"With my blessing."

Jules sighed. "I wasn't going to break a confidence, but Chris just made me angry. I'll let you in on a secret but keep it in this room. Pelosi is going ahead with the impeachment but not a word until the official announcement."

Kat realized that Jules was sharing a corporate secret and decided to keep it light. "Of course, Jules, abuse his family jewels. I understand they are not of much use anyways, but not until after the meeting. I'd rather not hear the screams. You know, not even some of my fellow big pocket donors to the DNC can get verifiable information of any secret plan to oust him before the election. We must assume that he is the candidate. Only Weld has indicated any interest in challenging him from within and he has no chance. Moderate Republicans are totally extinct or are drifting to the opposition like this Lincoln Group."

"That's it!" Chris burst out.

"What is?" Kat reflected on what might have resulted in his burst of enthusiasm, coming up empty.

Chris continued, "Sorry, thinking to myself. But listen. I've been keeping in touch with Kat's side operation that is looking at data trends to keep abreast of political developments. On the surface, it looks like Trump is in trouble. Perhaps that is why so many Dems have come out of the woodwork to run. They sense vulnerability. And yet, there is this underlying anxiety, probably emerging from the last election when no one thought America could elect a lunatic for President. In 1964, it proved impossible, not even close. Goldwater lost in a landslide. Every reasonable pundit concluded that the far right was dead and buried, that the new default position for American politics would be moderate liberalism, that the Keynesian economic worldview was the new norm. The old disputes and conflicts had at last been settled. Now, a half century later, the world has been turned upside down. The politics of selfishness and egregious greed are the new norm. Only the House remains in Democratic control, and for how long? We are one crisis away from Republicans cementing complete dominance. A surge in migration at the Southern border, an open military conflict to rouse traditional fears, an economy that continues to grow despite ruinous policies, and maybe they stay in charge another four years. At the end of that time, will there be anything left to democracy? Really, do you think so?"

"Funny." Josh added with an expression reflecting deep thought. "Up north, in a civilized country, we have been amazed at what we see in the States. I cannot count the times I heard my fellow Canucks say something like *'what is wrong with those fucking people.'* We loved Obama. We thought Trump would be buried. We surely thought there would be mass marches in the streets by this time in his reign. He literally craps on every democratic tradition, the things that made America what it is. Despite that, at least 40 percent of the likely voters still adore him, love him even more. Maybe I have been away too long, but it is like some alien virus has infected American minds. And what if Ginsburg dies before the next election, the hard right will take over the Supreme Court."

Peter looked at his old friend. "You know, perhaps you fled north for the wrong reasons, but I know a lot of people who now wish they had followed you. Even among my old colleagues, we often joke about what our prospects would be if we applied for Canadian citizenship."

Josh smiled. "It would help if you knew a Canadian citizen who might vouch for you. Too bad you don't."

"You really are a total fuck, you know that?"

"Okay boys," Kat interrupted, "time to put your weapons back in your pants. But I have listened to my brother's spiel on the hard-right's long campaign to dominate American politics so often that that I could tell the story by heart. I hate to admit this publicly, but he is spot on, as the locals here would say. Let me throw something out and see if it takes."

"I thought the business cliché was 'run it up the flagpole.'" Chris chuckled.

"I cannot believe I once looked upon you with awe. Of course, I was six years old at the time. Bert and Ernie on Sesame Street seemed profound. Anyways, listen to this. Suppose we forget about the short term?"

"Really Kat?" Chris looked dubious.

"Hear me out." Kat looked thoughtful. "For the most part, we leave the politicking to the pros, except to feed the Dems, and maybe this Lincoln group, information and analysis they might use. The question is, where do we focus our energies? I have this sense that we should rather focus on the long term but what does that mean exactly?"

Kat paused and it was Josh who responded. "I was thinking of something as I listened to the earlier discussion about working with Muslim girls, hooking in the next generation. That was a longer-term perspective, for sure. I know Chris well enough now to realize that we think alike, have the same take on how the hard-right won the battle for America's soul."

Jules reached out and touched Josh's arm. "My poor boy, there is still time to save you, we have an anti-Chris vaccination."

"Sorry, Josh, everyone is a comedienne or thinks she is." Chris struggled to defend himself. "Please continue! I sense you are on to something."

"It's nothing revolutionary. Basically, the other side won the battle of ideas. They have convinced the American people that greed is a traditional American virtue, that inequality is fair, economic failure is always a personal problem, government is always evil, that only institutions organized around a profit motive make sense, that guns bring security, and systemic killing is the equivalent of peace. They have tainted words like liberalism or democratic socialism. They have effectively plucked people's fears and forged associations that now are almost hardwired. What else can explain why the States are the only advanced country without some form of access to medical care while paying twice as much for substandard health outcomes, why no one blinks at the gun carnage in the streets, or levels of inequality that spawned the French Revolution but are looked at as normal in the States. They won the war of ideas. Time to fight back, take the longer view. Focus on those coming of age with levels of angst and despair that just may be unprecedented."

"Even with the election next year," Kat did not necessarily want a quick decision and tried a counter-argument, "you agree that we should focus on a big idea campaign and not the most crucial election of our lives."

Chris, however, quickly added his support. "Wait, I was reading some of the analysis your people produced recently, Kat. Young people are open to new ideas. The brainwashed folk now residing in The Villages in Florida and Sun City in Arizona are dying off. Only one quarter of young adults are proud to be Americans as opposed to almost two-thirds of the older geezers. This is the vanguard of the future, the ones who will decide whether we survive as a democracy. In case you missed this late breaking news but, for the first time, the US has fallen out of the top twenty nations ranked by the strength of the democratic institutions. We are hurtling toward banana republic status as we speak."

Kat made a sound that caught the attention of the others. "Sorry, guess I was thinking out loud, about a briefing I got in preparation for this trip. Chris, do you remember April Song and Pamela Stuart?"

"Of course, April had a crush on me, smart girl."

"She's engaged now, finally realizing just how freaking ancient you are, but that's not the point. They have updated estimates of the distribution of ideological perspectives. Using something they called statistical cluster analysis, they have come up with the following distributions. Some 45 percent of the population are what they call 'blues.' They are your liberal to progressive types, urban and women and young and African American. Then there are 35 percent 'reds,' older and whiter and rural and evangelical. The most interesting are the 'purples.' They are more difficult to categorize, embrace an eclectic mix of positions, and contain a lot of other non-African minorities . . . Asian and Latino."

Peter hit the table with his hand. "No wonder those Republicans are doing everything they can to suppress voting. A ten percent advantage is huge."

"Wow!" Josh whistled. "Things are not as hopeless as I thought. Keep the blues in line and win the hearts of the purples and not even the Russians can steal the next election."

Then Chris spoke up once more. "Yes, go after the ideas. It might influence the campaign, but the impact will be more enduring. Most campaign propoganda is negative. Let's get people thinking radical thoughts again, like government help is not Socialism and surely not Communism. I have ideas popping in my head right now."

Peter quickly added, "And I can bring a lot of old colleagues who are also upset at what has happened. They don't want to see this country swirl down into the crapper. You elites don't know how real people think but we do. We rub hands with the evildoers all the time."

Kat leaned back. "I don't mind agreeing with Peter, but I really hate to agree with Chris. No problem, I'll just evade all internal conflict by assuming this was Josh's idea."

"Damn," Peter smiled. "Wish you hadn't said that. I was enthusiastic since I believe we can attribute it to Chris and not Josh." Peter smiled.

"Oh, damn, I'll take the credit." Jules laughed.

"Good," Kat said with finality. "That was easy, we have a vision. Now, let's focus on detail, that's where the devil lurks."

Chris raised a hand. "Speaking of the devil, a moment to comment on his personal representative on Earth, who is Charles Senior or more commonly known as the man who sired Kat, Kay, and me. We would argue that he is not our biological father except for the fact that Mother was such a good Catholic. I still argue for virgin births, in my case for sure. And we can definitely argue that he is not our father in any real sense."

"Thanks, dear brother, and your point?"

Chris sighed, his thoughts suddenly seemed ridiculous to him, but he plowed forward. "The real dangers likely reside with the other group. Those who intend to confront entrenched, extremist beliefs in the Middle East. But we are not without our own vulnerabilities. Our sainted father, in effect, warned me to back off or else."

"Or else, what?" Peter said in a dismissive tone. "Will he spank you?"

Kat weighed in, thinking that support of her brother on this would add to the merit of his warning. "Peter, don't treat this cavalierly. Our father is a fanatic. I believe he has tried to kill me at least once and that he did get our sister-in-law."

"Over political differences? Hell, my dad and I fought all the time. We were Italian. But he would never really harm me, and we never stopped loving one another."

Jules stepped up; her words issued in a monotone that carried great weight. "Kat and Chris may sound paranoid but, believe me, they are not. It is personal with the Patriarch, beyond reason. He thinks they have betrayed him and anyone in their orbit is in danger. You should see the security I have in my place. So, before you commit, think hard on what they are saying."

Peter and Josh looked at one another, Peter spoke first, "Hell, I've gone up against bad guys more than once. I know fear, pants-wetting fear. No problem, I'm in."

Josh spoke softly, "I did all my running away a long time ago. No more."

Chris leaned forward. "Okay then, but before we get to into the devil's lair, one last point. Those hard conservatives from the

1950s and '60s, when they started out to win the battle of ideas and everything seemed against them, argued that they needed to borrow some ideas from the Bolsheviks."

"What?" Peter guffawed.

"Just listen. I'm not talking about worker ownership of the means of production, nimrod. I'm talking about the need for a vanguard of devoted leaders who would work to change the world. Maybe we are a little like that."

Kat laughed. "Okay, comrade. Just don't tell my business colleagues that I'm part of some Commie cell. Now to work."

CHAPTER 12

BALIOL COLLEGE REDUX

Karen Fisher and Professor Ali-Hussein sat at opposite ends of a large conference table. It was an impressive room, with floor to ceiling bookcases filled with volumes seemingly published in centuries past. Large domed windows looked out over a green rectangle that was crisscrossed with paths along which students and scholars typically strolled, most seemingly lost in thought. Others were engrossed in animated conversation while several scurried along as if fame and fortune were to be found on the other side of the quadrangle.

Cate Connelly looked about her with some awe. As others chose their seats, she walked along the length of the room gazing at the book titles. She reached out at one point before hesitating to touch a volume of interest.

"Don't be shy, sample the wares," Ali-Hussein said. "These are here for public use though seldom are anymore with so much available on-line. I fear these treasures remain mostly for decorative purposes except for us slightly older folks. Still, some of us like the feel of the room."

"Wow," Cate exclaimed, "Meena has told me about what it meant for her to study here. I am beginning to see what she meant. There is a special feel to this place."

Ali spoke with almost in a reverent tone. "I was so privileged to have experienced this place as a young scholar. Perhaps that is why I am excited about this project. I know that there are many girls from my back home who could thrive here if they only had a chance and by chance I mean if they could only envision this as a possibility. I . . . well, let's not get carried away with personal reflections. We are here to talk specifically about the new joint initiative between Oxford and ISO to take steps to alter the culture that keeps Muslim women chained to the past. Karen, do you want to say a few introductory words?"

"Thanks, Ali. In some respects, the University is taking the lead on this one. We at ISO are providing the logistical support and infrastructure to make it happen. But I am committed to this on a personal level, not that I am either Muslim or from the Middle East. In a very loose way, I can relate to what this is all about. You look at me and see a typical white Brit, educated and with all the advantages. For those of you who do not know my background, let me fill in a couple of details. I was born and raised in Birmingham, lived in council housing surrounded by struggling families who were spiraling down as the economy changed and the coal industry tanked. So many girls like me dropped out of school, got the preggies, went on the dole, and spent their days pushing a pram around the neighborhood."

"But you are here," Rachel sounded quizzical? "How?"

"Good question. I often think back to my early days, as a little girl. In some ways, I felt different, not fitting in with my culture. Partly, that was being a lesbian but that hit me more as a teen, though I knew something was amiss early on. I always had curiosity about the bigger world and what to do with feelings that didn't fit with where I was from. At some point, early on, I gravitated toward the area library. I must say, it was not oversubscribed, as the economists would say. There was one lady, a Miss Michaels, who befriended me, probably because she was not that busy and I was always around the place. I often read there, it was a safe place and carrying books around got you picked on . . . attacked for putting on airs and things like that. It could get you beaten up. You were supposed to be proud of your working-class roots and hate the educated elite. Anyways, she would spend time with me, just talking about life and things beyond Birmingham. She was the first to mention the possibility of uni to me, sorry, I mean university to you Americans."

"No, I got it." Rachel smiled. "I watch a lot of PBS shows, tons of British empire productions. And I get your story. We were raised in an Irish ghetto. It was not unheard of to escape the cultural prison, but not easy either. Getting into a Seven Sister's college and then Johns Hopkins Medical School was rare indeed."

"Did you have a Miss Michaels?"

"No," Rachel laughed, "how I hate to admit this now, but it was my brother Josh. He was my inspiration. While he introduced me to the local library, he often brought books home to me. I became more hooked than he was. He had sports but the life of the mind just captured me. Then later, it was an escape . . . but we don't need to go there. I take it you didn't read his memoir."

Karen looked a bit flustered. "Chris sent me a copy. I think I'll get to it now. In any case, the point is that breaking out of one's confining culture can be a universal phenomenon. It might not be obvious who can do it early on. I probably looked and talked like a lot of the girls in my neighborhood. I know I felt so out of sorts when I first made it to uni on a council scholarship. I was still a bit rough when Chris hired me after I had graduated. He surely had better applicants, more qualified on paper."

"He saw some potential in you?" Cate asked.

"Ha! He was ready to chuck me out the door when a funny thing happened. I know I keep repeating this story, but it did change my life. I knew how bad this was going when he asked me one final hypothetical question—how would I deal with a certain challenge? I thought I was already toast so I answered truthfully and not according to some script. I saw him physically blanch and thought that's it, he's going to call security. I recall starting to apologize for wasting his time and getting up to leave when he told me to sit back down. I thought he was going to lecture me for being rude but then we just started talking, really talking."

Overcome with curiosity, Rachel asked, "What was this hypothetical and, more important, what was your response?"

Karen laughed aloud. "Damn, I love this part. The scenario was something about me being his assistant in a meeting when he was making a fool of himself, what would I do as his assistant."

"And your answer?" Cate asked with great curiosity.

"I didn't blink an eye. I told him I would take him out of the room, rip his balls off, and not return them until he got his act together."

The room was silent for a moment and then Kay broke out into laughter. "Perfect for Chris. See, you had great instincts. And I've done that on more than one occasion but, of course, never bothered to give him his balls back."

Ali was also laughing even though she had heard the story before. "One of the biggest challenges will be finding young girls who have the talent and spirit to break away while they are still young. Maybe we can come up with a similar set of questions to identify the winners?"

Karen became serious again. "Bottom line. I have a sense, based on a roughly equivalent experience, of both the importance of this initiative as well as the difficulties it entails. I also know that Ali, Azita, and Deena have been working with the Singletons in the Panjshir Valley and the Guptas in Kabul on some prototype programs. It is sort of a rural and urban variations on the theme. So, for our guests, and for me, how about an update?"

"I am turning this over to Deena." Ali offered. "She and her sister have been in the field more than I."

Deena cleared her throat. She loved working with Professor Ali-Hussein. Despite her academic standing at Oxford, and her association with the royal family in Jordon, she had little in the way of an ego. She did not hoard credit and always deferred to others in areas where she did not have a comparative advantage. In truth, Deena felt a stronger attraction, beyond respect and one bordering on the physical. She had been alone since an ill-fated liaison with Karen had broken up. For the most part, she was fine going it alone. Her work was enough, she kept telling herself. No need to complicate things. Yet, at night, in the darkness and privacy of her own thoughts, she wondered. Ali, however, remained a mystery to her, always polite and inviting but not to the point where any real intimacy was suggested. "Yes, let me give an overview and then open it up to Q and A. That's the best way to drill down into what we know and, more to the point, what we don't know. I leave all that we don't know to my sister. That is her area of expertise." Deena delivered her dry comment at her sibling's expense absent any outward expression.

It was Kay who guffawed. "That is a classic Chris witticism."

"I know," beamed Deena, "I stole it from him. I'll be serious now. In truth, my dear sister and I have checked things out in the Afghan sites. People in both are enthusiastic. What they do day-to-day is often subtle, it demands that you be there to get a true understanding. But here is an outline. Each site has initiated informal parenting classes, sometimes one-on-one and sometimes small groups. They cover some of the usual topics including health issues, but a lot is focused on early stimulation and learning opportunities as the brain is developing. We all know the critical importance of the pre-natal period and the birth-to-three years. They are trying to impart small tricks to keep infants engaged with the world. And more than that, they try to give subtle cues that girls have wider opportunities than they ever had. That's the toughest nut to crack and all is trial and error."

Azita joined in. "Let me just add that some of the curriculum, if that is the correct term, is proactive and positive. But some is preventative in nature. We want not only to identify medical issues that might stunt development but also reduce stresses that have a toxic effect on brain development. We cannot remove all stresses, such as war and terrorism, but we might be able to do something about malnutrition and violence within households. We have an example of what I am talking about right here at the table. I am sure that my older sister, had she not been so neglected early on, might have developed normally." Her delivery was deadpan.

"While we are on that topic of abnormal development . . ." Deena started to respond.

"Okay," Ali raised her hand. "We are all entertained but let's keep the sibling rivalry under control. And I thought I had problems with my sisters."

"We will behave." Deena asserted with a smile, satisfied in her own mind that she won this round of sibling back and forth. "If you look at the program overall, you will see that we are developing interventions aimed at several stages of development. Moreover, some of our efforts are designed for the family, not just the child. You must shape, or perhaps reshape, the people around the child, and not just the child if you want to create a new cultural experience. And that is the point of all this, to open up new opportunities and possibilities for those who otherwise will be left behind."

"Can I ask a question this early?" Meena Muhaisen, Cate's partner, asked.

"Of course," Deena and Azita answered simultaneously and then laughed.

"Not Kabul, but out in the villages, perhaps in the north. Let's say you are successful in getting young girls to consider new and exciting options. Let's say you open up a greater world to them. Then what? Is it not worse to open up possibilities that lead nowhere? I mean, I can see this working in Amman but out the remote villages I'm not so sure."

Azita took up things at this point. "Lots of things will have benefits no matter what they do with their lives. Take family planning, for example. There is a lot of research to confirm that family sizes are smaller when the female has a more universal understanding of things. Expanding worldviews is a goal in itself. There is more, though. The most ambitious subplot to our agenda involves identifying the nuggets—young girls who have the capacity to change the world. If we find them, we can support them along the way. Ultimately, and this is what Ali is working on, we can get some of these girls to secondary and university level schools in Britain, perhaps a few even here at Oxford. Think about how things might change if we train a cohort of future female leaders here and they go back. Even if they stay at home, they can raise the aspiration levels of females within the Muslim community."

Ali then spoke, "Don't forget, we are developing the prototypes in Afghanistan, a tough incubator, but we intend to expand to, how should I put it, many other of the less advanced parts of the Islamic world. The true test is whether we can make this work without unleashing a backlash from the Mullahs. Of course, we will need a great deal of help from talented people as we refine the prototypes, people who get what we are trying and are tactful. Such people do not fall off trees." Her meaning was clear, and Rachel looked at her daughter. "Part of this effort is designed to broaden the perspectives of the next generation, even if just a little. We who live in the modern world have little concept of just how narrow and confining life is when all you see is one culture with no access to media or the internet or people who think and act differently. You come to fear everything that is different."

Rachel made a small sound and people looked in her direction. "Sorry, something just hit me. I recall Josh telling me of a friend he met in Toronto. An American who had spent two years in India as a Peace Corps volunteer, and then wound up also fleeing the States as they came for him to fight in Nam. The emigres were drawn to one another as you might imagine. One of this guy's stories about India stuck with my brother. In the rural area where he worked, this fellow described seeing cultural change in real time. The elders mostly spoke a local dialect and had a worldview that seldom extended beyond the immediate place in which they lived. Bombay, now Mumbai, might as well have been on the far side of the moon to them. The adults, or next generation at the time, spoke Hindi and could converse about national issues. They would read newspapers, in fact. The youth were in school, often could speak and read some English and were aware of events around the world, not in any sophisticated sense of course, but they had some awareness. There was no program designed to introduce these changes. It was just education and radios and movies now reaching out to rural India. The old, encrusted culture was making away for a vibrant future. Look how quickly that country has burst onto the international scene in terms of economic development. Want your computer fixed, someone in India is giving you technical assistance, someone who might have been behind a bullock-driven plow a generation or two earlier. That story Josh shared always stayed with me, gave me some hope."

Cate cocked her head. "I find myself getting excited about all this. I joined the Foreign Service to make a difference, lobbied for Middle East assignments that others tried to avoid and then found myself stuck in airconditioned consulates and embassies. Not exactly the change agent status I was seeking. On the other hand, this sounds promising. Getting out and working with real people was something I could only dream of doing. But tell me, has there been any blowback? Are you sugarcoating what is going on? In the service, we hear lots of optimism but become cynical after a bit."

"A good instinct," Deena said. "Before you make any decisions, visit our pilot sites, at least the one in Kabul. We get young people who want to work with us, that is not difficult. But we need some people with experience and language skills, and maturity. We need leaders, like you can be."

Rachel had been relatively circumspect to this point, mostly listening. "I would love to go to Kabul. I'm a natural sceptic and need to see things first-hand."

Azita took a big breath. "Before we get carried away, I must stress the dangers. They are real. I cannot think of the price the people close to me have paid. Our brother was killed fighting the Taliban. Our parents were murdered in their sleep by these extremists as an act of revenge for the work they were doing. Karen almost died from bullet wounds while trying to rescue us, and my dear sister here was shot in the head one day as I stood next to her. You will be putting yourself in danger every day." Then the girl sighed. "Even as I sit here, I worry about my husband. He is in Kabul right now, probably safe but I cannot help but worry."

"And yet, we must admit, though Ahmad faces some dangers in our troubled country, he is better off there." Deena deadpanned.

"What?" Azita responded and immediately realized that was an error.

"Sure, he is safe from his shrew of a wife who makes his life a living hell." Deena laughed at her own wit.

"Aaack," Azita responded. "It is clear that the bullet which struck my sister's head left permanent brain damage."

"Girls!" Kay shouted as several around the table snickered at the display. "I love you both, but I swear I will put you over my knee. You always regress when together."

Ali continued to smile. "That's all right, Kay. I suspect that, instinctively, they hope merely to keep our discussion light. We deal with so much horror and despair that I think we have developed our own way of coping, a good way, even if a bit childish." Ali raised a hand to dissuade any counter argument from either Azita or Deena. "Now, before we descend into verbal anarchy, I want to say a bit more about the intergenerational aspect of this program. It is closest to my heart because it potentially provides some girls with an opportunity that I enjoyed simply due to good fortune. I can remember some girls that I managed to befriend who were, how shall I put it, born to families with neither wealth nor connections. They often were the offspring of low-level workers around our house. Some of them were bright, very bright. Their prospects, however, were bleak . . . a future of marriage and children and household drudgery. Oh, a couple of the girls managed to become teachers or clericals, but they could have been so much more. I was too young to register the unfairness at the time, but the inequalities built into life scarred me as I got older. In an early conversation with Chris, he used a term, the birth lottery."

"That sounds clever." Kay observed.

"I thought so. I asked him to explain what he meant. He told me it was simple, that some kids will be given every advantage simply by being born to the right parents while even more intelligent and skilled kids will struggle and perhaps fail simply due to an unfair advantage given their birth family. Really, what chance does a kid born to a crackhead mother have? And what unearned advantages to a child born to parents who are Oxford or Cambridge scholars. I stored that conversation in my head, vowing to deal with that someday. Now is the time."

"Wait?" said Rachel. "Tell me again how this is going to work?"

"It is simple and difficult at the same time. We will be the talent scouts in the Muslim girls' world. As we work in poor urban areas and poor rural areas, we will keep our eyes out for the golden nuggets. The schools that Deena has developed are perfect for that task. We will work with the teachers to sort out native talent. Then we will try to nurture it, bring it along both cognitively and emotionally. Success is not only talent but also will, discipline, and self-confidence. For most, their potential will only take them to completion of the upper grades of primary school or, for those with some talent, university in Afghanistan. But some might be good enough to go all the way."

"Meaning?" someone asked.

"We will prepare them in terms of language, behaviors, resources, and so forth. We will find spaces in places like Oxford and Cambridge for the best of the best and look for spaces at other universities throughout the British Isles and our former colonies. Just the other day, I was negotiating with officials from Durham and York Universities. The higher-ups are open to the idea, just as Sir Howard, our venerable leader here at Baliol, has been from the get-go. Perhaps a little bit of guilt from their colonial past but some seem to believe that immigrant students work harder and appreciate the opportunity to advance even more than those who need not fight for it. Besides, some success stories will counter the negative stereotypes of Muslims in society. No matter what the reasoning is, there is willingness to try this, especially when we pay the bills. It won't be cheap, this is an expensive undertaking, like a Rhodes or Gates scholarship program but not for elite Americans but for disadvantaged Muslim girls. It is the payoff that excites me. Think down the line, a new generation of leaders who both know the hard-scrabble realities of the real world and yet who possess the knowledge and skills to transform that reality. A few strong people can make a huge difference."

Karen decided the time was ripe to get to the bottom line. "Listen, no one expects anyone to make a decision based on what we say here. I do want some experienced, mature individuals who can contribute to the development of this program. Right now, it is a small part of what we do but it might become our future, who knows. I will need good people to make it a reality, people like you. However, I'm sure you want to talk this over among yourselves. But if you want to explore this further, we can set up a site visit almost immediately. I can get emergency visas and all that crap. But again, talk it over."

Rachel, Cate, and Meena looked at one another. Almost imperceptible to the others, they nodded their heads. Then Rachel spoke, "Karen, set up the site visits. Then we can chat about the future. But I am confused by one thing. You seem sold on us already, why? You haven't asked about our credentials and skills."

Karen smiled. "Perhaps I've learned something from the Chris Crawford approach to hiring, go with your gut. In truth, we know quite a bit about you, we've vetted your backgrounds online. Everyone's life is an open book these days. Hell, a top pediatric doc, a Foreign Service veteran who is fluent in several languages, and a Jordanian who, like Ali, is well connected and a graduate of this overrated university. What's not to love."

With that, any remaining uncertainty evaporated from the room.

CHAPTER 13

A BONDING

"How many chairs do we need?" Amar asked her husband.

"I believe a dozen. Let me do a quick count of the adults. There is us with Azita and Deena. Ahmad is still in Kabul, much to Azita's distress. I never thought she would fall so hard for any guy. No matter, then we have Kay and Karen. On the Connelly side we have Josh and Rachel along with her partner, Usha. Then there is Cate and her partner, Meena. And we can't forget Josh's friend, Peter."

"Then there is your regular top staff."

"Guess there will be more than a dozen. You know, I'm a bit nervous."

"You? Why?" Amar inquired.

"It's been some months since I met Josh and began recruiting his people. Now it is finally coming together. The old team works well together, how will this work. Change can bring cultural conflict. That's why I thought this evening was a good idea, launching the new initiative more formally. Now, I'm thinking my plan for an intimate get-acquainted evening is getting away from me. Are we ready to bond, be friends?"

"Not to worry, you are just so popular. Either that, or the lure of free food and spirits once again has proved seductive." Amar gave him a quick peck on his cheek. "In any case, you will be fine, it will be fine. After all, you can charm the pants off anyone. You got me out of my pants."

"Hell, that was easy." He immediately regretted his wit.

Amar wacked him in the stomach. "You deserved that." She smiled. "However, thanks for letting me cater most of the food. I'm not used to big groups like this."

"Well," Chris smiled in his charmingly crooked way, "I would get stuck in the kitchen cleaning up crap, a task way beyond my pay level."

"My, my," Amar smiled back at him, planting a kiss on his cheek, "you are getting wise as your dotage approaches. And here I thought you were hopeless beyond repair. Then again, now that I think on it, just about everything is way beyond your pay level. Damn good thing you've hired good people."

"I am disappointed in one thing, though."

"What?" Amar asked, temporarily forgetting that he was seldom serious.

"That you didn't bring the food in from the Hairy Hare." Chris could not suppress a smirk.

"Ha, ha, but think of this, my dear. You don't have that many friends that you can sacrifice any to food poisoning."

"Good point, my dear. And that reminds me. I've arranged a romantic dinner for two, just you and I, at the Hare. You know, after things settle down a bit. Then, after our romantic feast, we can find this remote place I know about where I can, you know, dispose of your body."

"My god, you still think you're witty, don't you? It is always an inspiration to watch your delusional thinking patterns."

Chris walked up behind his spouse and wrapped his arms around her. "My dear wife, never forget that you chose me above all others."

Despite her best intentions, Amar giggled. "Oh dear, you had to remind me of my one horrendous lapse in judgment. Then again, come to think on it, my first attempt at marriage didn't turn out particularly good either. Perhaps I am stumbling on a great truth here."

"Which is?" Chris began to nibble at her ear.

Despite herself, Amar lost her train of thought. A familiar warmth spread through her body that yet surprised her. *Damn,* she thought, *he still knows how to push my buttons.* Just as she considered whether there might be time to enjoy a carnal moment or two, the doorbell pierced her reverie. "Saved by the bell," she said as she untangled herself from his grasp. On opening the door, she yelled back, "It's Karen."

"Tell her to go away while I ravage your body," Chris yelled with dramatic effect.

"Hah," Karen responded as she entered, "I wouldn't have to go far. I would say 15 seconds should do the trick."

"Why, oh why, dear Lord, does every woman in my life think they're hilarious."

"And thank you, dear Lord," Karen gave Chris a quick kiss on the cheek as she walked toward the drinks, "for giving me such excellent comedic material to work with. You are so freaking easy."

"Oy vey, it's going to be a long evening." Chris glanced to see if Karen were watching before pinching his wife's derriere.

"Stop that," Amar complained as she giggled.

"By the way, what was that great truth?"

"Truth?" She was puzzled.

"Yes, you said you were stumbling on to a great truth just as you were about to rip off my clothes and jump my bones a few minutes ago. Surely you must remember your epiphany unless lust has overwhelmed you."

"Oh yeah," Amar smiled. "I recall now. It really wasn't so original after all. Every woman gets it." Then she paused for effect. "My epiphany is that men are way overrated, hardly worth our bother. Now, do something useful and within your skill level. Get the rest of the food ready."

* * *

The food had been set out in buffet style, with guests picking and choosing selections among the vegetarian and non-vegetarian offerings according to their fashion. As was the practice in such an arrangement, small knots of people congregated in various parts of the expansive living area to eat and talk. Chris noticed that his American guests were chatting together separately from the British contingent. Perhaps he should have structured things differently. Oh well, live and learn. He would take the evening in different direction soon enough.

When the food portion of the evening was coming to an end, he pulled Amar aside. "Okay, let's get everyone together."

"Oh, you have a plan. This should be interesting."

Ignoring his wife's sarcasm, Chris spoke in a commanding voice. "All right, now that everyone has eaten my food and consumed copious amounts of fine spirits, fun time is over. I want to pull all into a large circle."

When the restructuring of the guests had been completed, Chris and Amar ensuring that the various natural groupings were no longer together, he began again. "Most of you have now met but not all since we have some late arrivals. So, let me quickly reintroduce everyone. Everyone knows Amar, my real boss in life. I saved her from a life of degradation but that is another story. Then we have my two adoptive daughters, Azita and Deena, both of whom are working closely with the lovely Shahed Al-Hussein, a colleague from Oxford who heads our Muslim girl's initiative."

Shahed smiled. "I must tell you that Chris did not save me from a dissolute life."

"Nope," Chris laughed aloud, "she remains as dissolute as ever."

"By the way, where are the younger girls?" Karen Fisher asked as she suddenly realized they were absent.

"Good point, the younger girls are with friends tonight. Amar and I thought they would be bored with us. And speaking of boring people, I should point out Karen Fisher, another woman whom I rescued from a sordid life of dissipation and depravity."

"Oh brother," Karen sighed loudly, "and to think I almost died saving his sorry behind."

"Most of you know that Karen is running my organization into the ground these days." Chris said to general laughter. "Let's see, we also have Carlotta Ciganda, head of human services and Josef Spiglanin, our logistical specialist in central office. Now, most of you know Kay Crawford, my sister and now head of health services. But let's move to our guests from across the pond. We have Kat, my brilliant younger sibling whose financial genius is paying more and more of our bills. Then we have some guests from Canada. Josh Connelly is emeritus from the University of British Columbia and a fine thinker of social issues. He's helping me with some strategic thinking and writing."

"It's a dirty job but someone has to bail him out." Kay was pleased with her witty riposte.

"Joining him, at long last, is his wife, Connie Chen. She has torn herself away from her research in biochemistry to check out what nonsense her husband is into this time. Then we have another woman who, I am told, has tortured poor Joshua just as the women in my life torture me. His sister, Rachel, is a retired physician who has joined our medical services team while her partner, Usha Nayer, is a lawyer skilled in international law and will help Shahed in that arena. Next, we have Rachel's daughter, Cate, and her partner Meena. Cate had been with the American State Department and Meena with the Jordanian government. They have considerable experience in the Middle East and will be valuable additions to Shaheed's team as they try to uplift Muslim girls from their cultural shackles."

Josh spoke up, "I should introduce Peter Favulli who is unknown to some of you. Peter was my good friend when we were just kids. We met playing football even if he was the slowest running back in the Boston area. But, to my good fortune later in life, we remained friends when I later ran into trouble. He had a career with the FBI and still has great contacts, which might become quite useful over the next year."

Chris cleared his throat, a signal that he would be getting serious. "Intermittently, as we've put things together over these past weeks and months, I know some of you have gotten to know one another. But we haven't had many opportunities to get together as a group, at least not socially. I thought this might be an opportune time to take stock and share thoughts and aspirations with one another but in an informal way. By that, I'm not talking about future projects, we've been focusing on plans enough. I want us to share a bit about ourselves, what we have faced in life, and where we, as individuals, think we are going." He paused, perhaps hoping someone would take the initiative.

It was Amar that spoke up. "You have the best idea of what you have in mind. You start." Then she rolled her eyes in an exaggerated manner. "I can't believe I encouraged him."

"Fair enough." Instead of speaking, he looked at his hands as if he realized he hadn't thought this through very well. After some moments, he looked up at the assembly. "Okay, we are entering 2020, less than one year out from what may be the most important election in America's history. My country of origin seems to be coming apart at the seams in virulent divisions that appear beyond repair. Similar divisions have reared up here in Britain with Brexit winning the day. The whole post World War II international order that has, with fits and starts, moved humanity mostly forward over the course of more than half a century is endangered. So-called leaders like Trump and Johnson want to pull us back into a vicious form of tribalism that can do nothing more than rekindle the despair of the dark ages. But you don't need me to tell you that. You are smart people and can see that for yourselves. What is in my heart tonight is something different. It is something reflected in the faces I see about this room."

Chris looked at his hands again, before clearing his throat. If anyone looked closely, they might have caught moisture forming in the corners of his eyes. "Out there, beyond our little band gathered here, our so-called leaders play on our anxieties and prejudices, the things that drive us apart, keep us looking at the wrong things, focusing on fears rather than opportunities. In the States, and here in England, working-class white folks are told to blame the guy and gal who doesn't look and think like them for all their problems. Forget about the rigged system that is redistributing untold amounts of treasure to the elite through regressive tax laws, impoverished labor laws, and tattered safety nets. No, keep focusing on the person who doesn't have the same skin color, or who speaks with an accent, or who might celebrate a different vision of god or sing different songs on their ethnic holidays."

When Chris hesitated for a moment, Karen Fisher spoke up with a slightly exaggerated Cockney accent. "Well, Gov, I just want you to know I've forgiven you ungrateful colonists for disrespecting the Crown."

Chris was glad for her lightness. "And we thank you. You have a generous heart, that is if we ever locate it."

Amar then spoke. "My husband is right, which is something I seldom admit. Since this whole Brexit thing, I've worried about my girls, Azita and Deena, every time they go to London, never mind back home to Afghanistan. I keep thinking some crazy will take it into his head to attack them just because he doesn't know who to blame for his unhappiness and frustration. Sometimes, even here in Oxford . . ." Then she stopped, looking back at Chris.

"So do I, dear, so do I. But I don't want to focus on what is wrong, we could go all night on that. My real point is sitting next to you, and across from you. Look around. We come in several colors—white, brown, yellow—and ethnicities. We have gathered from across the globe, and from different cultures and spiritual traditions and ways of looking at things. We love differently and we live differently. And yet, we come together for a common aspiration. At least I think we have, and that's probably what I want to explore here."

"Hmmm." Carlotta was obviously considering Chris's words. "How would you express what brings you here, but in fifteen words or less?"

Chris considered his words and started slowly. "Many things, of course. But there is one thing that has always driven me. I wonder if my sisters would agree that it is our hatred for our father, that this is a way for the three of us to spite his beliefs and what he represents."

Kay picked up her brother's theme. "My father, our father, would hate the very concept of this room. The rainbow of ethnicities and races and beliefs found within these four walls. He is more sophisticated than your traditional Nazi or Aryan thug but only to the extent that he's enveloped his belief system within an evolutionary vision that sounds sophisticated to some untrained minds. Man, he would say, are conscience and therefore capable of advancing evolution in a direct way. You shouldn't let natural selection play out but should employ our gifts to help create the next step of mankind. Conveniently, that converts into promoting values and perspectives that people who look and think exactly like him embrace. Funny how that works out."

"Many of you know what Chris and I survived as children." It was Kat who had spoken. "There was physical, emotional, and . . . sexual abuse." Then she stopped, embarrassed by what she let out in public.

Kay rescued her. "But mostly, there was a steady stream of propaganda, of indoctrination. I was never as close to my brother as when we, as kids, huddled under a blanket at night to read things our father would beat us for having if he knew and to discuss ideas that were anathema to him. Chris pushed me to rebel and for that, I am grateful. I'm not sure that fully explains my cultural escape but, then again, I really have no explanation."

Josh broke in and all eyes turned to him. "Let me play devil's advocate for a moment, maybe push the discussion away from personal vendettas. Isn't the inexorable march of technology a way of controlling evolution? When Alan Turing conceptualized the essence of the computer when breaking the enigma code in World War II, he set the species along a totally different path. He knew that artificial intelligence was a matter of time. So, what does that say about natural selection? Some early mammal, was it the shrew, could never think that if he could just make this small physiological adaptation to his environment, homo sapiens would arise just a few million years down the road. But we can entertain notions of the future, speculate at least."

Chris took a deep breath. Perhaps this gathering would work after all. Then he saw Usha Nayer, Josh's sister-in-law, act as if she were about to speak. He wanted everyone to get involved, especially those more peripheral to why they had gathered here. "Go ahead, Usha, don't hold back."

She smiled, looking at her partner Rachel. "As Rachel and Josh know, I am a lawyer who seldom holds back."

"Believe me, I can vouch for that," Josh said with a smile.

Usha gave him a mockingly withering look. "I was thinking about my own culture. I was raised when India was still a rather awful place for women, still not that great but better. When I realized I preferred females as partners, my road to independence suddenly was harder, much harder indeed. It even included a sham marriage for a while, a long time ago, to Josh for those who do not know. We do not often admit that in public, but I feel safe here. For a while, I struggled with my parents and my culture. But, at some point, I came to see positive things."

"Like what? I'm really curious." Amar inquired.

"There is something soothing about traditions that go back so far. Hinduism, at least the earliest records of it, goes back some 4,000 years or so. It provided sense to people whose lives were tenuous indeed. Hinduism hardly makes sense even to me, but underlying all were some simple notions of dharma, karma, reincarnation, and moksha. Dharma was a kind of cosmic law underlying what was considered right behavior and social order; karma was a reckoning of a person's actions in this and previous lives; reincarnation was, as you all know, the notion of rebirth based on karma, while moksha is what we all strive for . . . the release from life's toil and the experience of paradise, if you will. Oh, I never believed in the specifics of course, at least not by the time of college, but the sense of timelessness gave me, what is the word, perspective."

Karen almost shouted. "Perspective. I was sitting here trying to think about my background and what it gave me. Unlike most of you, I was an average delinquent from the midlands."

"Me, too," Josh threw out, "but not from the midlands since I don't know where that is."

"The middle part of England. Bother, our colonials are an ignorant lot." Karen smiled broadly. "But my mom would drag me off to the Church of England. Can you believe it?"

"I'm just shocked you didn't burst into flames, isn't that what is supposed to happen to Satan's helpers." Chris could not resist.

"Ah, sod-off, you bloody wanker," she issued with her best affected accent. "As I was saying, she would drag me there and I would go even after my siblings stopped. I suppose I wanted to believe in something beyond myself. It was not going to be the high Church of England, but that sentiment was there, and I even sought out courses in religious history at Durham. What fascinated me was this notion that spiritual conviction was found wherever people, even primitives, came together. We had ancestors believing in animism almost as soon as they could communicate. Forget about Stonehenge, there is an early burial site in Ireland called New Grange that goes back some 9,000 years where rituals were carried out, probably with astral connections, though that is uncertain. The point is this, even primitives were compelled to look beyond themselves."

Amar jumped in. "Like Usha, I was raised with stories of Brahma and Vishnu and Shiva. I think my father was too educated to raise me with traditional religious convictions but, perhaps because of my mother's simple sense of faith, I wanted something to hold on to. As Azita knows, I spent time up in Kashmir, near a Buddhist temple. The site was very isolated. I loved it. It was a temple to me. You felt so near the sky where all the celestial wonders seemed so close, as if you could reach out and touch the fields of stars. On one hand, I could understand a belief in the panoply of Hindu gods and goddesses. Life was complex and all these deities had roles to help mere mortals deal with such things."

"You once told me they were like the Catholic saints. Many of which were associated with given roles and to which the faithful prayed when they needed specific help," Azita said as she gazed with affection toward her adoptive mother. "I never forgot that. It helped me see how close we are despite the beliefs that separate us on paper."

Shahed Al-Hussein spoke up excitedly. "Yes, yes, religious evolution has always fascinated me as well. Our rich primitive spiritual aspirations which were one with nature evolved to more abstract concepts of Monism with the emergence of the first Abrahamic traditions. First, there was Judaism in the centuries before the common era and then Christianity, an offshoot of the Judaic tradition. The pluralism of earlier religious forms became more abstract and unified. Now that was real revolution."

Usha interrupted. "That is true enough but then we saw another burst of spiritual innovation some five and six centuries before Christ. There was this intense period in Asia where Jainism, Confucianism, and Taoism all started around 500 to 600 BCE. During that period, Prince Siddhartha achieved Shakyamuni, or enlightenment, and began a life of preaching to his followers, much like Christ did later on. By the way, we know him as the Buddha. This was a time when another wave of urbanization and advanced trade increased exchanges across cultures. As different cultures intermingled through trade, they inadvertently created petri dishes for creative thought."

"And don't forget Muhammed," Shahed added. "He appeared some five centuries after Christ to start the third leg of the Abrahamic religious tradition. Soon, his followers were marauding east and west converting many by persuasion and by the sword. They almost swallowed up Europe by the 8th century."

"I just thought of something," Deena nodded. "We moved to one god, more ineffable than substantive. Islam put an exclamation point on all that. According to our law, you are not permitted to portray God or His prophet in any physical way. He is beyond that."

"So true." Amar mused. "But what I remember were my discussions with the Buddhists monks from a monastery where my family spent the hot summers. It was a retreat in Kashmir, near the Himalayas. Creed and doctrine and abstractions didn't seem to matter any longer. They had this simplicity and peace and love that touched me. I recall one day, sitting by myself after a long discussion with a small group of them. When I returned to our family retreat I told my parents I was becoming a Buddhist. My father just smiled though my mother was upset."

"Did you actually become one?" Kay was curious.

"Well, I never went through any ceremony. It was just something that happened in my heart. In the end, spirituality might take many forms, but what touched the heart is paramount."

Peter Favulli suddenly made a sound. When everyone turned in his direction, he blushed. "Okay, tell me this. How the hell did I get involved with so many religious scholars? Now, here is a test for you. How many of you know what the Baltimore Catechism is?"

When everyone gave him a blank stare, Josh spoke up, "You will have to forgive my religiously illiterate friend here. He seldom got out of his own neighborhood as a kid. He is referring to a basic primer we Catholics were drilled in back in the early days."

Carlotta looked puzzled. "I was raised Catholic and never heard of the Baltimore thing."

At this, Jules laughed. "We used to beat up Catholics just for sport in my ghetto."

"Really?" Peter asked.

"No," Jules laughed aloud. "But this whole discussion makes me realize just how different my upbringing was. Not many of you probably have been to a Southern Baptist Church service. No matter, let me tell you that concepts like Monism and ineffable spirit and whatever were not found there. It was pure emotion that came from one's gut. I'm not sure I ever believed, but I felt something profound during those experiences. I had to go since I didn't want to face my mother's wrath. And the singing, there was none better."

Chris made a disapproving sound. "Don't listen to Jules. Her parents were the definition of love. I wanted to trade places with her as teens."

"All this makes me feel like I missed something," Connie offered whimsically but with a sense of disappointed. "My parents told me something about Confucius and a little Shintoism, but I never saw the inside of any place of worship. No rites, no mystery. We were devoted to science. I almost feel I missed something now."

Josh pointed at his wife. "Ah, my favorite atheist. And yet, as spiritual as anyone in this room. And there lies the modern tragedy, or maybe the traditional tragedy of religious affiliation. Associating with a formal religious tradition does squat to make you a better person. It seems to be uncorrelated with morality in my book, based only on personal experience, of course."

"Worse than that," Chris said loudly so that all looked at him. "So much of what we find amoral in America today can be traced back to religious revivalism from the post-World War II period. For example, there was a James Fifield, a congregational minister from California, who became the darling of big business. He spoke at an early Associations of Manufacturers national conference and argued that God himself favored free market principles. It was a kind of old-style Calvinism where economic success was a sign of God's favor. Nurtured by theorists like Ludwig von Mises and Murray Rothbard, the Rational Expectations School turned to big money for support. A marriage soon was made with people like J. Howard Pew of Sun Oil and later the Koch family. Their wealth, now blessed by God's representatives on Earth, began to fund every right-wing cause around including the John Birch Society. A guy name Criswell, from Texas, did the same for Jules's Baptist movement, eventually turning the South Republican at the local level. Along comes Billy Graham to give that movement national appeal and respectability. But danger always lurked. Abraham Vereide organized something called the Worldwide Evangelization for Christ. His dominant theme, all needs were to be met through God, with no appeal to men. The lesson, government should stay out of the compassion business, that was between God and man alone. By 1953, the foundations of the new moral order were in place. The National Association of Evangelicals held a huge march of freedom on July 4th. Religion was now wedded to patriotism and big business. The spearhead of the revolution that would taste political success with Reagan in 1980 and now threatens democracy itself with the Trump fiasco had been launched."

Kay looked at her brother. "Chris, life seemed simpler back when we were kids. There was one church, the Roman one. There were good guys and bad guys. We were on the side of the angels while those atheistic Commies defined evil. And we knew where everyone stood in life. The Irish were at the top, then all those other white Catholics though we had doubts about Italians . . . sorry, Peter, no offense."

"No offense taken." Peter smiled. "I didn't much like you Paddies if the truth be known."

Rachel looked relieved. "Then came the WASPs and Jews since we seldom thought about minorities or Muslims. They were hardly on our radar screen. So simple. I hate to admit it but sometimes I feel having to figure stuff out is just too hard."

Josh gave a half laugh. "I know. Immigrants back then might be that new Greek family that opened a restaurant nearby. We focused on other white ethnics, those culturally close to us, to fix our position in the world. Were the Polish better than the Lithuanians or was it the reverse? The Italians clearly were of less value than both of those groups but surely better than the Puerto Ricans. Then there were the debates about where to stick the French and German Catholics, probably above the Polacks though some vets still hated the krauts who, no matter what, were preferred to the Limeys in my neighborhood. If an Englishman walked into my dad's bar, he would get tossed out on his ass. A black man was more welcome. I haven't thought of such things in so many years, but the web of hate was so intricate and so . . . omnipresent."

Peter Favulli snorted. "I have no idea what you are babbling about since there was never any doubt in my neighborhood. The Italians were at the top of the heap."

"That might be the point of it all." Josh looked about the room. "And by that I don't mean that the Wops were tops."

"Oh no." Rachel threw her head back as if in despair. "I fear my brother the professor is about to start one of his lectures."

"Hah. If this were a class, you wouldn't have gotten past the entrance test."

"Don't worry, Rachel, you can cheat off my answers. I steal the questions beforehand." Karen smirked.

"Are you two children finished?" Josh tried to look serious, but his smile betrayed him. This was a banter he always enjoyed. "As you can see, I have a difficult life."

"Well," Karen interrupted the good-natured ribbing, "I haven't heard this lecture before. What were you going to say, Josh?"

"No lecture, just a simple point. As different as we all seem, in terms of color and culture and religions and so forth, we all came from the same place." Then Josh paused.

"Shit," Cate said, "he's waiting for a cue. And by that you mean . . .?"

"Think about it. We all came of age amidst tribal conflicts. Sunni and Shiite, or Pashtuns and Uzbecks, black and white and Latino, the ethnic neighborhoods of my youth . . ."

Usha chimed in. "And don't forget the caste system of India . . . it was drilled into us as kids. Simply put, it went Brahmins, Kshatriya, Vaishya, Sudra, and the untouchables, who were still above the Muslims and English. To translate, it went priests, warriors, landowners and merchants, commoners, and workers, and those who did the crap jobs."

"And we had the different color barriers, languages, and religious groups," Amar noted. "It was as bad as where Josh grew up, tribalism gone amok."

"Hah," Connie decided she had something to add. "In my childhood, we Chinese had our own complex tribal system and the various hatreds with the Koreans, Japanese, Mongols, South Asians, and whomever were legendary."

Chris seemed excited. "But here we are, in this room. Each of us had been exposed to the rawest forms of prejudice and hate in our early years. Each of us had to somehow fight past what our own cultures told us to believe. Each of us did it . . . somehow! We did it in ways we don't even understand or appreciate, each of us wants to bring this gift we enjoy to others."

"Wait, gift? What gift again?" Rachel looked perplexed.

"We enjoy the gift of connectivity. I think each of us sees the big picture. We feel we are part of the human fabric, not one color or pattern in a kaleidoscope of different weaves poorly stitched together. For me, that is everything. That is what we are all about, why I fought so hard to free myself from my father. The Morae stitched for each of us a most complex fabric, the patterns interwoven in the most complex ways."

"I see," Azita said quietly. "Most religions and cultures taught us about ordered worlds where most things were already decided. If you were born of a certain caste, or in a specific tribe or family, of surely of one sex or the other, your life was determined. There was, at best, limited opportunity. I think . . . I think it is becoming clearer now. My life, and Deena's life, is all about opportunity."

"Absolutely," Shahed joined in. "I used to walk around with an inflated ego because of what I accomplished. Excelling at Cambridge and joining the faculty at Oxford. But I never faced the challenges that 99 percent of Muslim girls do. I was born of the elite."

"As was I," Rachel's partner, Meena, blurted out as if discovering a latent truth. "I see what this is all about, what you are trying to do, more clearly now. We need to bring opportunity to all."

Kay spoke, "You know, tactics, strategies, and people change but vision is everything. In the end, you need to know what you are about. Think about what we have talked about tonight. Keep the discussion going. You know, my father and I are enemies now, seriously so. But we probably agree on a lot. There are real differences across individuals and groups. That is not to be summarily denied. He would select one group and expect that favored tribe to advance evolution and all our prospects as a species. I chose a slightly different vision, to break through all our artificial differences and lift all up. In my simple mind and heart, this room is a microcosm of it all."

* * *

Later, people had divided into small groups. Chris noticed that they were no longer only talking to those with whom they were most familiar. The new visitors from across the pond were intermingled with the others. He looked with satisfaction at the intensity of various discussions as individuals shared stories of both their pasts and what they envisioned as future challenges.

Josh sidled up to Chris. "Not bad. I see why you are so effective."

"What?"

"Sure, you can make people laugh and you can make people think. That is fairly rare." Josh put a hand on Chris's shoulder.

"No better than you, I suspect." Chris grinned.

"The important thing is that I think a team has been formed tonight. I wasn't sure until now, but I think so. I especially worried about my sister. You do know that she is the real talent in my family?"

"Of that, Josh, I never had a doubt."

"Another skill I see, you can insult people and they still love you." Josh laughed heartily.

"This has been good, but I worry about a lot. I've tried to keep my loved ones from spending too much time in harm's way.

"Harm's way?" Josh was not entirely sure he understood.

"Azita and Deena are from Afghanistan. I still recall the day I first met Azita, just an urchin of eleven or so. I flew into the Panjshir Valley to pull my sister out of there, as if she would have obeyed me, and to fire Amar for being complicit with Kay being in this dangerous place to begin with. Whom do I meet when I got off the plane was this kid who was more mature than I and spoke better English? She won my heart in a half hour."

"What, so you kidnapped her and took her home?"

"Not exactly. Her father was a doctor who trained Azita from a young age and lied to escape the Taliban to help the Northern Alliance. He and his wife were soon murdered by the crazies. By the way, instead of firing Amar, I ended up marrying her. Don't ask how she managed that. So, we spirited Azita out of the country, her elder sister, Deena, followed later. Ever since, they've insisted on returning. On one occasion, a nut tried to kill them, Deena almost died."

Josh sighed. "You do know that Trump is pulling out of Afghanistan since he can't figure out how to make a buck there."

"I do." Chris grunted. "This is always such a hard thing for liberals like us. We hate war but see the necessity on occasion. And this has been such a long one."

Josh whistled. "No shit. We've been at it since 2001, but the fighting goes back decades. The last I heard there have been 2,300 American military deaths and over 20,000 wounded. We have spent almost one trillion dollars there with only 12 to 15 percent of this total going for economic and infrastructure development. Hell, that was more than was spent on the Marshal plan even adjusting for inflation. It takes . . . something to keep at it."

Chris looked at the ceiling. "I have doubts every single day. Is all we do doomed to failure? How silly that we can even entertain the possibility of bringing Western institutions to a land that has only known tribalism, monarchy, communisms, and

Sharia law. Did the West ever know what it was trying to do . . . defeat the Taliban, defeat ISIS or Al Qaeda, create a democracy, shift the power balance in the area, and what else? There were probably as many agendas as there were political and military actors with their fingers in the pot."

"Let me just say one thing," Josh murmured. "I could be your father and I have seen more defeat and futility than you. Hell, I escaped from the US to avoid what I thought was the height of absurdity, the Vietnam War. Yet, I looked at the faces in this room tonight and saw what you saw."

"Which was?" Chris looked dubious.

"Hope. You can sense it. There is a restlessness among the young. Think about climate change and Greta Thunberg. Think about the education movement among traditionally ignored parts of the population and inspirations like Malala Yousafzai and Azita and Deena. You are on to something, my friend. My sister and her family can see it, I'm now sure of that. And I can see it."

"Sure you're not suffering a sixties acid flashback." Chris smiled.

"Hah, you never know but I was more of a political type, not a counterculture guy." Then Josh cocked his head as he often did when his mind had wandered in a different direction.

"Oh, oh," Chis sighed, "where is your mind wandering now. I've been around you long enough to learn your tells."

"Hmmm, guess I better not play poker with you. But yeah, when we were talking I kept going back to this stubborn thought.

We all were talking if we had free will, as if we had something to say about who we are and what we do in life."

"You talk as if that is a most absurd notion." Chris tried to look serious. "Yup. A drug addled brain working overtime, for sure."

"Bite me." Josh chuckled loud enough so that those near the two men glanced in their direction. "Now, hear me out. There are some theoretical physicists who posit an infinite number of special universes. Our reality is only one of all possibilities. Then, is it not reasonable to presume that there are an infinite number of temporal realities and we are fixed in just one point in a continuum of probable alternatives."

"And so?" Chris thought he knew where Josh was going but chose not to presume.

"Think about it. If this is so, future points in time already exist. I mean, God would already know what will happen since such a being must know all. That would only be possible if all future temporal moments already existed. This perspective is called eternalism by the eggheads, determinism, or pre-determinism by the religious oriented. Huh, what do you think?"

Chris let out a guffaw. "You must have been a great teacher. I knew there was a reason I had to meet you when I read your books. Having said that, you also are crazier than I am."

Josh's crooked smile spread over his face. "Now that is the highest compliment I can receive."

CHAPTER 14

KABUL (2020) DAY 1

Azita and Deena always experienced a frisson of excitement when they were back in Kabul, especially when they had the opportunity to spend time with Bahiri and Ferhana Gupta, who now ran the expanded medical facility and education center situated in the very site where they had grown up and where their father had practiced medicine. When the sisters had first stumbled upon the Gupta's medical facility several years earlier while seeking out their childhood home, they had been thrilled to see the site had remained dedicated to the healing arts. They were further astounded to realize that Ferhana had been a former neighbor of theirs who managed to escape to India before the Taliban took over. Inspired by Pamir Masoud, she studied medicine in Mumbai where she met and married Bahiri.

Upon first discovering their father's old clinic and their home, it had looked pretty much the same as they recalled it. Inspired by new ideas from Azita and Deena, and additional resources from Chris's international organization, it had expanded in just a few years into a sprawling set of buildings with medical facilities for indigent families, a public health initiative, outreach programs for girls with professional aspirations, and a community development program. Every day was a beehive of activity, but Deena was always drawn to the rooms filled with computers that girls, and some young boys, could use to expand their awareness of the wider world and broader avocational possibilities. The tutors were available to all, though mostly for the young girls, to whet their appetite for learning while encouraging their parents to accept and nurture the growing ambitions in their female offspring. Over time, the expanding staff had learned to leverage the exuberance of the youth flocking to this new technology to reach their more skeptical parents.

Josh Connelly and Peter Favulli had stayed behind with Chris to focus on a fast-emerging set of political challenges. There was post-Brexit regret in Great Britain. In America, the four-year cycle of ideological and political self-inflicted torture was now approaching. Josh and Chris were joined by Atle Bergstrom, April Song, Josef Spiglanin, and Pamela Stuart. This is what Chris considered his brain trust, younger whiz kids astute in quantitative analysis while he and Josh would now sift the data for meaning. They would be in continuous touch with Ricky and Kat back in the States to sound their interpretations out with more impressionistic input.

This work would provide Chris not only with material for more scholarly work that he would co-author with Joshua Connelly but, more importantly, with ideas and material to share with allies in the coming political conflict that was better known as the 2020 Presidential election. Connecting with others had always been Chris Crawford's strength. His easy manner and natural intelligence enabled him to reach others who might be cautious at first. It was his authentic willingness to listen that cemented new working relationships, and to help without demanding the limelight or credit. Chris was particularly excited to work with new initiatives developing among traditional Republican groups that had not gone over to the dark side of the crazies such as QAnon and the hate groups such as the Aryan Nation. The Lincoln Project and Vets Against Trump particularly intrigued him.

The mood of this team was not upbeat, however. After three years of horrendous gaffs, scandals, and demonstrable ineptness, Donald Trump remained a viable candidate for reelection. No matter what happened, his base of support remained stable, perhaps even more devoted than four years earlier. Perhaps, as Trump once claimed, he could shoot someone on 5th Avenue and not lose any votes. After his approval rating briefly fell into the upper 30 percent range early in his administration, it crept up just above 40 percent again where it stubbornly remained. Acute tribalism was as entrenched as ever. The allegiance of white working-class folk remained solid, their fears of losing whatever yet existed of their privilege in a multi-cultural country dominated all other concerns. For them, destroying the environment, succumbing to climate change, and becoming a pariah in the world meant nothing if Trump continued to hate the same people they did. They would do without themselves if the hated others never got a dime of help.

Normally mild mannered, this reality would set Josh off onto an occasional rant. He had grown up in an Irish ghetto. His people were working-class folks who struggled economically and had lives full of angst and uncertainty. They had their prejudices and their limitations for sure. Then Josh would get wound up. But they still knew, at the end of the day, that they should not throw their allegiance and support behind men and a party that made no pretense to any aspiration other than to advance the interests of society's winners and who fully embraced the one percent whose aim was to keep workers unorganized and economically desperate so that they would be grateful for any crumb thrown in their direction. *By god,* he would rant, *today's white working-class morons could not find their self-interest with GPS, a guide dog, and Google Earth.*

On occasion, Chris also would lose his affable demeanor and boil over with frustration. *How stupid can Americans be,* he would rage to no one in particular. Then he would calm down and consider that Biden would bring few of the negatives that Hillary Clinton had, if unfairly, in his mind. There was so much material that the Democrats could hurl at Trump, from his compulsive lying to the fact that the only way Trump could hold a 2016 campaign reunion was to have it in a federal prison. But all that seemed not to matter. If Trump's artificially pumped-up economic prosperity continued with help from horrendous levels of deficit spending, the average American seemed not to care. The rest of the world might look on in horror as the American deficit exploded but Joe six pack still focused on who would get to the Super Bowl.

One day, Chris was venting with Kay about his political concerns. She had grown increasingly fond of her brother after many years of estrangement, even admitting that she loved him when no one could hear. She had stumbled upon something of possible solace she might share with him. "Listen, Chris, this might help. Something is happening in China right now. Rumors are flying through the global medical community. A strange kind of pneumonia has erupted that defies easy diagnosis. It's mostly in Wuhan Province but there are strong indications that it has broken out." When Josh rolled his eyes, she hastened on. "This could be important. The Chinese authorities put a lid on it but that is now impossible. This ain't Mao's China after all. They are responsible people at the end of the day. And here's the kicker, they now think it is highly contagious via airborne transmission and a few cases have cropped up outside China."

Chris continued to stare. "Okay, so what?"

"You still don't get it, do you nimrod? We are talking a possible global pandemic here . . . something we haven't seen since the Spanish Flu of a century ago. It would be like God looking down and saying to you, Chris Crawford, I hear your prayers, my son. I'm sending you the worst plague possible to end Trump's chances." Finally, Chris smiled. Then, Kay added without a hint of a smile. "It's too early to tell, but this might be big, really big."

Over the weeks following the bonding dinner at Chris and Amar's Oxford home, the several individuals that had followed Josh from Canada to England were absorbed rather seamlessly into the international operations Chris had started when he first graduated from Oxford. First Chris, and later Karen, guided the original concept of coordinated and multidimensional service initiatives through several iterations. They tried things and then adapted and evolved. Even today, it still retained a strong medical component but now stressed more of an intergenerational approach. The work focused on identifying and recruiting future female leaders in cultures that had long denied any substantive role for women. Many times, Karen and Chris and the program leadership noted that nothing was more important than convincing this part of the world that half of their population could be more than child bearers and unpaid domestic help. Too much talent resided with the female half of the Muslim world.

As 2019 segued into 2020, Azita and Deena led a field trip through several sites in the Middle East and the Horn of Africa. These were periodic ventures to look at operations, assess and learn, and then update practices and strategies. In the past, they had been led by Karen and Carlotta and other senior management staff. They now were increasingly preoccupied with other administrative responsibilities and no longer could take the time for these more routine trips. Azita and Deena were now viewed more as program leaders than very capable staff.

The two women took a special pride in bringing the new people from across the pond into the fold. Rachel brought her medical talents to the program and found herself thrilled to feel so relevant again. It was like being a young doctor once more. Cate and Meena jumped into the community organization work that Ahmad had taken a lead role in fostering. Connie Chen, who had followed Josh reluctantly to England, found herself less interested in her research as an emeritus chemistry professor and threw herself into the task of working to interest young Muslim girls in science. Usha Nayer decided, with some reservations, to accompany the team though not sure of her role. Soon, though, she found a niche talking up possible careers in the law with Muslim girls and trying to get a head around the intricacies of Sharia Law to see if she could help with legal issues in helping those being persecuted for wanting to seek new opportunities. As they travelled from site to site, each new member of the team responded to the needs around them and began to see roles for themselves.

This new talent brought fresh perspectives into the program but profited from their new roles. In one way or another, they found themselves reinvigorated by this exciting new vision and the challenges it offered. They were infused with new energy and new goals. They were not just doing a job any longer, no matter how demanding or satisfying it might have been. They no longer labored among people whose routines were upset when their favorite sports team lost. Now they were encountering real need and suffering daily. They saw the extended bellies of starving children in the Horn of Africa, the listless eyes of babies about to die and the hopeless stares of mothers with nothing to possibly stave off the inevitable end. They saw communities wracked by hate based upon historical events that happened centuries ago and whose relevance has never been muted by time or reason. As if a curtain had been raised, they saw a way to make their remaining futures count for something more than lounging at the pool or another round of golf. They saw the possibility of an avocation being done out of love, not duty.

* * *

The team gathered in a luxury hotel for the night after another long day in the clinic, visiting with government officials and other medical and service providers, and seeing a few notable sites that Azita and Deena wished to share. Azita hated the fact that Karen insisted they stay at a luxury hotel when in Kabul. Whenever Azita complained, Karen simply responded that she had no choice, this was one thing Chris had insisted upon. Karen added that this was one decision of his on which she agreed. Given the notoriety that now surrounded the Masoud name, their activities on the part of girls, it had become dangerous. They could only remain if they followed the rules. Azita grumbled but agreed.

After dinner, they met in the largest room, the one Rachel had selected. She kept joking that she had to immerse herself slowly into her new world. She had only known top schools, as a scholarship prodigy, and top medical facilities, as a hotshot physician. She kept laughing that she could not go cold turkey but would get there. Rachel, Cate, and Meena all sat on the bed. Amar and Usha, who had bonded during this trip given their common cultural origins, sat together on a small couch. Carlotta and Connie found available chairs. Azita and Deena made do with places on the floor.

Rachel spoke first. "I see that everyone has found the drinks, assuming they imbibe. Thank Karen for insisting on a western hotel."

"By the way, where is Ahmad?" Amar asked. "Isn't he joining us?"

Azita chuckled. "No, he is a coward. He told me that we would be more comfortable if our gathering were all female. But I suspect he feared being the only male so I'm going with the coward hypothesis."

Rachel then looked about with concern. "Listen, I can call room service and get more chairs."

"No, no," Deena responded quickly, "we are used to this. Besides, my younger sister was always the spoiled one. She still needs some toughening up."

"Me?" Azita gasped. "You should have seen my much older sibling when we were young. She loafed and moped around the house all day doing nothing."

"Nothing? Why, I helped mother with the chores. All you did was stick your nose in your books."

"And helped Papa in the clinic." Azita warmed to their ancient battle.

"So you say, but where's the proof of that? All I know is that you disappeared when there was real work to be done." Deena was not about to surrender.

"Girls." Amar yelled with sufficient volume to quell the rising dispute. "I have listened to this squabble a thousand times. Our guests do not need to hear it."

"You're correct, Mother. That would be ungracious, especially since my stubborn sister refuses to admit she is wrong." Deena snuck in the final word as Azita scowled.

"Aaargh," was all that Amar could get out, though she laughed as she emitted this sound.

Connie laughed. "Doesn't bother me. I've had to watch my husband and his sister trade barbs for years. For two of the most intelligent people I know, it is amazing how quickly they can regress."

"Really," Amar expressed with genuine surprise, "from what I've seen they get along famously."

"Cate here knows the truth." Rachel admitted sheepishly. "She loved her uncle to bits and visited him all the time while I avoided him like the bubonic plague for decades."

"There has to be a back story here."

"Not an original one, or maybe it is." Rachel paused a moment and then realized there was no going back. "Here's the thing. I did worship him as a young girl. He was older, an athlete, charming and sweet to me. All the neighborhood girls swooned over him. And he protected me from Dad when he had too much to drink, he could get nasty."

"He sounds perfect. Maybe your standards are too high." Amar smiled.

"Well, then things changed." Rachel took a big sip of her drink. "Josh was the local football hero. Scouts from Notre Dame and other schools were looking at him. Then, one day, he crippled a kid during a game. Just one of those things, it's a rough sport, but he couldn't forgive himself. So, he quit the game, just like that. Dad was furious. Then, to make matters worse, he went to a secular college, not a Catholic one. Dad and Mom were outraged. Then he got involved in left wing politics and protests against the war. Dad went beyond outrage. The fights in the house . . ."

Amar intruded softly. "I didn't mean to . . ."

"No, no, I don't mind. It's all in his memoir. He is incredibly open about everything. Well, to keep this short and sweet, one day he disappeared. He was simply gone. None of us heard for months. He was in Canada and that was that. I was still a kid. I was hurt beyond hurt, felt abandoned to deal with what remained of our broken home. I thought him beyond selfish. Of course, I didn't know what he was going through at the time, what demons were chasing him . . ." Rachel paused.

"I did." Usha added. "I knew him long before Connie. Bottom line, he felt he couldn't return to the States. Some of the things he did as a college revolutionary were more than naughty, no question. He was another casualty of that stupid war—some died, some were wounded, and some got lifetime scars. But you had to live through it, I guess. The thing is, Rachel, he never stopped loving you. He talked to me about you all the time. But he was a guy. They are hopeless when it comes to emotions."

"No shit." Carlotta emoted. "And if I ever get a guy, I'll make sure he is not an emotional eunuch."

Amar laughed aloud. "Right there, my sweet Carlotta. That is why you have not yet nailed a guy. You are too picky. Do you think that Chris was marriage material when I met him?"

"But you married him right away. You must have loved him very much," Azita said. "I mean, that's the way it looked to me."

"Look at this. I am being lectured on matters of love by my daughter who comes from a society where marriages are yet arranged."

"As is yours," Azita responded a bit defensively.

"Not as much anymore. However, in my case, I wanted to bring you and Deena away with us. You were orphaned and had so much promise. Chris and I could see that."

"But wait," Azita looked at Amar directly, "you didn't just marry him to rescue us? No, I can't believe that." When Amar did not respond right away, Azita added defiantly, "I don't believe you did, not for a moment."

"Wow, you are like a dog with a bone."

"Tell me you loved him." Azita now stared at her adoptive mother.

After another silence, Amar sighed. "Okay, okay, more than you can ever imagine. But for heaven's sake, don't go telling him that."

"Good." Carlotta threw her head back. "Now that we have determined that Amar lacks total judgment in men, we can move on and I can continue looking for Mr. Perfect."

At this Deena laughed. "I am so happy Ahmad decided not to join us. He would have rushed screaming from the room by now."

Everyone laughed heartedly.

Carlotta turned serious. "Perhaps now that we have finished up with gossip hour, we can get some work done. As you know, we will split up the day after tomorrow with several of you flying by helicopter up to the Panjshir Valley for the day. Once there, Deena and I will show you a more rural Afghan site. Then back home to England for all of us. So, tomorrow is our final full day as a whole group."

"Yes." Deena picked up the theme. "This trip north will be a different view of Afghanistan for some of you. It will be rural, a real trip back in time. You will get a better feel of the country than you get in Kabul. Besides, my father, our father," she nodded to her sister, "grew up near the site being managed by Dr. Singletary and his wife, Agnes. This will give me a chance to show off my favorite girls school."

Carlotta again took the lead. "So, Amar and I were chatting earlier. This being the last stop before we head back to England, what are your impressions so far? Any overall feelings, questions? We will do a more formal briefing with Chris, Karen, Kay, and Shahed when we get back, but this is a chance for a quick informal sharing of impressions. Anyone want to start? This is pretty informal . . . anything you want to share."

There was the usual looking at one another before Connie Chen cleared her throat. "Perhaps I can begin. I was the reluctant member of this group. I was not thrilled back in Vancouver when my husband brought this Professor Crawford to dinner one evening. That evening was fine, it was where that pleasant evening led, to talk about joining some international effort to save the world. All I knew was my lab and the University of British Columbia. I didn't even get to the downtown area all that much. But, as Amar must also know all too well, never marry an Irishman, they are way too charming."

"And stubborn," Amar added.

"Hell, yes." Connie agreed. "Somehow I agreed to his joining Chris at Oxford, but I would stay uninvolved to continue my post retirement research at the University. Then I get talked into visiting Oxford myself. Big mistake. I met all of you and then we had that dinner at Amar's place. Next I knew, I'm on a plane to the Mideast."

"Still a big mistake."

Connie smiled. "Well, I was going to ask Usha what she knew about divorce law but . . . this whole thing has been pretty amazing."

"How so?" Rachel asked her sister-in-law.

"I could have spent my life engrossed in enzymes, proteins, and amino acids. As fascinating as such things are, I've seen a new world these past weeks, even seen new research possibilities. But here's the big thing. I am used to smart students who take their studies as a matter of course. They expect to be where they are. Then, in some of the worst places imaginable, I've seen girls so eager to be learning, so thirsty to understand the broader world. I guess one day captures it all. I can't even recall which site it was, there have been many, but I recall watching the faces on those young girls . . . so eager just for the chance to learn." She hesitated, seeming to fight some internal emotion.

"Guess you don't need my divorce advice," Usha said lightly.

Connie cracked a tiny smile. "Not today. I'm not an emotional woman but that night I wept in my hotel room. I am not even sure why, maybe because I realize how blessed my life has been when so many others . . . well, you know. Since then, I've been thinking about ways to make chemistry and biology more exciting for these girls. Education here is still regimented. I want them to see the miracles embedded in the world of life around them. I want to nurture the excitement of learning and discovering no matter where they land."

"Yes," Usha added, "I've noticed some fine minds on this trip. We think of this place as backward. Wait, I didn't mean to put it that way . . ." she glanced at Azita and Deena.

"No matter, Usha." Azita smiled. "Deena and I will insult India later."

"And you are not too old for a spanking, young lady." Amar mockingly raised a fist.

"I was trying to say that I much better appreciate some of the things we chatted about at Amar's place. "Attributes like intelligence, inquisitiveness, and initiative are not the exclusive property of any one group of people, any so-called tribe. They are found everywhere. I saw some talent I thought might make good lawyers."

Rachel guffawed. "Usha! I hope you realize that I have no problem telling people that I married a woman. That's now fine even in polite society. But telling them I married a lawyer . . . that's still difficult."

"Yes, dear, we'll discuss this later . . . in bed."

Rachel continued, wanting to change the topic. "I knew all about that so-called Irish charm and thought myself immunized to my brother's version of it. But damn it, I was this little sister following him around like a puppy dog. Then, some fifty-plus years later, I'm that same girl. I mean . . . you know Irishmen are full of it, but you still follow them. They can be so convincing."

"Hmmm. Perhaps I should take a trip to Ireland to find me one of them," Carlotta mused aloud.

"Talk to me before you book your flight." Rachel smirked. "Like the rest of you, I'm so glad I came. I have watched Azita and Deena very closely as they do their work. When they are not squabbling with each other, they are inspiring. Each is so gifted. There is something special about this work. I focused on pediatric cancer at Children's Hospital at the University of Wisconsin and did research at the Carbone Center there. That work was rewarding, for sure. But when Josh beckoned me to look at what you are doing, he hit me at a vulnerable moment. I was thinking that maybe my best days were behind me, silly I know, but there it is. More than that, I knew there were tons of very smart doctors and researchers waiting to take my place. You have no idea how incestuous the world of medical research can be."

Amar gave her a puzzled look. "And that means?"

Rachel considered for a moment. "Often, you pursue a line of research and realize that there are many others out there poking around in the same area. Driven by paranoia that is rampant in academia, you work around the clock to get something published before the other guys. The discovery was probably inevitable, but you are killing yourself for the credit, a momentary pleasure before you are off on the next chase. Moments like Fleming's accidental discovery of penicillin don't happen in modern times. Sometimes I think Jonas Salk was the last lone wolf. I guess . . . I guess I wanted to go back to what pushed me toward medicine in the first place."

"Which was?" Cate chimed in.

"To help people. To feel needed and useful and rediscover that sense of purpose."

"I get that." Cate leaned forward as she gazed at Meena seated next to her. "My partner here and I have talked a lot about this. I drifted into the State Department for questionable reasons. Really, what was a linguistic major to do? I didn't have the chops for medicine which made me feel so guilty, having this world class mom."

"Cate, my dear, remember what Amar said? I also can still spank you."

"I know the script, Mom. You are proud of me. But when you are a kid, you dismiss such words as obligatory Mom speak. I envisioned the Foreign Service would give me adventure and sound impressive to others. No, I'm not good enough at science to be my Mom, but I'm great at languages and using that skill to save the world. The previews, however, turned out more exciting than the main feature."

"But you met me. That would never have happened were you not assigned to Jordan," Meena said.

Cate leaned over to kiss her partner on the cheek. "So true, sweetheart. On the other hand, I was not saving the world. No way. I did manage to wiggle my way into that part of the embassy that got me working with in-country development projects, but only on the paperwork end. Occasionally, I could kibitz on other's work and ideas, but I wanted to do some original thinking on my own. Besides, perhaps then . . ."

Meena interrupted. "I'll take over now. Dear Cate and I have been together too long, so I know what is coming out of her mouth next. Surely, we would all be embarrassed to see her mother spank her in public."

"Thank you, Meena." Rachel smiled. "I knew from the moment you stepped off that plan with my daughter in Vancouver that you were going to be a keeper."

Meena smiled at Rachel and began. "I've thought hard about things on this trip, hardly realizing how transformative it would be for some of us. For me, it was like this. I was born to privilege, much like Ali. In fact, she and I are connected to the royal family. Since it is a large family tree, we cannot recall meeting earlier though we must have at some function or another. No matter, I was educated, given a job in government, and then spent my time keeping busy and hiding my sexuality. That driftless existence ended when I met Cate which happened when I ran a project through the American Embassy. That meeting changed my life . . . freed me up in terms of my sexuality but professionally I was still adrift. I wanted more."

"Are you finding it now?" Carlotta asked.

"Hah, can't you tell by my smile. What is amazing is how little I knew about my culture and about the world around me. Let me be clear on that. I knew a lot about England and Europe and the West. But I knew almost nothing about life in my country outside of Amman, the capital. While I could tell you all about the 6,000 years of recorded history of my home city, about the Ammonites and all the other ancient tribes, I knew nothing about how rural people in my country lived or what they thought. About such things, I had not a clue."

Cate smiled. "That was a good thing. I was counting on you being clueless. How else could I have landed a beauty like you."

As the two smiled fondly at one another, Usha laughed. "I know that look. I think we may have to hose down the two of them."

"Enough," Carlotta mumbled. "All this sexual tension between couples is not doing me any good. On the other hand, this feedback is great. I would suggest, in order not to inflate the egos of certain men we know any further, that we not shower Chris and Josh with any effusive thanks for the role they played in all this."

"Amen," said Amar. "I already have this full-time job of keeping Chris's inflated sense of self-worth in check." Amar then looked at her adoptive daughter. "Zita," she called her by her family nickname, "you have been noticeably quiet tonight. What's up?"

"Me? Nothing." But she squirmed uncomfortably.

"Ladies, my daughter must go down as the world's worst liar. We're among friends unless it is something you and I need to talk through."

Azita took an exaggerated sigh. "It's . . . well, how can I put it. Let's see . . . wow. I'm having difficulty here."

"Oh my God," Deena blurted out. "You're pregnant. That's it, isn't it?"

"Damn you, sister!" Azita was smiling broadly.

Amar sprung up and hugged her daughter, followed by the others. When the hubbub died down, Amar, Deena, and Azita found themselves at the hotel window looking out over the lights of the city. "When did you find out?"

"Just today. But I knew in some way. I felt differently."

"And missing a period is a clue," Deena laughed.

"Hah, hah, sister. But you are right. They had pregnancy test kits at the clinic, so I confirmed my suspicions. I think I was in my own world tonight."

"Of course, dear. Wait, have you told Ahmad?"

"Oh yes, but I told him not to blab until I had a chance to share it with you. He's ecstatic. That's the reason he is not here, he wanted to get in touch with his family. But I think that was just an excuse not to be stuck with a bunch of women. He's rather a coward in that sense."

Amar looked out the window over the city. "It looks so peaceful out there, doesn't it? No sirens, no guns, nothing. And all these positive feelings in the room tonight. I just have a good feeling about everything. Am I just a hopeless romantic?"

Azita hugged Amar. "You married Chris; you must be hopeless. But you know what he would say. Be wary of happiness, bad things lurk right behind."

"Pshaw, that's his Irish pessimism talking. Things are going to be good."

* * *

In the darkness, a young man worked his way through mostly silent side streets. He avoided the main thoroughfares even though he was not sure why. No one would pay him any attention. He was just another figure among many. But he knew what was in his heart and that infused him with caution and excitement. On the morrow, he would exact his revenge. He would slay the infidel girls who had escaped the Taliban so many years ago and then consummate his older brother's attempt to exact the vengeance of Allah. He would not fail, nor would he succumb as his brother did to an ill-considered suicide mission. No, he hoped for a long career of battle against the enemies of Islam. It was written such. He knew it. And if he died, that would be all right. Martyrdom was a blessing for those who realized that life was a brief illusion. One's rightness with God is all that counted.

He had been here many times before, waiting for them to return as he knew they would. The Kabul media made a fuss about their presence and the so-called "good works" that brought them fleeting glory. It was like moths flitting toward the flame. He rather enjoyed his newly found notoriety among God's warriors, some of it attached to the deaths of his father some two decades ago and his brother just a few years ago. They had both perished pursuing these elusive infidels. That would end tomorrow. He knew their routine from the past several days when they would arrive and which buildings they did their work. He was ready.

Suddenly, he was there. It was mostly dark, but lights flickered in a couple of buildings. There was always someone around. No matter, he just wanted one more look before judgment day. He looked up at the stars above, surely Allah looked upon him with favor. He must. There could be no other fate!

PART III

THE FIRST BLOW

CHAPTER 15

KABUL DAY 2

Bahiri and Ferhana Gupta welcomed a contingent of visitors on another bright, sunny morning. Fortunately, being winter, the weather was tolerable, even chilly in the mornings. Rachel wondered what it would be like to work there in the summer months. She was used to Wisconsin weather, cold and snow for several months, then a pleasant transitional season to be followed by humidity and mosquitos. She smiled at herself. She had loved Madison, the liberal atmosphere, the physical beauty, an educated population, and an abundance of cultural possibilities. All those blessings were wrapped in a city of manageable size. *But yeah,* she said to herself as she listened to the Gupta's explain the medical challenges they faced, *the winters did suck.*

She recalled the first time she visited Arizona. It was between semesters and the weather was ideal, high's in the low seventies and chilly nights. *Lovely,* she thought. Then she returned for a conference in June. The heat stunned her. She considered it possible to fry an egg on her own forehead. The small print, she concluded, was everything. Always ask about conditions during the time of year no one talked about. Extending that thought, she bet that no one bragged about Kabul in July. The hard surfaces must crackle under a relentless sun while your skin hardened to a brittle shell and every organ in your body screamed for moisture. And all those things that crawled such as scorpions and lizards and snakes. What kind of snakes did they have here? Yes, she would have to read the small print before committing to this as a post-retirement life.

Ahmad had been beaming this morning. Rachel found his exuberance to be enchanting. It was obvious he could not wait to be a father. She recalled her own pregnancy with Cate. She was nearly as excited for him and envious since her own marriage had been a hollow sham. She had married the scion of a wealthy family who wanted a trophy wife . . . someone pretty and successful that he might parade around in society and at functions as an adornment to his overall success. But when she behaved as if she intended to have a real career for herself, that proved a bridge too far for him. The final straw came when he realized she could not be controlled. He wandered off into a series of mistresses though Rachel later concluded that would have happened in any case. Even before the birth of Cate, she envisioned life as a single mother. That destiny seemed an inevitability. Still, she could never abort the living thing inside her. Was she yet that much of a Catholic? She birthed a baby girl absent any joy. And true to form, the marriage collapsed in due course when she found her husband in bed with one of her close colleagues.

With time, though, her maternal instincts kicked in. Motherhood was better than she had imagined. In truth, she never thought herself any good at it. Her career was demanding, and she lived with constant guilt that she was shortchanging her daughter. But she found herself marveling at this homunculus she had produced in her own body as it pretended to be a human being and evolved right in front of her. At some point, during a grade school recital, she cried unashamedly and told herself that this was the greatest thing she had accomplished in life. She now felt a similar set of reservations. Could she handle the challenges of working under these conditions? The inducement of contributing while working with her daughter was very compelling.

Her conviction wavered from day to day but, in the end, she really wanted to give this a shot. Whatever else came into play, she desperately wanted to remain a part of her daughter's life. And then, there was Josh. She hated to admit it, but she felt some tug to prove herself to her older sibling. What in god's name remained to be proved? She had been showered with professional laurels and kudos all her life. Still, she wanted to prove herself to him on his turf. Was this his turf? Not really, she said to herself, but it was close enough.

Turf was never a physical location, she said to herself. Then it struck her, why Josh continued to frustrate her so. Even after their reconnection, she had remained angry at him on some deeper level. What was that all about? They had reconciled, she had become part of his life again. She loved his wife, Connie, and Cate continued to adore him. What was eating at her? The bottom line was that he had gone about doing wonderful things with his life even as she spent hours virtually torturing him in her mind from afar. Why hadn't he dissolved into a puddle of guilt and regret after he fled the States with no word? Damn him. *Maybe he had*, she thought, *but she had not seen it.*

No, he had gone on to do wonderful things in his teaching, policy consultation, and writing. What greater tribute to his impact than this internationally known philanthropist and service innovator seeking him out to become part of his senior team. Then she caught herself. This was silly. He did not sit around reliving the past five decades. He embraced her and continued to live his life unfettered by second thoughts. Men were like that, emotional eunuchs. She could do the same. She could join his life and contribute to it. And this was where he was, where his life now was, so it would have to do. Then she kicked herself mentally one more time. She was worrying about scorpions and snakes while he was comfortable back in Oxford. When it came to her brother, she had always tied herself in knots. Here she was, of retirement age, and she yet felt as if she were seeking his approval. Some scripts simply refused to die.

While Rachel had found a solid relationship with another woman, Usha, there was always a nagging doubt as to how things might have transpired had she married well the first time around. Could she have experienced the look in Azita's eyes when Ahmad was around? Her expression vacillating between affection and respect and pure joy. For each other, they must be what people called soulmates. She often wondered what they meant by such an appellation. Was this thing merely lust by another name, something to make their carnal desires more acceptable in polite society? No, she had concluded after much thought, it was something real and irreplaceable. She had a very satisfying relationship with her partner, no doubt, but would she call Usha a soulmate?

Whenever she thought hard on this topic, she would conclude that the problem was her ethnicity. Her biological father was Irish while her mother had been Russian or Lithuanian or of some uncertain providence from that part of the globe. Neither bequeathed much emotional capacity, if any, upon her. Other than her devotion to Josh when she was a little girl, and before he broke her heart, she had never experienced close ties except for Cate. She seldom felt sharp emotions, cared much except for doing a superb job as a healer, had few close friends. But was that normal? How could she know without opening herself to the world?

Maybe she would be given a do-over in retirement. After all, her brother seemed happy in his marriage. Her brother! For most of his life he never displayed an ordinary emotion, at best relying on professional consorts and arrangements for what passed as a human attachment. He did not come out of his shell until she trooped up to Vancouver as he was about to retire from the University. Over several intense days, she managed to extract a reasonable version of a human from a man who skated by with his charm and cleverness. Stunningly, there was a real person there, one that married Connie. Perhaps she could find her real self. That would be nice, she mused, before turning to the tasks at hand, as she always did.

* * *

The young man had hardly slept the night before, nor the night before that. He had been going on adrenalin for days now. But that was all right. In a few hours it would hardly matter if he lived or not. His work would be complete. Of course, he would prefer to survive, escape detection. But if that were not Allah's will, so be it. He was content in doing God's work. A man could do no more than that.

He had collected the package the night before. His contacts had gone over the arrangements again, where he would go, the route he would take, and the scrutiny he would give the site before proceeding. Again, he went through the protocols for arming the explosive device and making his escape. Once again, he asked if it would be better if he were to remain with the device to ensure that nothing went amiss. It would ensure that he would meet Allah in paradise that very day. He was not afraid. He was ready, his heart was confident in that. It had been ready since the day his older brother died in a similar mission.

And yet, he was glad at some level when they said no. He should not sacrifice himself, they told him. That might be necessary if he were attacking a well-guarded target of opportunity, where security would be tight. This was not the case here even with the visitors of some note being in the vicinity. Oh, there may be a few guards, private security, and perhaps some local police, but they would not be expecting any problems. Kabul had been quiet for some time. People were relaxing, becoming confident that the worst was behind them. There were even hints about impending peace talks between the Taliban and the government. All he had to do was casually walk up to the entrance, trigger the device, and calmly walk away. The trick, as they repeated endlessly, was in being casual, as if nothing were out of the ordinary. He was just a young man going about his innocuous morning chores.

On this day, all those who had defied Allah's will would be reminded that nothing was in the past. God's warriors would never abandon their quest for divine justice. This young warrior must survive to carry on the work. Yes, that was ordained. Perhaps all the pain he had suffered was merely part of God's plan, to prepare him for a life of honor and glory. He surely had been forged in this crucible of anguish, made indomitable of purpose though the sacrifices of those he loved so dearly.

At times, he questioned whether violence was the path he should take in life. He had come across Mullahs who argued with considerable passion that Islam was a religion of peace, that the Prophet would never sanction the slaughter of innocents in his name. They could be persuasive, and such sentiments tugged at his heart. When such doubts were not easily dismissed, other thoughts crowded in. The Americans and other Westerners came into their land, dropped their bombs, and sent their soldiers to kill his people. How many did Usama Bin Laden kill? Perhaps three thousand Americans. How many had the Americans slaughtered in return? Too many to count. They did not mourn the consequences of their actions since we Muslims were not considered human, not worthy of their tears. He recalled his friend from those bad times, an innocent boy who was shot while playing in the street. The Americans said it was an unfortunate accident, an outcome of the fog of war. But the adults who lived near there had another story. These American kids playing at being warriors were bored and fearful, taking their rage out in target practice on defenseless children. In the end, who would punish them?

He could not quite recall what his father looked like, merely a hazy recollection of an awesome warrior always carrying a fearsome weapon even in his own village. He had heard the stories of his bravery often. As a young man, even younger than he was now, he fought the godless Russians. Rumor had it that he had brought down two, perhaps three, helicopters with surface to air missiles. His reputation was further burnished by his personal bravery in killing many soldiers as the Russian military headed north as their masters in Moscow finally accepted that Afghanistan had become their personal Vietnam.

Then came the day that they had sought revenge against the Masoud family who had defiled the honor of Allah by working with the *Shura Nazar* against God's own people . . . the Taliban. It was a holy Fatwa that sent them that night when the family was more vulnerable as they visited the original family village away from the British military camp. These helpers of the foreign infidels had to be punished according to Sharia Law. There was no debate on the matter. It had been sanctioned by the Mullahs. The parents had proved easy prey as dawn broke that morning, but the girls somehow had escaped into the nearby hills. When his father and the other men had tracked them down, he alone cornered them as security guards sent to rescue the girls fired upon his fellow warriors for God. Then, when he was about to realize Allah's justice, one of the girls pulled out a gun and shot him through the chest. That was the story he had been told many times. But none of those who witnessed it were sure which girl it had been. So, they both had to die.

He remembered his brother more completely. Older by quite a few years, his male sibling had been a demigod to him. He trained with those who would take back control of Allah's chosen land one day. Now it was ISIS. The names, he concluded, meant little. It was the shared purpose that counted. That is the essential lesson imparted to him by the one male figure he respected. A man needed something in which to believe. Without that, he was adrift and meaningless. All you needed was a cause and a family and some tribe with whom to bond. The boy found all that in these men who swore to remake the land in God's image. He could remember crying tears as he swore his allegiance even as a kid.

Yet, when his brother went off one day with conviction burning in his eyes, all he told him was that prayers were needed. He was going to right things that had been wronged in the past. He would make the world whole that day and rectify errors that tilted the universe in a jarring way. Just wait for him to return, he said, and then they would celebrate. He waited all day and into the night. When the men came to him, there was sadness in their eyes. He knew even before the words were spoken. But on this day, that tilted universe would finally and irrevocably be righted. He knew it. In his heart, it was written so.

* * *

During a break from seeing patients and discussing medical challenges unique to this area, Ferhana took Rachel and Ahmad to see where the Masoud family had lived until they made their way to join the *Shura Nazar* when that embattled group was the last holdout against a religious tyranny. Ahmad had not seen it since he was a chubby boy with a crush on Azita who simply ignored this smelly, obnoxious boy. He reveled in the memories as Rachel remarked on how modest and unassuming it was. While Pamir Masoud was now a hero to many, his life when he lived among us apparently was quite ordinary.

"You must understand," Ferhana told them, "that Pamir and Madeena were saints to me. He was not only a healer but the kindest man I knew and so ahead of his time. It is difficult to imagine that he grew up dirt poor in a remote mountain area in the north. His life sparkled with promise and accomplishment until the Taliban murdered him. And Madeena had taught mathematics until women were shunted back to the kitchen and bedroom. So sad, but she lives anew through her daughters."

"They must have been a joy to her even as her life shriveled in comparison to what it had been."

"Hah!" Ferhana blurted out. "Azita and Deena were such a burden to her. Azita would do no chores and merely followed her Papa around bothering him to distraction to teach her all things medical. Deena was older and a beauty, but she was resentful of her younger sister. She thought her parents favored the younger sibling, spoiling her. She became jealous and the two fought all the time."

"Oh yes," Ahmad added. "I came to this house with my father a number of times. Poor Pamir was also at his wits end."

"Oh, Ahmad, I remember you. You also were a spoiled little boy, and so chubby, who followed Azita around with a moonstruck look on your face. But she would not give you the time of day."

"I couldn't blame her. I was lazy, fat, and had all the charm of an oafish cow," he said.

"And look at you now, lean, handsome, accomplished, and a father to be. You must be so thrilled."

Ahmad beamed. "It is a dream come true. I'm not religious but even I thanked Allah when I found out."

"By the way, where is the mother to be? I have not seen her this morning," Ferhana asked.

"She will be along. She wanted to send some messages back to Oxford this morning and I assume share the good news with friends. Perhaps she has morning sickness. Is it too early for that? Wow, I know so little." His thoughts seemed to jump from topic to topic. "You know, I must say she is happier about this than I imagined she would be."

"I don't understand," Rachel asked, "you thought she might not be thrilled?"

"She is different, special in a way. She has always had this sense of purpose in life, to do good. First, it was to heal and now it is more about passing off the fire inside her to other Muslim girls who might otherwise never experience it. It might not be a divine purpose, but she always will be devoted to something that is beyond her own happiness. I think, after she grew up, that she thought that she had been too selfish as a child. I guess, well, I think part of her thought that motherhood might be a distraction from what really counts in life, another form of selfishness. Does that make sense?"

"Hah, that makes perfect sense, you have no idea. One day, she will realize this is her greatest gift, to others and to herself." Rachel had a faraway look in her eyes.

Ferhana spoke next. "But let us hope she doesn't have girls. As I said, she and her sister were such a grief to her mother, and a blessing of course. But the two were always fighting. Madeena would complain to me and tell me to make sure I had boys and not girls, which I did. Bahiri and I have two boys, one in high school and one in university. But I miss not having a girl, I must say." Ferhana looked about her wistfully. "Oh, I have such memories of this place. Pamir would let me help him as if I were a nurse. I did not know much but he insisted on paying me. Perhaps that is where Azita first got the idea of becoming a doctor though she was a tyke at the time. Women were increasingly restricted by this time and the Taliban were making things even worse. Her father took great risks in letting me help, before I escaped to school in India. He was such a good and kind man. And such a risk-taker. His escape to the Northern Alliance during the worst of the troubled times is still talked about today."

"And the times are no longer troubled?" Rachel asked as Bahiri and Amar joined them.

Amar tried to sound gruff. "Here are the shirkers. You see how hard it is to get good help, Bahiri."

"I do, and my good wife is the worst offender," the good doctor replied with a broad smile.

Ferhana made a mocking gesture. "And how many times have I found my husband napping when there is work to be done."

"My dear, what looks like napping is a man thinking very hard, so hard indeed."

"All I can say is that men may think hard but they seldom have thoughts worth hearing." Ferhana shook her finger at her husband but could not suppress a smile. "But we were talking about Pamir and Madeena. Oh, how I wish, Bahiri, that you would have gotten a chance to meet them, they were saints for sure."

"And they produced two saints in their daughters, that is a fact," Bahiri added.

"A fact indeed," Amar said.

After a few more memories, the group walked back to the main building. As they approached the entrance, Rachel noticed a young man with a bicycle watching them intently. His eyes bore in on the group. She had grown accustomed to stares on the trip, it was a price that Westerners experienced when visiting out-of-the-way places in developing countries. When the locals are not expecting to see you, it is easy to become an object of curiosity. And yet, this was not the look of curiosity. No, it was something more sinister. The man's eyes burned rather evidencing a fire that could only be described as hate.

* * *

The young man watched as the group made their way back into the main building. *They were not all there,* he told himself. Why was that? He must have missed the others somehow, especially one of the two sisters. Which one did he not see, Azita or Deena Masoud. He was never sure which was which. But they must both be there; this was all about them. Where else could they be? Still, he hesitated. Should he make certain? He had not counted on this. For so long he had dreamed of his revenge. Now he was so close. Everything in him screamed that he should make sure his targets were there. But he couldn't wait. No, it was time. The female infidels must be inside. *Where else would they be,* he repeated to himself.

He stared at them until they disappeared into the building. Then he paused, a final moment of uncertainty seized him. Was this the moment? Would there ever be a good moment? His life would never be the same again. His body tingled and his mind started to shut down as if paralyzed. He shook his head, every man faces an existential moment, the decision that determines his future and his fate. If he stepped away now, turned his back on this moment, his life would be a torment of continuing regret.

Deciding, he leaned over the bike to reach into his large package. His hands shook, so dangerous given the sacred task before him. He forced himself to summon up the faces of all those known to him who had been killed by the bombs and bullets of the foreigners. One last time, he envisioned what America would do if Muslims had carried out the same carnage on their shores. They would seek an incalculable revenge. Their hands would not tremble. His certainty rose, his body calmed. He went about preparing his package before calmly slipping away.

* * *

When they entered the building, Rachel stopped Ahmad. "Did you see that young man standing outside the front door?"

"I did notice him. Why do you mention it?"

"There was something about the way he looked at me, at us. It was unnerving."

"Rachel, I wouldn't be overly concerned. He might be a local kid, not used to seeing Western devils. Perhaps he is simply curious. Or perhaps he thinks you attractive."

"Ahmad, I am old enough to be his grandmother. I doubt very much that he finds me attractive. But you are probably correct. If I'm going to work in these lands, I must adjust. The thing is, I have been invisible all my life. A woman of some notoriety perhaps, but I could go about my business and just blend in, especially after female surgeons became more the norm. It takes some getting used to when others look upon you as an exhibit in the zoo."

Ahmad laughed. "Oh, yes. I know the problem. When I first went to England, I had the same paranoia. All these white people are looking at me. But I got over it soon enough."

"How?"

"Easy, I just assumed that the women were staring because I was so hot and the men because they were jealous of this new and sexy competition in their midst." He smiled.

Rachel let out an involuntary laugh. "Sorry, I'm just so sure that was it."

Ahmad tried to frown. "Ah yes, Azita had the same reaction when I told her. I am surrounded by unbelieving infidels. No paradise for you, I fear."

"Oh, my dear friend, I fear paradise is not in my future."

"And why would you say such a thing?"

"Well," Rachel thought about that as if it were a serious inquiry, "for one thing, I avoided my brother all those years. I blamed him, of course, but I was equally at fault. I was so angry when I thought he had abandoned me. It just . . . never occurred to me what he must have been going through. Okay, that's not quite true. I had a sense of it, but I was too focused on me . . . my needs. Selfish, I suppose."

"No, very human, I think."

"Ahmad, you are wise beyond your years. Azita is so lucky to have you."

"Now," he smiled broadly, "that is a message my dear wife needs to hear from you. I tell her that all the time and she just laughs."

"And I will tell her when I see her next." Rachel smiled. "And when I see my brother next, I will give him the biggest hug possible and tell him I love him."

Ahmad nodded. "That is good. He will appreciate that, I am sure."

"No way," Rachel laughed once more. "He's an Irishman. They hate all displays of affection. It will drive him crazy. All the better, I suppose."

At that moment, a door opened and Amar and Ferhana appeared. "Here they are." Amar said to Ferhana. "Rachel, come with us, we have an interesting case we want you to see. Deena, you come as well. You will find this fascinating."

Deena had been listening to Ahmad and Rachel's conversation. She hesitated, seldom finding medical issues fascinating, mostly nauseating. She opened her mouth to beg off, saying that she had some matters to discuss with Ahmad. But those words, for some reason, never emerged. Rather, she oddly felt an obligation to follow her mother's request, "Okay."

Rachel took one step toward the two doctors before stopping. "I'll be there in a moment. One thing I want to check first."

"Okay, see you in a moment or two." Ferhana retreated deeper into the building with Deena reluctantly following while Amar hesitated to wait for Rachel with whom she had grown close in the past few weeks.

"Ahmad, forgive my paranoia, but I just want to check outside one more time."

"Fair enough," he said with the hint of a patronizing smile. "Perhaps it is worth checking out. That boy did have a bike with a large package strapped to the back. It could hide . . . bad things."

Rachel followed Ahmad outside. The bicycle was just next to the entrance, but the young man was nowhere to be seen. Two security guards lounged nearby. Ahmad was going to chastise them but merely walked over to check it out himself. He looked about him one more time to see if the boy was anywhere in sight. No. Suddenly, a small knot of fear locked into the pit of his stomach. Peering into the larger package, the knot washed over him in a full panic.

* * *

Azita reproached herself for running so late, she had spent way too much time communicating on her computer. She had intended to be at the clinic an hour earlier. She found a cab outside the hotel and thought about the reasons she might employ to excuse her tardiness. She could always claim morning sickness. Then again, who would believe that an Afghan woman would be slowed up by something so trivial. Her countrywomen were a hardy lot. They would labor in their homes and in the fields until the baby was due and hardly take any time off to complete their birthing duty. This was not a land for the soft.

She really didn't need any excuses. It was not as if she had spent the morning lounging in bed. No, she had been in touch with Chris, Kay, Karen, and others back in Oxford. She was pleased with the way things had been going and wanted to update everyone. She had ended with a cheery note that when the field visit to the Panjshir Valley was completed, they would all gather and head back home. She was so excited to have everyone back together again.

She was still thinking on this conversation, smiling, when the taxi seemed to pitch and almost lose control. She fell forward, hitting her head on the headrest in front of her. It took a moment for her to recover, to become aware of a large cloud rising somewhere ahead of her. Calculating direction and approximate distance, her heart seized up with total dread.

"No, no, no!" That was all she could utter.

* * *

Sir Charles Howard, Don of Baliol College at Oxford, looked about those seated at his conference table. He was pleased. Before him sat two of his favorite colleagues, Christopher Crawford and Shahed Al-Hussein. In addition, they had invited emeritus Professor Jeremiah Joshua Connelly from the University of British Columbia, Doctor Kristen (Kay) Crawford, and Karen Fisher. He enjoyed these people. In a world of continuous bickering, this group tended to stay on target and, more surprisingly, remain civil even as they kidded with one another endlessly. Sir Charles loved academia, it had been his life and the lives of his forbears. But he did recognize one failing of his colleagues. They were all clever and articulate, with all that talent and intelligence typically being brought to bear on the most trivial of issues. There were days when he would look about at his peers and colleagues and desperately wish he had become a plumber.

But not today. Chris had been bringing them up to date on a call he had received from Azita a bit earlier that morning. All was going well in the tour of field sites. The newer recruits from across the pond were fitting in nicely, he nodded at Josh as he said this. But most importantly, his operatives in the field were identifying prospects for the new program headed by Professor Ali-Hussein. These were young Muslim girls, some from impoverished backgrounds who had demonstrated remarkable intelligence and a keen interest in learning. They discussed the next step in this initiative, bringing some of them to England to improve their English and see how they would accommodate to the cultural challenges. A select few would be invited to stay and continue their education. The hope was that more prodigies like Azita and Deena were to be discovered. They were all convinced that there was a treasure trove of undiscovered talent out there.

Then, a side door opened, and the Don's administrative assistant approached him. "A call, sir."

"Can't it wait?" Sir Howard looked annoyed.

"I fear not. You better take it." She looked briefly at Chris before turning back to the Don.

Chris sensed disaster. The minutes the Don was out of the room seemed endless. *Why was he imagining the worst? Why?*

The same door opened. The Don entered, his face even more white than normal, a visage so stricken on his face so as discredit any doubt that the news was bad. "Chris, can you come with me. News from Afghanistan, I fear."

Chris could sense his heart stop. "It's bad!"

The Don simply nodded.

CHAPTER 16

ENGLAND

To Chris, Jeremiah Joshua Connelly seemed to have aged at least a decade in just a few days. His new friend had always looked to him the perfect combination of the eminent man of the academy who also was a citizen of the world. While he may have put on a few pounds, his face remained lean with those craggy lines that suggested wisdom and experience as opposed to length of years and hard living. The hair was silver and long enough to give off that indifferent look to style or fashion. It was the *'I'm way too busy to worry about a haircut'* look. Now, however, the lines on his face made him look haggard and the disheveled hair appeared more from carelessness than choice.

Chris was afraid to look in a mirror, reluctant to acknowledge the years he had added in the past week or so. They already had been through an emotional ringer. What was left to say. How many more ways could he apologize to his new friend for binging his beloved sister, Rachel, into harm's way. The guilt had wracked him since he absorbed the news. In truth, he had only partially embraced the horror since his body and mind shut down at the words describing an explosion that ripped through part of the medical and services facility killing several including Ahmad Zubair and Rachel Connelly. Amar Singh and Ferhana Gupta were also injured.

It could have been worse, as he was told later. Ahmad, realizing what the bicycle and package meant, desperately tried to get the package away from the clinic. He jumped on the vehicle and started pumping furiously. He only got so far before the device did what it was intended to do. His frantic efforts saved many lives inside the building, certainly Amar's. Ferhana had already started toward the rear of the clinic and was only slightly injured.

Rachel, unfortunately, was still outside, looking on without comprehending what was going on. She had no experience with terrorism, it was not part of her ordinary existence. Ahmad was shouting something at her, but she could not understand the words. Was he speaking Arabic? Farsi? In the end, she had no chance even if she had comprehended his warning. Her death was instantaneous.

Many of those inside had heard some yelling from the front of the building. Some walked quickly in that direction, others continued their work. Something was amiss, but what? On occasion, Islamic traditionalists would cause a ruckus, usually no more than a nuisance, protesting the work they were doing with women. It was probably no more than that.

Amar approached the entranceway when the world exploded about her. She was blown backward. Smoke and debris and the screams of the dying penetrated Amar's consciousness. No, this had not happened. They had talked and planned and anticipated such things, but never did she permit the reality of it to seize her brain. Even now, it was not real. She was suspended in air, without pain, and understood nothing about events surrounding her. All was illusory, her awareness trapped in disbelief with a hint of horror attached. Soon, however, the terror of the moment pushed away the illusory phantasma, pain replaced numbness, and the desperate cries and smells became real. She reached about her and felt mostly cement and wood and rubble. But there was something soft as well. It posed a mystery for her, out of place. She forced her mind to identify these substances that seemed so foreign. Why was this so important to her, perhaps the need to find certainty in a world suddenly without definition? Then it came to her. She was touching human flesh, disembodied flesh and bone, random body parts. She pushed away the horror and blackness came.

Azita finally made her way to the site on foot, the taxi driver having refused to go any closer. It was not easy fighting through rescue vehicles and police. Kabul was used to such things. The citizens and first responders knew how to respond quickly. Some arms, probably out of kindness, tried to restrain her but Azita was wild with fear and anger and wild surmise. She would not be dissuaded. No power would dissuade her. She kept screaming that she was a doctor and pushed forward. It was not real. It could not be real. She would soon awake, of that she was certain. She tried forcing herself out of the nightmare engulfing her.

Sometimes that happened, more often when she was young. She would experience nocturnal journeys into a personal hell where she was forced to relive her family tragedies. Several were the same. There would be a knock on the door of her childhood home in Kabul. She would answer to find a smiling man she did not know. *I have good news,* he would say, *your brother, Majeed, is home from fighting the Taliban.* With joy she would rush past the bearer of good news only to find a coffin outside her sanctuary. The dream drifted after that but always was dominated by this bitter sense of pain and loss.

Her most common dream was situated in a rural village, perhaps her father's traditional family village in the north, but that was never clear. She would be lost, running through village streets in search of something just outside her comprehension. No one would help, everything looked the same, endless byways that stretched beyond the limits of any such place she knew. In the end, she heard her parents screaming for her at the end of a dirt street that looked identical to all the others she had been down. But she knew this to be different. She had to get to the home at the end of this nameless path. She ran as hard as she could with feet that seemed incapable of movement, as if she were mired in quicksand that was dragging her down, down, ever down. Exhausted and frantic, she made a final lunge while willing herself through the abode's doors only to scream herself awake without seeing what waited inside.

She first made her way into the rubble toward the front of the building. Instinct told her to help the wounded. But instinct be damned. She found Ferhana who was bleeding but was conscious, a nurse from the clinic was tending to her. "I am okay, I think," she uttered without Azita asking.

“Where is Amar and Ahmad?” Azita managed to ask through gasping sobs.

“My husband is helping Amar. Ahmad . . .” She said nothing but pointed back toward the door and started to weep.

Azita was frozen, whom to see first? The condition of her husband struck her as more ominous, so she made her way back outside the rubble that had been a place of healing an hour earlier. Looking about frantically, she could not see her husband. It seemed a kaleidoscope moving figures, groaning victims, and lifeless bodies. All was blurry. Of course, the tears kept her from seeing anything with clarity. She walked further away from what had been the clinic entrance. Something in the confusion caught her eye. It was a body so disfigured that it was beyond recognition. Slowly, she walked toward it, dread increasing with each step. It was the tattered clothes. She raced through each possible denial but stared at the clothes. They were what Ahmad’s had put on that morning. She sank to her knees and wailed. After some moment, she forced her body up, and with tears streaming down her face, she went to help the wounded, and to find her mother.

* * *

Of such happenings and more, Chris would come to know later. In that first call, in the office of Sir Charles at Baliol College, he merely learned that his life would no longer be the same. Now, days later, he was walking with Josh along the river as it wound through Christ Church Meadows, the ribbon of water that would make its way through London and eventually to the sea. It was a place that Amar loved to walk when she had things to contemplate and figure out. Chris thought the magic of the place might work for him. He had much to consider these days.

The aftermath had been a blur. There was the scramble to arrange a medical team to descend on Kabul, stabilize Amar and Ferhana, and get them back to London where they received emergency surgery. Ferhana's injuries proved more serious than originally thought while Amar was in serious condition from the outset. All the foreigners stationed in Kabul, including those in the Panjshir Valley site, were evacuated. This included Bahiri Gupta along with Dr. Archibald Singletary and his wife, Agnes. In the confusion of the moment, all forms of conspiracies infected Chris, and his more sanguine associate, Karen Fisher. Perhaps the Islamic extremists were about to attack all their sites in Afghanistan or the Mideast. Perhaps the highly publicized push to elevate Muslim girls and young women had been a bridge too far. In the immediate aftermath, there had been no broader threats nor any group taking responsibility for the Kabul attack. Chris had relaxed some but wanted to assess the overall situation with some care.

"Josh," he began, "I am so . . ."

"Stop, just stop right there." His face bordered on fury at some unseen and unknowable enemy. Then it softened, as were the words that followed. "Listen, do you remember me telling you what the Morae are?"

"Vaguely," Chris whispered. "You explained they are representations of fate. But surely . . ."

Josh cut him off. "This is not a time for logic. I need that . . . sense of destiny right now. I brought her here more than you did. Never forget that. I must believe it was destined to happen, maybe for some reason I'll never understand."

"Don't you dare take away my guilt," Chris said more sharply than he meant. "Sometimes I feel like a damn general sending troops into harm's way while I sit in some safe bunker. My god, I've lost your sister and Azita's husband. My wife . . . my wife . . . I almost lost her for Christ's sake. If that had . . ." No more words came, his sentiments struck him as self-absorbed.

Chris thought back to the first couple of days after their return from Afghanistan. Kay provided continuous care and brought in a team of top surgeons to repair the damage. Azita's fight to be in the operating room flared into sharp words between them.

"No," Kay had yelled at her, "you are in no shape to help."

"No shape," she screamed back, "who tended to her right after . . . on the plane. I have no injuries. I need to be there."

"You have no physical injuries . . . no physical injuries. But, my dear, you are wounded, believe me."

"Damn you," she excreted through clenched lips and ran from the room to appeal to Chris, her father. But he backed the judgment of his sister without hesitation or reservation. That struck Azita as even a greater betrayal for some reason. After that, Azita and Chris had few words for one another as they sat by Amar's side during the first, post-surgical hours. Chris would look at the daughter he so loved but she seldom met his gaze, and never addressed him. She remained impassive, a stone of silence absent human expression.

Josh broke through Chris's reverie as the two continued their walk by the water, disrupting the latter's memories of the aftermath. "Where are you? You look lost."

"You know, Amar got me coming here, to this stretch along the river. I mean, I knew it was a favorite place of the locals but hell, I never went for the usual attractions. But she was right about this one, about so much. She told me how the river was her metaphor for life. *'You knew the ultimate destination,'* she explained to me, *'it would disappear into the sea to be no more. But, from here, you could never guess at the twists and turns you might encounter along the journey.'* I took her words to mean that therein lies the mystery of existence. We know the end, oblivion, yet we act as if we will go on forever. We pretend immortality when mortality is the one constant of existence. For Christ's sake, where do dreams come from, ambitions, aspirations. How futile everything is. If there are these Morae, they hide their piece of fabric well after they're done messing with our fates. Only they know the pattern, what has been woven for each of us. Selfish of them, no?"

"Whoa," Josh interrupted. "I'm the one who should be screaming at the fates. But I think it is compassionate of them. Think about it for a moment. Would any of us want to know beforehand?"

"I suppose not." Chris looked at the older man with obvious anguish spreading across his face. "Why in god's name aren't you screaming at me, hitting me, suing me for god's sake?"

Josh managed a smile. "Suing you? There is a thought. You are richer than Croesus, or at least everyone I know all combined. But sue you for what, trying to save humanity? I think not, tempting as the suggestion might be. My favorite charity, yachts for retired academics, is not doing well, so a contribution there would be welcome."

"You didn't answer my question." Chris persisted. "You should know you can't bullshit another Irishman with humor."

Josh looked at the river for a long time. "I haven't because I'm not sure there is any blame. Pain, yes. Culpability, no. You know what I kept thinking when the shock wore off, when I realized it had happened. I felt cheated, as if I were the one who had been wronged by the fates."

"That's not . . ." Chris tried.

"Let me finish. You read my memoir. I ran away from my past and from the people closest to me for decades. It was Rachel, for the most part, who yanked me out of my emotional exile. In that moment, as she dragged me from my cocoon, I thought she was a royal pain in the ass for doing that. After, I loved her for it. Then, I was semi-retired and had time for her, but she was still the top doc and researcher back in Wisconsin. So, I deferred my desire for a real connection to the day when she also would retire." A tremor crossed his lips. "You know, she never admitted this but I'm certain she stepped down earlier than she intended just to reconnect with me, so we could be a family again. She missed what we had as kids. And . . . so did I."

Chris came to the rescue. "And this, this bringing her to England was a way to get closer to her. Am I hearing you right?"

"Absolutely. This seemed perfect. If she could be recruited we might be together at long last. Maybe there would be a role for Usha as well. I figured even Connie would find a place, though, to be honest, I never could understand her research. No matter, it would all be perfect in my twisted head. You must understand. The greatest pain of going into exile to escape the war was losing Rachel. There was a bitter price to pay for being a pretend revolutionary."

"Pretend revolutionary ... pretend? You were burning down buildings, for Christ's sake."

"Okay, okay, but that wasn't me and we had no freaking chance of stopping the insanity of war. That was all these events sweeping me along to the point where I no longer was in control. I was a kid and had to escape before I became something I detested." Then he paused as if he had an epiphany. "Now that I consider it, maybe I was on the verge of denying my fate . . . I think." Then he hurried on when he saw Chris about to ask a question. "After reconnecting with my sister, I kept thinking about what we had as kids. Our old man was a grade-A SOB, our mother just cold and remote. But we had one another. Even with the age difference, we could share things. She was a precocious little shit. I really wanted to capture some of those moments again. She would follow me around and drive me a bit crazy but still . . . she would ask me all these questions. Oh yeah, I would make up answers that she eventually realized were BS but kept on asking. She was so amazing. Even as a child, she absorbed so much, was the parent while I remained a child. Still, there were moments when I felt like I was shaping this young mind, creating this person who might change the world in some way. Maybe that's where the thirst for teaching came from, those early moments with Rachel."

"I get it," Josh whispered.

"Do you?" But Josh did not wait for a response. "I had this vision, these images of Rachel and I finally getting back to that intimacy, the sharing we once had. Maybe you cannot do it. Maybe, those moments of intimacy and discovery are only permitted the young and unformed when all that is good is still ahead of us. Perhaps we get too cynical and jaded with the years. But, damn it, I wanted the chance." His body shuddered at this point.

Chris put his arms around the other man who cried without shame.

* * *

Ferhana had been released earlier and was settled to convalesce in the Crawford spacious home. She protested at being waited on but Bahiri insisted on playing the caretaker role.

"I don't need you fussing over me like I'm a cripple."

"Your injuries were more severe than we thought. You must rest," he would counter.

"Have you forgotten? You are an Indian boy. You don't mother females. You expect them to mother you."

Bahiri would try to look exasperated before responding with, "and who is the one who taught me how chauvinistic that was. Besides, these are doctor's orders."

"What doctor? Not you, I hope."

"No, Dr. Crawford."

"Chris? He's no real doctor."

"No, silly, Kristen, his sister, who is a very fine doctor."

Ferhana would pout, knowing defeat. "You mean Kay, no one calls her Kristen. I will talk to her." But then she would let her husband fuss over her, smiling when he could not see.

This was a ritualistic dialogue played out several times a day, the sequence and wording varying somewhat but not significantly. The dynamic altered when Amar was brought home. She was still in a condition that needed care and plenty of care was available. Ferhana insisted on being ambulatory and began to assist in Amar's recovery. Agnes and her husband were also available, even as they lobbied with increasing vigor to return to their clinic in the Panjshir Valley. Kay, when not consumed with her other responsibilities, assumed overall care. Then there was Azita, usually at her bedside, even when Amar was sleeping, watching her mother with a penetrating stare that hid a turmoil within.

Chris walked in Amar's room late that evening when only Azita was there. For a while, the two looked upon the woman whose chest heaved in continuous testimony that she had escaped death, for the moment at least. Occasionally, Chris would glance at his daughter, who kept her focus on her mother. He tried to find words to open a dialogue, but they escaped him. The man of many words was without any. How could that be? Partly he sensed that a wall suddenly had been erected around this young woman he impulsively had brought into his life so many years ago. Now, he would sacrifice his existence for her in a moment. What had happened to that unattached, hedonistic guy who had vowed never to get tied down by family and commitments? Oh, no, he might sacrifice himself for principles and values but not for mere relationships. That was for the other guys, the weak and shallow ones. And here he was, watching over his wounded wife whom he adored and trying to find words for the adopted daughter whose smile would melt his heart. But where were those words? For Christ's sake, he was Irish, they should come as water over the falls.

Chris became aware of someone approaching from behind. An arm made its way through his and he knew the identity of this presence even without looking. Kay spoke in a low voice. "Listen, you two, Amar doesn't need your mother-hen attention. She need's rest. Besides, I sedated her so that she could rest undisturbed."

"C'mon, Kay, how can a few words from the light of this women's life not speed the healing process."

"You're right, dear brother. A few words from the light of Amar's life would do wonders. But George Clooney isn't available right now."

"Great," Chis sighed for effect. "I have a sister who thinks she's a comedian and a daughter who won't speak to me."

"I am the funny one in this family and Azita . . ." Kay felt awkward, not knowing how to finish her thought. Azita kept her gaze on Amar.

After more silence, Chris spoke in a soft voice to his wife who remained asleep, her breathing regular and undisturbed. "Hey, sweetheart, I'll be leaving in a moment but, before doing that, a few thoughts." He paused as if deciding where to go next. "Well, you'll be happy to know that the Chicago gang will arrive soon . . . Kat and Ricky and Jules. Yeah, they had a bit of trouble getting away but are desperate to see you and Azita. Great news about her pregnancy amidst everything else, isn't it?" He sensed Azita's head swivel toward him for a moment, but he kept his gaze on his spouse. "It will be good to gather again, maybe we can get you out of this bed and down to the Hairy Hare for a group meal. I know how much you love the place." He snickered at his own joke. "I am torn, sweetheart. I want you up and about and I want you to stay exactly where you are. That sounds stupid, doesn't it? Consider the source I suppose. Mr. logic here cannot decide what the hell he wants. Thing is, when you are in bed, I know you are safe. It kills me that I've put you in harm's way, all of you. And now, every fear that has kept me up at night, worried to death, has come to pass. Do you have any idea how much I wish it were me in that bed or . . ."? He felt Kay squeeze his hand. "The pain, Amar, the pain at night, when I lay in bed going over and over what I've done in life and to the people I love. Can you imagine my anguish? Of course you do. You are the most sensitive women I know." Chris risked a glance at Azita, but her head remained fixed on her adoptive mother. "Last night I was thinking about something Robert E. Lee was supposed to have said when he mused about loving his soldiers but also realizing that he would do things that would destroy that very thing he loved so much. I have felt like that for so long. I love what I've helped create and what you all do, since I do nothing of consequence on my own. I love you all so much, but I knew this day would come. It had to. I am Irish after all. I knew it was just a matter of time . . ." His voice rose but he caught himself when Kay squeezed his hand again. "Funny, you do things to protect yourself, your conscience. Inside, you say things about how diligent you have been about security and how, after all, each person has made their own choice knowing the risks. I even tell myself that I could do nothing to stop them. You, Kay, Azita, Deena and all the rest would go on without me, as if I had nothing to say about things. These are sacrifices that flow naturally from you, contributions to an insane world you are compelled to make. And yet, at the end of the day, all that is crap. I cannot wash away the guilt that consumes me and overwhelms me in the dead of night. It is my fault. I am to blame. Ahmad and Rachel's blood are on my hands. I bear the guilt." He reached out with his free hand to touch his wife. "Please forgive me. I can't ask the others but you . . . please forgive me."

There was silence for what seemed like a long time, probably just seconds though. Some moments seem to get frozen with uncertainty as each person embraces the emotions about them. As if to end the drama playing out, the prone figure on the bed sighed deeply. "Enough." Amar managed to say with effort. "If my dear husband doesn't stop whining this very moment and let me sleep, I swear I will get out of this bed and kick him in the family jewels." Kay laughed aloud before Amar continued. "Now, all of you, just go away and let me sleep."

* * *

Not long afterward, Kay caught up to Azita as she was about to enter the room that Azita and Deena were sharing during these days. "A word, if I may."

Azita looked wary but nodded and they walked to an unoccupied room in the sprawling house. She spoke first as if trying to control the anticipated dialogue. "Just don't ask me how I'm doing. I'll explode if another person asks."

"That's not it." Kay had her game face on which threw Azita off balance a bit. "What I want to know is why you are being such an asshole to my brother . . . your adoptive father, if I'm permitted to remind you."

"I am not."

"Oh please, you can hardly look at him. You do not speak to him except in monosyllabic responses. There is enough frost when you are around him to create ice cubes. What the hell is wrong?"

"You mean what is wrong . . . with me, don't you? As if I am to blame." Azita's lip quivered slightly but she brought it under control.

"No," Kay started, "okay yes. What the hell is wrong with you? Don't you see, the man is dissolving. I have never seen him like this. Listen to me, young lady, if anyone is going to make his life a misery, that person will be me. Do you understand?" The final words burst from her mouth with more intensity than she intended.

"I am not angry with Father . . ."

"Well, you could have fooled me. You've been avoiding him like the plague, stonewalling his every approach. What happened to the loving Azita I once knew?" Kay struggled for composure. "Listen to me, you are hurt and angry. I get that, we get that. You have every right to be. But don't take it out . . ."

"I'm not, damn it!" She shouted, looking around to see if anyone was in the vicinity. "I'm not." In a softer voice.

Kay looked into Azita'a eyes. "Then who, or what, is pissing you off. And be honest. Even though you are all grown up and one of the best healers I know, I won't hesitate to put you over my knees and beat the living crap out of you. I am still your aunt."

A tear slowly made its way out of the corner of Azita's left eye. In an uncertain voice, she said, "Kay, you should know better than to make threats you would never keep, that you're too kind to keep." The young woman wiped away the tear and looked upward as if searching for a lost thought. "I'm . . . I am mostly angry at myself. Chris is . . . just an easy target, a way to avoid the hard things."

"What hard things?"

Now more tears flowed and Azita made no attempt to hide them. "Like what am I going to do with the baby inside me? And do not tell me it is a legacy of Ahmad, that it will be a testament to our love. I know that. But it is also a reminder. Damn it, Kay. First, I killed Ben who was merely a boy who loved me so, but I could not love him back in the same way. And now I've killed Ahmad whom I loved dearly, so much so that I managed to kill him as well."

"Zita," Kay used the familiar, affectionate name, "you know that's . . ."

"Silly, absurd, ridiculous, all of those things. That's what you're going to say. I can hear all the arguments in my head, all the adult arguments that someone of reason and science must obey." She paused, trying to find a thought that would not make her look like the emotional female she suddenly felt herself to be. "Here is something you cannot deny or explain away. He would not have been there were it not for me. No, no, had I rebuffed his advances when we were students, Ahmad would have married a regular girl and had several children and worked with his father to build the family businesses. He would be alive today. I'm . . . I am like the kiss of death suddenly. I . . . should put a sign on me. Men, stay away if you value your life."

"Do you hear yourself?"

"Just don't start lecturing me on my feelings. You are not one to lecture me. You left your husband and are letting him raise your kids. So, don't pretend to be holier than me."

"Bullshit!" Kay yelled, stung by what she knew to be the truth. "Someone has to straighten you out and since you won't listen to Chris these days, and your mother is too ill, I suppose it's up to me." Deena suddenly appeared, apparently drawn by the raised voices. "Before you all left on this last trip, Ahmad talked to Deena and me, didn't he?" Kay turned to Deena.

Deena looked a bit confused but, to Kay's relief, nodded affirmatively. "Yes, I remember."

Thankful for the support, Kay went on. "He went on at some length about what his life would have been like had he not met you. And you are right about one thing. He did see a future in his father's world of investments and business. That was the future all laid out before him. And guess what, he hated that thought, abhorred it. He knew it would be a life of misery, one of filial duty. He was just fortunate there were other siblings to fill that role and that you came along to rescue him. Don't you see, can't you see . . ."

"What?" Azita said softly though she already guessed the answer.

"You saved him. You gave him these years of purpose and happiness. He was so happy being with you, doing this common work. It made his life complete, full."

"Our aunt is right about that, you know." Deena stepped up to Kay's surprise. "You made Ahmad so happy. He lived the life he wanted, that he dreamed about. Never forget that."

"And never forget that so many go through life without ever chasing their dream, many never discover what they even are. You cannot imagine enduring a life of quiet desperation. Think about Deena if she had been forced into marriage with some man, only because she could not envision another possibility. Or you not being able to heal others. Which would you pick . . . a long life of merely existing or a short life of completion and fulfillment? Think about that!"

"I don't have to think very hard," Azita managed to say.

"I'm going to say one thing to you. Do *not* make any decisions right now, especially about the baby. Everything is too raw. Do you understand, do you?" Azita nodded. "Now go with your sister, get some rest. I can yell at you some more in the morning." As the two young women walked into their room, Kay called out in an exaggerated whisper. "And for god's sake, be nice to your father. Someone has to and it won't be me." Kay thought she saw a brief smile cross Azita's lips.

She walked back to the room she was staying in. *That was one helluva pep talk,* she said to herself. But how did it apply to herself. Was she happy and content? Gradually, an uneasy sense of loss embraced her. *I need to call Jamie, hear his voice . . . yes. I need to do that.*

CHAPTER 17

FEBRUARY

As soon as Chris and his group entered his favorite establishment, the Hairy Hare, he was waived into a private room. Several of the patrons enjoying a respite from the blustery weather outside called out "professor" as he made his way smiling and waving past the bar and toward a mahogany door marked *for private use only.*

Kat grimaced. "My god, do you live here now?"

Chris laughed. "Dear sister, you are so jealous that I am the one who gets all this public adoration."

"Fair enough," Kat retorted with a smile, "just don't forget who makes all the family money."

Chris could now command excellent personal service almost anywhere in the area, perhaps even London. He had grown in notoriety and stature over the recent years as his international work and his crossover writings received increased attention and admiration. He periodically appeared on the BBC to weigh in on political and social matters both in the UK and the US. His passionate arguments against Brexit in his new home and against the Trump phenomenon in his original home were not universally appreciated, especially his Brexit opinions, but they were quite acceptable in a college town. He had become a local celebrity. The fact that he and his sister were two surviving siblings of a wealthy American family who had chosen to relocate to merry old England had not escaped notice among the locals.

He sometimes thought about selecting a new location for his more social gatherings. He had to admit that critics of the Hairy Hare had their points. The food was passable but not exceptional and it was not upper crust by any imagination. He might well select a more prestigious setting if he were into impressing guests. The Hare would not do that by a long shot. But he was loyal, those born under the Taurus sign were that if nothing else, or so he was told, though he only snuck into the Taurus month by a mere day. And he was Irish, in part at least, the part about which he cared. The sons of Eire were stubborn if nothing else. Of that, he had no doubt. They had to be to survive centuries of persecution by those who wished to destroy their culture and remove them permanently from the earth. Ironically, those persecutors of his people were the very same group he now lived among. *Should he feel guilty about that*? He sometimes wondered.

As they settled around a table, Chris looked over his stateside guests more closely. He had not been back to his ancestral home as often in recent months. His onerous work schedule of writing, academic work, and a continuing involvement in his international work, which he couldn't quite let go, left him little spare time. Even Kat seemed to have aged a few years of late.

She always struck Chris as being a female version of Dorian Gray, always youthful and full of energy. Early on in life, she reminded him of the eldest, Chuck, with similar physical features and her disposition, more on the creative and kind side of the spectrum. Chris always felt that those good qualities killed Chuck in the end. He was too kind and sensitive. No way could he avoid that sense of failure forced upon him when, as the eldest male offspring, he could not meet Father's expectations. Suicide proved an available option he could not ignore. Kat's early signs of similar goodness and sensitivity well disguised a core of steel.

In the end, Kat proved to be more of a hybrid offspring as she matured. She had their mother's fine, elegant physical features but their father's sharp mind and killer instincts. As the youngest, by several years, little had been expected of her, except to be an ornament on the family tree. Then, she burst out of her cocoon with fury and purpose to take control of the family empire in a family coup. He looked more closely at her as she casually chatted with Kay. What if she had embraced the patriarch's values? He and his twin sibling could never have resisted such a father-daughter alliance. That pair would have continued to direct most of the family fortune to the right-wing causes and characters favored by the neo-Fascists that were struggling for control of their original home. Chris shuddered at the thought. Now, though, for the first time, he noticed more worry lines on her face. Even with Ricky at her side, she had to be worn by the stresses of keeping it all together. He could have helped more. *Perhaps he should make an offer.*

He shook that off and shifted his gaze to Ricky, who had dropped everything else to be with them at this hour. Despite growing up in a West Chicago ghetto, Ricky always carried himself with grace and assurance. He never lacked conviction, feeling free to break Chris's nose in a basketball camp the first day they met. A frustrated Chris had swung first, a blow to which Ricky responded to great effect. Smiling, he merely reached down and pulled Chis up while remarking that a crooked nose *would be an improvement for a white guy.* Chris, however, would not show defeat. He stuffed his nose with cotton and finished the game despite being in considerable pain before heading to a local emergency room. Ricky accompanied him and a lifelong friendship was born. More importantly, he got to meet Ricky's parents, the loving and supportive family his own domineering father would never tolerate, nor understand. No, the patriarch of the Crawford clan was a firm believer that achievement was a product of suffering, character an outcome of challenge, success a consequence of pure will. Love and affection were signs of softness. Chris now looked closely at his long-time friend. Ricky's deep brown face was more handsome and assured than ever. He had earned his spot as a polished businessman welcomed as an equal by financial titans around the globe. He must challenge the preconceptions of so many new business associates when they finally met Richard Jackson in person.

Chris's gaze shifted to Jules, Ricky's sister. She was the perfect on-camera network personality. Her lighter, ebony complexion was not off-putting in the least to audiences, there were many black faces in today's media. Besides, her smooth delivery and perfect pitch seemed made for primetime. What many failed to recognize was that her winning smile and easy, unforced sensuality masked an acute mind. She wrapped hard-hitting stories inside a nonthreatening demeanor, lulling some viewers into accepting material they might ordinarily reject. Chris scratched his memory to recall where their early love relationship had gone off the rails. She had rejected him, that was for sure. He was good enough for a lover, but as a lifelong mate, a white boy, she had to think on that one. After all, she had mountains to climb and almost unconsciously held to a feeling that wedding a white boy violated a tribal rule. By the time she realized the silliness of that and what she had passed on, it was too late. Chris went to Afghanistan on a rescue mission and came back with a wife and an adopted daughter. Chris smiled, *that must have blown her mind.* But maybe it was for the best. After all, her own marriage did not work out. Perhaps she was not destined for domestic bliss; not all women are.

Then his gaze shifted to Kay. When he was young, he had speculated whether Ricky and Kay might connect romantically. That never happened though they had always liked one another. Later, he realized that Kay never seemed that interested in boys. She was devoted to her studies as she drove herself to become a physician. Well, that was the prevailing explanation he embraced, she was too busy. Secretly, though, he wondered if her avoidance of romantic entanglements went deeper. Then she married Jamie, had two children of her own, and all seemed settled, until it was not. After dabbling with a couple of lesbian relationships, she now seemed rootless again. She was yet immersed in healing, now with an international focus rather than being buried in one of the worst emergency room situations imaginable as she had been earlier in her career. And yet, Chris sensed a change in his sister. He was considering what that change might signify when a voice intruded into his musings.

"Hey, where are you?" It was Kat. "Aren't you our leader, you look lost."

"Oh, yes, sorry. As you can imagine, I'm a bit preoccupied these days. Azita has really been struck by Ahmad's death as you can imagine. She has been cold to me since . . ."

Kay broke in. "Talk to her again. That's all I'll say for now."

"Okay," Chris said slowly. "Then there is the loss of Rachel Connelly. Kat, you didn't get to meet her, but she was a great person. I've been dealing with Josh, her brother, and Cate, her daughter, and the whole Canadian contingent. God, I feel like shit."

Kat gave him her steely look. "My god, you really inherited the full measure of that Irish crap . . . you apparently got Kay and my shares of the Catholic guilt along with your own. Now give it a break. Everyone is an adult. Everyone knew the risks. You forced no one to do anything they didn't want to do."

Chris flushed with embarrassment and then anger. "When did you become the family Rottweiler?"

"When you started acting like a child." Kat shot back.

Chris blinked before holding up his arms in a surrender sign. "Got it."

Jules broke the tension. "You know, I was so pleased to see how good Amar looked. Not sure what I was expecting but she will be up and about soon. And while she is recovering, do try and be a good husband for a change."

Chris welcomed the change in tone. "Hey, I'm always a saint." His claim was greeted with groans from around the table.

"But Azita does seem depressed, not that anyone can blame her. That is apparent." Jules added.

Kay made a sound, and all looked in her direction. "My bad. This is awkward. Okay, listen, this needs to stay with us unless she brings it up. Zita's pregnancy was supposed to be happy news and now she is torn about going through with it. Personally, I don't think she is thinking all that straight but who would under the circumstances."

"I get it, I really get it. We'll let her work that out for herself." Kat looked extremely tired for a moment but smiled as if to suggest a segue toward a lighter mood. "I do have one question here, though."

"Which is?" Chris took the bait.

"You do realize that our family is rich, don't you? I mean, really . . ."

"What?" Chris feigned ignorance even as he guessed where she was headed.

"What I'm saying is that you could afford to host us at a better venue." Kat deadpanned.

"For visitors I respect, I would. For you guys, lucky I haven't taken you to Curry-In-A-Box."

Kay rolled her eyes. "I see we are sliding downhill into the usual family insults. I, for one, want to hear what is going on in the States."

Kat looked at Jules and her husband before realizing they expected her to give the summary. "Let me start, at least. Let's see, there are two levels, the national and the personal or family. Let me start with the national. We have the combatants . . . Biden and Trump. Mixed feelings on Biden as you know, he is old and not liked by the progressive wing. However, he doesn't scare the money people. I've talked to many of my peers, even the few with a conscience. They would have been torn by a Bernie candidacy and you know that money is everything these days. Joe may not inspire passion, but he'll do well on the money front."

"What's your feeling about the general national mood?" Kay asked anxiously.

"Not good. The market is doing great, the economy perking along. You and I know it is mostly a result of debt-financed artificial stimulation that cannot last forever but Joe Six-Pack doesn't see it that way. He has a job. It doesn't pay crap, he might not get health care, and he likely is one accident away from living in his freaking car. Yet, he thinks Trump is doing a good job. You add the single-issue voters, abortion foes, and gun nuts and outright racists and I think we are in a heap of trouble."

"Fuck." Chris exploded. "What is wrong with people. He is a malignant narcissist, chronic liar, a misogynist and nativist and bullying maniac, not to mention that he is dumb beyond measure and totally incompetent."

"Come on," Jules cut in. "You know as well as anyone that most Americans are entertained by reruns of Jerry Springer. We are not a sophisticated people. You know the biggest criticism I get from the network brass. They keep telling me that I'm talking over my audience. I am already down to a fourth-grade level, which is still two levels above Donald. If I listened to the brass, my delivery would never get beyond 'run, spot, run.' Sometimes I want to cry."

"I hate to agree with my wife, and especially my sister, but they are spot on, as you Brits would say. It's not just that Americans are, in general, dumber than dirt, which is true. It's also that Trump will do anything to stay in office and now is working within the halls of power."

"Like what . . . what will he do?" Kay asked, being less politically involved than others around the table.

"Oh, some of it is obvious. He will continue working with the Russians, the Ukrainians, and every other despotic regime who might help him out. He's shut down any investigations of foreign meddling, eviscerated the Congressional oversight capabilities and, through his surrogates, launched a systemic campaign of voter suppression among minority voters. I wish African Americans the best of luck finding a polling place next November or even find themselves still on the voting rolls. It is Jim Crow with a vengeance with only suburban and rural white folk permitted to vote. The GOP will probably introduce a new literacy test where you are forbidden to vote if you can read above the 8th grade level, since then you are probably too smart to fall for their lies." Ricky paused, deciding if he should continue.

Kay whistled. "But we are talking about the United States, not some banana republic."

At that, Kat, Ricky, and Jules all laughed simultaneously. “Chris,” Kat fought to control her laughter, “I thought you said you trained your twin in the reality of American politics. I mean, that’s what you told me.”

“I tried,” he said with weariness, “I tried but some students are just uneducable.”

“Oh, bite me,” Kay responded to the jibes.

Chris ignored his sister’s protest. “The scary thing is that the entire election comes down to just a few swing states. Long gone are the days when most states were in play. Remember that Florida, Pennsylvania, Michigan, and Wisconsin were all decided by narrow margins in an election where a lot of minorities didn’t vote. Even if these groups are more motivated this time around, Republicans will try their best to make sure they don’t cast a ballot. A lot of their tactics work. In Wisconsin, Democratic candidates got 200,000 more votes than the GOP but only picked up one seat in state elections last time around. This is gerrymandering run amok. The electoral college is a form of national gerrymandering, don’t forget that Hillary got three million more votes than orange top and still lost. The right wing is sitting up nights coming up with schemes to steal this thing.”

Ricky jumped in. “Maybe they won’t have to cheat all that much. Listen, this maniac has a cult-like adoration among his base who think this depraved moron was sent by god to save us. I would not be surprised if they showed up at the polls armed with automatic weapons, just to intimidate voters. Ah, where are the Black Panthers when we need them? I think we can only be saved by some disaster that shakes things up. Anyone got one of those?"

There was silence around the table. Then Kay spoke up with some trepidation. "Maybe I can suggest something, but it is still speculation at this point."

When she paused, Kat tried to reassure her. "Please, anything is welcome, even something stupid."

"Okay, don't laugh. There is something going on in China that we, in the medical field, are worried about. I've mentioned this to a few folks already, including Chris."

"China?" Chris seemed perplexed. "That flu thing?"

"Okay, buster, we are now in my area, so you keep quiet while I finish."

"Yes, sis. I know my place."

Kay glared at him to make sure he was finished. "There is an outbreak of something with flu-like or pneumonia-like symptoms. Apparently, it is a SARS-like virus but one that we are now sure is spread through airborne contagion. I told this to my dear brother a while back but apparently it didn't make an impression. You know, some people are uneducable."

"Oh yeah, I remember now that you mentioned it."

"Well, put it back in that mind of yours. We now know more. It is out of China and around the world. This is the thing about airborne infections. Once the cat is out of the bag, you cannot stuff it back in. We are in the honeymoon period between that point when our ass is already cooked but before we realize the heat has been turned up and a meltdown is unavoidable. It cannot be stopped now. It is just a matter of time before we all know the bad news."

"What bad news?" Kat asked, still a bit confused.

"That a pandemic will engulf the world, like the Spanish flu. A bit before our time but at least 20 million perished globally in that one with over 650,000 in the US. We have better technologies now but there's always so much uncertainty. Bottom line, countries will have two choices. They can let it rage throughout until it dies out on its own, the herd immunity response, or lockdown the country, the containment response. Either way, the impact on the economy may make the 2008 slowdown look like a speed bump."

"Holy shit," Chris whispered. "If you are right, we know how Trump will respond. He'll lie and try to bully his way through this. He will not listen to the experts, figuring he's the smartest guy in the room. That's the danger of narcissists, they don't know how stupid they are. We know he is an incompetent ass but with this might just reveal how bad he is."

Kay picked up on the theme. "He will lead us into a total debacle. Of course, the cost to us might be incalculable. And don't forget, Chris, we have Boris Johnson on this side of the pond, a Trump wannabe. Granted, he's not as dumb as Trump, who is? Still, we may not escape disaster. Thank god for Merkel in Germany. She's a scientist and will be the lead in the EU."

The conversation went on about how all this might evolve and what they could do to prepare for it, use this impending disaster to change the political fortunes of the country. Kat talked much about working with disaffected Republicans who now hated Trump even more than she did. At some point, she sensed they were running out of fresh ideas. "Listen, I mentioned at the beginning that we had two levels of intelligence to report."

"Oh yeah, go ahead." Chris encouraged her.

She took a deep breath. "There is the question of our dear Pater. There is always the question of Father. If anything, he has become more unstable I sense. Hard to tell since I'm not in contact but I have some sources and the bits and pieces I get worry me."

"Like . . ." Chris pushed her along.

"Like, he is reaching out to extremist groups, not the usual right-wing political organizations but the violent whackos. This conversation makes me more worried. What if this pandemic thing is a real disaster, as Kay believes. The prospect of Trump losing, of Father seeing his dreams of an autocratic coup failing at the last moment, could set him off."

"Set him off how?" Kat asked.

Kat seemed to close within herself as if troubled by the words on her lips. "He will turn his wrath on to us, the family that he thinks betrayed him."

"You did betray him." Ricky reminded them.

Kat sighed loudly. "I wish this were all just paranoia. But sometimes people really are out to get you. We all agree that he killed Beverly, somehow, not personally but had her killed when he realized she was spying on him. Then there were a couple of worrisome incidents, a car that seemed to aim for me one dark night and some phone calls to my private number telling me to 'watch my step.' From trac-phones, untraceable. I've had the offices and my home swept."

"And?"

"Nothing yet but I'm sure I've been followed. I'm hypervigilant now and I can see some familiar-looking men hanging around, familiar-looking cars that always appear to be going where I am."

"Well, Kat, you are still hot," Chris tried, "maybe you got male admirers."

Kat nailed her brother with a withering look. "This is fucking serious."

"Yes, sorry."

"More than anything, I want to stop Trump this fall. But I am deathly afraid the cost to our family will be incalculable."

"Wait." Chris suddenly was on board with just how serious his younger sister was. The thought of losing her coursed through him like a frigid wave on the coast of Scotland. "Relocate here. Get out of Chicago with Mother. Do it. You can run things from here."

She raised a hand for him to stop. "Okay, listen to me. I am not letting that asshole run me out of my town. Do you think I was able to wrest control of the family company from him because I was a chicken shit? That is my country he's attacking. I'm not going anywhere: I'm hanging tough and going to save it. Understand!"

Chris looked at her, wondering if she realized that her words were a slap in the face to him. That was exactly what he had done, as had Josh. They both ran away from America many years ago, to escape from things they could not face.

* * *

Later, Chris returned to meet with Karen Fisher and others who had survived what now was termed the Afghan incident. For a moment, he pondered over our habit of selecting neutral terms to designate horrific moments. Was that self-deception or something more deeply healing . . . an essential balm to ward off devastating psychic effects associated with assaults upon our sanity? If so, Chris was not sure it was working. He could not bring back Ahmad and Rachel, no matter how desperately he wished to turn back the clock. Ferhana and Bahiri were showing signs of PTSD as they continually lamented the death or injury of several staff members at their clinic. Even as Amar healed physically, he knew she was suffering nightmares that prevented healing sleep.

They met at a large conference room at the university, this was less social and more formal. He had arrived first while Karen Fisher and Carlotta Ciganda would be bringing the others along. He had been in this room many times but never had paid all that much attention to the ornate portraits enclosed in gilt-painted frames that adorned the walls. It was all well designed to display the intimate connection between the academy and Britain's destiny. Surely, some of these distinguished-looking individuals had played a role in the oppression of his ancestral homeland, others had played a part in England's 15th century civil war. He mused on whether they might be loyalists or roundheads, devoted followers of Charles most likely. As he scanned the walls he could envision many being part of the East India Company, a private enterprise that divided and conquered the subcontinent that was his wife's homeland. Other portraits paid homage to those who had tried in vain to keep control of some ungrateful colonists in North America by hunting down those pesky revolutionaries to hang them for treason. He doubted that any of these honored men had played a role in England's ill-fated effort to control Afghanistan, a venture that ended with the massacre of an entire British army. How odd, he mused, that this place, this institution, had prepared individuals whose destinies and fate were so linked with his own family's past. Then he recognized the portrait of John Churchill, statesman and military hero who, as the first Duke of Marlborough, became one of the richest men in the land under Queen Anne. But his eventual claim to fame was assured by a future issue of the Churchill line named Winston. Most prominent was a portrait of the Duke of Wellington, the man credited with finally stopping Napoleon. Where were the more recent men of honor? They must be in some other room.

Chris snapped out of his reverie. He was not looking forward to this session. Emotions were still raw, his guilt over the death of Rachel Connelly yet a fresh wound. Instinctively, he distinguished the loss of Ahmad from Rachel. He saw his son-in-law as a kind of soldier who knew the risks going into battle. Josh's sister was a different case altogether. Why had she joined her brother? Was she really committed? Was this merely a way of cementing a filial relationship that had been rent apart by early domestic trauma? If so, perhaps he should have been more direct and explained the risks in more dramatic terms. Yes, they were all adults, responsible for their choices, but he had the advantage of intimate knowledge of the risks. Had he been completely transparent, or had he permitted his desire to absorb these fascinating people into his world to dissuade him from total honesty. Why couldn't he decide these things? Was he losing his edge?

He refused to concede ground to any apprehensions of personal vulnerability. Deep inside, he might harbor self-doubt but that was not necessarily a bad thing. Look at Trump, he seemed incapable of any self-reflection. That surely was a devastating pathology. No, some deep doubt prevented one from descending into total hubris. He took a deep breath. Decisions had to be made. He had convinced himself that it would be best to release Usha, Cate, and Meena while reassigning Archie and Agnes to less dangerous sites. He thought Ferhana might argue to return to Afghanistan with her husband. He might fail to convince them otherwise, but he would try. He remained unsure about what Josh intended to do, or even how Josh was dealing with his loss. *The damn Irish*, Chris thought, *so hard to read.* In any case, the bottom line was this . . . he would try to do whatever he could to keep everyone out of harm's way.

At that moment, the door opened as Karen led the group into the room. *Showtime,* Chris told himself. A thousand other times he had said the same thing to himself before audiences big and small, important and not so important. He had inevitably managed to kick himself into action. Not today. Today, it was different.

"Thanks for coming by." That sounded stupid even to Chris. After all, were they likely not to come? "I . . . I've talked with each of you individually, but we haven't had a group session. I thought it is time we had one to, you know, think things through collectively. I mean . . . each of us must make their own decision but . . . you know . . . sometimes it is good to air things out in a group." Suddenly, and for once in his public life, he struggled for words. "What I'm trying to say is that we need to share things . . . see what I mean."

Karen looked at the man she so admired as if he had lost his wits. "What in god's name are you babbling about?'

"This is hard," Chris said defensively.

"Of course it's hard. But shit happens, right?" Karen said in her take-no- prisoners style. It was why he hired her so long ago when she had no apparent qualifications for any position. "Listen, you nimrod, we've been talking among ourselves before heading over here."

"But . . ." Chris tried as he realized he would quickly lose control.

"But nothing. Remember my job interview back in the dark ages? That question you asked me about how I would handle you if you screwed up in a meeting. I said I would take you outside the room and rip you a new one. Well, I am more confident now . . . no need to leave the room. I can do the job right here."

"Oh shit." He managed to get out.

"Here's the thing, you imbecile. You are moping about and taking all this on yourself. Well, suck it up, buttercup. The world does not revolve around you. I mean, I get it. Most males, particularly the alpha types, think that the sun rises and sets over their scrotum but here is the truth . . . the sun will rise and set anyways. There are things we cannot control. No one, not even you, can make the world right, or keep everyone safe, or even decide what others do with their lives. I love you, you cretin, but sometimes you can be infuriatingly stupid . . . and stubborn. Got that, buster."

Carlotta could not suppress a smile as Chris looked on blankly. "My colleague here promised to be tactful, but I see she is what she is. Listen, Chris, we've all been talking among ourselves. There is all the pain and anguish you can imagine. But there is something else as well, a truth we cannot ignore. The thing is that none of us can dictate our future. We can only make each decision in our lives according to how we see the world. For me, I grew up Catholic before becoming an ersatz revolutionary in college. But you never totally lose those early lessons. What I never lost was this sense that we all are part of something bigger, that we cannot fully understand nor surely not control. You can't dictate outcomes, my dear. You can, however, do what god meant for you to do."

"Amar would take me out at night to look at the night sky."

"What?" Carlotta seemed confused by the apparent non sequitur.

"Sorry," he said quietly, "give me some rope there. Amar would take me out to look at the stars. She knew a lot, her brother being a cosmologist. No matter, she told me to look hard at the universe, thing about the immensity of it all, and how little we really knew. With billions of galaxies and trillions of stars, we might only be seeing a fraction of it all. That humbled me, sometimes I need to be reminded of our insignificance. Slow learner, I suppose."

Karen spoke again but with less intensity. "You understand what we are trying to say then. No one is blaming you. We might as well blame God, or Allah, and you surely are no deity. No one is confused on that score." A small chuckle rippled through the gathering. "The thing is, we are mere cogs in things larger than ourselves. Hell, that time I got shot foolishly saving your sorry ass near Azita's family village, I was told that bullet missed a major artery by a fraction of an inch. The tiniest shift of position and I would have bled out before the copter got back to the camp. Thing is, I chose to go after you and the girls. And I would do it again, in a heartbeat, even if I weren't sure where that bullet would hit me next time around. Now who is the slow learner."

"Really?" Chris said lamely.

"Of course, you bloody idiot. After all, I'm sure you would have erected a monument in my memory."

"Well," he finally cracked a smile, "maybe a tiny one, more likely a small plaque."

"Bloody sot." Karen managed a small smile.

Cate spoke up in a tentative voice. "Let me say something now." She looked about the room uncertainly. "Maybe I'm wrong but here is what I think . . . we think." She quickly glanced Meena then back at Chris. "You've been carrying around this hurt. We can all see it. I can see it. You haven't been able to look me in the eyes. Chris, look at me." She paused until his gaze slowly rose from examining his own hands to focusing on her eyes. "While I will miss my mother more than anything, I do know one thing. She died doing what she wanted to do . . . heal others. We talked on this trip, more intimately than we had ever done before. She was getting it finally. She was getting what I was all about. You see, she thought my joining the State Department and doing foreign service was all about running away from her and my worthless father. But now she was understanding that I was running toward something. I mean, I was getting closer to who and what I was supposed to be . . . my fate as you will. And that is what so many in this room are all about, seeking our real fate. We have one, I'm now sure of that. Not all of us get to stumble over it or have the guts to go after it. The fortunate few do. We are those lucky few." She paused to collect herself. "If you want the truth, my mother did join us on this trip probably for the wrong reasons—to get closer to her brother and certainly to me. One thing is clear, she didn't come here to follow you, Chris. Sure, my uncle talked you up but, in the end, she did not know you from a hole in the wall. She came for me, Meena, and for Josh . . . to reconnect with a family she had once lost, or thought she had."

"But the cost . . ." Chris tried one final time.

"Just stop it. For such a smart man, you can be so dense. She was seeing her future, she was understanding me, and Josh, and my relationship with Meena. My god, can't you understand how precious that is? I'd give anything to have more time with her, but what I had in these past weeks has been a treasure beyond measure. Please understand that . . . please. We got something we might never have experienced, something irreplaceable."

Chris's voice cracked but he managed the words. "I do get it . . . I am slow but I'm not beyond hope." Chris looked about the room. He saw heads looking at him with unflinching conviction, some were nodding. He knew, beyond doubt, that there was no way he was going to keep them out of harm's way. He simply would have to endure whatever came his way.

* * *

The next morning, Kat and Ricky and Jules stopped by to say goodbye before heading to the airport to take the corporate jet back to Chicago. There were lots of hugs and promises to stay safe and assurances that they all would meet again. Chris had insisted on driving them, he was strangely reluctant to let them go. Some ominous premonitions had grabbed his insides, refusing to release its icy grip.

At the building which afforded access to the private planes of the wealthy, they seemed to linger. Perhaps all were reluctant to part, more so than was normally the case. But, in the end, it was time.

Chris hugged Jules who whispered in his ear, "You take good care of Amar. Damn, I wish I could dislike her, but she is so good for you. What possessed her to marry so poorly."

"Luck of the Irish," Chris responded as their bodies separated, much to Chris's relief since he always felt that physical tug around her. "And you be safe, just go after mobsters and political crooks in your reporting for a while, okay?"

"Hell, no." She laughed. "I'm going after your father and that turd in the White House."

Chris moved on to Ricky who preempted any display of emotion with a plea. "You're not going to kiss me, are you?"

Chris laughed. "Relax, I'm going to challenge you to a one-on-one game when I get to Chicago next. This time, I'll beat your ass or else . . ."

"Or else what?" Ricky seemed unimpressed.

"I'll break your nose for a change."

"Enough dreaming the impossible dream," Kat interrupted, "time for us to be on our way." She put out a hand as if a shake would do but Chris pulled her into an embrace.

"You are still my little sister. You may have all these business barracudas fooled, but I remember the shy wallflower you once were. Got that?"

"Yeah, so?" She wasn't sure where he was going.

"So, don't try to be a freaking hero all the time. Be careful. No unnecessary chances. Understand!"

"Right, big brother."

And then they were gone.

CHAPTER 18

CALCULATIONS

In the aftermath, many private and collective calculations took place. They happened in separate places and in different ways but were driven by common questions. How would each person respond to the events about them, the smaller matters that consume our daily moments and the large issues that determine national destinies?

The young Islamic warrior was back in the North, in the harsh mountains and parched land where only the hardened and driven survived. He was beyond anguish. He had kept his ambitions secret except for family and close associates. No one knew that he had dedicated his life to Allah and the Fatwa that had been declared against the infidel females who had spit in the prophet's eye with their blasphemy. Though he was among friends, it was yet dangerous to be free with information. This had traditionally been the land that had stood against the Taliban when they were the strongest. Even in the time of ISIS, the tribal currents and complex relationships made paranoia a necessary approach to life and people. Better to keep one's own counsel.

Yet, everywhere he went he saw people staring at him, laughing at him, deriding him with eyes filled with contempt. He had failed. His bomb had missed his targets, first and foremost the Masoud girls and secondarily those that ran this clinic in the name of the family patriarch, Pamir Masoud. Azita had not been there, her sister had managed to escape again. It was his fault, he should have made sure, he should have waited until he was certain. No, he was too eager, his thirst for vengeance so fresh in his mouth. Perhaps he could not believe that Allah would let him down like this, to bring him so close and yet deny him satisfaction in that last moment. Ah, it hit him, perhaps that was his miscalculation. Allah was not there to do his bidding. Rather, he was there to do Allah's will.

Unable to stand the anguish inside, he took the pistol he had been given in Kabul for protection on his assignment and stole into the countryside. He wandered over the crusted earth up the hills into the higher levels from which the peaks soared above him. There, he found the cave where the girls had sought refuge after their parents had been assassinated in Allah's name for their sins. Near here, the foreigners came to rescue them and where his father had been struck down in Allah's service. But he did not know exactly where this tragedy occurred. He had been taken to the spot as a young boy but now the landscape seemed indistinguishable. There was nothing to mark this place that was sacred to him but apparently to few others. In a land with so much blood, where the soil was perpetually tinged with a reddish hue, no single contribution of one's life source meant all that much.

He found the cave easily enough, the place where those blasphemous girls had hidden, shivering with fear, as his father and the other warriors had searched for them. They had sat in this very spot, probably believing that their end was only a matter of time. But they escaped, and they escaped again years later when his older brother had tracked them down during that ceremony over the new school for girls in Pamir Masoud's ancestral village. He sat against the cave wall. *My god,* he screamed internally, *what deity protects these blasphemers, these infidels.*

He had been down this futile debate before, but it proved impossible to escape. Perhaps he just could not see Allah's plan. Perhaps simply killing them was too simple, or even poor strategy. Think of that Malala Yousafzai. Did a bullet to the head silence her? No, it made her an international hero and gave her a bigger platform to spout her heretical nonsense. Who could support educating girls? That was blasphemous for sure. They were meant to breed and to serve men. That was all there was to it. Besides, females were evil incarnate, always seducing him to defy Allah's commandments . . . enticing him to pollute his own body. He could see their mischievous glances even behind the veil. He was certain they were there.

But why wasn't Allah's message clear to him. Why could he not hear it within his heart? Why did Allah not help his family realize their revenge? Were they not worthy? Were they being tested? He could not understand why Allah's words did not fill his head with encouragement and lead him to a righteous fate. Why? Why? Why? Perhaps he was not worthy, perhaps his family had failed in God's eyes. That might explain the divine silence.

He searched his memories. They had obeyed the commandments and the law. They had followed the true edicts of the true and holy Mullahs. They had fought against the infidels and foreigners who had polluted their land. All was blameless. They should have been rewarded. He should have been rewarded. A blackness descended over him. He looked at the pistol in his hand for a long time, then slowly raised it in a shaking hand.

He heard a loud bang then the reverberation of the sound flowed down the valley and across to adjacent mountains. He tried to focus. No pain, no blood, he sensed his breathing. The bullet somehow had missed his head. This had been a test, all up to this point was a test. Perhaps that was God's message. He would be spared self-destruction for a greater purpose . . . a truly felicitous fate.

* * *

The objects of the young man's obsessions were thousands of kilometers away, safely ensconced in the secure academic town of Oxford England. They were meeting in the office of professor Shahed Al-Hussein.

"What is next?" the comely Jordanian said as she leaned over her desk.

Deena looked at her, as she often did, with a mixture of unrequited longing and guilt. Ali was not married, had never been married. That was strange for a woman of the Mid-East, no matter how cosmopolitan. Yet, this intelligent and sophisticated beauty had never given off any interest in relationships or evinced even a hint of sensual need. Was she even human? Deena could never totally suppress this curiosity that found its way with considerable stealth into the crevices of her mind. Though she had never offered a hint of interest toward her, Deena could not push away the thought of Ali as a possible partner. Deena's ventures into the world of lesbian relationships had dissolved with time, she was never totally sure why. It was probably her work, the long absences visiting field sites. That was probably it. She had suppressed thoughts of romantic relationships but with Shahed, they would have a common culture, shared interests to cement any relationship. Deena imperceptibly shook her head to clear such thoughts as Shahed spoke.

"I've been thinking. We are identifying quite a few girls back in our target areas who have all the talent in the world but never would escape their cultural prisons without help. What we don't have, or have enough of, are situations and opportunities for them here and in America or the EU. I mean, we can see signs of attitudinal change, surely relative to the worst days of the religious extremism, but we need more role models."

Deena cocked her head slightly. "You have a plan?"

"Thoughts more than a plan, but you have to be on board. The press has been getting more interested in why Ahmad and Rachel sacrificed their lives. It is self-interest for them, most of them. Listen, there is a human-interest story here that we can use. I will tell it openly and honestly. Think about Malala and all she has been able to do by being shot while going to school in Pakistan."

"You want to use Ahmad's memory for publicity? Is that what you suggest?"

Shahed looked Azita in the eyes without flinching. "I want to ensure that his sacrifice means something. I talked with Julianna, I mean Jules, Chris's friend. She wants to play up this story with the American media. We can advance our cause so much, and Jules has media contacts everywhere. Think about the possibilities, he left behind his wife and the child he will never see. As crass as it sounds, this is the way to reach all those people who would care less about girls in what they consider backwater places in the world."

"And keep me, us, here, right?" Suddenly, Azita burst with an emotion seldom displayed. "I'm not a child, damn it. I can figure things out. This is a way to keep me from going back."

"Everything is not about you," Shahed shot back, her own temper breaking through her normal calm.

"But this is. I can see it now. This is typical Chris. He won't let me go back but he cannot stop me, so you have come up with this charade."

Deena put a hand on her sister's arm. "Zita, please . . ."

Azita pulled her arm away. "No, you just want to exploit Ahmad's memory and me as the grieving pregnant widow. It is good stuff, guaranteed to bring tears to people as they drink their pints and eat their fish and chips. And then, in a while, you can drag me out with my big belly, that will make some great photo ops."

"Stop it," Shahed shouted rising from her seat. "Think for a moment, just think. You have a Fatwa on your head, both of you, at least that is what we are told."

Tears now flowed down Azita's cheeks. "Any stupid Mullah can issue one of those. They can just bugger off. I am not backing down. Do you think Ahmad would want that?"

"Yes, I do." The words came from her sister. "I know he would, until the baby is born, for sure."

"You're all ganging up on me." Azita's eyes flared with anger as she spun on her sibling. "There won't be a baby. I will end that soon enough. What use will I be for your publicity thing then?" With that she spun and left the room, slamming the door behind her.

There was a long silence. "Well," Shahed finally said, "I probably could have handled that better. By the way, was she serious about aborting the baby? Would she?"

Deena seemed far away. "I don't know. I can't get through her pain right now, maybe because I've never loved someone as she has." Deena looked directly into Shahed's eyes.

"Go talk to your sister."

Deena did not move, merely continued to stare into Ali's brown eyes which narrowed imperceptibly with concern. "Listen, Deena, there is something I need to say . . . maybe I should have said it some time ago." Ali briefly looked at her hands before resuming. "I'm not a lesbian. Maybe I didn't have to say . . ."

"But I never . . ."

"No, Deena, you never . . . I know that. But I can see what is in your eyes. I've been approached by men of course, but also by several women over the years. I can see it coming. Better to make things clear with those I'm working with."

"Of course, I understand. And you were right, the thought was there."

"And to answer the question you never asked, why no man, or woman? Good question. I've been attracted, yes, I have. Maybe my standards are too high. When I've calculated the pros and cons, I always concluded that a relationship would take too much out of me, take me away from my life's work. You must realize that men are hardly worth the bother, surely you do. Women are more difficult to turn away but still. Does that make sense?"

Deena cocked her head as she did when experiencing a small epiphany. "Yes, yes it does. Now I better go and have my sister yell at me, she rather likes that, it will calm her down. And by the will of Allah, she will have that baby even if I must beat her to a bloody pulp to make her think straight. I want a niece or nephew."

* * *

Charles Crawford Senior took his place in a comfortable chair. He hated Las Vegas, the shallowness of it, the crass and superficial glitz it represented. But it was a place to make money and he had made his share by investing in the unending greed sought by those seeking the 'big score' amidst all the glamor. How stupid could these people be, he would think. On rare occasions during a business visit, he might stroll through the casino floor, aware of all the tricks used to keep the victims playing a losing game. Those obsessed with the slot machines fascinated him the most. He would watch them as they continuously fed money into these mechanisms and then stare at the columns as they spun to a stop. Their eyes seemed glazed, unseeing. That stare was interrupted only by the occasional win that merely fed their desperate need to part with more of their money. In the end, the house always won. So many fools but that is exactly what made him and his co-conspirators so wealthy. Only those who ran the games won in the end. It was like the gold prospectors of old. Those panning the streams mostly left with little or nothing. Those who profited greatly were those supplying liquor, women, and other supplies to the desperate men.

Charles gazed out the expansive window at the light bejeweled city blinking below. He barely listened to the other men who filled this penthouse office. Their small talk was inevitably transactional, how they had employed their wiles to increase their wealth. He wondered if any of them had any relationships with anything other than money. He could not imagine that any had a real human attachment. Sometimes that caught him up, the loneliness in his life. For he was alone, no family. There were business associates, of course, and those who identified with his ideological obsessions. But those were utilitarian relations. Was there anyone who wanted to be with him? He searched his mind and came up with no one.

A rotund man in his eighties spoke in a way that indicated they were about to get serious. "It is always a pleasure to get together with like-minded gentlemen. You know, the resources we command. Just us in this room would exceed the GDP of some rather large countries. Quite an accomplishment, considering where I started, where some of you started." The man looked directly at Charles who basked in the indirect praise. "But we all know full well that it is one thing to accumulate wealth and power, another thing to keep it. We all know that, or we would not be here. We are here to remain up-to-date on where we are and . . ."

"To get to keep more of our money." Came from a voice to appreciative laughter.

"Of course," the octogenarian said. "We all know the old saw . . . you have to spend money to make money. So true, we sometimes must spend some to keep more. The 2017 tax bill by itself justified Trump, no matter how crazy he is. But yes, I do expect you to open your wallets. We want a billion-dollar war chest at the start of the serious campaigning, and we can only fleece the little guy for so much. But let's start with something John here wants to say, something that is bothering him."

The younger man cleared his throat. "There's been more talk recently about this Corona virus or Covid-19 or whatever you call it. I've been talking to financial types in Asia. This is serious, they say. People I trust say the eggheads may be right and this could disrupt everything. Of course, as we all know, one man's disaster is another's opportunity. If we do have this pandemic thing, the short-term pain might be offset by some longer-term benefits. Can you imagine the money to be made if we had the rights to a vaccine? Well, that will be way more likely if we keep the goddamn Democrats from power. Those morons will go on and on about the public good. Shit, we have over population to begin with. A pandemic might just weed out the unnecessary flotsam of society."

"Hear, hear!" Another voice was heard.

"Like I said, all will be easier if our boy stays in power. Who's he going to turn to if the economy goes into the crapper? He won't try any silly jobs program or infrastructure repair scheme. Hell no, he will help us out by priming the pump with even more tax cuts and corporate bailouts. I wish he wasn't such a loose cannon, but he does have his uses."

"That's the problem, he is not totally our boy and he's way more than just a loose cannon. He's dumber than a sack of rocks," Charles said.

"True, but he has our instincts. He won't be swayed by some bullshit liberal nonsense." This observation came from a tall, angular man with a sharp face. "But here is what I worry about. We all agree that 'it's the economy, stupid,' right? If the average guy can pay the rent and watch football on the weekend, he could care about anything else. Sure, those Bolshevik academic types can write their papers about the 1 percent getting richer and richer but the asshole scrapping by in his 1,000 square foot apartment isn't reading that shit. He cares more about the liberals helping some niggers by giving them stuff with his tax dollars than he is about paying his own rent. In the end, that's what he cannot stand, the fact that others will get something. The average working-class white stiff only wants to keep ahead of those closest to him in the economic struggle to survive. Heaven help us if they ever figure things out and cooperate with one another. We're fucked then."

Charles winced at the language. He was not above employing colorful language but not in ordinary conversation. Did these men think it made them sound tough? Hardly, Charles thought, it made them sound juvenile. "Listen to me," Charles asserted in his deep, commanding voice, "I'll tell you exactly what is going to happen. There is a good chance that we will see another Spanish Flu type thing. You know that Bill Gates has been harping about this for years now. I hate his politics, but he is no dummy. Unfortunately, our boy may have great instincts that we appreciate and can use but he won't listen to people who know anything. He will revert to form by trying to bluster through this."

"Meaning?"

"He'll yell and deny and try to bully his way through the crisis as the body count mounts. And when the bodies pile up too high, he'll blame the Chinese or Obama or whomever his Evangelical nutcase supporters have picked out that week . . . gays probably. But here's the thing. The economy may well tank. We could easily see a double-digit drop in GDP and unemployment above 10 percent. Think about that, gentlemen. That is Trump's ace in the hole—the economy. If he doesn't have that, what does he have? No wall, no deficit reduction, Obamacare still hanging on, what does he have? Pure hate can only take him so far."

"We'd be screwed," the octogenarian who convened the meeting interjected.

"You would think so, wouldn't you?"

"You have a plan, don't you?" The angular man smiled.

"Gentlemen, I always have a plan. Life is little more than a complex chess game. The key is to think several moves ahead, be strategic. That's how we amassed our fortunes, and how we will keep our treasures."

An older man with a bald head asked. "And your plan?"

Charles leaned back in his chair. He did not want to reveal too much but enough to keep these potential allies interested. He might need their money. "Let me talk in hypotheticals. Let us say that all transpires as we say it might. Pandemic and a tanking economy and a scared electorate. What is our fallback position, what is always our default position?" He looked around as everyone looked on without expression.

"We're not in school here," someone said with more than a hint of exasperation.

"Gentlemen, I am disappointed. Race. Tribe. That ultimate sense of belonging."

"You mean appeal to racism," came a voice from the other side of the room. "I am not a racist."

"Don't be naïve, Harold. I was on some of your corporate boards. I never saw a black or brown face in the room. Just listen to me. If things go south, a primal instinct takes over—fear and the need to survive. We can shower the unwashed with benefits to tie them over but there are too many of them, it costs too much, and the longer-term consequences are catastrophic. How many trillions of debt do you want on the public ledger? We never managed to fully turn back the new deal, just slow it down for the most part. What we need if things get sketchy for Donald is civil unrest, and I mean real civil unrest. Then Donald can ride into a second term as the restorer of law and order, but only if he can keep it together long enough."

"Sounds a lot like 1930s Germany to me, disorder and battles in the streets. Total chaos. My father worked with Hitler, he had stories," one of two brothers in the room added.

"Exactly," Charles said with conviction, not being sure where the last speaker was heading.

"And you can dial this up?"

Charles smiled. "It's is not that easy, of course. I've been in contact with people whom you really do not want to know. They would be scum to us but share some of our, let's say, convictions. They, in turn, know others who have friends in law enforcement around the country. Let us say there were a few outrageous incidents around the country where negroes were killed by the police, unarmed and innocent men. If Donald has accomplished one thing, he has stoked tribal hatreds. It wouldn't take much, a lit match shall we say, to set the fires burning. We then have the perfect scenario, an easy target for all our anxieties and a hero to save the day. I thought immigrants might do the trick but who knew how complacent and sympathy invoking they would be. Those damn toddlers in cages screwed that one for us."

"I'm not seeing it." The octogenarian pondered. "How can you be sure of the unrest?"

"Oh, for Christ's sake, you don't leave such things to chance. You have people in place who make sure there is chaos and destruction in the streets. A firebomb here and there, some police overreaction, and the game is on. It won't take much to give an excuse to bring in troops, declare martial law, or whatever it is called."

The angular man yet looked puzzled. "And how exactly are you getting cops? I think that's what you are implying . . . to kill innocent blacks."

Again, Charles smiled. "Well, you first have to find some that believe as you do. That is not hard, not hard at all. Then, you merely need to convince them to put up with some inconvenience until the Donald is reelected. In a second term, the law will be what we say it is. They will be pardoned and rewarded. And by the way, you will be expected to pony up for what all this will cost. Revolution does not come on the cheap."

"And if all this fails . . . if he doesn't win? We cannot have that. Don't forget, he has made a lot of mistakes and I don't think the Russians will be as effective this time."

"Oh please." Charles now sounded a bit exasperated. "By the time we get through manipulating things, people will be convinced that democracy is a sham. There is no way he is leaving the White House. No way, for sure if Ginsburg croaks and we get to pack the court!"

* * *

In another penthouse office suite, another group was meeting. Kat, Jules, and Ricky casually sat around with drinks they felt well-deserved at the end of another day's labor in the respective worlds. They were not often together. Ricky too often was off on business trips for the Crawford family financial empire and Jules was occupied with her network assignments. These respites when all were in town were precious occasions to both reminisce and to take stock. Kat embraced such moments with her husband and sister-in-law. They seemed to make up for vague regrets recalled from her childhood where Ricky and Jules would visit her older brother. To the young Katerina, they seemed exciting, exotic, and slightly taboo. She instinctively understood that her domineering father was most displeased and her mother uneasy. But their visits gave her a connection to a world she would not otherwise have seen. Perhaps that was the source of her own path away from the doctrines imposed by the patriarch. Now, so many years later, it was difficult to recapture youthful epiphanies.

"So," Jules was saying, "what is the latest intelligence on the machinations of the evil one? I need more dirt."

Kat pointed at her sister-in-law in a teasing fashion. "Hey, I don't give it away. First, have you heard anything recent from Oxford? You are in contact with Chris more than I am."

"You know why that is," Ricky offered with a sly grin, "she is still carrying a torch for him."

"I am not," Jules huffed. "You are a shit, still a shit that is."

"No sibling squabbles. I can vouch from experience that no one wins," Kat intervened.

"True enough." But she gave her brother the finger as a parting shot. "The best news is that Amar really has recovered quite quickly, though there is lingering damage. Given who she is, though, she is back doing her healing magic, at least part-time. Great therapy for her. Azita has privileges so she is working alongside her mother in the hospital while working on her big project. Chris still worries that she is a bit depressed, but everyone is hopeful she'll keep the baby."

"Was she really considering aborting the fetus?" Ricky seemed surprised.

"Apparently, but that may have passed, at least she hasn't done it yet. Right now, Amar, Azita, and Kay increasingly are worried about this Covid thing. It suddenly is breaking out in Europe, big time in the Mediterranean area like Italy and Spain but also in the poor, migrant communities of England. It's an all-hands-on-deck-thing. That will keep everyone occupied but the big battle is still ahead . . . will she and Deena go back to their homeland. Chris is convinced they are targets and is beside himself. But other than tying her down, what can he do? She is aflame with a passion to reach girls who are not as fortunate as they are, as is Deena. Wow, I love them both."

Ricky endorsed his sister's comment. "They are inspirations for sure. I'm reminded of a famous Ben Franklin saying, *Justice will not be served until those who are unaffected are as outraged as those who are.*"

Jules looked at her brother with an amazed expression. "My word, and I thought you never studied anything but numbers in school. As I remember it, I had to explain to you what black power meant."

"Shows how little you know of your big brother."

Kat seemed thoughtful. "Why I chose not to have kids. If they are not always squabbling like infants, they are off somewhere getting into trouble. How can you worry about saving the world when you are consumed with those so close to you? Speaking of those close to you, mother is coming by."

"Great," Jules and Ricky said simultaneously.

"Yeah, she wants to share something about Father, but wouldn't tell me over the phone. From what I am told, he is off in Vegas meeting with those of the 1 percent with whom I share nothing other than a skill for making money. They clearly are plotting the triumph of Trump."

"How do you keep tabs on his doings?' Jules asked.

"Sorry, my dear. If I told you I would have to kill you and you are the one member of the Jackson clan that I adore."

"She ain't kidding about that," Ricky observed with a grin.

"Let's just say that I have people on the inside of his world, not as close as I would like, not like Beverly was until the SOB . . . well, you know. But listen, what really worries me is that he apparently has been in touch with the armed crazies, the Aryan Nation, and the like. I've thought about it. I think he is thinking ahead, contingency planning for the possibility of the Trump bid to stay in power going awry. Father thinks he is too close now, he will never permit his plans to evaporate now, never. He would bring the country down first."

"Isn't that just a bit paranoid?" Ricky tried.

"No, not in the least," Kat affirmed. "You didn't grow up with him. He will stop at nothing."

"I smell a story here." Jules leaned forward.

"Exactly why you are here, other than the fact that I like you better than your brother." She ignored the finger Ricky sent in her direction. "I've redirected the staff Chris hired when he was here from mining data to convincing people that Trump is destroying the country to now tracking what the whack jobs are doing. We also are beginning to help folks like Steve Schmidt, Rick Wilson, and George Conway at the Lincoln Project, along with other emerging groups of disaffected Republicans. The thing now is that we need to stay ahead of their game if we can, and hit people emotionally with hard messages, not appeal to reason. Those reformed Republicans are way better than Democrats at that, always have been."

"Wait," Jules seemed concerned, "will your dad figure out that you are the source of stuff that the opposition is using, that I am using in my media reports?"

"Probably."

Jules grimaced. "Isn't that a dangerous game? We should never forget Beverly."

"I'm just saying, if he is connecting with the crazies, he could use them on . . . his own family." Jules was about to continue when a door opened, and a prim woman led a distinguished-looking elderly woman into the room.

"Mother," Kat exclaimed with sincere warmth, "lovely to see you."

After the greetings and usual endearments along with updated information from England, Mary Kelly turned serious. "I've gotten phone calls from Charles, but I never answer them. So, he's sent me a bunch of texts and emails. I've printed some of them out."

"Wait," Kat seemed dubious, "you mastered the technology. You didn't even use email a few months ago."

"Well, a gentleman neighbor helped me out."

"And how friendly are you with this gentleman neighbor, Mother?" Kat could not resist a mischievous grin.

"Get on with you. I can still put you over my knee, young lady."

Jules laughed. "A non-denial denial if I ever heard one."

"Just look at these." Mary tried to get them on track. "Charles talks about being lonely, missing me and the family. He talks about regrets. I don't know what to make of all this. He almost sounds . . . human."

The others passed some of the messages back and forth. Kat finally took a big sigh. "Mother, I'm not sure what you were hoping I would say to all this. I don't believe he has changed at all. Perhaps I am too jaded, but he might just want to use you, get back to your private money or, worse, use you to spy on me and the twins. I'm sorry . . ."

"Oh dear . . . nothing to be sorry for, nothing at all. That's a relief. If he were serious, I might feel a tinge of guilt. You know us Irish Catholics. But you have to remember that I knew he was a total shit long before you."

Kat, Ricky, and Jules looked at each other for a moment before breaking out into raucous laughter. "I love you, Mary," Jules said and hugged the white-haired women.

"Oh, don't make such a fuss." Mary protested. "But, Julianna, you are a dear. My son married very well but he would have done just as well if he had taken you as his wife."

"If I hadn't let him slip away you mean," Jules said but so low that no one heard her.

Mary kept her thoughts on Charles Senior. “It is just so hard to imagine now, but early on my husband had some charm about him. Oh yes, people were drawn to him, and this was before he had real money, of his own that is. Then again, a lot of those, what do you call them . . .”

“Sociopaths,” Kat added.

“Yes, a lot of those can have charm. Trump doesn’t have any, charm that is, but most of them do. We all knew, the money people that is, that Trump was a con man. But he was not even good at that. He had no charm. Just a bully. If his father hadn’t kept bailing him out, he would have had to get a real job, not that he was qualified to do anything. But Charles had the gift when he was young. He could be so charming when I met him. Swept me off my feet. My parents had reservations, but I was in love . . . silly me. And so was he, with my money.”

“Mary, I’ve seen pictures of you as a young woman. You were a heartbreaker,” Jules said.

“Ancient history, but he didn’t care about that. It was only power and money for him. The pretense of caring didn’t even last that long. He just kept getting harder over time, more bitter and angry. It got worse as you, Kat, and the twins did not follow him in life. You were never more than extensions of his will, as I was. He’s never forgiven us, any of us, for betraying him, at least as he sees it. These pleas for help . . . I think they mean just the opposite.”

There was a pause as everyone looked at each other, wondering if they were all thinking the same thing. Ricky spoke, “Personally, I think you are on to something, Mary. Perhaps it is a last chance to regain control of things. Charles must see himself as coming toward the latter part of his life."

"That's putting it too delicately, Richard. He and I are fossils," Mary huffed.

Ricky smiled but then turned pensive. "You know, I seldom really listened to Chris's BS, but for some reason I remember him talking about Richard Feynman, the great physicist. There was a lot of crap about molecular movement and probabilities and entropy I didn't get but one thing stuck. Your position along the arrow of life divides how you look at things, your attitudes. Looking back, you have memories and missed opportunities and regrets and some good things. But forward you have hope and aspiration and dreams and possibilities. But the farther you move along that temporal arrow, you've accumulated more regrets and missed opportunities. There are fewer hopes and aspirations. You get a bit desperate."

"Oh, my god," Kat moaned, "you sound like my brother."

Kat stood and walked to the window. All eyes followed her as she looked out at the Chicago night before spinning around. "But I fear my husband may be on to something. Father may well be comparing what is with what should be in his mind. God, he may be thinking about balancing things in his twisted mind."

They all looked at one another but no one spoke for a long time.

* * *

Chris met with Karen Fisher, Josh Connelly, and Peter Favulli in his university office.

"What?" Josh seemed disappointed. "No Hairy Hare?"

Chris tried to laugh but lightness failed him. "The way I feel right now, maybe I better stay away from pubs, I might take up permanent residence."

"God, I know what you mean." Josh sighed deeply. "Want to know what's funny? Several times a day I want to give a call to Rachel . . . maybe to tell her a joke or because I'm reminded of something from our childhood. Then it hits me . . . I cannot. She's no longer there. For decades I had virtually no contact with her and it hardly mattered. Now that I want to . . . I can't. I think god plays with us just for fun."

"This is not god's fault, its mine." Chris grimaced.

"Enough of that," Karen said with more than a hint of exasperation. "I won't go over all that again. I've got work to do if nothing else." Then she paused and blushed slightly. "Oh buggers, I'm sounding like a shit I suppose, so selfish."

Chris seemed to react momentarily before relaxing. "Ah, my dear, you are what you are, which is good right now, since we need someone no-nonsense to keep things going while some of us mope all day. But, you know, you can't fool me. Behind that tough girl exterior, you have the softest heart of all of us."

"Perhaps, but if I hear any more apologies or whining, I swear I'll rearrange your family jewels so much you'll be looking for sex change operations."

The men around the table looked momentarily taken aback before Chris lightened the mood. "And gentlemen, listen to me carefully, she is just the woman to do that."

When Josh stopped laughing, he added, “God, I know why Chris hired you. If I weren’t married already, I’d snap you up.”

“Good luck with that, Grandpa.” She shot back with a broad grin. “But you are a little long in the tooth for me and besides, I’m on the other team.” Then she looked at him more closely. “But you were probably a catch back in the day.”

Peter Favulli laughed the loudest. “She is a gem, Chris. She would have been a great G-man in my day, they are mostly wimps now. Or maybe a spook for the agency. Yup, I can see that.”

“Spook?” Karen asked suspiciously.

Chris gave Karen a look that said ‘thank you’ as he said, “He means a spy for the CIA, going around covertly taking out threats to the US and before he denies that we ever did that, at least not since our failed attempts at Castro, what are you hearing from your contacts back home?”

“So freaking depressing,” Peter started. “You might have thought with the Mueller investigation and the impeachment stuff on Russian collaboration, that Trump would dial the election interference back. No way, he only knows how to cheat.”

“What have you heard, my friend?” Josh asked.

“My sources don’t know just how the Trump people are involved, but a Ukrainian National, Andrii Derkach, is heading up another version of the IRA.”

“The Irish are involved?” Karen asked incredulously.

“Oops, sorry. I keep falling into old habits of using acronyms. The IRA is the Internet Research Agency which is a Russian troll factory for hacking the Dems and spreading misinformation. They are kicking into high gear now that it is officially election season."

"I don't get it." Chris shook his head. "A normal politician would back off, afraid of the negative publicity given that everyone is on to this scheme, or at least is looking for it."

"Ah, there's the rub. Trump and today's Republicans are not normal. Here's the speculation I hear. Despite everything, all the bad publicity, Trump remains amazingly positive with his base. He has them convinced that all bad news is fake news. He has lost almost no support. But even he knows it will be close, or his people do. His team will pull out all the stops. Being clinically nuts, he doesn't even see this as illegal, it is just business as usual. Like Nixon, he assumes everyone is a crook, so it is okay to lie and cheat."

"I think even Nixon knew he was doing wrong." Josh offered.

Peter shook his head. "Thing is, to feel guilt you need a conscience. Trump is a bona fide sociopath. But that is not the scary thing. He and some of his devoted acolytes are fully prepared to foment a coup to stay in power. A few scare tactics and the need for law and order, you get the picture. If that fails they'll try to get friendly courts to undermine the Constitution. After that, full out insurrection, perhaps martial law. It all starts slowly, with the evisceration of the oversight committees, the packing of the appeals courts. The end game might be made for the movies stuff. More recently, Senator Sasse has brought back the idea of overturning the 17th amendment."

"What?" Karen asked.

Josh answered absentmindedly as he picked up his friend's theme, "The amendment that requires direct election of Senators. We've only been doing that for little more than a century. That would give Trump great control. In the end, you're talking the Nazi takeover in Germany, that's his game plan."

"Everyone thinks so," Peter said, obviously warming up to the topic. "But I have a different take. Yeah, Trump was supposed to have had a copy of Mein Kampf next to his bed but come on, he couldn't read that. No one could. No, my guess is that he is taking a plan out of Putin's playbook. Remember Alexander Litvinenko?"

"Yeah, vaguely," Josh said as he nodded.

"He had been an FSB agent working on corruption. In the later 1990s he started looking at Putin and his buddies. They brought him upon sham charges, but Putin wasn't strong enough yet and he got off. Still, he knew it was a matter of time, so he escaped to London and became a British citizen. He kept up his investigations, writing about things like the assassination of oligarch and Putin enemy, Boris Berezovsky, and the attempted assassination of Anna Politkovsky. But worse, he was uncovering evidence that Putin was behind some bombings in Moscow and other big cities that were being used to vault Putin to uncontested control of the country."

"Now I remember," Chris exclaimed. "They knocked him off, right?"

"Bingo! Putin ordered him taken out, presumably the task being done by FSB agent Andrei Lugoyov. It was all John

LeCarre spy novel stuff, radiation poison hidden in an umbrella that was injected in him in public on a rainy day in London."

"It's always raining in this place. They never got the assassin, though, right?"

"Right. He fled back to Moscow where the Brits couldn't reach him. After that, there has not been an effective opposition. There is one guy, Alexei Navalney. He is going after Putin publicly. My buddies from the Bureau have a pool on which month they get to him."

"Shit," Chris exploded, "this makes sense. Trump loves Putin, of course he would follow his lead. He's probably using the hotline, does that still exist, to chat with Putin about which poisons one might use to knock off your political enemies. But wait, you don't think that Trump really would knock people off in the States, the ones on his enemies list."

"Trump?" Peter mused. "I don't think he's quite there yet, but if things go south on him, who knows. Think about the press, how he vilifies journalists. If I were one of them, I would be updating my will right now. I mean if he gets backed into a corner . . ."

"My guess," Josh piped up, "is that he would use surrogates, or at least his minions would. But I'm a little rusty on American politics."

Chris bolted up. "Josh, if you would, let's collaborate over the next few months. You have every right to say no, with Rachel and all, but I need someone at my side who thinks like me."

Josh smiled. “Hah, no one thinks like you, but I’m glad you asked. I was afraid you were pushing me away, with Rachel and all.”

“And Peter, I have no right to ask this of you, but would you go to Chicago? For one thing, I have people working with my sister on political stuff and you would be a great asset. But, and this is more important, I’m scared shitless for my family. Our father is a true believer and he . . . there is no telling what he might do.”

“Good plan. My wife, Laura is actually missing me though that will last a couple of weeks and then she’ll be giving me honey-do lists, guaranteed to push me out the door again.” Peter reached out and shook his hand. “Besides, I was thinking I wanted to get back to cold beer.”

CHAPTER 19

TOYNBEE HALL

Shahed watched as Kay, Amar, Azita, Deena gathered in her office, along with Cate Connelly and Meena Muhaisin who were last minute additions. "First, I keep thinking about your mother, Cate. I did not get to know Rachel well but understand she was a remarkable woman."

Cate lowered her head slightly. "She was. I'm here . . . well, I feel I want to honor her memory in some way. I think . . ." She struggled to find the right words. "I think she was finding herself in the last weeks of her life. I mean, she had always been a great doc and loved what she did, but I had never seen her so excited as during our last . . . trip." Meena took Cate's hand.

As Cate fell silent, Shahed said softly, "I think I understand totally. No need for explanations. Just so glad you are here. Listen, I've been called by the Warden of Toynbee Hall. His name is the Reverend Professor Luke Geoghegan. He is also a Barnett fellow and spent time in the States some years ago as a Harkness fellow. Good chap, you will like him."

"Yes," Deena added, "Azita and I have been there often. They serve a huge Muslim immigrant population among other poor groups. We need to be working with them, not just identifying talented Muslim girls in oppressive regimes in the Mideast but right here in England. Let us never forget that people take the chains that bind them even as they emigrate. Culture is a powerful thing, more powerful than laws since it imprisons the imagination and the heart."

"Exactly, but let me add something to the agenda, which is why I insisted that Kay and Amar, who is looking so well by the way . . ."

"Thank you," Amar said, "I really had the best of medical help though I yet tire easily."

"Of course, we'll see that you do nothing more than you want to take on, and not even that. But here is what's on my mind. You've probably been seeing the warnings from the WHO and the NHS about this virus. There is no doubt. We have a global pandemic breaking over us."

Kay spoke up, "The official stuff scares me . . . a lot. The unofficial stuff is worse. Whispers are being heard that the highest intelligence services are warning their governments that this can be as bad as 1918 pandemic. Some leaders are listening, some are not, the right-leaning ones are very resistant."

"They're worried about the economic impacts of any response," Shahed said, "but your sources, Kay, seem better than mine."

"Well, Chris and Jules have their uses, both are very well connected as is Kat, my little sister. You have heard us say this before, but we still shake our collective heads at how powerful she has become. I guess the lesson here is to beware the quiet ones."

Amar looked puzzled. "What can you tell us, Kay? I suddenly feel way out of the loop."

"You've been doing what you had to do, rest. But here is the worst of it, Trump knew at the end of January that this would be bad. There is little question on that. He knew and he's been in public denial ever since. What was that one case from China nonsense, or it will disappear like magic one day. Then there was the warm weather will kill it, and bleach is the cure all." Kay had her angry face on. "You can guess why . . . the election."

"Of course," Shahed said, "even I could see that head in the sand . . ."

Kay interrupted. "You mean up his ass, don't you?"

"I'll stick with 'in the sand' reaction . . . my genteel upbringing you know. But Boris is no better, well, everyone is better than Trump. But Boris does not want an economic downturn in the post-Brexit era. Bad for the next election. You can see what will come. Places like China, Japan, and South Korea will stop this scourge. America, us, and places like India won't . . . no real leadership and way too much divisiveness within the population. That can be a bad thing in this situation. Pushing people in strong democracies is always like herding cats but the failure to lead, lying about an impending national and global crisis, is negligent homicide. And I use that phrase advisedly." Anger flashed across Shahed's face to be replaced with a purposeful expression. "Here is my pitch . . . we should help the folk at

Toynbee respond to this thing impending crisis. We can use their infrastructure to help create responsive strategies which I'm hoping you docs can handle. Deena and I can work out the cultural challenges of working with immigrant populations. They do not all trust the NHS or the government in general. And in a pandemic, you cannot have weak points. Thoughts?"

Kay nodded. "I agree about weak points in a pandemic. It is like allowing people to pee in one section of the pool."

Amar tried to suppress a smile as she asked, "Is Karen on board, Carlotta?"

"Yes, it is a go on all counts."

"Is this central to our program?" Azita asked tentatively, doubt finding expression in her voice.

Shahed responded quickly, as if expecting this question, "I've thought hard about that. You know how I got thinking about reaching out to better incorporate those Muslim girls we typically would cast aside as second-class citizens? I'll answer my own question. One day, as a younger scholar, I ran into a quote by Steven Jay Gould, the paleontologist and evolutionary biologist I so admired which said, *I am, somehow, less interested in the weight and convolutions of Einstein's brain than in the near certainty that people of equal talent have lived and died in fields and sweatshops.* You know what struck me about that? Again, I'll answer. We can lose the brightest of the next generation when they are buried by culture or political repression. But we can also lose them when they are left to die because no one tried to save them. That's just the way I feel."

"Isn't that what we were planning to do…" Azita seemed unconvinced.

"Yes and no. We were totally focused oversees. We were missing the challenges at home. This virus has brought that omission home to me at least. Plenty of undiscovered treasures in our own backyard I suspect." Ali offered with conviction.

"I'm with you." Kay affirmed and other heads nodded.

"Great, let me bring Amar and Kay up-to-date on what Toynbee Hall is all about. Great history, really. It was created in 1884 by Samuel Barnett and his wife, Henrietta. He was a vicar in the Church of England, and she was a teacher and social reformer. They were not happy with the piecemeal and individualized approach to helping the vulnerable and sought something more systemic. A bit like Chris in a way, they fixed on a university extension concept where the educated class, like Oxford students, might live among the poor and dispossessed and develop systemic responses to their plight. This was a notion first pushed by Arnold Toynbee, a social reformer who unfortunately died way too young at twenty-nine. In any case, the hope was to generate the seeds of broader social reform. This was in sharp contrast to existing interventions which focused on individual pathologies and stressed personal redemption."

"I take it the place was named after this Arnold Toynbee?" Deena inquired.

Ali continued, "You got it. So, because many of the involved students and scholars spent time at the Hall as residents, it became known as a settlement house. How could you create new methods for addressing poverty and disadvantage or generating new opportunities unless you really knew the target population and lived with them. Wow, there's something most of my Oxford colleagues have forgotten. Few of them get any closer to the poor they purportedly care about than a bunch of secondary data sources. And I'm afraid that numbers can only tell you so much, but you know the game—keep grinding out journal articles. Field work is way too labor intensive."

"But you've managed to do well at Oxford and violate the rules of the academy." Kay addressed Ali with genuine curiosity.

"I'm not naïve. I work hard, this is my life, all of my life." Shahed glanced at Deena as she said this. "But I'm also female, a Muslim, and most importantly, well connected to the Jordanian Royal Family and now the Crawford clan who are also quite generous. With all that diversity and those connections going for me I can be unconventional. I don't have to worry about research grants, and I bring a lot of positive publicity to this crusty institution with the fastest growing demographic in Britain. I make them look as if they care."

Kay chuckled. "Don't you run into resentments from male colleagues?"

"Of course. Feminism runs shallow in these waters. But I have a secret weapon. I just threaten to issue a Fatwa on them, that shut's them up." As soon as the words were out of her mouth, she looked toward Zita and Deena and whispered. "Sorry, that was insensitive."

But Azita smiled. "No, please, it is all right. I found that funny. I might use it myself."

Amar joined in with her own chuckle. “Can I use one of these on my husband?”

“And my brother,” Kay added quickly.

“Back to business.” Shahed took control. “Toynbee Hall proved a success. Others emerged. A few years later, Hull House opened in Chicago and a similar effort was launched in Tokyo in 1901. But what impressed me most about the early history is the famous folk that came through here. Future PM Clement Attlee cut his teeth here as did the great reformer Lord William Beveridge. The good Lord Beveridge, by the way, issued the report toward the end of World War II that created the National Health Service and much of the social safety net we now enjoy. Even more recently, when Tony Blair announced a war on child poverty in the UK, he came to Toynbee to launch it. It is sacred ground.”

Cate responded to the brief history lesson. “Wow. I had heard about Hull House, and Jane Hull, but not Toynbee Hall. Not surprising, we Americans are like the Russians used to be. We either invented something or claim that we invented it. Otherwise, it doesn’t exist.”

Everyone laughed but Kay remained aware that Azita had been quiet throughout. Kay had long felt like more than an aunt to this young woman. In her heart, she loved her as a daughter, often returning in her mind’s eye to those desperate and turbulent days in the Panjshir Valley in 2001 when they feared the Taliban would somehow overcome the final resistance to their complete control of the country. Doctor Pamir Masoud and his family appeared out of nowhere, having made a miraculous journey from Kabul to Kunduz and then, when the moment was right, through the front lines to the Northern Alliance, the *Shura Nazar*. With him were his wife, Madeena, his son, Majeeb, and these two girls, the teenage Deena and the eleven-year-old medical prodigy called Azita. As a male caught up with a sense of obligation, Majeeb went off to fight and die with the Northern Alliance. The Taliban found revenge on what they saw as the treachery of Pamir and Madeena, even as their hold on the country melted away in the military response to 9/11 by the Americans and British. These two fetching girls were left on their own, bright and engaging and alone and yet hopeful. In her heart, Kay wanted to take them away, save them, but that seemed beyond her at the time. Then, magic struck when her brother, a bachelor who never showed the least interest in domesticity married Amar, rescued the girls, and took them back to England where they might thrive. Being their aunt would have to do though she sometimes wondered what had been lost in not having the chance to be their mother.

"Zita," Kay used her familiar name. "What are you thinking?" Kay and Amar had chatted on several occasions since the Kabul incident that the young woman had remained uncommunicative. At first, they assumed it was a reaction to her husband's sudden death. That was understandable. That segued into an agonizing internal debate about the baby inside her. All initially were astounded that she even considered ending the pregnancy. There were talks between sisters and between mother and daughter but the deliberations within Azita's head remained hers alone. No one was permitted deep inside her struggle to find a way through conflicted emotions and divided paths to the future.

"Yes, what are you thinking?" Ali added when Azita remained silent.

After more time had passed absent a response, Deena chimed in. "Will I have to beat you like the Taliban to get a response from you?"

At that, Azita cracked a small smile. "As if you could." Then she cleared her throat. "Yes, I have been struggling inside but already my debate is different. Okay, I may ramble here so be patient. I . . . I had been so surprised by my feelings toward Ahmad. I never thought that any man, except for my sainted father and maybe Chris, could match my expectations for what a man should be, but seldom were. I think that is the curse of growing up with perfect parents—you idealize marriage and relationships. I can still recall being confused when I first felt . . . well, you know. Was this my body, really? How had I lost control of it so?" Then she laughed which relaxed all in the room. Azita was glad there were no males at this meeting.

Kay fought back a sarcastic comment at the mention of her brother while Amar desperately wanted to sweep her daughter into her arms. In the end, neither did anything. Oddly, it was Meena who urged her on. "Go ahead, Zita, you are among people who care and who know that love is never simple."

Something about that statement reached Azita. "You're right. Of course." She went on with more confidence. "In the first few days and weeks after getting back, I was consumed with grief and anger. Yes, I thought ending the pregnancy was an answer. I would not be reminded of Ahmad and what I had lost. And there was this other thing . . ."

"What other thing?" Amar gently asked her.

"Having a child alone seemed overwhelming. I would never be poor and would have all kinds of help but that answered nothing in my head. How could I achieve all that I wanted with this . . . responsibility? Would it drag me down? You see, it was Ahmad that wanted the baby, a baby. He was paternal while I . . . just wanted to please him in the end. Does that make sense?" Instinctively, she looked directly at Shahed as she finished.

The silence became excruciating as the moments ticked on. Finally, Shahed leaned forward. "If I had a euro for every time I was asked about marriage and children, especially from my large family, I would not need to toil away in the university." Then she chuckled. "Somewhere early on, I had your struggle, Azita. Could I be a wife and mother and do all the things in life that I wanted, no needed, to do? I chose the monastic route. Was it worth it? Was it necessary?" Shahed then looked away and it was clear nothing more would be offered.

Azita asked in a whisper. "Well?" Then immediately continued. "No, don't answer. No one can answer for my heart." Azita stood and walked to the window overlooking the green quadrangle below. "I remember when life was easy, though I didn't know it at the time. I would walk across those green spaces concerned with anatomy or chemistry or some such thing. That all seems like a fairy tale now." She swung around toward the group. "I'm keeping the baby. I made that decision some time ago. I kept my counsel until I was sure. But what I worried about has come to pass. As this pandemic has unfolded I keep thinking, should I get involved? Can I risk getting infected? I now must be concerned about more than myself. I was tying myself into knots, even this morning. I wanted to run away . . . I . . . but no, that stops now. No running. Life is risk. Period." She took a deep breathe.

Amar said tentatively. "Dear, no one would . . ."

But Azita cut her off. "No, I really know what I must do. Yes, I have decided. I am with you. I back down from nothing."

At that, Amar rose, crossed the room, and enveloped her daughter in an embrace. She did not agree with her daughter's decision to put herself in harm's way during the pregnancy, but she would respect it.

* * *

Toynbee Hall was located on Commercial Street in the East End of London. When this fine Victorian building was erected, this area of the city was known as Whitechapel, a name better known for being the hunting ground of Jack the Ripper. Then, it was a haven for prostitution, crime, disease, and despair. Things had improved over the 135 years since the Hall went into business, but the area remained a refuge for those settling to the bottom of the social and economic heap.

The Reverend Professor Luke Geoghegan met the contingent as it arrived. The first thing he insisted was that they call him Luke, no Reverend and certainly no Professor even though he taught an occasional course at Kings College-London. His eyes seem to twinkle with mirth. His olive colored complexion and jet-black hair suggested that he was not of pure Anglo-Saxon stock. When Kay checked on his background, she found that his father had been Irish and his mother from India. Though of modest beginnings, he himself had spent time on the British dole to get by some rough patches in life. He managed to get a degree from Durham University, later undertaking religious studies to become a minister in the Church of England, and a social reformer of some repute. He had also done his homework. When introduced to Azita, he went out of his way to mention that he had spent six months at the University of Wisconsin as a Harkness fellow, where she had done her internship in pediatric medicine.

When the preliminary introductions were over, they gathered around a conference table and got down to work. Luke had prepared a power point presentation where he flashed several slides up on the screen. Some focused on where the immigrant populations were spatially located in the area. Other graphs located where the Covid cases were erupting, where hospitalizations were on the rise, and the seriousness of cases. The storyline was apparent, the virus spared no one, but the poor and those marginalized from the greater society were disproportionately at risk.

As he finished his slides, he segued into a short speech. The storyline is obvious. The virus is hitting the poor hard. They are more concentrated, are in occupations where working from home is not an option and are less likely to be responsive to government public health announcements, either because of literacy issues or suspicions of all things governmental. When they do get sick they sometimes are reluctant to get medical help for a variety of reasons and surely cannot afford options outside the NHS. Have you seen the projections from Neil Ferguson, the epidemiologist?"

"Yes," Kay nodded, "Chris knows him well, so I've been in touch."

"He puts what they call the preliminary R-naught rate above 1, especially in the densely populated urban areas. That means it will spread fast and the government will have to do a general lockdown. Boris is bad but not as dumb as Trump, he will do something to respond."

"My question is, how can we help?" Amar asked.

At this, Luke's face lit up. "In so many ways. The resources of the NHS will be stretched for sure. We need people to go into hot spots to do testing, basic instruction in wearing masks and hygiene, telling people the symptoms to look out for, and encouraging them to trust the authorities. And we need people to communicate with community leaders who can pass the word on, communicate in their own language. Many of these people need to trust the messenger."

Suddenly, Cate brightened. "I was wondering what I might do here. But now I see. All my work in the Foreign Service in the Mideast, my linguistic training in college and the Mideast. I can help here."

Luke's eyes twinkled once again. "That was obvious to me. Here's the challenge. We have volunteers, we've always had them. But mostly they have focused on parenting, education, job training, and things related to combating social exclusion. We never focused much on health since we relied on the NHS for that. And maybe we were lazy in the past. We let too many people come to us. Now we will have to go to them, out into the neighborhoods and the homes. We might not be able to use the social infrastructure we used in the past, like the schools and community centers. Those are likely to be shut down or the crowds severely limited."

Kay spoke, "Well, we've been in tough spots before in some tough neighborhoods around the world. I'm thinking we can do this and be creative in how we do it."

"And careful," Amar added, looking directly at Azita.

* * *

Later, Deena, Azita, Cate, and Meena were driving back to Oxford, reflecting on the day and the tour of the East end they had taken after their meetings. They would be back after the weekend to kick things into gear. They were reflective for a while, not saying much as they worked to clear out of the city. It was not as difficult as expected as many businesses were already closed. The virus was taking its commercial toll.

Deena, who was driving, noticed the change. "Wow, I thought we would still be stuck in traffic. I guess there is always a silver lining to these things."

"There is a silver lining for Chris and Amar," Azita said with a hint of irritation.

"What do you mean?" Deena asked as alarm bells sounded inside her.

"Isn't it clear, Bahiri and Ferhana, as well as Archie and Agnes get to go back to Afghanistan this very weekend. It will kill me to say goodbye to them not knowing when I'll see them again."

"I am glad we'll be back in time for their going away party tonight," Cate said brightly.

"Now Chris has a wonderful excuse to keep me here. It is just convenient for him," Azita continued, ignoring Cate's attempt at lightness.

Deena was fully exasperated. "Cate and Meena, let me explain something about my sister here. If you are going to work with her closely, this is something you need to know. Yes, she is exceptionally talented. At the same time, she rather thinks the sun rises and sets over her sainted presence. Oh yes, I am sure that God said that Chris needed an excuse to keep Azita safe, so he unleashed a global pandemic on the world. Anyone besides my self-absorbed sister buy that?"

"Oh, I am so sure you were adopted." Azita glared at her sister. "No one as mean as you could have come from my parents."

"Okay," Meena yelled, "everyone just calm down. Cate here is an only child. She has always thought that a disadvantage. I've always thought it a blessing, no one to point out all your faults. I have several siblings so I can tell you about familial torture from personal experience."

"But I do have Meena here to point out all my faults," Cate snuck in.

Meena guffawed. "Hah, I'll let that bit of humor slide. In some ways I feel like an outsider here. Think about it. I did not lose a mother. I did not lose a husband. And I can go back to my homeland any time I want. So, what do I know of the pain and loss you feel? Azita and Deena, I can only sense what loss you have faced from afar, what you are struggling with. I can guess but I do not know, not really. But with Cate, it is as personal and raw as it gets. When you love someone, you absorb their pain. She has been brave in public but at night, in the privacy of our room, I hear her crying. There is nothing, nothing worse than witnessing the pain of a loved one knowing there is nothing you can do."

"You're wrong," Cate said.

"What?"

"You are wrong about not being able to do anything," Cate said with slow words. "True, it is the most difficult at night, lying in bed in the dark. That is when the regrets sneak back in, when the reality of loss is most present. For me, I keep thinking of this opportunity I thought I had to work with Mom. She never really saw me as an adult. I had her on this pedestal, never thinking that I measured up to this gal from a working-class family who worked her way to the top. No matter what she said, I felt I never lived up to what . . . oh, you don't need to hear that broken record. But if she could see me working with people, using my language skills, that's what I was good at. She would really be proud of me."

"Oh, silly girl. I saw how she looked at you. No mother was prouder. But I'm still not sure about how I was wrong?" Meena asked.

"You said there was nothing you can do. Really. At night, when the loss feels unbearable, I sense your presence next to me, feel your touch. You have no idea what that means."

They rode in silence for a bit. Deena broke the silence. "My god, Zita, why do we fight so often? It is like we are children again, driving everyone around us to distraction with our incessant squabbling."

"I know, I know," Azita said with sincerity. "If you had just admitted that I was always right, everything would have been perfect."

Nothing was said for several seconds before Deena pulled the car abruptly into a parking lot at the side of the road. When the car came to a stop she turned to her sister. "You really are such a shit." With that, she threw her arms around Azita's neck and embraced her. "Let me say this one more time just in case you missed it the previous hundred. I am so sorry about Ahmad. You cannot imagine the hollowness inside me. And in case you are too dense to figure out why I hurt so much, it is because he brought you such joy and completion. I never thought you would find someone good enough. I never thought there was anyone good enough. Can you believe that? It is true. I never thought there would be anyone good enough for someone like you. And why did we fight? Because you were and are special. Our parents saw that, people in the community, everyone saw that. Worst of all, I saw that."

"Oh Deena, don't be such a sot, that's such rubbish. We are simply different, that is all. And you never thought that I was jealous of your beauty, how everyone fawned over you?"

"Oh posh," Deena protested, "there are lots of pretty girls but few geniuses. Besides, you grew into rather a beauty yourself."

"Aha," Azita yelled as if in triumph, "you are admitting that I was the ugly duckling as a child . . ."

Cate interrupted from the back seat. "That's it. I can see where this is going. So, let me say two things. First, everyone has something they would change. But we have one thing going for us that no one else has."

"And that is?" Meena asked.

"Each other, silly. We have each other. I'm thinking the four of us will become good friends, just a hunch on my part."

"I agree," Deena said with emphasis. "And your second point."

"That we are needed here for the time being, to fight the pandemic among people we care about. There will come a time when we must go back into harm's way and, when that time comes, we will go together. Agreed?" Cate looked at Azita.

After a pause that seemed too long for Cate, Azita spoke, "Yes, I agree. I do agree. I meant it back at Toynbee when I said I was fully in. Let us not forget. We don't have to go back to Afghanistan to be in harm's way. I am so aware of that now." She looked at her stomach which she rubbed. Everyone understood.

Deena started the car again. "Let's keep going. We don't want to miss the party."

PART IV

THE END GAME

CHAPTER 20

BEGINNING OF THE END

Ricky Jackson's voice was a welcome relief to Chris. With the pandemic now operating in full force, travel seemed unwise and he missed the banter the two had shared for several decades now. They both thrived on insults. Chris had long thought that this was a male thing. Women did not seem capable of going for the jugular unless they meant it, which they did often enough. Mostly, though, females shared actual information, much of it on their relationships which Chris's thought tedious in the extreme. To his amazement, those of the female persuasion spent a disproportionate amount of time complimenting one another, at least to each other's face. What was with that?

Men were different. They skewered one another verbally with the ease associated with an ordinary greeting. It was a habit born on the school playgrounds which followed them through life. The one-upmanship omnipresent on the streets was a world that a boy either mastered or was, at best, condemned to coruscating ridicule and social oblivion. You could never show that the other guy had gotten to you, a clever retort was your best defense. If you showed hurt, it was over. You might as well surrender your balls to all the other guys on the block. You were finished.

True, Chris thought, the women around him cut him no slack but it was a form of gentle jesting, lacking the bite he most associated with his closer male companions, yet still capable of emasculating him whenever his hubris threatened to break out into the open. His siblings certainly were good at the art of verbal jousting. He wondered why he had been so unlucky. But then he thought about it more deeply. While there was nothing he could do about his siblings, the other females in his life were there by choice, his choice. The women to whom he responded favorably had always been the ones that could go toe-to-toe with him. He quickly grew bored with the others, those that were nice to him. He remembered a series of women early in his life who tried to seduce him with feminine wiles. Being a man, he permitted himself to be bedded by a few who played the coquettish card but inevitably regretted that weakness by the following morning at the latest. Wit, intelligence, and a bit of spunk, or quite a bit of spunk, were what he wanted.

He looked forward to this conversation with his oldest male friend. "Ricky, my boy, screwed up any international financial deals yet this morning?" Chris started.

"Listen, not a social call, something's come up." Ricky's voice was no nonsense.

"Go ahead." Chris straightened in his chair. They always started out conversations with a few insults, so this business first dance caught his attention.

"We've had an incident." He paused but started again before Chris could wrap his head about the serious tone. "Kat's in the hospital. Don't panic, she will be fine. They said she'll be released later today most likely. It's the circumstances that worry me the most."

"Which are?" Chris prompted at another pause.

"As I often do, I stopped in the lobby to get her favorite high-octane Starbucks. She thrives on caffeine and finds the office stuff rather weak. She took a couple of sips but then got so caught up in a business call that it got cold. As I went to check up on some Asian market numbers, I threw what remained out, thinking I'd send someone to get more. A few minutes later, there were sounds from her office. She was bent over with pain. Clearly, it was serious, and I called 911. The docs say it was poison, but they are not sure which one yet. And the cops have been grilling me since everyone knows I brought her the coffee. Maybe it came from somewhere else, but we can't come up with an alternative scenario. It also looks bad that I threw out the coffee and the cup, like I was getting rid of evidence."

"Wait, how would they get poison into the drink?"

"I've been racking my brain and trying to come up with coherent answers for Chicago's finest. You know they always suspect the husband, especially when he is black. Anyway, the folk behind the counter were the usual workers but I suppose one of them could be bought."

"Bought by my Father?" Chris's brain was focusing on the obvious.

"Who else? The more I think on it, the more possible that sounds. I heard my name called indicating the drinks were ready, but I was on a call. It was a couple of minutes before I retrieved them."

"Enough time for someone to spike her drink but how would they know which one? You seem okay."

"I drank all of mine, I'm fine. But anyone familiar with our routine would know she has the fancy crap while I have straight caffeine."

Thoughts continued to race through Chris's head. "Did you notice anyone hanging around the counter?"

"Sure, more than one. But everyone was wearing a face mask, all in suits. I wasn't paying any fucking attention to them. It wasn't like I was saying to myself . . . this is the morning they'll go after my wife."

"Easy buddy. We're all stressed here."

"Yeah, sorry. Thing is, if Kat had not been distracted, if she had drunk all of it . . . the docs said she might be gone. Anyways, the cops asked me the same damn questions over and over. I could tell they didn't believe me. I wanted to scream at them that I would have come up with better answers if I had really done it. In fact, I may have called one a moronic cretin."

"Way to go, you idiot. You can't blame them I suppose. They always suspect those closest to the victim, no matter their color. Don't you watch any of those true crime shows? There are a million of them on these days."

"I know, I know," Ricky protested, "but you are not black. "Sometimes I just feel myself tightening up. I can see them looking at me saying, *who is this nigger in the $2,000 dollar suit trying to act like a white man.* I see it in their eyes, they just want to bring me down."

"Okay, I'm sorry. I can never be in your skin, never. Still, hell if I will visit you in the slammer just because you pissed them off. Just be smart here, buddy."

Chris could hear Ricky's voice lighten a bit. "This helps, talking to you, and you can imagine how much I hate admitting that. But the whole situation is worrisome, it feels like an escalation. Perhaps your father is panicking with the economy tanking and the Trump people panicking. Could that be it?"

"That's what I'm thinking. The problem is that the top cops know about the family feud. When we tried to get them to look at Father for my sister-in-law's suspicious death, they just thought we were out for revenge. Not sure they will take our suspicions seriously. Get Peter Favulli on this. This is precisely why I sent him back."

"Way ahead of you. He's the first guy I called. He is already consulting with our security. And Chris?"

"Yeah?"

"You be careful. What we have long feared might be starting."

* * *

A week after his conversation with Ricky, Josh popped his head into his office to ask if he could borrow Chris's car. They went through their usual banter where Chris expressed doubt about Josh's ability to navigate driving on the wrong side of the road and why hadn't he gotten his own vehicle by now. But, in the end, he threw the keys to his new friend and made his typical joke about not paying for any speeding tickets. In truth, it was Chris who drove fast and racked up the traffic violations. He had come a long way from his early days when he preferred to be driven in London traffic by a native. Now he drove like a native himself and like a certifiable maniac. Josh, being wary as a newcomer to a stick shift and British driving habits, was a cautious driver, often going below posted limits.

Chris still remembered well that moment when he noticed several calls from Karen, Carlotta, and Connie. He had missed them since it was his habit to mute the phone when deep in serious writing. It was either that or stay up at night to find the solace he desired. He was about to call one of them back when his phone now rang, and Carlotta's name popped up. He answered to hear her say something like *thank god* before she breathlessly told him that she would pick him up in a few minutes. Josh was in the hospital, a car crash. She said more but his mind went blank.

All the way, his heart was in his throat. He pumped Carlotta but all she could say is that it could have been worse. The car was rather totaled, but the driver would survive. Josh would *survive,* what did that mean? It still sounded ominous. What if he were crippled or in a coma or . . . all kinds of terrible fates crossed his mind. How could he have let his guard down. He had grown fond of Josh in such a short time. He also had found his sister, Rachel, quite fascinating, but she was taken in that Kabul incident before he really could get to know her. Why did he still call it an incident? It was a devastating act of terrorism.

Josh was a kindred spirit, the brother he never had. He had loved his older brother, Chuck, but they were different people. There was little to bond them together other than a mutual disgust with their father. Worse, he saw himself as the destroyer of the Connelly clan, first Rachel and now Joshua. Who's next, Cate? Would he wipe them all out? Maybe even the lovely Meena, or Connie, Josh's wife, who made it to England when her university research permitted it. Why spare any of them. He hated himself for looking up Josh. How could he know that reaching out would result in such evil consequences? Then again, how could he not know. There was a curse on him, the family. They were paying a price for sins about which he was unaware. Maybe those are the worse kind.

By the time they made it to the hospital, he found Josh awake and talkative, and surrounded by his wife and niece, along with Karen. They all looked relieved that Carlotta had tracked him down. When she first had trouble, bad thoughts about multiple targets crossed their minds. They were passed thinking this was just an unfortunate accident. On seeing him, Josh managed a weak smile but clearly was suffering from injuries that required two casts, one on an arm and another on a foot, and bandages to cover facial wounds.

"Afraid I ruined your Jag." He managed to say with a grimace.

Chris, relieved that it was not his worst fear, tried to be light. "Last time I let you borrow my car."

But Karen flashed him her famous "shut the fuck up" glare. "This is serious. The brakes failed but he was going slow. If he had made it to the M system, who knows. And if you had been driving, we'd be planning your wake right now."

"The brakes failed my ass?" Suddenly it swept over him. He should have been driving. He would have going like a bat out of hell. He was the target. "What happened, Josh?"

"Again, sorry about your car."

"Screw the car. Just fill me in on everything that happened." Chris already had his dark speculations. Still, he was looking for an affirmation of his suspicions.

"I should have stopped right away. But I was on my way to Cambridge to see an old student who teaches there. I was extremely excited about it." He paused as if something was bothering him.

"Perhaps we should let him rest," Cate said.

"No, no. Let me say just this. I sensed the brakes were soft from the start, but I thought maybe they were always like that since I don't drive fancy cars. I was thinking about stopping to check them out when I approached one of those roundabouts. I sped up a bit to get into the traffic flow when I realized I had no brakes at all. I think I swerved out of my lane and got hit by an adjacent car in such a way that I flipped over. Next thing, I was looking up at rescue workers. There was nothing I could do, really."

"Josh, you just rest, okay. Don't worry about the stupid car."

"Kay and Azita are on the way. They were at Toynbee," Karen offered.

"See, you will soon be in the best of hands. My sister and daughter would torture me, but they will baby you and make sure you get the best of help. You rest now, see you later."

When they left the emergency room, a nurse said that a detective from Scotland Yard wished to speak with them. Chris preempted the British cop by first saying, "The brakes were sabotaged, weren't they?"

"Detective Inspector Reynolds, sir. You are Professor Crawford, I presume. I have seen your picture in the media. And yes, that is what it looks like from a cursory inspection at the scene. We'll look more carefully but, at this point, we are thinking attempted murder. You do not seem surprised. Can we speak in private?" When they found a private area, the detective continued, "I have two big questions. Was Mr. Connelly the target and who might have wanted him dead?"

"You'll find that the car is registered to me, Josh just borrowed it. I am sure I was the target, and the most likely perp is my father, though not directly. Though, to be fair, it could be an Islamic extremist. I've upset a few people through my activities."

"Yes," he said deliberately. "So I gather, so I gather."

* * *

One of the rooms in Chris's Oxford home became facetiously known as the recovery room. Kay and Amar now treated Josh when they were about. His head injury was a bit more severe than originally thought and took a while to fully heal. The headaches persisted. In addition, his broken bones slowed him up a bit though he was soon up and about. His Irish wit remained, however, and people would gather in his room at night where

Azita and Deena would discuss their work in the immigrant slums of East London, sometimes being joined by Amar. Chris sometimes would sit in on these sessions to learn what his adopted daughters were doing. Eventually, they stopped talking about themselves and got Josh talking about his own life, especially his younger days before he fled the United States for Canada to escape the war and his apparent destiny.

Deena and Azita resonated to the story of his flight and the challenges that ensued. There were so many differences between their stories and yet, for some reason, the girls could relate to this man who might be their grandfather. They could relate to the twinkle in his eyes and the soft intelligence and kindness of his voice. He came across as a man at peace with himself and his life. The loss of his sister remained a savage disruption to his emotional equanimity, but he managed not to let it overwhelm him. His wife would sit as the girls elicited stories about fighting on the side of the angels during America's ill-fated war in Vietnam, breaking the law and stealing money from the Irish mafia to support their juvenile revolutionary efforts. To them, he remained a romantic figure fighting for peace and justice. His wife would sometimes smile and roll her eyes when she thought his embellishments a bit much. At the same time, losing him would have been unbearable for her.

The two girls were quite taken with his flight from America as a young man, what they would call his Hegira. They shared some of their own Hegira moments when the family fled from Kabul and the clutches of the Taliban. For Josh, his own journey north was a frigid ride in a poorly heated VW bug to Canada. The cost was not in blood but in torn relationships, philosophical conflict, and emotional trauma. The two girls seemed to understand both the differences and the connections. These evening discussions led to a form of bonding that tied all more closely.

One evening, when the usual crowd had been thinned out by other duties, only Azita, Deena, Cate and Meena were there for the evening visit with Josh. They all seemed subdued. Not even the quick wit of their Irish hero could perk them up. When a few of his best witticisms fell flat he knew something was wrong.

"What's up?" he asked. "I can't get you gals to smile tonight. I have always been able to get women to laugh, usually at me but still."

The four looked at each other. It was Cate that spoke up. "I'm going to say something. You can yell at me later, but the others need to know." She looked around but took silence as permission to continue. "Azita and Deena have been getting death threats."

"What? From whom? Wait, of course you don't know. Tell me all."

Azita sighed and reached into her blouse to pull out two letters. She looked at them as if she did not believe their reality but, assured that they were not a figment of her imagination, handed them over to her new friend. "It's probably nothing."

Josh looked at each in turn. Letters had been cut from magazines to create short messages:

A Fatwa has been declared upon you. Make your peace now!

In the second:

Your days are numbered. Prepare to meet Allah's judgment!

Deena also tried to be nonchalant. "Threats are nothing to us. So many have opposed our work. It is something we must live with."

Suddenly, Josh was totally serious, the twinkle in his eyes were gone. "You've got to tell Chris and the others."

"No," Azita said forcefully. "He, they, have enough to worry about. Deena and I have talked about this. It is not serious; of that we are certain. Just some more cranks."

Josh could feel his Irish temper rising. "Cranks? Cranks? Haven't you been paying attention? My sister and your husband are blown to bits with Amar seriously injured. Someone tries to poison Chris's sister. And I am almost done in though the real target undoubtedly was Chris. And you are dismissing this as a couple of crank letters. What in god's name are you thinking?"

"Thank you, Josh, that's what I've been trying to bat into their brains." Cate issued these words with obvious relief. "And the other thing, there's more than these two. There are six that I know of, and I might not have been told except I came across one of these at Toynbee Hall. Then they had to tell me."

Josh sat up in his chair. He wished he could easily rise to his full height but that was too much effort. "I'm going to try to remain calm here. But we are telling everyone, the police for sure, and Chris, and maybe the Prime Minister and the Queen and perhaps God himself. Already you have screwed up by just handling the letters. There might have been DNA or fingerprints or whatever. But that's not the point."

"What is the point?" Deena immediately realized she sounded defensive if not a bit petulant and ridiculous.

"I'll tell you the point, young lady. It is not up to us to figure out what is a real and what is not a real threat. I mean, really, what if houses in your neighborhood were burning down night after night. What would you do if you saw smoke coming from your house . . . stand around debating whether it was a real fire or not? Is that what you would do?"

"But Chris and Amar will make such a fuss," Azita tried.

"Really, that is your big worry, that the two people who love you more than anything might make a fuss. Well, just think about the fuss they will make when they put toe tags on you in the morgue." When Azita blanched, Josh realized he may have gone a bit far. He went on in a lower voice. "Are you going to tell them? Because if you don't, I will, and you can hate me all you want."

Deena sighed. "No, no, you are right. I think sometimes we deny reality."

Cate let out a small clap. "Oh, thank God. This has been killing me, but we were getting so close as friends and I didn't want to jeopardize that by breaking a confidence."

Josh leaned back in his chair. "This has been good for me, an epiphany that one needs to experience every once in a while."

"You lost me," Cate said quizzically.

"Easy enough. Every once in a while I revisit my decision not to have children. I think that maybe it would not have been so bad. I mean, it always seemed like such a huge responsibility and I never thought I had the right stuff to be a parent."

"Oh, that is silly," it was Meena adding her voice.

"No, no. I was convinced of that when I was young, that I would hate being a father and bad at it to boot. But I had begun to second-guess myself recently. However, this brings the wisdom of my initial decision home to me."

"What are you talking about?" Cate looked at him dubiously.

"The thing is that you so easily fall in love with some young people, sentiments that I suspect possesses even more force when they are part of your family." He looked at the four women around him. "And you realize to lose any of them would completely destroy whatever remains of your heart. I am not sure I'm strong enough to bear that. My god, I've only known you for weeks and . . . I'll just say that I shudder at what might be in front of us."

* * *

Peter Favulli was always surprised when Chris Crawford answered his own phone. He was used to important people being protected by layers of gatekeepers. Of course, Chris insisted he was not an important person, but Peter had seen enough of him in the media, including television, to scoff at his weak attempts at self-deprecation. Peter often marveled at the similarities between Chris and his childhood friend, Josh Connelly. Though about a generation apart in age, they had so many similarities—the same sense of humor, the quick wit, the eclectic minds, and an inquisitive approach to life. He hated to admit this but perhaps there was this thing about Celtic charm, a traitorous thought that a full-blooded Italian like himself could never admit in public.

"Damn Chris, you always catch me off guard when you answer the phone."

"I don't understand," Chris chuckled, "it is my number. Whom did you expect to answer my phone, the freaking queen?"

"I expect voice mail or, more likely, some lackey."

Chris grunted. "Hell, I asked my wife early on if she would perform lackey services for me and all she did was knee me in the family jewels."

At that, Peter laughed out loud. "Oh man, you should have married an Italian lass or, better yet, gotten one of those mail order brides from the Philippines."

"Yeah, well, talk about bait and switch. I got mine from India, they were supposed to service their men well. Hah! But enough about our troubles with women, I assume you are calling because you have something to report." Chris adopted his business tone.

"That I have. First, after the mysterious poisoning, I suggested a more obvious security detail. But she and Ricky will have nothing to do with that. They will permit me and another retiree from the agency to check out things. They are not totally absent the self-preservation instinct."

Chris made an unintelligible sound before speaking clearly. "I think I know what's going on. Kat and Kay, no matter how badly Father treated them in the past, cannot believe that this asshole would do them bodily harm. While he hates all of us . . . his enemies as he sees it . . . females are hardly worth his bother.

Then again, to be bested by the weaker sex might psyche him up even more."

"Ah yes, which brings me to another matter." Peter sounded deadly serious now. "Part of my paranoia pushed me to check out the obvious things, like the cars used by the obvious targets."

"Did you find a bomb under Kat's car? I worry about that."

Peter kept his monotone. "No, no, nothing so Hollywood-ish. But I did find a GPS tracker under Jules's car."

"A tracker?" Chris was not expecting that.

"By the way, she still likes you. And I don't mind saying, if I were twenty years younger and single . . . well, she is hot."

"Simmer down, Romeo. What do you make of the tracker?"

"It's obvious. Your father, our most likely perp, is doing basic surveillance, wants to keep tabs on what the enemy is up to. You guys are the enemy, by the way."

Chris let out a reluctant grunt. "And brilliance like that is why you G-men got the big bucks."

"Hah, wish I had gotten paid as well back then as you're paying me now. But I was a dedicated public servant." Then Peter segued both in tone and content. "Here is my take, or at least one possible take on things. These things that have been happening might only be intended to scare, not to kill."

"Really, I don't buy it. What if Kat had drunk all the coffee, or I had been driving my car. And the bomb in Kabul, that device was completely intended to kill."

"Oh no, the bomb was a real terrorist act, no doubt. The guys behind that were Islamic extremists. But the other events might have been intended to plant fear in you. Right? We don't know how much poison was in Kat's coffee since it was thrown out. Maybe it was just intended to sicken her. And cut brakes, not a certain way to kill someone. In fact, very sloppy for a hit. Cops will figure it out and your odds of a fatality are less than 50-50, except if a mad man is driving."

"Exactly, like me."

"I'm just giving you my professional judgment here. For the sake of argument, let us say that the guy behind all this is your father, except for Kabul. I'm thinking that he wants to see what he can achieve with scare tactics before escalating things. I mean, really, doesn't that make sense?"

"Sure," Chris scoffed, "if we were talking about a human being. But we're not. We are talking about a sociopath, an animal. But then again, perhaps I'm not objective here."

"You think?" Peter tried not to sound too sarcastic. "Anyway, think about that. In the meantime, I've got some promising news. I've had my buddy keeping tabs on your father. At some point, it hit us that he uses the same driver all the time. Okay, why not try to connect with this guy. It's a long shot but so isn't getting a bug in his place that won't be discovered. That could be worse since you might get disinformation."

"My head is beginning to spin but go ahead."

"It goes like this. You find his favorite watering hole, sidle up to him in the bar, and strike up a casual conversation. You talk sports, agree that the Packers suck the big one and, once he is relaxed, mention that you have seen him chauffeuring this rich guy. What's that like . . . blah, blah, blah. At that point, you play off where he is. If he thinks his employer walks on water, tough going but money might work. If he thinks he is a schmuck, you've got a good chance of reeling him in."

"And?"

"Bingo. The guy's name is Rogers but it's not. It is Rodriguez. However, he changed his name to fit better with the elite. His family was from Mexico, but you could never tell. He's been here a long time. And he despises your dad for reasons you can well imagine. Drivers get great insights and info from their employers. They are with them a lot and their bosses relax about them. Everyone needs someone to vent with and apparently your dad doesn't have anyone close. That's how we got one of the mob bosses in New York, through his driver."

"No shit."

Peter went on. "I'm serious. Some of my agency buddies brought down a major mafia family head in New York by getting to his driver. The boss thought the car was safe and would talk freely with his driver about whacking this guy and that guy. But they had bugged the car and the boss treated his driver like a son, was very free with him. You couldn't make this stuff up."

"And Rogers . . . or Rodriguez?"

"He's in. Will wear a wire and all. He has a family, so I promised him some of your money. Hope you don't mind."

"No problem, I'll just ask Kat for a raise." Chris chuckled.

"Damn, you are lucky."

"What do you mean, Peter? I can barely sleep at night worrying about everyone around me."

"Okay, you've got a point there. But you can go to your sister for a bottomless source of money. I've got three sisters. The best one off financially is married to a guy with a trash hauling business on Long Island and I'm 90 percent sure he is mobbed up. Anyway, what's next?"

"Well, I think I'm going to call Kat and Jules and try to scare the crap out of them."

Peter laughed out loud. "Good luck with that."

"Hey, a little respect here. I can be very persuasive." Chris tried.

"I'm sure you can, but we're talking about smart, tough broads here. You, my friend, are toast."

CHAPTER 21

ESCALATION

Peter Favulli felt useful again. He had recruited several retired colleagues to help with security work on behalf of the Crawford family in Chicago. He liked the thought of working with a team again, as he had done throughout his career. Almost immediately, he wondered if he needed more men. Perhaps this assignment eventually would encompass those attached to the Crawford clan who were operating in England as well, though getting the kind of people he would want in another country might be tricky. Still, he had contacts in the UK. He had found the recruiting process less onerous than he had supposed, retirees often were bored and missed the old life.

His wife and children, however, were not thrilled with this retirement choice. It did keep him out of the house, which was a good thing in his wife's view. However, she had visions of lazing away their golden years on a beach somewhere while his offspring worried more about his safety, just as they had when they were children and yet old enough to realize he had a dangerous job. He kept the specifics of what he was doing from them, sharing only that a filthy rich family had hired him to provide private security. Easy money and no risks, he lied to his loved ones. At the worst, it was work involving the usual financial espionage. You know the filthy rich, they are paranoid that someone will steal their secrets and, worse, their money. This is like taking money from children, he assured all in his family who would listen. No one, however, totally believed him.

His deception worked well enough until one of his daughters who had followed him into the agency as a career choice did some digging herself. *Financial espionage my ass,* she yelled at him over the phone, *this is the damn family that is one bad hair day away from killing each other outright. Hell, the old man in this made for Netflix mini-series is suspected of financially supporting a bunch of right-wing whack jobs.* Peter had no good response. He merely asked her to keep this secret and reminded her how close he was to Josh. *The guy who dodged the draft and beat several felonies as a minor-league terrorist,* she responded with frustration. *You could do better in the friend department. You just can't give up the life, I know it.* Then Peter heard his daughter grunt in frustration and the phone click. He had been about to tell her that she would be the same one day.

She would keep his secret, that he knew. She was part of the agency and members of that fraternity had a kind of loyalty that went deep, as deep as blood connections in some cases. Someday he would explain his connection to Josh more completely. He would tell her that he was the guy who ran him down from behind on the five-yard line as time ran out in the championship football game their junior year in high school. Her father was this close to being a hero in the Italian community, but it was not to be. He was still a hero, he guessed, just not a legend. However, his athletic shortcoming led to an off-field connection that deepened the following year when Josh unintentionally crippled another player and walked away from football and a likely scholarship to Notre Dame. His respect and connection with him deepened. This kid was more than a Mick who could play football, much more. He would explain that to his daughter someday. And all that anti-war stuff. Someday he would tell his daughter just how close he came to following the same path.

He was sitting in a stakeout of a staff member of Charles Senior, the man who drove him around town and served as bodyguards and daily companion. His new relationship with James Rogers, aka Jesus Rodriguez, was paying off. When he and Rogers met in the watering hole that had become their meeting place, Peter was told to keep tabs on a beefy guy named John Stokowski, a hulking former football player who ran to 6' 5" and upwards of 280 pounds, with a bald head and a jowly face. Rogers was certain that this hulk was a courier of some sort with some unbelievably bad guys who looked an awful lot like poster boys for the Aryan Nation. Then again, there were a lot of whackos running around the streets these days and many of them looked like character actors straight out of central casting.

The election of Obama in 2008 had inflamed the paranoia of that portion of the nation dedicated to the proposition that the white race were God's chosen people. All others were suspect, including Southern Italians and other Mediterranean types, depending on who was sharing their well-honed prejudices. When Peter was first with the agency, these groups were a nuisance but not a threat. Presumed danger then came from the left. That began to change after the 1980 election. The neo-liberal revolution brought in by Reagan resulted in a massive transfer of wealth to those at the top of the economic pyramid. Whereas the elite had garnered less than 10 percent of the pie in 1979, it's share had grown to almost a quarter of a larger pie by the time that a black man occupied the White House, a black President whose major social reform was to extend health coverage to more Americans. That happened just before the Republicans surged back into control of Congress howling with rage that most Americans might finally secure a benefit that every other advanced nation provided as a right of citizenship. The economic elite soon found they could keep those they were fleecing distracted by fanning historic racial and ethnic animosities. It was like taking candy from babies.

A perfect storm had been brewing in recent years. Guns had always been plentiful, but now the 2nd Amendment had been twisted to consider a well-regulated militia to be any gang of thugs who rode motorcycles and felt they needed an AR-15 for security whenever they ventured out in public. In recent years, they would brandish their military grade weapons as they purchased their favorite perfumed hair conditioner in Walgreens. At the same time, economic opportunities for those without higher degrees had disappeared, moving oversees where labor was cheaper. It was an outmigration abetted by Republican backed legislation that eased the creation of dummy corporations and tax havens. The greatest insult of all was the taxation of income for the privileged at lower rates than those imposed on ordinary working stiffs. Often, hedge fund managers who might count their annual take in the tens of millions, paid proportionately less than schoolteachers. Somehow, the working white stiffs missed all that, tending to blame liberals and nigger-lovers for their economic struggles. That was the easy target sold to them by fat cats who laughed all the way to the bank.

Peter would shake his head. How could those stiffs not notice they were being hosed big time by the very people they flocked to vote for on election day? It never seemed to matter that policy under Republican Congressional control favored those who needed the least help but got the most. Unions were eviscerated, tax breaks mostly helped the top 1 percent, pay rates for average Americans stalled or fell even as the productivity of average workers continued to rise dramatically, and the safety net kept fraying at the edges. If the purpose of American economic and social policy were, by conscious design, to create an anxious, desperate, and vulnerable workforce, one could not have done a better job. Young whites without college degrees looked to the future with increasing anxiety, and with good reason. Even those with degrees often started out burdened by crushing debt and anxieties about what lay ahead.

Even back when Peter went one direction and Josh took a more radical route, he knew there was justification in the path his good friend had taken. Peter was simply more effective at suppressing and compartmentalizing his doubts about the system he served. Later, he would think back to what he had seen. For two generations, huge proportions of black males were systemically disenfranchised by punitive sentencing for crimes more likely to be committed by those of color, by the abuse of discretion at every turn of the so-called Justice system, and by the impoverishment of services and educational systems in poor and minority neighborhoods. Even the hero of the black community, Bill Clinton, supported sentencing reforms that served to warehouse African American prisoners for atrociously long sentences. Soon, the US had 25 percent of all incarcerated citizens, disproportionately minorities, despite having only 4 percent of the world's population. The country had become one large Gulag. Toward the end of his career, Peter would joke to himself when he met a young black agent and law school graduate . . . *how did this one escape our efforts to destroy the black community?*

Nixon and his jackals knew what they were doing. They were countering what they saw as the sinister effects of expanding voting rights to minorities. The founding fathers implicitly intended to keep power among white and privileged males. Slowly, that eroded and by the voting rights acts of the 1960s, white dominance at the polls faced a legitimate threat. When incarceration and the consequent eradication of voting rights had reached its feasible limits, and the fiscal costs of institutionally warehousing much of an entire racial group were better appreciated, access to the polls was more directly attacked. Gerrymandering and new hurdles to voting were imposed in those states controlled by Republicans. And it worked, Peter mused.

Peter saw all this happening over the years, but he never had Josh's courage to fight back. After all, he had a wife and a family and a career that he loved in many ways. But he did fight back in one way. When his colleagues pushed to go after this radical college student who likely committed a series of felonies in opposition to the war, Peter found some way to thwart their efforts. He would do what he could to protect Josh despite his qualms. Eventually, delay became neglect, and neglect fell victim to the statute of limitations. So what if a few draft offices were burned down. It was a stupid war to begin with, he just hoped that Josh's crimes were no worse than property crimes. He would never look too closely.

Now, with the incendiary language of a Donald Trump, white grievance melded with bleak prospects for most in America. Peter thought how fortunate he was that he was retired, not required to serve under a President who so tarnished the highest office in the land. But what amazed him so was how many Americans could be manipulated so easily and pay such a high price for their gullibility. Forget about a decaying infrastructure and a fraying safety net or soaring national debt that will cripple our children for generations to come. Who cares about a planet burning up to an uninhabitable cinder, or environmental destruction that cannot be repaired, or the outrageous abuse of public lands once held in trust as they were sold off for private gain?

All that pales next to what most average Americans care about—money. Since the mid-1970s, some $50 trillion dollars had been shifted from the bulk of hardworking folk into the hands of the economic elite absent any significant protest. It has been the greatest heist in history. And Joe Six-Pack did not seem to care. Inexplicably, he rather applauded his own economic rape. The elite could always distract the white working class by pointing out that they were, by definition, better than the black or brown man they saw on the streets. White working-class schmucks, it pained Peter to see, sold out their futures for the illusion of psychological superiority . . . the worst deal imaginable.

Peter broke out of his reverie. Wow, he thought. If he had seen the future back in the 1960s, as Josh apparently had, he would have jumped on that revolutionary bandwagon. He came close but he never did, or not with sufficient clarity and commitment at least. The lure of a good career and family and future was too promising to forfeit for some vague sense of political righteousness. Moreover, the economy still served the middle class, the rape of American workers would not begin for another decade or so. Besides, they were all kids, really. What made them think they were smarter than the adults who ran the world? Now Josh could look at that question from the perspective of adulthood and a career working amidst those very adults who ran things. For some reason, an epiphany washed over him in that moment. Sure, there were some good and competent people in high places but so many were fools who could barely tie their own shoelaces unaided. He recalled his early days in the agency when he looked forward to meeting those people who made the world run. Late in his career, he was still searching for them.

That was not it, Peter told himself as he mused about his life choices early on. It was not that he took the easy road. His lingering discomfort was a matter of torn loyalties and a world about him that offered only ambiguous choices. Both he and Josh were grounded in a Catholic ethic that told them to do the right thing, that compassion toward others and seeking the moral high ground was the highest virtue. Those were not common sentiments in their respective cultures, but it was the peculiar strain of Catholicism which they had embraced unlike so many of their peers. It helped bring them together as friends. Josh focused on such ideals with a clarity Peter never found. He was torn by an inherent loyalty to country and culture that he could not quite shake back then.

Suddenly, Peter noticed a familiar car come into view. As it passed, he saw the driver glance quickly in his direction and nod. That must mean he wants to chat again, Peter told himself. He would have to get to the watering hole tonight. Time to switch to diet cokes since the beers were not helping his battle of the bulge. But now the task at hand. He turned on a remote sound detecting device he had brought. He knew there were better technological options, but this is what he had on hand. The patrician of the Crawford clan emerged from the back seat and shook hands with the beefy-looking biker. It was a comical scene to Peter. One man looked as if he had just stepped out of Forbes magazine, tall and slim with silver hair while impeccably groomed and dressed. The other seemed perfect for the cover of *Biker Illustrated* with a black leather jacket, scraggly facial hair, shaved head, and chains draped over his torso. Peter was sure that man was well armed.

After a few minutes, Peter kicked himself for not going out of his way to get the better technology he needed. Rodriguez obviously had been told to stay in the car as the two men walked about a parking lot talking. A stiff breeze created even more distortion. Perhaps he could get more when he had a chance to listen to the recording, and when the tech wizards could eliminate some background noise. He doubted it, however. What he heard were scattered phrases such as *fifty thousand dollars now and . . . after it is done.* Later, there were words indicating a timeline and then something that fascinated Peter. *What about your contacts abroad, are they on board?* Then Peter's heart sank, were they talking about England? *Everything you need is in this packet.* An envelope was handed over to the biker model. Then the word *destroy.* Destroy what, the envelope? Peter was left worried and unsatisfied. Perhaps Rodriguez had more information for him.

* * *

Peter saw the driver as soon as he entered their set meeting place. He wondered if he should be switching locations every so often or if that might be excessively paranoid. A suspicious nature had come with his years in the agency but not everyone was a super sleuth. James Bond was, in the end, mere fiction. The decision to succumb to complete paranoia could wait.

"How are things going?" The driver asked as Peter joined him in a booth where they might have some privacy.

"Pretty good," Peter responded, "still vertical and taking nourishment."

"That I can see." The driver glanced toward Peter's expanding middle.

"Opened myself for that one. And you?"

"Okay." Then the driver went directly to the point. The longer they were together, the more likely a wrong person would see them. "Did you hear the conversation?"

"Some, but the ambient noise gave me problems. I did figure out that something is going down, the details and cash were in the package that Charles Senior gave to the biker guy. I followed this character after, but he just went to some bar and met up with his cronies. Looked to me as if nothing more would happen on this day at least. Can you fill me in?"

"Wish I could. I tried to prompt the old man by asking if things went well and even took a bit of a risk by noting that these biker guys didn't look like his usual business partners."

"Ooh, be careful," Peter warned.

"I keep it light, never push. Then again, I never get much back. He talks a lot. I think he's lonely. His words, though, are never terribly coherent. You know, it is like he is talking to himself and yet manages to keep his real secrets to himself. Damn frustrating."

"What do you remember?"

"Mostly phrases and bits that might be part of a longer conversation he's having with himself. Stuff like *I gave them plenty of chances* then silence followed by *no one would blame me given how I was provoked* and later *and I had such hopes but the betrayal, the betrayal.* I asked him who had betrayed him. But he merely looked at me as if he were just realizing I was there or that he was talking out loud. Then he gave me that look that told me it was none of my damn business."

Peter took a sip of his beer, his prior decision to switch to diet coke already forgotten. "Really, be careful. Don't make him suspicious. I was told that his daughter-in-law died under mysterious circumstances. Others in the family are convinced that this harmless-looking old man had her killed because she was spying for the kids. That really spiked my own paranoia."

Rodriguez whistled. "Did not know that. When I go to work for someone, maybe I should ask for a resume, like asking for where the bodies are buried."

"Let me try this. If I were to speculate that he was planning to knock off more of his own family, would you tell me I was bat-shit crazy?"

The driver paused, sipped his own beer, and then responded. "I would tell you that you were crazy if you did not think that. Once you get beyond that surface charm, he is a scary dude . . . real scary."

"I think that is what's happening. Trump's falling prospects are pushing him to the edge. He may have gone around the bend already."

"Now, that could be," the driver said with emphasis. "He does go on about politics. Why in god's name he thinks I agree with him is a puzzle, perhaps just because I don't look or sound Latino at all. Using an alias, Rogers rather than Rodriguez, got me in his door. So, he never holds back with me about politics and I just nod at all the shit he spews forth. Sometimes I'll give him a *got that right.* He goes on this rant about protecting the real America and how close they are to taking over. This election will decide all. But more recently, he is getting worried. I can tell that, real worried. But I've been wondering, something I've been noodling."

"What?" Peter prompted him when he hesitated.

"Ah, there is a gal who works as a domestic for him. She's from South America somewhere and real cute so I've been cozying up to her."

"Thought you were married and had three kids." Peter immediately wished he had not said that.

"True enough but, at the end of the day, I'm a guy. But what's important is that I think she dislikes the SOB even more than I do. And she hears everything, or more than I do at least. Like I said, the guy strikes me as lonely, no one is close to him. He has what he calls associates, people who think like he does or are obsessed with power and money like he is. But people he can talk to, be open with, he's got nada there. So, I think when he is rattling around that penthouse place of his, he talks to her. I'm not even sure he realizes she understands and speaks English. Turns out he does speak a bit of Spanish."

"Why in the world would he hire a Latina?" Peter was confused.

Rodriguez laughed. "You haven't seen her. Anyway, he just talks or that's what she told me. I'm going to push her to listen more carefully."

"Rodriguez, I hope you understand that I'm not asking you to do this."

"Got it, and I hope you understand that I can't stand this asshole. And neither can Martina, that's her name, no alias even. You should hear what he says about our former countrymen, all immigrants in fact. Revolting. She's only working with him now because she wants to help me."

"I can well imagine. Trump followers are like a cult and I think Charles Senior is a Hitler wannabe or the Jim Jones character. I worry about this Martina woman."

"Jones?"

Peter realized he had been obtuse. "The cult leader who had 900 followers drink the poisoned Kool Aide in Guyana."

"Right." Rodriguez nodded his head as if sharing that concern. "Oh, and one more thing he said in the car. Maybe you can make sense of it. It was something like *and they thought they were safe by getting out of the country. Like that will work.* Then he laughed."

Peter stared at the man across from him. He knew exactly what that meant.

* * *

Kat looked at her older brother on a computer screen. She thought he looked worn and a bit older. What bothered her most was that the twinkle in his eyes had been extinguished. He had always sustained the twinkle, his wit, even when experiencing the bumps in life. Now, he seemed worn down. "You look like shit."

"Why thank you, dear, and may I compliment you on your fresh as a daisy looks."

"Fair enough, but I only say that because I care. You do realize that."

Chris smiled wanly. "I thought keeping my family in England would ease my worries. No such luck. With the Covid thing now hitting England as bad as America, it is now so clear that stupid, conservative asshats cannot manage a paper bag, never mind a pandemic. I now think my people would be safer in Afghanistan. Kay is working mostly in a hospital with patients, but Amar and Azita and even Deena have been working out of this Toynbee Hall in East London. They are out among the poorest of the poor, trying to change behaviors and nip things in the bud."

Kat tried to lighten him up. "You are surrounded by strong women who are willing to take risks for their beliefs. You would not have it any other way."

"Try me," he shouted back. "Just try me. Do you remember when I was a dissolute young man? Maybe not since you were rather young then. But my biggest worry was how to dump my latest female conquest without her taking a contract out on my life. That depraved lifestyle is looking mighty attractive to me right now."

"Bull . . . shit." She separated the two words for emphasis. "You love your family."

"Maybe so, but love can be way overrated. What they never tell you is how painful it is, how much worry and concern it dumps on your miserable existence. They ought to put a disclaimer on all those match sites for the lonely. Something like finding a soulmate comes with serious side effects such as insomnia, heartburn, and occasional bouts of diarrhea."

"Yeah, yeah, but I've got important stuff to talk about, which does not include listening to your whining. That friend of yours, or friend of a friend, you sent to us really knows his stuff. He's beginning to develop contacts with people on the inside. Father's driver will even wear a wire."

"Yeah, Peter has been a lifelong friend of Josh Connelly. He's a good man, but we know that spying on Father has its risks."

"He knows that. He is a pro after all. But here's the thing. Peter is convinced that Father is losing it, he might be planning something bad. He may have set something in motion."

"Damn, Kat, you be careful. They never identified any poison when you got sick, but I must think it was an attempt on your life. And you are important to me just in case you've forgotten."

"Why thank you," Kat replied with a bit of emotion.

"After all, you are keeping me rich enough to live in the style to which I'm entitled so I kind of want you around."

"Sure, asshole, and I love you too," She gave him the middle finger through cyberspace, a gesture which ended when Ricky stuck his head into the screen shot and kissed his wife.

"Hey, bro, how's things on the other side of the pond?"

"Same as on your side, screwed beyond belief by our illustrious leaders." Chris smiled broadly at his lifelong friend. "At least our Boris is not mentally unstable, he just has values that suck."

"Lucky you." Ricky laughed. "Maybe I'll steal the corporate jet and come over to see you. Gotta run now, though."

"Where's he off to?" Chris asked his sister after Ricky disappeared.

"Oh, some meeting." She shrugged.

"Does he go alone? No security?"

"Do you walk across the Oxford campus with armed bodyguards?" Kat retorted.

"No, but we're far away from our maniac Father."

"Right, as if geographical distance is going to make any difference. He hates you most of all," Kat said with deadly seriousness.

"What do you mean?" Chris retorted. "You're the one that engineered the hostile takeover of his financial empire. Since he has no freaking heart, that hurt him where it counts the most . . . his wallet. "

Kat paused just a moment looking for a response. "I do agree with you on the no-heart thing, but you wounded his ego. You have to admit he has the ego the size of an elephant."

"Me?"

Kat scoffed at her brother's reluctance to embrace the obvious. "Come on, don't play dumb. Just think about it. After Chuck, you were the male heir. We girls did not count. You were the one he kept trying to pull back in. He never came to me, never."

"That's because he knew how stubborn you were, how hopeless it would be to go after you," Chris tried.

"Hah, you're the most Irish of us all, you stubborn Mick. This is a man possessed. He'll go after you no matter where you are. We have stepped things up here, had more sweeps for bugs, put in more surveillance cameras, hired more security. I've brought our mother to live with me though she is spitting mad at being treated like child, as she puts it."

For a few minutes more they continued discussing things they had done and should be doing when Kat suddenly looked around. "What the hell was that?" A moment later, she shrieked, "Oh no!"

Then she was gone from the screen as Chris yelled his sister's name repeatedly to no avail.

CHAPTER 22

REFLECTIONS

Kay, Chris, Azita, and Deena were seated in Kat's corporate jet that had been sent to bring them back to the States. It had taken a short discussion to convince Chris's adoptive children to leave their work. They were terribly sorry about Ricky, whom they found charming and full of interesting stories of Chris as a young man. More than anything, Chris was close to him so he must be a good man. Still, they were not sure why they were going, were not they outsiders to a private tragedy? That debate ended when Kat called personally to say how much she wanted them in Chicago and what type of strings she had to pull to get them cleared during the international flight impediments. Amar would stay behind to look after the children and manage the Toynbee project in their absence.

For some time after take-off, none spoke, each lost in their own thoughts as the land disappeared under the cloud cover that inevitably covered England at this time of year. Soon enough, the heavy mist gradually broke to reveal intermittent sightings of dappled sunlight on the endless waters of the Atlantic Ocean. Kay broke the silence to everyone's relief. "Any further word from the authorities or Peter?"

"Peter got the FBI involved immediately. The explosion destroyed several cars in that area of the parking garage. It was a big device, no one situated anywhere near Ricky's car would escape. It was immediately seen as a terrorist incident even though no group took responsibility. Shit, we told them who was responsible. No secret there. They recalled Beverly's so-called suspicious suicide after Kat reminded them. When we tried to convince the authorities that was murder, they humored us and simply went through the motions. We did get the coroner to list her death as undetermined but eventually the case went cold. I just don't think they want to tangle with Father, he is too powerful and wealthy. It was easier for them to employ their usual tunnel vision—this is just a family feud that has devolved into intense paranoia. Our obsession with Beverly was nuts in their view. The woman was distraught and killed herself, end of story."

Kay grimaced at her brother. "Well, it didn't really help when you tried to strangle Father at Beverly's services."

Chris rolled his eyes. "Thanks for reminding me. Yeah, that Celtic temper of mine. The thing is, they now have evidence that there also was a bomb under Kat's car, even though she seldom used the thing. That might account for the widespread damage and the other victims. An innocent man walking to his car also was killed instantly. A couple an aisle away were wounded, the woman later succumbed. Kat felt the tremor way up in her penthouse. In any case, Kat is beside herself with grief and guilt."

Kay wanted to change the subject suddenly but was driven by curiosity, the need to understand. "I could see Father going after Kat but why Ricky? It looks as if he didn't care who he got."

"Putting something under her car made little sense. She never uses it; a service takes her about town when she needs to go out. But Ricky drives himself often, drove himself . . ." Chris stumbled on the correct verb tense. "And why him? To get at me. I'm sure of it."

"Don't go there, Chris."

His gaze swung toward his sister; her eyes were filled with fury. "There's no way to avoid this. It's the proverbial elephant. That SOB knew how much Ricky meant to me, how far back we go. He probably blames Ricky and Jules for me going rogue on him. Getting him was a way of hitting back at me and Kat. He knew that . . . you can be sure of that."

"And you don't think Ricky's death affected me? Let me tell you . . ."

"I'm sorry, sorry." Chris cut his sister off. "I'm self-absorbed as usual."

At that moment, Azita spoke, "I don't want us to fight, please. We all hurt, and we are frightened. Things are happening around us that we barely comprehend." She paused to look out the window. "Earlier in this flight, I was thinking back to my first trip in an airplane, when you took me from my homeland to England. I was still pretty much a child and scared for sure. I was yet hurting from losing my family, only Deena was left to me. But there was also such hope. The future . . ."

"Yes, I remember that as if it happened yesterday." Chris smiled. "I kept thinking about how much my life had changed, like overnight. I flew into the Panjshir Valley to yank my idiot sister here from her own stupid decisions and to fire Amar for not listening to me."

"And how did that work out for you?" Kay smiled, mostly because the conversation had turned away from a focus on pain and loss.

Chris also smiled. "A total disaster except for you two gals. You have brought such joy to my life."

"And not your wonderful wife and your devoted sister here, who puts up with you without complaint?" Deena said mischievously.

"Without complaint, without complaint," Chris stammered as if stunned by her words. "Did you say she puts up with me without complaint?"

"Absolutely, isn't that right, Azita?"

Azita nodded her head. "That's how I see it."

Chris smiled broadly. "Oy vey, I see when I'm beaten. The burden of being surrounded by females, no man should have to endure such pain." His daughters chuckled despite their overall grief as he continued before they could say anything. "That trip was like two decades ago. I suppose it could have turned out worse, though I can't see how. I lost my carefree bachelor life and wound up with two brats to raise. And Kay here. She used to be a minor irritant bothering me from Chicago but after that she was in my face all the time. Poor me."

Kay reached over and smacked her brother on the arm. "Hey, do you think we can open that exit door and push him out without causing the plane to crash."

"Excellent thought," Azita looked serious, "but perhaps a bit risky. But I do remember that day in the camp. I was eleven. Already I was helping my father with the worst patients and had figured out what I wanted in life, to do what Pamir did. And yet, I was so innocent."

"How innocent?" Deena prompted her as if anticipating the answer.

"So innocent in fact that I was awed by you." Azita looked at Chris and smiled.

"As well as you should have been," he tried.

Deena looked at her sister. "I was just a teen at the time and so jealous of my little sister, the protégé and prodigy. How insufferable you were." Azita stuck her tongue out at her sister but remained silent. "See that. But even then things were changing for me. All the praise about being so pretty since I would have my pick of boys. That sounded ridiculous to me. Inside my body, I knew I was different in ways that I could not talk about. Even as I felt inferior to you, sister, I knew I could not go on as I had, just feeling sorry for myself. I would have to become my own woman, like you were. Maybe that's what changed me . . . jealousy. How odd."

"Yes, very odd." Azita deadpanned. "You really had no chance of competing with me."

Deena playfully hit her sister on her shoulder. "That's it, crash or no, I'm opening that door and out you go."

Kay laughed. "Oh, how I've enjoyed watching the two of you over the years. You both are so accomplished and yet can be so playful with one another. You two have a love that is rare, so rare."

"Oh, I think not." Azita asserted. "I mean, yes we love each other when Deena behaves that is. But it is not so rare as you say. The two of you love each other, we can see that." She pointed to Kay and Chris.

"Thanks for the thought, but we Crawford kids have had a hard road. How odd, all that money and all those advantages and it is freaking amazing that we made it." Kay paused as if deciding whether to drop the topic, but she plowed ahead. "Let me say this. Chris and I leaned on one another as youngsters. But I think I . . ." Her voice caught but she caught hold of her emotions. "Maybe it's the emotions of the moment but I have to say this now. It's my fault that Chris and I grew apart."

Chris looked dubious. "What the hell are you talking about?"

"Just listen, nimrod. We drifted apart when I hit puberty. That was when Father started . . ." She was not sure how to phrase it.

"He raped you," Azita said without emotion. "We know. I'm no longer sure how but we know."

Kay stared at her and smiled grimly. "For some reason, I wanted to protect you from such things, but you've seen more of life than any of us. How silly of me. Yes, he raped me, and later Kat, so many times I lost count. The thing is that I felt so helpless. Mother sank into alcohol for a long time to escape. Our older brother, Chuck, could never stand up to Father, a fact that led him to kill himself in the end. And I wanted to turn to Chris here but, in the end, I couldn't. So many times, so many, I would stand outside your room, thinking about how I would tell you what he had done to me. I never did. As you got older, you were off with Ricky and Jules more and more, you found a substitute family. I began to hate you for not guessing what had happened, what was happening. Eventually, I would tell you and, even after that, I still blamed you for not having guessed earlier. Now, there's a classic female trick for you."

"Not a trick, I think . . . more just a human way of coping." Chris murmured. "Probably better you never told me in the moment. I would have killed him. Justifiable for sure but they still would have thrown my ass in jail. And they call it justice, right."

Kay felt a tear making its way down her cheek and then another. "You know, if our father were here right now, I'm not sure I could confront him. I'd still probably freeze right up. It's a freaking sickness."

"And you think I'm any better." Chris yet felt a sting of bitterness. "The few times I brought Ricky and Jules over to our place, mother tried but *pater noster* treated them like shit. I was furious beyond words but did nothing, nothing . . . just spent more time away from the house. Funny, I felt guilty about taking a basketball scholarship to Princeton because the tuition and fees for him would be pocket change. Maybe some other kid could have used it, but I did not want to take a dime from him. Silly, since I had grown up in luxury, but I had a chance at independence I could not pass up. I would get by with little more than the black kids on the team though mother sent me money which I mostly saved. I never talked about my family with the other players. They probably thought I was orphaned. No one came to see me play. Same with the Rhodes Scholarship in the beginning, until Mom's trust fund kicked in." Chris looked directly at his sister. "I think . . . I think I was just too focused on surviving our dysfunctional family, breaking away from it, to look out for you. I just thought you had it together, with your studies and all. You seemed self-contained . . . that you knew what you wanted . . . where you were going. God, I'm so sorry."

Kay let out a small sigh. "Not your fault. Okay, I did despise you. No, I hated myself for being so weak. That's what living with a monster does. You become objects in their orbit, spinning around him while obsessing with how to survive. We never understood what was going on, except for poor Chuck probably. We saw our brother's agony well enough. How could Father not see that his demands were killing his oldest son. But I guess the thing was that he never saw anything beyond himself and his own will . . . his own world."

They were silent for a few moments before Chris ventured forth as if talking to himself. "I think that's the thing. When you are reasonably normal and, don't laugh now, I put myself in that category . . ."

"Should we vote on that?" Azita said with a tiny, sad smile

"A spanking is in your future for sure, young lady." Chris inwardly was thankful at that moment for her playfulness. "But listen. When you think you are normal, you expect everyone else to see the world as you do. Then you are amazed that they don't.

For years you can talk as if you are inhabiting the same universe, seeing a similar reality but no. You cannot really communicate, not in a meaningful way. It's just impossible."

"Yeah, have you ever tried talking to a Trump nut?" Kay said mostly to herself.

"Exactly," Chris said with meaning. "I had a conversation with Josh recently where we delved into that very topic . . . why did reason and evidence fail so badly when talking with today's Republicans? He had an explanation that made sense to me. The short version . . ."

"Thank god!" Kay interrupted.

Chris responded with feigned exasperation. "The short version is that they are authoritarian in character. That's simple enough but what we miss is that there are several kinds of authoritarianism. There is the *conventional* or *traditional* form. They are the ones that respect old fashion social norms, values, and morality. You would see them in church on Sunday. Then there are the *submissive authoritarians* who favor uncritical, respectful, obedient, and submissive support for existing authorities and institutions. They are the ones that went ballistic when Colin Kaepernick took a knee during the national anthem."

"Colin who?" Deena asked wondering if she were the only one who was clueless.

"I'll explain later, dear," Kay said quickly, "he's on a roll, best not to interrupt."

"Finally, and why do I feel as if I'm casting pearls before swine, there are the *aggressive authoritarians.* They are the ones who totally favor strict, harsh, tough, punitive, and coercive social control. But here's the thing, normal folk, and I'm talking about me here . . ."

"Of course, we knew that." Deena was getting into the playful back and forth.

"As I was saying, the normal folk have trouble interacting and even understanding these authoritarian types. What is more surprising is that the authoritarians can't even understand one another. I bet there are a lot of church-going moralists eating their heart out at the thought of a depraved pedophile like Trump heading the party. Remember that Trump and McCain clashed so badly, Romney has broken away from him. Some authoritarian types need rigid beliefs. To question anything is to question everything and that cannot be permitted. What grabs me is the emergence of organizations like the Lincoln Group, reasonable Republicans who are all in to stop the Trump machine. Thankfully, some Republicans remain sane and evidence driven."

"Fine," Kay said, thinking back to the discussions they had as kids before they drifted apart. "but how do you explain the huge approval rating Trump enjoys among all Republicans? Some 85 percent of them think he's doing a bang-up job on Covid. How bizarre is that?"

"Good point, and from such an unlikely source."

"Bite me, dear brother."

"The party has shifted over the years. The GOP of the 1950s was dominated by the traditional types, respect for morality and marriage and a balanced budget, but also not opposing those institutions that strengthened the middle class like social security and some unionization. Look at the 1956 GOP platform." Chris could see that Azita and Deena were mostly placating him at this point, simply thrilled that the topic had turned away from private pain to a discussion of public issues. "Okay, just listen. For all kinds of reasons, the Republicans kept lurching to the right. Now, the vast majority are full-blown *aggressive authoritarians* or, as Josh and I like to refer to them as, neo-Nazis."

Kay grunted. "Damn, I'm going to have to separate the two of you, you feed off one another."

"The brother I never had." The words were out when Chris realized they were an aspersion on his deceased elder brother. Kay's expression did not change. "My guess is that as your average white conservative saw their world falling apart, they saw increasing threat all about them. They faced more job insecurity, declining real wages, competition from foreigners and minorities seeking an equal place at the table. They no longer had the inside track and that infuriated them. Their America was white and Christian, maybe even Protestant. But they saw it disappearing and they were hell bent on hanging on to it. Probably the worst thing in their minds was the disrespect they felt coming from the educated classes, the so-called experts. They hated the elite for looking down on them and taking away their one claim to any superiority . . . minorities. If those lesser people had rights and opportunities, what in god's name was left to them? It must have been like the southern states when Lincoln was elected in 1860. In their eyes, their world was endangered. It was only a matter of time until it was all over."

"But it's not." Deena tried to get involved. "Am I wrong on that?"

Kay answered, "No, dear, you are not wrong and, I hate to admit it, but that is my brother's point. Their world is not falling apart but they believe it is. Your average white working-class guy believes that all these newcomers, immigrants, and blacks, and even women are elbowing their way into the queue so that he can't advance. He feels stuck and it's making him angry."

"And therefore, they follow demagogues and populists who promise a return to glory and a dominant place in society," Azita added.

Chris was always amazed at his two daughters. "Absolutely. But the amazing thing is that they follow politicians who, in fact, are making their lives more difficult. They vote against their self- interest. That drives us crazy but, then again, we cannot see their world, surely cannot experience it. It is one dominated by fear and hate, and an uncontrolled wish to lash out at enemies. I swear, the typical Trump cult member is driven by a fanatical desire to stick it to guys like me."

"You mean pedantic, elitist, eggheads who think they know it all." Kay smiled.

"Exactly, asshole." Chris smiled back at her.

Azita looked on thoughtfully. "This discussion reminds me of my youth, our youth, and life under the Taliban. These aggressive authoritarians you talk about. That was my life. That was Deena's life. I was nearly killed for reading a notice in a public square when girls were not supposed to read. Deena would have been killed for certain for loving the wrong person, another woman, in their hate-filled eyes. They would have beheaded her or perhaps stoned her to death, just for the way she chose to love. Our dear, sweet brother was killed fighting against these monsters and then, and then, my mother and father were murdered in their beds without an ounce of mercy. What was their sin, what sin did they commit? They merely wanted their children to have the opportunity to be what we could be. Was that so bad? Really, I ask you. Was that so awful?"

"Of course not, dear," Kay whispered though she realized her words were not necessary.

"Even then, they were not done. They came within an inch of murdering the dearest person left to me, my sister Deena, and they did reach out to kill the one man I came to love. What is next, will they wait for my child to be born so they can exact revenge on this innocent. Really, where does their hate end? How much fear can you force into your heart? I sometimes want to scream at the fates we must endure in this miserable existence just because we want to heal, or educate, or love, or be the person that God wishes us to be. How can people hate such things?"

"I wish I had an answer," Chris murmured, taken aback by his adopted daughter's level of emotion.

For several moments, only the groan of the plane could be heard before Azita fought back tears to continue. "Sometimes I despair. What is happening in America and in Afghanistan are reflections of the same dynamics, the same hates and fears. How sad, how hopeless."

"Sad perhaps, but not hopeless." Kay corrected her niece.

"Perhaps, but I have listened to Chris and Josh talking about what is happening with Trump in America and Johnson in England. It makes me so sad. When Deena and I made it to London and Oxford so many years ago, I thought we had escaped all the insanity, the killing, the blind intolerance, and the mad fury. Sure, we might go back into harm's way but by choice, to try to make the world a better place. To even think that it is now following us into our sanctuary, I shudder, and I'm sure that Deena does as well. Where might we run next? Will the world be overcome with insanity? Will there be no place to run? It almost makes me think, in moments of black thoughts, that my Ben and your older brother were right. Why fight against what cannot be defeated? Just escape all this nonsense."

Now the silence, except for that relentless groan of the jet engine seemed to continue for an indefinite period.

Chris spoke with deliberation, his words spreading out like molasses. "I am supposed to tell you that you are wrong. I am supposed to use my gift for marshalling facts and arguments, I suppose, to convince you that there is hope for the future. I'm not sure I can anymore. The dearest brother a man could have was compelled to kill himself by his own father, a man who was driven by an obsessive fanaticism for money and power. Your Ben did the same because of personal demons. My sister-in-law, Beverly, as sweet a girl as you could imagine as we discovered too late, was pushed to her death. That is what we believe at least. Her sin was that she sided with me, I mean with us in the family feud. Now Ricky has been blown to bits, my dearest and oldest friend. The pieces of him were scraped off the garage floor so he could be cremated. I also struggle with this. And Ahmad and Rachel, the good Lord did not make better people." His voice cracked. "For the first time, I am having trouble . . ."

"But we must." It was Deena in a voice so low she could not be heard.

"What did you say?" Kay asked.

Deena looked at each person in the plane before asserting in a clear voice. "This is not the first time we've had this discussion. We must go on."

Chris seemed a bit baffled by her words. "You can say that knowing the price you almost paid."

"That is precisely why I can say it, why I can feel like I do. I came as close to death as one can. So, I know the expected price as few others can. Just listen to me. You've heard the story of me and Azita as girls. I was the witless one, the one with no ambition and drive, the one who would get by with her looks. And my sister, here, she was the anointed one by our father from early on. It was clear she had an intelligence and drive that everyone saw would propel her to success one day. And poor Deena, at least she is pretty, she can get any man she wants except for that small detail that I didn't want any of them. For a long time, I pouted, felt sorry for myself, and hated my little sister. There were many a time I would be helping mother preparing the food. When I'd be cutting vegetable with a sharp knife I would fantasize about using it on myself." She looked at Azita. "Okay, I'll admit that I sometimes thought about using it on you."

"The knife?"

"No, a secret spell that only lesbians know about. Of course the knife. But mostly I fantasized about slicing through my wrists . . . one cut and the pain would soon be over. And that was the promise of redemption inside, that the pain would be over. It's hard for me to recall precisely how all that changed. I think, one day, I said to myself that you were not all that much smarter than I. You recall that I read a lot, well a lot of silly stuff but not all silly stuff. Majeeb liked history and I read his stuff and I knew I was cleverer than he was. It just struck me that I didn't have to compete with you, at least not directly. I could just be my own person, follow my own fate. So, I dove into the studies that mother was so willing to provide. She was waiting for me to do that. How did she know? I mean, it took a while but soon I found my dream."

"To be an educator," Azita said with a broad smile.

"Exactly, the Afghanistan Malala."

"I love that but what does it tell us about the world's slide into fascism and hate?"

"Ooh," Deena sniffed, "for such a bright man, you can be so slow sometimes."

"Why, thank you, I love you as well."

"It is simple. In all our lives, there are moments when things look dark. You cannot see how it will turn out."

Azita suddenly burst in. "Oh yes, I remember one day by the river in Oxford, when mother and I were walking and I was down about something, I no longer even recall why. She told me to look at the river. It twisted and turned, she said. You can only see a little bit ahead when it likely will meander out of your sight. But you still know that it continues its uneven course all the way to the sea. And that is our lives, each of ours. The twists and turns will be different, and sometimes the current will race and froth and become extremely dangerous. But it gets to the end of the journey, where it is supposed to reach, eventually. That story might well be written already."

"But what, dear Zita, if all these rivers are going in very different directions, pulling each of us apart?"

"I have thought of that. No matter. We can only master our own way. Our biggest sin is if we beach ourselves on some random bank, saying the journey is too difficult or dangerous to go on. That is the only sin against God we can make."

Deena said excitedly, "Yes, my sister is so right. We will never forget that awful day when we fled into the hills after the Taliban killed our parents. We wound up in a cave, alone, knowing that they were searching for us. We could hear them in the distance, or what we thought was them." Then Deena smiled. "That was them but some of the noises turned out to be you and some of our villagers, but that was like a turn in the river no one could expect."

"So very true," Azita said. "So very, very true."

Deena looked thoughtful. "Those hours after the assassination of our parents have remained with me all these years. Nothing in my life is so present to me like those moments. Every emotion was seared into my core. I had utter fear, total despair, and a sense of futility that was beyond all reckoning. There was no way out, none that I could see. And yet, and yet . . ."

"And yet what, dear?" Kay asked.

"I never once considered giving up. I had black thoughts on other occasions, when I felt trapped by my culture in a life that involved marriage and domestic and sexual slavery. But not then. Is that odd to you?"

"Not to me," Chris joined in. "I would read about men in war, imprisoned in Gulag's or tortured in POW camps. They seldom seemed to despair. They wanted to survive above all else. But why? What drove them when we read about suburban teenagers killing themselves because someone called them fat? Perhaps I will understand life when I understand that."

"I cannot answer your conundrum, Father," Azita said thoughtfully. "All I know is this. You must keep your heart open to what you know to be true and let the waters take you there. You simply must believe that the fates will take you all the way to the sea. In the end, after all else, you trust in God, or Fate, or sheer instinct that you are doing the right thing. None of us can do other than that."

CHAPTER 23

CHICAGO

The remains of Ricky were in a simple vase situated on a table in front of a window that looked out over Lake Michigan. Chris had insisted moving it to this location so that he might look at it and then out across the lake. Water had been his refuge as a kid, so reflective of the various moods that had swept over him—rage, determination, serenity, and exuberance. Somehow, he found every emotion expressed in the surface of this immense body of liquid, itself a complex interaction of color and movement dictated by wind, light, and clouds. Remarkable, he thought, how this aggregation of a simple molecule could mutate into so many representations of one's internal state and even reflect the world about him.

Perhaps his ability to appreciate this liquid landscape suggested a greater artistic bent than even he had ever admitted he might possess. While he was foremost an academic and a philanthropic entrepreneur of sorts, he loved to write, express himself in words. Now that his position in the academy was secure, he wrote for broader audiences, and drew more upon real life rather than the 'literature,' which represented the bible for his academic colleagues. That cost him points among his more conventional colleagues within the academy as did his growing fame and notoriety in the outside world. His appearances on BBC and in American spots often hosted by Jules for network TV generated jealousy among some colleagues. Again, some of his peers considered this crass and even undignified for a true intellectual. It was a form of pandering in their eyes. Believing that reaching out to the public was an obligation for members of the academy, he could care less.

Of his remaining siblings, he was the one who had the most difficulty deciding who he was, what he was. Kat was the disciplined and organized one, an excellent Chief Executive Officer who blended skill with numbers and a sense of organizational awareness and management skills. She had their father's business skills but blended them with an innate sense for collaboration as opposed to the usual zero-sum mentality that infected financial types. Chris often wondered where that came from, since she seemed to be a late bloomer, though some of her skills clearly were bequeathed from their father, a fact she was loath to acknowledge. Kay had always been the physician, the healer, excelling in the sciences. She could have gone the research route but could not tear herself away from people and direct healing. That was it, he sometimes thought. She dedicated herself to repairing damage to others mostly because she felt so much damage within herself. He would have to ask her one day if she retained any regrets about not focusing on the laboratory.

And there was Charles Junior, Chuck, the eldest male. He clearly was tormented as his father's hope and thus the tragedy of the family. He had known what he wanted to be—a man of the arts. He had an innate esthetic sense about him, an appreciation of everything fine. He truly was his mother's child and, at the same time, a victim of his father's obsessions. The eldest was supposed to become the family head, the one to carry on the legacy. It was a classic case of primogeniture, in which the patriarch passionately believed. Remarkably, Charles Senior retained a sense of his Polish aristocratic roots that were seemingly erased in the chaos of World War II Poland as this proud people were first crushed by its two neighbors and then devoured by the Russian bear. The old aristocracy had been obliterated. Unfortunately, Junior was incapable of bearing the family title, even if it were not official and there was no aristocratic line to carry on. He tried, though, so eager to please a man who could not be satisfied. Chris and Kay watched from a distance as their elder sibling dissolved under the pressure until he finally discovered a way to escape in death. Only Kat and Chuck's wife understood the intimate horror of it all.

As Chris looked at the funeral vase set before the tableau of water and sky, he reflected on those early years. He had escaped as well, to a loving black family on the west side of Chicago. How odd was that, how separate were their cultures and worlds. Basketball had been what brought Ricky and Chris together, a fistfight on the first day they met launched a lifelong connection. Chris now tried to recall what had triggered his momentary flash of anger that day. He was not used to being bested on the court. But here was this athletic black kid, dark brown at least, whom he could not shake to get an open shot on the basket. Every move which worked so often in the past was thwarted by this super quick ballplayer who remained all over him. He had met his match on the court. In frustration, he lashed out . . . a foolish move that was promptly quelled by one quick punch from his opponent that sent him crumpling to the ground. What he did recall, as pain radiated from a broken nose, was this smiling young man reaching down to him. *You are quite good, I was having trouble keeping up with you,* this handsome opponent who had just flattened him was saying.

Within weeks, Chris was a fixture at the humble Jackson home. It possessed all the love and care absent from his own wealthy world. He was quickly infatuated with Julianna, Ricky's sister two years younger, who appeared to look upon him with a mixture of distrust and interest even after they fell into an uneasy relationship. The sex would not come for a while, and only reluctantly, but was intense when it did. Chris came to adore the parents who were hardworking and dedicated to raising decent children. What most impressed him is that the parents were focused on raising the children. They cared about their offspring and thought hard about the proper amounts of discipline and opportunity to foster their optimal development. He recalled eating there so often during high school, laughing and joking around the dinner table. In his home, the eating ritual often was done in an icy silence. He felt so guilty about imposing on their limited budget that he tried various ways of leaving money to offset the cost of feeding him, and often more to help generally but not so much as to look like charity. It was a difficult line to walk. In the end, he was found out, leading to a kindly scolding from Mr. Jackson about how welcome he was in their home and that his 'gifts' were more an insult than anything else. They knew, Chris had decided in that moment, that he was the poor one, not in money but in love.

"Reminiscing." A voice came from behind him.

Chris jumped at the sound before whirling to see Jules approaching. She never slowed until she embraced him deeply, burying her head in his shoulder. As she held on to him, he felt his body responding to her as it had for so many years. He solaced himself with the knowledge that she had rejected him, not the other way around. To his relief, she finally let go while brushing away several tears.

"Yeah," Chris responded, feeling his own eyes watering, "thinking about all those dinners at your house and my ill-fated effort to leave money for your parents."

Jules smiled. "Now that was stupid. Dad was angry with you about that, and he never got angry. Pretty stupid on your part."

"Well, I know that now, knew it even then. I mean at least after I was stupid enough to try it a dozen times. Damn, I should have given you the money."

"Me?" And then she scowled knowing where she was going.

"Of course, then it wouldn't have taken me so long to get into your pants." He tried to laugh but he found it hard.

"You are a shit but absolutely right on this one. I never should have given it to you for free," Jules said as she hit him in the stomach though it was a weak blow. Her heart was not in it.

Another voice came from the door. "Oh for crying out loud," Kat said as she looked on with a wry smile. She was holding her emotions together even as Chris could see the toll required to keep her composure. "They haven't been in the same room thirty seconds and she's already beating his brains out. Some things never change."

Kat entered the room with Kay, Peter, and two men he had not seen before. A taller angular man with thinning blond hair and a shorter square man with oriental features. Peter introduced them as special agents.

"These are two of the agency's best," Peter concluded the introductions. "They have some follow up questions."

Everyone found seats before the Asian agent, obviously the senior of the team, started. "Professor Crawford . . ."

"Chris, please. I only expect my sisters to address me as Professor or Your Eminence." Chris started with his usual gambit to disarm strangers . . . humor.

"Okay, Chris, can we speak to you in private?" Kat waived them toward an adjacent room where the questioning immediately started. "Tell us your suspicions."

"Suspicions? I'd say they are more than suspicions. You have no idea how sick our Father is? Besides being famous and rich as Croesus, he is a pathological bastard. I cannot imagine you've heard anything different from the others."

"But we want to hear it from you."

Chris breathed deeply before launching into his recitation of facts and surmises. It was a speech he had run through his mind countless times, usually in a virtual dialogue with his father. In his mind's eye, the monologue would be in response to his father denying that he had any bad intentions toward the family. When he came to a stop, the agent smiled. "I'm glad we taped that. It would have been difficult to keep up with you while taking actual notes."

"Yes, I can talk fast, that's what my students tell me, especially when I'm on a roll."

The taller, blond agent spoke for the first time. "I know you feel strongly about your convictions. But I must say that sometimes the obvious is not always true. We get accused of tunnel vision all the time and sometimes that accusation is accurate. Every top financial player makes enemies, people they have wronged or who believe they have been wronged by others. Could that have happened in this case?"

Chris paused as if he were considering the agent's comment seriously. That was for effect. "Anything is possible, of course. But while these elites may despise one another, few of them kill one another. Besides, Ricky was known as a straight shooter by everyone."

"True," the agent responded, "but sometimes a little man loses all in an investment gone bad. Someone of modest means who sees it all gone can be more dangerous than a wealthy guy who loses three times as much."

Chris battled against displaying his irritation. "Well, I know you must look into all possibilities. However, at the end of the day, the man behind this is Charles Crawford Senior and it has nothing to do with money, at least not directly. I would bet the lives of my children on that fact. Moreover, he will come after the rest of the family at some point. I know him. My sisters know him. I'm sure they said the same thing. He has gone over the edge. The private, twisted world in which he lives leaves him no other option. If he fears he is losing the big game, he will take it out on us, all of us. In his paranoid, self-centered world, we will bear the brunt of his fury."

The Asian agent looked befuddled. "The big game?"

Chris wished he had not gone there. This will make him look paranoid and silly. "Listen, bear with me on this. My father has been a force behind the worst of right-wing political movements for decades now. With Trump, and the sudden rise to acceptability of all the white nationalists out there, he finally can taste victory. But there are two things in his way. Trump is an incompetent moron but there is little he can do about that. And his family, his own children, are doing all they can to stop him, particularly with the money they have after engineering a hostile takeover of much of his empire. That he can do something about, and he has started. My immediate family is no safer in England. Perhaps what bothers him the most is some of the work we are doing in the Mideast, trying to find talented Muslim women we can help educate and bring into positions of power. In his eyes, that violates everything in which he believes. He hates women, he hates Islam, he hates people of color. And so, he hates me and mine."

"You seem very certain of this."

Chris leaned forward. "Mark my words. Either he will be dead, or I will be dead by election day. You can bet your pension on that." Then Chris realized what he had implied. "By the way, I have no plans to kill anyone."

The two agents looked at one another. "Listen Prof . . . Chris. We believe your version of events. Peter Favulli has a superb reputation in the agency, one of those retirees that is recalled with favor. We pay great attention to him. Plus, our own investigation seems to corroborate what you say. But your father is clever. Many right-wing nut cases are not very bright. They do things that are obvious and stupid and easily caught. I cannot reveal details, but there is chatter that a small right-wing team planted these devices. But they came from out of town, perhaps even another country, and have vanished into the wind. They are well-financed and have a network supporting them. And remarkably, they left no forensic evidence for us to use, at least we have not discovered any yet. If they were not pros themselves, they were helped by pros. But everyone leaves forensic clues and we'll find them eventually. However, until we catch them, and we will, it might be difficult to link your father directly to this affair. People as well-financed as they are can . . . disappear. You understand?"

Chris focused on his use of the word *affair* as if it were a social event. But he let that go. "Of course. And you must understand this. Unless you get to him soon, the body count will go up. My ashes will likely be sitting up there next to my best friend."

* * *

When Chris and the two agents returned to the other room, he was surprised to see that his mother was there, though Azita and Deena were still absent. After kissing his mother, he asked where his two girls were, realizing as he did that he was becoming a possessive parent of his two fully adult adoptive daughters.

Kat answered, "The sisters are in my office, talking to folks back in England. You can take them away from their work, but you cannot take the work away from them. They are so like me. I wish they were interested in making money. However, listen to what Mother has to say. You might be interested as well." Kat nodded toward the FBI agents.

Mary smiled wanly, as if she had been found stealing from the cookie jar. "It was nothing. I just went to confront your father."

"What?" Chris stuttered, for once at a loss for words.

"Mary, that was the craziest thing . . ." Kay started but had trouble finishing her own sentence.

Kat took over from her tongue-tied older siblings. "Mother, what in the world prompted you to do such a thing?"

"I just knew that my one remaining son would go off and do something just as crazy while in town, so I did it first, before he had a chance. Charles is less likely to kill me than he would you, Chris."

"And what in god's name leads you to believe that?"

"Simple, he sees me as little more than a harmless mistake he made early in life. He sees you as a danger to him now. Besides, you couldn't get within a half mile of him these days, he is surrounded by security."

"Good point," Chris looked at her. "So, just how did you get close to him?"

"My dear son, I lived with the man for almost half a century. I know his weaknesses, how he thinks, what he does. He is a creature of habit if I must say. On Sunday mornings, he goes to a certain Polish bakery. He would normally eat there in a patio arrangement they have but now, with the pandemic, I wasn't totally sure. Still, I took a chance that he would go himself to pick up his favorite bulkies. He loved to cut them in two, then smear butter and cream cheese on top and heat them so his topping would melt into the two halves of the dough. I cannot figure out how he has not had a coronary yet, or how he stays so thin."

"Oh, for Christ's sake," Chris uttered spontaneously.

"Christopher, such language. You know that I can still spank you." She gave him her best scowl.

"Fine, so what happened?"

"He was sitting outside the shop, eating his bulkie. He usually ate one there and brought the rest home. Of course, being who he is, they served that one as he liked it, extra butter and cream cheese and heated thoroughly. When I approached, three men stepped up to block my way, but he waived them off. He was pleasant enough, saying how nice it was to see me, how good I looked. When he finished with that bullshit . . . sorry, I'll spank myself later. When he finished with his obligatory niceties, I looked him straight in the eyes and told him that if he harmed anyone else I knew and loved, that I would kill him." Her eyes were cold blue as she said the words. "And you agents can write that down."

"What did he say?" Chris managed.

"He didn't respond so I repeated myself. I walked even closer to him and said the following in a voice that could not be misunderstood. *Remember this, Charles. Nothing is more passionate than love which has turned to hate . . . nothing.*"

"Then what?" Kat asked.

"He just gave me that grisly smile of his and looked away. It was over as far as I was concerned, so I got back in my cab and came back." She turned to the FBI agents. "By the way, he killed Richard Jackson, or had him killed at least."

"Wait, did he say anything?" The Asian agent perked up.

"No, silly, but I could see it in his eyes. I could tell that he wanted to tell me, rub it in, and maybe share his other fantasies. But he still has enough self-control left. He couldn't take the chance that I was, how do you put it, wired up. I could tell he wanted to confess, though. Everything is eating at him. I just hope he strokes out soon, or that you get the goods on him and throw his sorry ass in jail."

The agents admonished Mary about her actions which Chris knew was like arguing with the tides to change direction before their time. When they finished, she mumbled something about "being sorry for what she did" but no one believed she was at all contrite.

Chris fell into a chair. "Mother, if you keep doing stunts like that, Father won't stroke out, I will."

"Oh, Christopher." She always called him that when she was frustrated with him. "You were always one for the dramatics."

Kay laughed. "Though you are right about the dramatics, Mother, I must agree with Chris on what you did. That wasn't very smart."

"It was very smart." She snapped back. "I know what my son here would do if he got his Irish up. He'd go off and get himself killed like he almost did at Beverly's service. Besides, Charles knows that I'm deadly serious."

"What does that mean?" Chris was still shaken.

"That I would kill him, of course. Charles could tell I was deadly serious about that, which is why he couldn't look at me in the end. He knew all right."

* * *

The agents left, Mary Kelly went to take a nap, and Kat returned to her adjacent office to deal with some unavoidable business details as well as respond to messages of sympathy and condolences from all over the world which yet continued to arrive. Azita and Deena had rejoined Chris, Kay, Jules, and Peter. For a while, Chris merely watched the conversation around him, paying especial attention to Jules as she fingered the vase that held what remained of her brother. When he was growing up, he wondered how people coped with the loss of loved ones. Of course, there were the stories about young men who never returned from Vietnam, but they only existed in the periphery of his life, tragedies shared but before his time. The immediacy of death and loss remained mysteries to him. But no more. Now it was all so real. The body blows were becoming almost unbearable. Azita still had a hollow look in her eyes from the loss of her husband. He recalled Josh stuffing in the pain from the loss of his sister. Kat and Jules went about as if their lives continued, but he knew that each struggled to present themselves as whole and functioning persons to the world. There were times he did not know if he could refrain from bursting into tears.

"That's all I would have needed right now, to have mother go off and get herself killed," Chris said absentmindedly, suddenly feeling the need to say something, anything.

"Say," Peter asked, "was she serious about killing her ex-husband?"

Kat corrected him. "Not ex, they're still married. She despises him but it's a Catholic thing. She takes that 'til death do us part' thing very seriously. Perhaps that's why she is so eager to off him."

Peter groaned. "I'm going to need more people if I have to keep members of the family from becoming hitmen or, more precisely, hit grandmothers."

"Hilarious Peter." Chris smiled.

"Who's joking?"

Jules let out a chuckle. "Hell, add me to the list of possible assassins. That man killed my brother. I can see the headline on *Entertainment Tonight* now—*Network reporter goes psycho, guns down financier.* You have no freaking idea how angry I am."

"Okay, okay, the checkbook is open by the way." Chris nodded to Peter. "But here's what I need to know, what we all need to know, what is your assessment of the situation?"

"This is serious, and the agency thinks it's serious. You couldn't get them to buy into the murder scenario involving, who was it, your sister-in-law?"

"Yes, our older brother's wife. She remained close to Charles to report to us what he was doing and then mysteriously fell off her balcony. We never bought the accident or suicide explanation."

"Neither does the agency any longer. They are going to open that investigation up again," Peter affirmed.

Chris looked dubious. "Even under Trump's watch? My father supports all the right-wing nut cases."

"That maniac hasn't locked down the whole federal government just yet. Give him four more years and all bets are off. But for now, we can . . . listen to me say we." Peter chuckled. "I mean to say that the agency has not yet been turned into a Gestapo or NKVD. Your father has been seen with white nationalist leaders. These are people on the terrorist watch list, just as Josh was so many years ago. Of course, Josh we know was not really a terrorist but your dad, on the other hand, is consorting with some bad dudes."

Chris sighed. "I have two questions. How bad are they and can they reach to England or globally?"

Peter glanced at Azita and Deena but decided not to sugarcoat anything. "They are extremely bad dudes—drug dealers, the super-nativist types. And they are stone-cold killers, some of them are. For money, they would kill their own grandmothers. Their reach? We think of them as mainly located in North America, and international travel is hard these days. You can hop on a private plane of course . . . and there are Aryan types and skinheads in the UK. It would be easier to use their foreign counterparts. They don't exactly collaborate often but there are avenues of communication. We might have a chance of flagging communications about you across the pond. International chatter is monitored but you have to get lucky."

"A chance?" Kat asked.

"Best I can do. We don't catch everything unless we know where to listen. But this is something you can take to the bank. I'm going to be all over these guys so that you don't get swept under the rug. This whole Black Lives Matters movement has rather overwhelmed the agency now but I'm on them like flies on honey. What I worry about is that he will go after soft targets, or what he thinks are soft targets."

"What does that mean?" Jules asked.

"It means you." Peter looked at her coolly. "Everyone expects him to go after direct family—Kat, Kay, or Chris. But all that I hear about him tells me he might focus on those close to his prime targets. He got your brother, why wouldn't you be next."

Chris grunted. "Of course, that makes perfect sense. He will go after the people we love. That extends our pain. Kill us and it is over, assuming there is no afterlife. Kill someone we love, and the torture keeps on hurting each of us for a long, long time. But why plant something under Kat's car if she were not a real target?"

Peter responded instantly, "Simple, he wanted it to look as if she were a candidate, but he knew she didn't use that car. Classic misdirection of course."

"But . . ." Chris started.

Peter held up a hand. "Listen, it's always easy to overthink these things but I'm guessing he'll go for what I call associated targets. Jules, you are prime, close to Chris and Kat and a pain in the butt to him with your network exposes. Anyone else here?"

Kat thought for a moment. "If he leaves Mary alone, and I think he will even though she has promised to kill him. Besides Jules there might only be some staff that have uncovered data that we've used to attack him and his causes. He might go after them but there is no emotional connection so that seems unlikely."

Peter did not look convinced. "Perhaps, but the more I think on it, he might try England. He knows he's being watched here, and he has several targets there. Amar for sure, and I'm afraid your girls here."

"Women." Kay corrected him. "But there are several others such as Cate and Meena, Josh and his wife. Maybe they are long shots, but he just might go after what Peter says are softer targets but ones that will still hurt us."

Chris rose and looked out the window. "I still would feel safer if we got back to England."

Deena also spung to her feet. "Don't for a moment think that we are afraid, my sister and me. We have escaped shootings and bombings and our whole lives have been lived amidst threat. You either put those fears behind you or you live as a slave all your life. I guess I am a believer in fate. Allah has a destiny for me, for my sister and I, and we will not be dissuaded from where we are bound. Right, sister?"

When she looked at Azita, her sister looked lost in thought, but she soon realized everyone was looking at her. "I am so sorry. I've been preoccupied. It's probably nothing."

"What are you talking about, dear?" Kay asked.

"I'm sorry. I was skyping with mother earlier. We were just going over the work, what was going on," Azita then paused, "Damn it, she didn't look good. She looked tired and flushed and there was a cough. She brushed it off but . . ."

"That's it. We're heading back."

Kat responded, "Wait, don't overreact. It might be nothing, simply hard work."

Chris looked at Azita. "You saw her, even if only through cyberspace."

"I have seen so many who've been stricken by the virus, mostly in East London. I know the look. When I asked her to take her temp, she put me off. I agree, we need to go back."

"Chris," Jules said affirmatively, "I'm going with you. I've got some time and . . . hell, I don't have to explain to you."

He just smiled weakly. In his heart, he was glad. He wanted her to be with him.

CHAPTER 24

AMAR

Kay took a deep breath before entering Amar's hospital room. Even though familiar with the medical equipment that surrounded the half comatose body of her sister-in-law, she was shocked. This was her brother's wife, the woman who convinced her to take her medical skills to the heart of the beast during the height of the 2001 death struggle between the Taliban and the Northern Alliance. Memories flooded back to her, struggling daily with the wounded from the fighting, the refugees fleeing an oppressive regime, the constant worry about terror that might be unleashed by religious extremists. Despite all, she had never felt more alive. And then, suddenly there was the unexpected arrival of the Masoud family who somehow had made their way from Kabul to their medical site despite the paranoid watch of the Taliban Mullahs.

That was a turning point in so many ways, though it was not apparent in the moment. Pamir Masoud was an excellent medical hand for sure, but it was his steady hand, the reputation he had since his clan was from this region, and his cultural knowledge that brought order and direction to their work. More than that, that insignificant-looking man brought his family; a competent wife who stepped in with the refugees, an older daughter who immediately began working with children, especially the girls, to get them back to some form of learning curriculum, and a son whom she never got to know. Much to his parents' angst, he went off to fight the Taliban who kept encroaching closer from the south and west. His devotion to his country and to freedom were beyond question. Unfortunately, his personal bravery was greater than his military skills, and soon he perished. The father, Pamir, had anticipated this fate but knew there was nothing to be done.

The memory that gripped Kay the most was that of the younger daughter, Azita. She seemed a mere child yet had a presence about her of a young adult. She followed her father around absorbing his medical skills and knowledge like the proverbial sponge. Now this urchin no longer had to sneak around while learning from her father. There were no Taliban mullahs to accuse her of sinning or worse. Whenever Kay would speak to this eleven-year old, she would respond with the English vocabulary that would shame some of her Western peers, though yet heavily accented. And yet, there was something childlike that remained in her, the obvious devotion she had for Pamir, the incessant squabbles with her older sibling, and even the inevitable mother-daughter butting of wills. Kay soon forgot the child's age and lack of formal education and began using her as an assistant when she was not helping her father.

Sometimes, when the day was over, she and Azita would talk about medicine and Kay's adventures in a Chicago Emergency Room. Kay marveled at the way Azita would talk about a future as a doctor even during the darkest hours when their prospects appeared more appropriately measured in days rather than decades. Kay soon realized she was imagining this naïf as her own child. That fantasy always caught her off guard. She had never thought of herself as maternal but this image of raising this girl to adulthood, shaping her future, was not easily shaken.

As Kay looked down on Amar, she recalled how the two of them prepared for the arrival of Chris so long ago. Kay knew he was furious with her for disobeying him and traveling to the most dangerous site in his international operations. The two women were also certain that he was equally furious with Amar whom he undoubtedly blamed for leading his sister astray. Kay told Amar that her witty and charming brother did have a bit of Irish in him. Once roused, he could get ornery, nothing Kay could not handle of course, though she harbored serious doubts in this instance. Still, they thought it better they be elsewhere when he first arrived, especially if his Irish were already up. Give him time to cool his heels. They both managed to be occupied when Chris and Karen Fisher landed by helicopter, only this eleven-year-old girl was there to greet him. In retrospect, Kay smiled at the memory of that day, it worked like a charm.

One word broke through her barrier protecting her mind's eye and her memories. "Kay."

She whirled about. A man stood there highly disguised with protective medical gear and face shields but there was no mistaking his identity. Kay looked into the eyes of her former husband. "Jamie?"

Impulsively, Kay rushed to him and embraced. He pulled back slightly before giving in to it. "That breaks several hospital rules but what the hell. It has been too long."

"My bad, *mea culpa*, I've been overwhelmed and then my brother-in-law was killed. We immediately came back from the States when we heard. The damn visitor restrictions are punitive, I got in claiming to be her personal physician."

"You mean Chris hasn't seen her?"

"No, he's going nuts out there, as are the girls." Then she realized that maybe he had some pull. "Are you in charge here, of her case?"

"As a matter of fact, I made sure of that. Karen got in touch when things went south. At first, we thought we might just quarantine her. She is young, perhaps her symptoms would be manageable. I know she lied to her daughter over Skype in the very beginning, saying she was merely tired. She didn't want to worry her daughters and thought she could just tough her way through it. But with the injuries she suffered in Kabul, she was compromised. She has lung damage from the toxic fumes she inhaled from the blast. Well, you see the consequences. When I knew how serious this was, I made sure I took charge."

"Oh, Jamie, thank you. I don't know . . . I mean." Kay struggled for words. "What . . . I mean. Hell, I'm a freaking doctor and I can't ask the question, get a simple sentence out. My brain is frozen."

"Kay, I'm not going to lie. There is hope but she is terribly ill, and we still know so little about this virus. I've made sure she's gotten the full arsenal, all that we have but her lungs aren't strong enough. That bombing in Kabul is not helping. I'm afraid things are getting beyond us, I'm sorry."

Kay began to cry, and Jamie embraced her again. "I'll have to prepare them."

"Kay, it is not over."

She looked at him sharply. "You're not talking to an idiot."

He looked at her gently, with affection. "Don't I know that." After hugging her in silence, he continued. "I'll make sure everyone gets in to see her. Azita is easy, she's a physician. And Chris's foundation has donated to this place, that must be worth something. I'll take care of it, but we have to get everyone tested."

"They've taken swabs from everyone, and everyone's temp," Kay said quickly, turning to the patient. "This is so unfair. She is the nicest woman I know and so good for Chris. I shouldn't say this out loud but I'm closer to her than I am to Kat, my own freaking sister. Makes you wonder."

"What?" Jamie said quietly with his arm around her.

"What the fuck is wrong with god." There was more than a hint of venom in her words.

Jamie squeezed her closer and she put her head on his shoulder as he responded to her frustration. "I look about at all the suffering and wonder the same thing."

"I suppose as doctors, given what we've seen in war zones, death becomes a common commodity. And philosophically, we know we never cheat it, we merely postpone the inevitable. And yet, yet, there are times when I am infuriated. There are lives that deserve their full allotment of time, they have so much to give. And there are those . . ."

"No need to finish that thought. I'm totally with you."

Kay spun around to face Jamie. "Why did we stop being we?"

She could tell he was trying to smile even through his facial protection. "We didn't. You did."

Kay let her head fall forward into his chest. "True enough. I was a hopeless idiot."

At this Jamie laughed. "No argument here, but one question."

"Go ahead," she prompted.

"When did you begin to talk like a drunken sailor? See, you need my guidance."

Jamie felt her body tremble but could not tell if she were crying or laughing.

* * *

Karen Fisher, Josh Connelly, and Shahed Al-Hussein joined Chris and the others waiting to see if they could see Amar. Shahed immediately went to embrace Deena and Azita, the three of them moving off to the side for a private conversation. Josh also stood a bit off to the side as Karen embraced Chris with unambiguous intensity. There would be no insults on this day, only expressions of the deep affection she felt for this man who had become her father, brother, and mentor after their years together. When Karen finally released him, Josh came forward to hug his new friend.

"Before coming here, I thought of so many sweet things to say, or encouraging words. But now that I'm here they all sound stupid in my head."

Chris smiled wanly back at him. "Now you know how I felt when we lost Rachel. There are no words sometimes, which is odd for a loquacious guy like me. I suppose, in these moments, you really don't need any."

"For Christ's sake," Karen was back in her feisty mode, "Amar is still with us, so no negative nonsense. Do you hear me?"

Chris walked over and gave Karen another hug. Normally, Chris would expect her to tell him to bugger off. But she embraced him back instead. He realized more than anyone that under her crusty shell was a sensitive person more capable of love than most. It was that unique amalgam of cynicism and sincerity that made her perfect for her role in his organization. She could look at things objectively and yet still bring a caring soul to the table. Chris recalled that it was Karen who organized a helicopter search party after he foolishly went off looking for Azita and Deena the day their parents had been killed and they had escaped into the hills. His impetuous move almost cost Karen her life when a bullet hit her as she helped Chris and the girls into the chopper, a British Tommy firing away with a machine gun to keep the Taliban at bay until they could make their escape. Chris smiled inside. She never held that over his head after the *I saved your ass, so you owe me* gambit. It simply was what you did for someone you loved.

When they parted, Chris turned to the group that had gathered. It included Jules, who had come with them back from America, Josh's spouse, Connie Chen, and Rachel's family, her partner Usha Nayer, daughter Cate, and daughter-in-law, Meena Muhaisin. There were also several from central office including Carlotta Ciganda. Other friends and colleagues had also collected. Chris let his eyes wander over the collection of people who now turned in his direction, becoming aware that he was about to address them all. "Part of me wants to thank all of you for being here and part of me wants to yell at you for being so foolish. I've seen better social distancing, but at least everyone is masked."

"You're someone to talk about safe practices," Karen said through a cracked voice, searching for her normal demeanor. "I've never seen you so touchy-feely." The crowd tittered.

"Good enough. I stand chastised, and by the woman who has chastised me more than any other . . ." He was going to finish the thought with *even more than my wife* but caught himself just in time. "Thank you for coming by and showing your love and concern. You know I appreciate this so much. Now, I am going to tell you to get the hell out of here, most of you at least, except for family. You are putting yourself at risk. Besides, visiting is extremely limited so there is little point being here and I desperately want all of you to be safe. Before you leave, though, there is something I want to say, something I want you all to think about. We have suffered unimaginable losses recently—

Rachel and Ahmad and Richard Jackson. My wife is critically ill, and my family has suffered earlier losses. Some of these tragedies are beyond our control. I suppose I could yell at the virus, but I doubt that would do any good. Some are the result of tribal hates born of religious fanaticism that seem alien and distant to most of us. And some are found closer to home, my home, my own family. Julianna Jackson, Ricky's brother, knows full well the price to be paid for extreme family discord."

Jules lowered her head. "You can say that again."

"Well, I think I can do something about some of this. I want to stop the programming we have in Afghanistan. Some of the history there is personal, the Masoud family is hated by some extremists. And second, I think it best to send Josh Connelly and all those who have accompanied him back to Canada, just until all is settled."

Cate spoke up, "Meena and I don't belong to Canada."

"Oh, I haven't thought this through totally, but hear me out. All of you know what happened to Ricky Jackson. And some of you know that Josh's good friend, Peter Favulli, has been doing his best to figure things out back there, and protect my family from . . . my own father. This may be hard to understand, if you come from a normal family with typical neuroses but mine is special. Kay, Kat, and I have become anathema to our own father. He hates us with a passion. He feels that we have betrayed him and the things in which he believes, things we find abominable. But the bottom line is this—we think he may be going after people close to me and my sisters. That is his way of torturing the three of us, hideous because he knows there are people we love almost more than our own lives. I'm just desperately afraid that the more you hang around Kay and me, the greater danger you'll be in. Frankly, I cannot stand the guilt."

"Even here in England?" Cate asked.

"Well, we are not certain, but we cannot take the chance. I cannot imagine my guilt if . . ."

"You are asking us to run away?" Meena asked.

"No," Chris tried, "I am asking you to be sensible." Chris heard his phone beep and he quickly checked a text. He looked a bit confused but returned his gaze to the crowd. "I can see Amar now. Please go back to Oxford and wait there. Talk about what I have said. Think about things seriously. Will you do that for me?" There were murmurs of assent as he went up to Jules. "We can go two at a time. Amar asked for you to accompany me. Then Azita and Deena."

"Me?"

"That is what Kay texted. I'll talk to the girls."

Twenty minutes later they made their way through security and the medical screening, adorned the proper protection, and were led to Amar's room. Chris could feel his breathing become labored. A frightening thought ran through his mind . . . was this the first symptom of Covid? No, he convinced himself, just anxiety.

"Why does Amar want to see the two of us together?" Chris whispered as they approached the room.

"I hope she doesn't think we're sleeping together and is jealous." Then immediately sensing that is not where she wanted to go so Jules quickly added. "Of course not, that would be absurd. She knows I have higher standards."

The sight of Amar bound up in medical equipment grabbed them, even after they had prepared themselves in advance. There are some things that defy preparation, that the mind cannot anticipate. Chris was glad he was masked. He was certain his facial responses would betray his reactions. Amar looked totally drawn, her face a portrait of struggle as she grasped for each breath of air.

"Hi," Chris tried to sound upbeat. "Seems I can't let you alone for one minute without you getting into some kind of trouble."

"I'm sorry," Amar's words came with difficulty. "I'm sure . . . I've been so much . . . trouble to you ever . . . since that day . . . we met."

"Stop that." Chris took her hand.

"I am very . . . tired. Just let me talk and then . . . I want to talk . . . to the girls."

"Of course," Chris responded as his heart cracked into pieces.

Amar summoned her strength. "I'm glad you came . . . Jules, so glad. I wanted to ask . . . to ask if you would . . . look after . . . Chris and the girls . . . the young ones. They will need . . . a woman and Chris . . . doesn't quite qualify. He tries . . . but . . ."

It was the last thing Jules expected. "Amar, you'll be around to raise them."

"No . . . I understand . . . my situation. Don't forget . . . I'm a doctor. Chris . . . loves you. And the girls . . . you are a hero . . . to them . . . a famous person."

Chris tried to find words, but his mind froze at that moment. All that came out was, "Amar, I love you."

"I know . . . I know . . . it's a mystery but I know." Her words were interrupted by deep breaths and coughs. "But . . . marry Jules . . . promise."

Chris struggled for what to say. Only one word emerged. "Yes."

"And Jules . . . will you?"

She waited too long to reply, as Chris desperately wished for her to lie. Finally, she squeaked out the words in a thick voice. "I promise."

"Thank you." She smiled. "Now, I want . . . to see the girls . . . all four of them . . . to hell with rules."

* * *

Karen Fisher had taken most of the original group back to the London headquarters of the International Services Organization which she now headed with only periodic input from Chris who still had an office there though he spent most of his time in Oxford these days. Kay had largely assumed Chris's management role with the program, particularly on the medical side, while Carlotta served as a deputy administrator. Karen thought it important that they have a place to talk through what Chris had said at the hospital and public places were not considered safe. Security issues had confronted them in a place they had considered a haven.

Jules, Chris, and Kay waited for Azita, Deena, and the two biological daughters, Liz and Emma, to return with Jamie who had accompanied them to the room. The wait was agony, and no one wanted to speak.

"Sis," Chris almost never called Kay that and she almost ignored him. "She's not making it, is she? Just be straight with me."

Kay looked at her brother for some moments but decided truth should triumph false hope in this instance. "Nothing's totally certain but there isn't much hope. If it had not been for the internal injuries from the bomb, she is young enough but . . . this is overwhelming her. I know it is killing me. God, I feel so impotent." They sat in silence for some moments before Kay spoke again, "Sorry about this but I have to ask. Did she ask you two for her favor?"

Chris and Jules looked at one another, neither willing to hazard a guess on what the favor was in case it was not what they supposed. Finally, Jules spoke, "About Chris and me? That favor?"

"Of course that favor. She was obsessing with Jamie and I about it earlier. She's not worried about dying at all, she doesn't care for herself. I think it is that Buddhist perspective she embraced as a child. She has a calmness about her, a kind of centeredness. I really should investigate it for myself. But the girls, the young ones, that's her worry. Frankly, they are just coming into womanhood and, not to be too blunt here, feels Chris will just screw things up with them."

"Good thing you're not being blunt." He wanted to say more but restrained himself, knowing anything said at this point would sound defensive.

"You're welcome. And so?"

"Yes," Jules responded. "I was blown away, but she seemed so serious."

"You did promise her. Didn't you?" Kay persisted.

"Sure, but what else could we say. I'm sure Chris was just being kind to his wife. He has the usual male faults, but he is kind. That, I will concede."

Chris turned on Jules. "Wait. How pathetic do you think I am?" There was irritation born of pain in his voice. "I could have weaseled my way around that moment if I wanted to."

"You're kidding me." Now Jules seemed irritated. "You would marry me, just for the kids."

"Of course not," he sputtered.

"I knew it," Jules said with an air of triumph.

"Not just for the kids but because I love you." At that moment Chris realized what he had said. In a lower voice, he repeated the words, "Because I love you. I always have."

"Oh." Jules managed to utter but nothing more.

"Surely you know that. You must, not that it matters. Let us never forget that you were the one that that turned me down," Chris said quietly. "Love is something you don't turn off."

"I never stopped loving you," Jules murmured.

"Really? I had no idea. I never thought you did."

Jules looked at him with an expression of incredulity. "Sometimes, for such a smart guy, you are such a moron."

Then, as if on cue, Jamie emerged from a corridor with the Azita, Deena, and the two younger girls. Liz and Emma were crying while the older ones had watery eyes. As they approached, Chis let out an expletive under his breath.

"What?" Kay asked.

"Just cursing our moronic Prime Minister. Azita and Deena, along with Amar, have been out trying to get poor families to practice common sense protective behaviors while dumbass Boris keeps encouraging people to work, and shop, and eat and drink in public places. He and Trump . . . total idiots. I'm a peaceful man, but there are days I want to strangle those morons."

Everyone hugged. Chris started to look for encouraging words but Azita cut him off. "Father, we all know. Mother has always been honest, she still is." Then she looked back and forth between Chris and Jules in a knowing way.

Chris looked as if he had more to say but he could see everyone knew. There was a calmness in their disposition that shocked him. Perhaps there was something about his wife's sense of destiny that had been absorbed by those around her. Some things are written, and we will know how each story ends when it is time. The final pattern of each life as spun by the Morae in good time.

It was a sunny, delightful Summer day in London. The pandemic had denuded the streets of the usual throngs, especially the hordes of American tourists who normally would be gawking at sights and looking in the wrong direction for traffic as they stepped off the curb. They decided to walk back to the office to join the others. As they ambled, Liz and Emma eventually got themselves under control, only the occasional sniffle could be heard from them.

Chris talked for a bit about his calls to Amar's brothers, one in Canada and the other in India. They were distraught that they could not be there. Her brother who taught cosmology in Canada talked to Chris about how he would show his sister the night sky and talk about the mysteries of the universe. Chris was gratified that he, in turn could relay back the fact that Amar had passed on those lessons to him. The two of them often walked at night while Amar pointed out items of interest and mused with considerable detail and passion on the lessons imparted by her brother. Chris confided in those moments how fortunate he felt to have this woman in his life. She was more than a wife and a doctor, she was a woman of depth and eclectic interests. She was a companion and soulmate. And she was a person of deep spirituality who complemented his casual cynicism. The call ended when Chris realized that Amar's brother was weeping more than sharing memories and thoughts.

Soon, Azita preoccupied them with stories of how Chris and Amar had met. It was a story all knew but seldom tired of hearing. She evoked a small chuckle with her tale about Kay pulling her aside just before Chris was to arrive by helicopter. *Listen, Azita, my brother will be hopping mad when he arrives. You be in the office to greet him. I'll be in the operating room while Amar is off treating some wounded in a nearby village, or that's what we'll tell him. You just look at him with those big eyes of yours. He'll melt. Inside, he's a softy.*

Chris managed a laugh. "I should be offended but it's the truth. And you did melt me that day."

Azita went on to recount this whirlwind relationship as she recalled it from her young eyes at the time. She could not possibly fathom what this woman whom she so admired could possibly see in this man, or any man for that matter. The small group was particularly amazed at her story of confronting Amar when she realized that a romance was blossoming. Azita continued to be amazed that someone as smart as Amar could possibly lose her reasoning over this American. He was good-looking, she granted him that, but he wasn't even a doctor, at least not the kind that did any good. So, what did have to offer her?

Then again, Azita noted to her audience, she was amazed when any woman fell for any guy, they were so … useless. Except for her father, males ranked low on the pecking order of homo sapiens. By the time Amar and Chris got married by the British Major who ran the outpost under wartime emergency powers, she had concluded that this Chris character had promise.

"Bollocks," Chris said with a laugh as she finished, "you saw me as prince charming from day one."

The mood had lightened considerably during their walk. Chris renewed his feelings of amazement toward Azita. She was eleven going on thirty-one when first he met her. Somehow, she had wisdom built in. Where did that come from? No more than a child who had never experienced more than her beleaguered country and culture. Oh, Chris could recall some bad moments when her real age emerged, especially when she and Deena clashed. Those moments were driven by the deep love they had for the other, of that he was convinced. Yet, there was a competition there, and that led to sparks if not fully combustible moments. It was the same with Chris and his own siblings. Love and rivalry were intertwined. In Chris's mind's eye, her journey whirled before him, from an orphaned girl in a remote area of Afghanistan through British Public School through Oxford University to further medical studies in the States. It was the stuff of Hollywood, Chris mused to himself.

They finally arrived back at the offices where Chris was surprised that everyone was yet gathered. He let Kay inform everyone of Amar's situation, which she did with a sensitivity that made Chris marvel. It was obvious that his sister had delivered bad news thousands of times. There were tears but the news surprised no one. Then, to Chris's mild surprise, Karen spoke for the group with measured sympathy. "Everyone here is deeply moved and saddened. Of course, you know that. Anything we can do for the family we will. That, too, should be no surprise. Perhaps there is one point that might surprise you, Chris. We talked about what you said before, about the dangers. To a person, everyone understands. But the thing is, no one cares about that. Okay, we care but no one is going to let it dictate the direction of their lives at this point. Bottom line . . . no one is leaving. And, for Christ's sake, don't bother to argue."

Chris didn't but it took him considerable time to fall asleep that night on a cot in his office. It seemed he had just shut his eyes when there was a soft knock on his door. It was Kay. "Time to go," she whispered.

He said nothing but he knew. Soon, Jamie led them through security to where Amar clung to life. Chris sat watching her struggle to breathe as she now lay in a deep coma. Every breath caused a jolt inside him, thinking that this surely would be the last one. But they continued. Where does she get the strength? He wondered. Where does any human get the strength to continue? It was a question he often asked himself.

He looked at her, hoping she might awaken so that he might have some last words with her. But what would he say? There are no words that can encompass so many years of love. As he felt, rather than saw, the first suggestion of morning light through the window, she took one final desperate breath. It was over.

He wept.

Kay had never seen her brother weep before.

CHAPTER 25

MUSINGS

Chris and Josh took advantage of a spectacular English day to amble aimlessly and talk. They first wandered along the Thames before reversing course to head across Christ Church Meadow along the Cherwell River. Their destination was unimportant though Chris had a vague notion they would end up at the botanical gardens. Both men realized that prior decisions ought to be revisited. Now that Rachel was gone, Josh and his entourage had to determine a future purpose. Karen had declared that everyone had decided to stay the course but Chris, for one, wondered if that had been a decision made in a moment of loss and pain.

Other matters were crowding in on Chris. The election in the US was fast approaching, raising all kinds of uncertainties including the prospect of an incumbent unwilling to accept the results. Could the current occupant of the White House launch an insurrection and foment a possible hostile takeover of the American democratic tradition. Anything was possible with this maniac. Chris also knew that Ali, Azita, and Deena would not long be preoccupied with their work through Toynbee Hall, as essential as it had been in the beginning. He worried that they would want to return to harm's way in a more direct fashion. He had no plan to stop them.

Josh also had much on his mind. He had grown fond of both Oxford and his new friend, Chris. He often looked at the younger man and envisioned him as the son he never had. In his youth, he found it easy to decide against siring his own children, opting for a vasectomy in his early twenties. He never looked back at that decision with a moment of regret until recently, as he came to know Cate more closely and now Chris. Could he have generated an offspring like one of them? His seed would then be carried on into the infinite future. But he dismissed such thoughts as nonsense. His kids probably would grow up to be raving conservatives, God's way of punishing him through an intolerable karma. No, he made a good decision. He never could figure out why people were so eager to have children, the burden seemed awesome to him. In life, his screwups fell upon him alone, for the most part at least. But burdened with responsibility for a child, failure was unacceptable. And yet, he now felt as if he were, in fact, Cate's father since her biological father had long being out of the picture. How odd life is?

Suddenly Josh realized they had both been lost in their thoughts. "So, I've been thinking about our President."

"Not mine. I'm a Brit now."

"Not mine either, I'm a Canuck. But you know the saying, America sneezes and the world catches the flu. Everyone knows this malignant narcissist must be stopped. Hell, the US formally leaves the Paris Accords on November 4, that date surely was picked with care. He either has another four years to destroy the world or we will turn the corner."

Chris looked thoughtful. "I know. For months and months, we have seen all the usual tactics to steal the election—voter purges and selective election restrictions, and the usual Russian antics. This time, it is the newsroom for American and European-based citizens created in St. Petersburgh by our good friends in the Russian Internet Research Agency. A few different characters but the same old song."

"Absolutely, but what I fear is that the final throw of the dice is out of our hands."

"Meaning?" Chris asked.

"The hard right is beginning to fear they are becoming cornered rats. It's not this election. They see a demographic tide moving against them. If they don't grab complete power now, their chance may be gone."

"Okay," Chris murmured thoughtfully, "I have my theory but what's yours."

"America's democracy has always been more tentative and vulnerable than most people admit. We had appointed Senators, no direct election of President but an electoral college, widespread legal proscriptions on political participation, and ex jure denials of voting rights to groups on the outs. Hell, in the beginning, many states had no direct voting for President. Despite Lincoln's claim at Gettysburg, in no way did we have a government of and by the people, certainly not for the people. It was for the favored few and that is what the GOP has fought to maintain. Now Republicans are scrambling to turn the clock back as they see their grip on power slipping away."

Chris again looked thoughtful. "What odds do you give for a refusal by Trump to abide by the results and the party to back him?"

Josh did not answer immediately. "Perhaps 50-50, maybe higher against if Ginsburg doesn't last. They will ram a far-right candidate through to the Court and then who knows. The occasional bouts of sanity by Roberts won't be enough to stop the drift of the Court to the hard right. Of course, the coup will be dressed up in semi-rationality. Don't be shocked if there are fake or manufactured problems on election day with intimidation and violence. That will be followed by assertions that the other side is doing it. Absent that, they will scream about fraud at the polls, with the radical left stealing the election."

Chris threw his head back. "Yup, they have been preparing the way for this move all along, building distrust of existing institutions. Classic!"

Josh continued as if Chris had not interrupted. "Normally, contested elections would get thrown to the House but not this time. If it is not an armed coup, they will rely upon friendly courts to give the takeover the patina of judicial approval. And voila, the end of the democratic experiment in America. I've been around longer than you and never has the country's institutions been in such danger as they are now. Sure, we risked being incinerated during the cold war, but the Russians were never going to take over the country. And Islamic terrorists, that was a laugh. All they could do was cause some isolated pain. The real danger has always been in the paranoid minds of the far right, the same morons who believed that fluoride in our water supply was a commie plot back in the 1950s. Those demented bastards have not changed one bit. They merely have gotten their own media outlets and control of a major political party."

Chris thought about this for a few moments. "In the last election, and up to now, Kat and I have supported the work of staff that has been gathering intelligence and evidence to help with the campaigns, mostly feeding it to allies for direct use. But I think it is time to move on now."

"Really, how so?"

"I saw this Andy Borowitz quote the other day. He talks about defeating Trump as a short-term goal. The challenge is how to educate the next several generations to feel compassion, behave civilly, and think analytically. Take the longer view. It is an unspeakable tragedy that 40 plus percent of Americans consistently vote against their self-interests and their children's futures. Beyond obvious right-wing propaganda outlets like Fox News, I am discouraged by the aggressive efforts run out of Hillsdale College, PragerU, and a bunch of so-called religious colleges. They want to institute a right-wing authoritarian government or a Western-style Taliban regime."

"Hmmm," Josh murmured. "I've got to think about that."

After some time walking in silence, Chris spoke, "Do you get the sense that there are small conversations going on all around us. Not this one precisely, but similar."

"Do you mean plots against us, like the villagers scheming to overthrow us and take over the kingdom?" Josh chuckled. "I hate to break this to you, but we don't have a kingdom. Well, you might but I don't."

Chris laughed out loud. "Oh no, nothing like that. But I feel that the past few weeks have been a time out of time where life has been suspended. I mean, we have been busy, all of us but to me it has had this feel of marking time, waiting for a shoe to drop." Chris sighed and then continued, "Think about it. You and I have been busy using my resources to generate analyses and arguments and feeding them back to the US to those trying to stop Trump and flip the senate but . . ."

When Chris stopped there, Josh prompted him. "But what?"

"Oh, I don't know. It doesn't feel like it is enough, like we fight with our minds while the battle is one of emotion and power. Worse, I sense defeat, this suffering of intolerable losses with the deaths of those close to us. I feel useless suddenly, and maybe a bit lost, as if things are getting away from me." He looked up at the sky. "I never thought I'd ever get married, you know. And then I did, and now she is gone. Part of me is no longer there. I miss Amar, I feel adrift most days. At night, the pain is unbearable. And then I think of you losing your sister and . . ."

"Okay, that's it. If you go into guilt mode one more time I swear I will take a swing at you. You may be younger than me, but I grew up on the mean streets of Boston where we fought our way to school and back. We kids didn't sit around eating caviar all day."

"Caviar?" Chris gave his friend a gentle punch on the arm. "I'll let you in on a secret. I've never eaten that stuff in my life."

Josh suddenly stopped and turned toward his companion. "There is something I've thought about a lot. For all the differences in our backgrounds, you from the elite and I from the real world, we could be brothers. Before you laugh, listen to me. We both are eggheads, love ideas, delayed marriage as long as we could, broke away from our fathers, were estranged from our siblings, ran away to foreign countries, and I'm sure there is more that I'm forgetting at the moment."

"That I'm drop dead handsome and you are not," Chris deadpanned.

"Your sisters are right, you are an asshole," Josh deadpanned back at him.

"Yeah, I see that, about our similarities and not about my better good looks. I think I know the origins of this apparent similarity."

"Which is?" Josh inquired, sensing that Chris had become serious once more.

"We both were cauterized from our emotional self," Chris said.

"Excuse me, Doctor Phil. That sounds like psychobabble."

Now Chris smiled. "Before I deck you, let me explain. We are both Irish, well half at least. You from your dad and me from my mom. Whatever else we are hardly counts. The black cloud dominates both of us."

"Black cloud?" Josh laughed. "I get you, totally. We are born with a combination of an inescapable sense of responsibility and this utter burden of guilt. What's the first thing you do every morning?" He waited for an answer.

"Apologize?"

"Of course!" Josh spoke with excitement. "We both apologize for merely breathing. Then we go about our days cataloguing all our sins of commission and those of the more insidious omission variety. By evening, we are utterly convinced that our worthless carcass is clearly destined for an eternity of shoveling coal into the fire pits of hell at the not-so-gentle behest of Beelzebub's pitch folk."

"And your point?"

Josh exhaled with exasperation. "Don't be so difficult. This is what drives guys like you and me. We walk around with the scourge of original sin embedded in our souls looking for redemption. I tried to save my country back in the '60s from a stupid war, an effort that cost me everything at the time. Now I'm here, still looking for some way to expiate sins I can't even define. I'm still trying to save the world to offset some divine accountant I cannot see but whom I know calculates our net moral worth on a daily basis. You would think that losing someone I loved would balance the scale or atone for my wickedness. But it doesn't even come close."

"You mean being estranged from Rachel and your parents?" Chris wanted to make sure.

"Mostly, and not seeing Cate as much as I would have liked. But there's a bit more . . ." Josh paused but Chris merely waited for him to collect an apparently difficult thought. "There was this girl in college. I know, everyone discounts connections at that age. Still, I've come to believe that each of us may have a person out there that is a soulmate. On rare occasions, we connect with them and, too often, they get away. Mine was Leni, a unique Irish and Egyptian beauty who absorbed my soul in college. But I was confused about commitment and caught up this radical revolution to save the world. You know. For years after I fled to Canada, I debated whether my personal hegira was motivated by a fear of jail, a fear of dying in some remote jungle, or the more prosaic fear of a commitment to this woman I loved too much."

"Commitment! That is every Irish male's worst nightmare." Chris grimaced.

"No shit, my friend." Josh agreed. "More than that, it is a fear of a conventional, ordinary life. You know, marriage and kids and a typical job."

"I recall the story from your memoir, but not this obsessive fear of conventionality." Chris said thoughtfully. "Did you ever decide what scared you most?"

"I suppose. The vision of an ordinary life bothered me but mostly I feared what I was becoming, someone whose frustrations were leading him to embrace violence. Shit, I was stealing money, setting fire to government buildings, and toying with explosives. It didn't take a freaking genius to figure out what was next. But even after making it to Toronto, I could have asked Leni to join me, my neurotic resistance to conventionality notwithstanding. I wrote maybe a dozen letters to her, pouring out my love. In the end, I never sent one of them. I just couldn't do it."

"I'm sorry," Chris asked gently, "what happened with her?"

"She stopped waiting for that letter, went on with her life. But I did track her down after some four decades. The web has some uses. We connected via cyberspace, but I was with Connie by then and Leni was happily married on her second try. But here is the thing. Our cyber connection was as intimate and intense as it ever had been. She was the same person that I remembered. And I, remarkably, was what she remembered though in an idealized way. She had never lost memory of me. Can you believe that? Funny, she was this rare combination of brilliance and innocence. She had this sharp wit that was tempered with sensitivity, the best human I ever met."

"Wow!" Was all Chris could say.

"Yeah, wow. It was as if our last conversation had taken place forty minutes ago, not forty years."

"Did you ever connect in person?"

"No, we set that ground rule right away. We knew what would happen. But I found out that she loved me, had never stopped loving me. That was enough. That was more than enough for me. Then she sickened and died of cancer."

That revelation came so quickly that Chris didn't quite know how to respond. He stumbled over his next words. "Seems to me you've . . . done enough . . . penance."

"Hah!" Josh exploded. "As if that were possible. I still have the guilt associated with my father and sister to deal with. I never reconciled with him and then he went and dropped dead. And it was only when Rachel pushed herself into my life after decades of neglect that I got to know her again. We were making up for lost time here, and now she's gone." He paused looking up at the sky as it he might find her there. But I have Cate, and now Meena. They are adults though I think of them as my children now. You know, after Meena became Cate's partner, she was shunned by many in her extended family. Her relations with the royal family have cooled, less from their rejection of her lifestyle as opposed to worry about public reaction in an Islamic country, even one that is rather secular."

"I didn't know."

"They wouldn't complain to her, but she senses the rejection. It hurts. Odd, I feel like a father for the first time. I am what I fought so hard not to be." Josh made a sound as if surprised. "Huh, you know what? I'm going to be with them, look after them. I broke my own father's heart, maybe this is a way to make amends. I will have a family at last."

Chris wanted to say something about they would more likely be looking after him in a few years but decided against that. Rather, Josh's comments generated thoughts on his own family. "Yes, I can see where breaking with a dad that you had once loved would be difficult. For me, the break with my father was essential to my survival. I never considered myself lucky but perhaps I have been. He is so flawed that hating him has been effortless. And I think I know part of his problem."

"This should be interesting." Josh looked at his friend intently.

"Charles Senior wants to be German, a member of the master race. But he was born Polish and had to hate those who crushed his country and family aspirations."

"Tough spot."

"Tough indeed. He embraced Fichte who saw Germans as a people fated by providence for supremacy, and Hegel who had them leading mankind to a dominant *culture.* Like Nietzsche, Father saw himself as being beyond the normal rules. And like Treitschke, Father embraced power as the highest personal and state virtue. He has been intoxicated with all that crap. It is part of his DNA. And you know what the Greeks say, character is destiny."

"The Greeks probably don't say that anymore," Josh dead-panned.

"The break was essential and costly. There were things from which there was no repair. I lost mother for a long time. But as I think on it, my original sin was walking away from my brother. Sure, I tried to take him with me to England, but I never did enough, not even close. And then one day he killed himself to no one's surprise. And like you and Cate, I stayed distant from my sisters for way too long. No good reason, my best guess is that I thought they might force me to man up and return home. I was way too cowardly to do that. Odd, really, but we have these remarkably high intellectual quotients, but our emotional quotients are in the gutter. So cowardly."

"No matter," Josh said with animation. "Here's the thing. Our families are now together, what's left of them at least. We have a do-over. Remember as kids, fighting in the playground for a do-over. We got it and I, for one, plan on not blowing it. We both can look back and see the forks in our lives where possible paths diverge. We could have gone this way or that. I sat in my VW Bug on a snowy night and flipped a stupid coin.

Would it be Canada or stay and fight? I still wonder if the toss had come up to stay. Would I have kept flipping until I got the right answer?"

Chris stopped walking and looked directly at his new friend. "I haven't learned much in life except that regrets don't help much."

"True," Josh said in a thoughtful voice. "It seems as if we are at another fork in the road, doesn't it?"

"I've been so afraid to ask this but here goes. I am assuming what Karen said is true. You and your family plan on staying. Am I wrong?"

"Absolutely, unless you get tired of supporting a bunch of mooches. Besides, as a teacher I like the idea of reaching the next generation, particularly if I can use your money to do it."

Chris chuckled and then embraced the older man. "Don't freak out at this, but I keep thinking of you as a surrogate father of sorts. My real one sucks."

"Well," Josh smiled, "I can handle that. I love it when the bar is set low."

* * *

Azita and Deena tracked down Ali in Bodleian Library. Their prey had not been in her office nor was she answering her phone. After a quick analysis of the situation, they fixed on the main research library at Oxford. This is where Ali secluded herself when she wished to do serious scholarship, something that was becoming more of a luxury in these hectic days. The two walked casually past the shops on High Street, then around St. Mary the Virgin's Cathedral to Radcliffe Square where Azita had often sought refuge to enjoy those rare warm and sunny days to think about things. On the other side of the square stood the library, an edifice of distinction among so many others. The library was nearly deserted, most students away or accessing the intellectual treasures stored there remotely. Memories of the bad days of the pandemic were yet fresh and fears of a return present. Ali was not hard to find. Most scholars were creatures of habit and she was no exception. They found her in a private alcove hunched over several texts splayed out on the table before her.

Ali looked up when the two women entered. Her initial look betrayed a hint of irritation, but it immediately dissolved into a smile. "Ah, I see I must find a new hiding spot."

Deena responded immediately, "I told my obnoxious sister that we would be intrusive, we can go."

"No, you didn't," Azita protested.

"Stop." Ali raised a hand. "I can always tell how much you two love one another by the amount of squabbling you do. It yet amazes me how two of the most accomplished women I know can dissolve into childlike squabbling so effortlessly, and so often."

"It's my sister's fault," Azita said in a low, quick voice.

"We really can go," Deena tried one more time as she ignored her sibling's comment.

"Come in, sit. I always have time for you two . . . time for a break in any case. What is on your mind?"

The siblings looked at one another before Deena spoke up. "We've been thinking . . ."

"Ah, that accounts for the pained expression on your faces." When neither woman responded to her light jest, Ali continued hurriedly. "So sorry, I've been hanging with Chris for much too long now. His wit is infectious, worse than the Covid scourge."

Azita smiled. "For certain, Chris is to blame, and you must have spent a lot of time with him in the past."

Ali looked uncomfortable as if she were considering a delicate rejoinder. What she said, however, proved mundane. "What's on your mind? Must be something rather important to track me down in my lair."

Azita remained silent, looking as if she had somehow stumbled into a forbidden topic. Rather, Deena spoke up. "We, I mean Azita and I, have been thinking about what to do next. The Toynbee project is well under way now and doesn't need our active . . ."

Then Azita broke in, somehow sensing that the moment to resolve an unstated issue was at hand. "My good sister will eventually get around to telling you that we are ready to go back to Afghanistan, and the other places, to get our project back on track."

"But you're pregnant?" Ali protested.

"No matter, there is yet time." Then Azita hesitated as she looked directly at the middle-aged woman who retained all the beauty of her youth. "By the way, my pregnancy reminds me of something. I . . . we . . . have a question, a personal one. Just why hasn't a beautiful and successful woman like you ever married? Most Muslim women don't escape."

"Such impertinence. I really should spank you both."

"But answer the question first," Deena asked. "We admit to our impertinence but so be it."

Ali sighed as she gestured to the books before her. "This has been my life's partner."

"And you never thought of Chris, back when you first met him?"

Ali didn't want to go there but realized it was better to get this off the table. "Way back in the beginning, I did notice him, had thoughts. I even thought of ways to be alone with him, more than once. But he had a . . . rakish reputation. He was considered a player, not serious husband material. In any case, he ran off to Afghanistan for some crisis and came back with a wife and an adopted child of all things. I put those thoughts away."

"But . . ."

"That's it. End of story. Besides, apparently there is an arrangement that he and Jules will wed someday. That was Amar's wish. Is that a problem for you two?"

"No, not at all." But Azita did not sound convincing.

Rather, Deena followed up. "I, we, think of Jules more as his third sister than a … partner for our father. Do you understand?"

"I suppose…" Ali offered cautiously.

"But you …"

"That's really it. No more! So, what is this thing about going back to the place where you almost died? And with an unborn child who is now well along. Are you insane?"

"I am past all the morning sickness stuff and besides, the women of my country worked until the day of the birth and went back to work right after."

Ali rolled her eyes. "Don't be so evasive. You know I'm not talking about work. I'm talking about you staying alive to the end of your pregnancy."

Deena blinked at the reproach. "Well, I did try to talk her out of it, saying that just I should go. But she is so stubborn as you know."

Azita angrily glanced at her sister but Ali spoke up. "Both of you listen to me. We have all gotten death threats for speaking out on behalf of Islamic women. Most of us have had Fatwas placed on our heads. That comes with the territory. But no one has ever tried to kill me. We know there are real people dedicated to your demise, the deaths of both of you. In the name of Allah, go back to the Middle East if you wish. Carry on our great work. It is my work as well. But do not go back to Kabul where you have real enemies. For my sake, do not go back there yet. Do you hear me?"

Deena opened her mouth but Azita cut her off. "I know you care . . . we know you care. But you must understand. If we don't go back, the terrorists win. It is more than that, though. If we do not show courage, how can we ask young girls to uproot themselves and do things they never imagined possible? We cannot ask them to risk all while we sit in safety here in England. You must understand that."

Ali's light brown face managed to flush with anger. "And you must understand that your work depends on you staying alive. Look at what Malala has accomplished, and she never went back to Pakistan."

This time Deena beat her sister to the punch. "We cannot speak for her, only for ourselves. This is what they call a moment of truth."

"Moment of truth?" Ali exploded. "More like a moment of insanity. Are the two of you on a suicide mission? Have you forgotten what happened to Ms. Mangale, right in Kabul . . . in the middle of the day?"

"What?" Deena sputtered as Azita heard her phone ring, glanced to see who was calling, and then answered it. "We remember. She was our friend. And we also know that she would never have run away, never."

Deena and Ali stared at one another until Azita spoke up. "That was Cate. She and Meena want to meet us in Radcliff Square. Let's go, this isn't getting us anywhere."

Deena and Azita talked strategy on the way to meet Cate and the others. They were not about to cave easily. When the two arrived, they found Cate and her partner waiting. They sat in a circle while observing the social distancing rules. Even if they violated the prescribed behaviors in the privacy of their own homes and offices, they were scrupulous in public.

"What's up?" Deena asked.

Cate and Meena glanced at each other before the former spoke. "We've been talking. Not just the two of us but Usha and Connie as well. We all can keep busy here. I mean Usha has been writing some comparative law articles of arcane differences between British and English law, something about how they have diverged over time. Interesting to lawyers, I'm sure. Connie has connected with chemistry researchers here at Oxford and Cambridge. She could even do a tutorial next spring. But they are restless."

"They?" Azita asked with a smile.

"We all are restless. Like you and us, they are enthralled with this larger vision. Can we reach out to the millions of Muslim girls and bring some along into professional roles? Usha was talking about the need for Muslim female lawyers. She remembers when female attorneys even in Canada were a rarity, now law schools are mostly female. Female Muslim lawyers remain scarce, however. Why not uncover females in the Islamic world interested in the law or politics. And Connie has similar feelings about science."

"Wait," Azita asked, "are you suggesting that the four of you want to work with us on the ground, in the Middle East?"

Meena responded, "Absolutely, I think you had us working on the back end of the process, when you had candidates here and in America, and in programs of study. But that won't happen for a while yet. We want in on the front end of the process . . . get this thing off the ground in a bigger way. You were making progress until Covid and . . . the unspeakable happened."

"So, you haven't forgotten about the bombing, the dangers?" Azita asked with a voice that trembled slightly.

"Not in the least," Cate responded as she looked into Azita's eyes with an unflinching look. "I'm not your naïve American, I worked in the Foreign Service."

"My God, your timing us perfect." Azita enthused.

"Not exactly sure what that means," Cate asserted, "but we'll have to face Chris, Karen, and Ali. They will not budge easily on this."

Meena smiled. "They will not have a chance against us."

"The six of us," Cate added.

* * *

At the same time, Kay and Jamie took a break from working with hospitalized Covid patients. They had been pressed into service given their experiences working under difficult, even dangerous, circumstances. It had been a long shift so the two wandered out into a courtyard adjacent to the hospital and found a secluded bench.

Jamie exhaled. "I thought we were out of the woods a few weeks ago, the trends were going down. Now we are backsliding."

Kay groaned behind her mask. "Same problem as in the States, nutty leadership. Boris wants to wish the virus away to keep his business cronies happy. And guess what, the damn virus is not listening. Did you ever realize that those very pols who always claim to be realists, who say they know how the real-world works, are the same ones that deny reality when it doesn't profit them? Amazing, isn't it?"

"I'll tell you what's amazing . . . working with you again."

Kay blushed, pleased that her reaction was hidden behind a mask. "No, these so-called leaders . . ."

"Forget them." Jaime stared at her. "These past few weeks, working with you again, reminds me of when we met in the Panjshir Valley all those years ago. The conditions were terrible but, in many ways, those were the happiest days of my life. Do you want to know why?"

"I can guess." Kay managed to get out. "I had a glimpse of happiness myself."

"Perhaps you can explain what went wrong then."

Kay pulled off her mask. "Shit, I'd have a better chance of being summoned by the Queen."

"Let me try or start at least. When we became lovers in the camp, and then married, I always felt I only had part of you. You never committed, not really. Want my instant analysis? Don't answer that, you're getting it anyway. You liked me but somehow couldn't take the emotional leap. You could not commit fully, and you yet suggested we get married. Even then, I thought you came up with this idea because you had this notion of adopting Azita and Deena. You loved those girls. But then your brother beat you to it."

"Oh, please . . ."

"Kay, there are many ways in which you are more talented than I, but not in understanding human emotions . . . or motivations. That part of the human experience is not a strength of your family, of any of you. When you finally shared how you were raised, I began to understand." Jamie leaned back on the bench they shared as Kay lowered her head. "I thought us having the twin girls would somehow add the missing pieces. Perhaps that is where I went wrong in reading the human heart. Can't nail them all I suppose."

Kay gasped. "Okay . . . okay. How can I apologize, Jamie? How can I make amends?"

"Kay, I'm not . . ."

"I know, but let me just say this, try to say it at least. Back then, you must understand, I wasn't . . . complete. I mean, think about it. I was raised in a home with a sociopath for a father and a mother, who, at the time, was missing in depression and alcoholism. Then I lost my twin brother who ran off to England and an older sibling, whom I adored, to suicide. And father, every memory of him was tarnished with violation and pain. Each time, I closed off another part of my heart. I couldn't let the hurt and disappointment in any longer. Males became conflated with pain in my head. Better to run away."

"Are you still running?

"I don't think I can, not anymore. Jamie, I must ask. Do the girls hate me? They must."

Jamie looked at his ex-wife for some moments. "No, they don't hate you. But they are confused. And sometimes, they think they did something wrong, so they blame themselves."

"Oh my god." Kay leaned in and sobbed on Jamie's chest.

* * *

Karen arrived home to her London apartment. It was not ostentatious but a very decent place in an upscale neighborhood. Never in her youth had she dreamt of such a nice place. She sometimes pinched herself with how things turned out. The only disappointment of late was Chris was no longer a big part of her life. He was the brother she always wished she had and now she was driven to make up excuses to call and talk to him. On the one hand, she reveled in the trust he showed in her. On the other, she just missed trading insults with him.

When she got to her apartment, she noticed something wrong. Very slowly she pushed open the door and looked inside. Yes, something was wrong. Her furnishings were in array, items smashed across the floor. Pictures that had adorned her walls were slashed while obscenities attacking her gender preferences and work with Muslims were scrawled across the walls. Slowly she entered, each step deeper into anxiety. Damn, what was wrong with her? She had been shot by the Taliban for Christ's sake. But the fear was palpable. She forced herself forward toward her bedroom door. Why was she doing this? Just call the police. As she stood, paralyzed in the middle of the room, a voice came from in back. She jumped and whirled.

"Oh my god, Mr. Shin, you frightened me." Karen relaxed at the sight of her neighbor, an Asian businessman who had always been polite but distant.

"So sorry. I was concerned. I heard strange sounds and looked out to see two men running down the hallway. I knew something was not correct but decided to wait for you. I think I should call the authorities." He still smiled but weakly.

Karen's phone rang at that moment. She saw it was Carlotta. As she answered, she mouthed to Mr. Shin, *yes, please call the police.*

"Karen, you'll never guess what has happened."

"Let me try. Your place has been trashed."

"Yours as well?" Carlotta seemed taken aback.

"Yup. What's going on? We don't have many enemies here in England, none that stay up nights cursing at our very presence. I've got to call Chris, find out if this might be his dad's work. But why? Just to create confusion, cause grief? Anyways, when you are finished with the coppers, come on over. If I'm not in my place I'll be across the hall at Mr. Shin's." She looked at her neighbor inquiringly as he finished his call to the authorities before mouthing, *"My wife and I will be happy to have you stay with us."*

Carlotta let out a grunt. "I've heard all the stories, but Chris's dad really is nuts."

"Nuttier than a fruitcake, for sure. My next call is to Chris to see what he thinks. See you soon. Frankly, I will feel better if we are together. I thought I was a tough nut, but this unnerves me."

* * *

Across the pond, Kat sat with her mother and Peter Favulli. Peter loved being in the inner sanctum of the Crawford Financial Empire. The combination living suite and headquarters were understated by the standards of the elite, but it still blew this son of a working-class family's mind. Whenever Peter visited, he could not resist looking out at Lake Michigan or southeast toward Navy Pier. There is something to being filthy rich he thought. But then he snapped back to why he was there. The members of this family needed his help.

Kat looked up from her mobile phone. "Jules just texted. She's here, getting off the elevator now."

Peter raised an eyebrow. "Tell me one thing. With all the international travel restrictions, how does she manage to criss-cross the Atlantic so easily?"

"Oh, Peter, haven't you figured out yet that the rich and connected don't follow rules." Mary Crawford said with a sly smile.

"Mother!" Kat tried to look cross. "You make us sound like spoiled children."

"And just how is that not true."

Peter adopted his own smile. He liked the matriarch of the Crawford clan. He could see how the children had escaped the frailties and self-absorption that afflicted most of the filthy rich.

Kat, after a moment of thought, was about to respond when she was saved by the outer door opening in through which Jules swept. "Greetings, Jules. Glad you are back. First, how is my brother doing? I hated not being with him at this time, losing Amar. I loved that woman."

Jules thought about an upbeat reply but hesitated. "Well, most days he seems fine. But I have not known him quite as long as you have."

"But you have known him better in many ways," Kat blurted out and then regretted the words.

"Yes," Jules replied slowly, "there are days when I can see through him. He's functioning and most people can't see it but there is a shitload of pain inside him. I find it awful to see. He still tries to be his witty self but . . ."

"All of us who love him know the truth," Mary said as she purposely looked from Kat to Jules.

There was a silence before Kat quietly said, "He told us, you know."

"What?" Jules pretended confusion.

"He told us about Amar's last wish," Kat said absent emotion.

"Oh." Jules looked about as if not knowing what to say.

Mary broke the uncomfortable silence. "My dear, I have known that my son loved you even before he did. Even in my bad years, I could see the obvious. Amar was a very bright lady. She saw it as well."

"So, it's okay with you, both of you?" Jules began to relax.

Kat laughed. "Of course. We're talking about my brother. Most men are helpless on their own, but he is worse than most. He needs you. And we love you. Mary and I have talked about this and we think it a grand idea. Hell, I know his pain. I miss Ricky every day. I still look about expecting him to be there." Her voice caught but she willed her way through the emotion. "I was stunned by how comforting marriage was. Hell, I would marry Peter here if he didn't already have a wife and twelve grandchildren."

"Only seven but the eighth is on the way," Peter murmured, clearly embarrassed.

"So, what did the two of you decide?" Kat went straight to the point with her businesslike efficiency.

"I put him off, told him I wanted to talk to you."

"And now you have," Mary spoke up with a bit of irritation in her voice. "And young lady, don't you break my son's heart a second time. You did it once before and you will feel my wrath if you do it again. Understand?"

Jules smiled at the matriarch she had come to love. "Understood."

"Good," Kat sounded as if that piece of business had been concluded. "Now to my crazy Father. Sorry, Mother."

"Bat-shit crazy is more like it."

Peter tried not to laugh as he realized he was up. "Crazy or not, the man is dangerous. I've tried to keep track of him and some of the people he has been consorting with. There is no doubt that he is stalking this family, and you, Jules. And get this, he knows about Chris and Jules contemplating marriage."

Jules exploded. "How could he possibly know? Does he read minds? And come to think about it, how do you know that he knows? Christ, this is straight out of a James Bond movie."

"I know because I have a CI in his household, that's a confidential informant by the way. Charles is careful around her, but he sometimes needs to chat aloud, and she seems safe to him. At least I hope so for her sake. He knows most things because he has someone spying in London and Oxford. I'm sure people are chatting about this openly and perhaps the walls have ears."

"I think this is too much like a Le Carre novel."

Peter continued, "Whatever, but here's what worries me. Trump is imploding, going off the rails. Our bat-shit crazy friend must be desperate, but he is not stupid in the way that cornered rats are cunning. He must see how desperate his cause must be. Trump likely cannot pull off a right-wing coup. He's alienated too many insiders. For someone like Charles Senior, it may well be the lost cause. When fanatics are faced with such a fate, they sometimes try to take everyone down with them. I saw these guys when I was with the agency. They lose their careers or something and they think that since they cannot be the protector they thought they were, they kill off their whole family. They believe it to be an act of kindness. I'm sure the profilers would see the patriarch like this."

"Makes perfect sense to me," Kat said without emotion.

"Listen, the people he is relying on for Armageddon are difficult to deal with. Maybe the agency could but I do not have their resources. They often meet in camps that I cannot approach, and my overweight retired friends from the agency don't look the part."

"Should I call the head of the FBI? Would that help to get them on board?"

"Couldn't hurt. I am working them hard and they are coming around, just not fast enough. With the election and all the crap going on, they are swamped at present. If I can just keep you safe for a while, I think we can get him."

"I've hated to give into paranoia," Kat said, then considered her next sentence. "It is time, I suppose. Let's upgrade the protection around us and get some more folk in England. We need to go to a full court press for a while. Yeah, I learned some basketball jargon from watching my brother in college. If Father wants war, so be it."

"Wow," Jules exclaimed, "it does feel like we are going to war."

CHAPTER 26

GOTTERDAMMERUNG

Charles Crawford Senior sat by himself in his penthouse suite. One light illuminated the room. His favorite composition, The Ride of the Valkyries from *Die Walkure,* broke the ominous silence that surrounded him. He preferred the solitude these days. This was so opposite to the style of his youth when he cherished the battles fought to gain supremacy in a virtual battleground where only the worthy and determined would survive. The raw excitement of intellectual and financial confrontation had always elevated him, motivated him, pushed him to excel and triumph. Those were heady days.

But now, increasingly, doubt had seeped into his world. Where were the rewards for all his efforts? What had a lifetime of striving availed him besides riches which seldom afforded him any solace and certainly no fundamental satisfaction. His family had abandoned him, and now opposed him bitterly, with a totality he yet found shocking. His worldview appeared under attack from all sides. It had all seemed within reach, it really had. America, among the world's advanced nations, had never succumbed to the collectivism that had infected all the others with their socialist guarantees of health and opportunity. What did they not understand about struggle and progress through conflict and conquest, not in war but in life's challenges? Nothing should be given, all earned. Then people would see and thus understand, absent illusion, both the necessity and the inevitability of racial purity.

He had been elated with Reagan, the man who with Phoenix-like aspirations articulated the promise he could easily trace back to Hayek, Friedman, Popper, von Mises, and other like-minded libertarians and free market enthusiasts who had been his intellectual heroes. Oh, how he wished to have been among those great thinkers, but he would not have reached his 10th birthday when they gathered in Switzerland after the war to set the world on a true path. Then, to his joyous surprise, American politics kept lurching to the right as the pundits incorrectly predicted disaster after disaster for the Republican Party. He would privately chuckle as right thinking never ended in political disaster but in a new orthodoxy for America. Collectivism was dying, though not quickly enough. Individualism and freedom became the new default position across the land or most of the land at least. The left hung on, squeaking out occasional victories but the hard right slowly succeeded in strangling the life out of most institutions including the judiciary, parts of the media, and state legislatures. If they could only do something about those remaining bastions of leftist thought—the universities.

One blemish on his hopes had come with the election of a black man to the highest office in the land. But even that could be a blessing in the inexorable march toward the promised land. Charles smiled to himself as he thought how Obama had paved the way for Donald Trump. Could such an inferior specimen possibly have risen to the top position if there had not been such an obvious affront to the real America, the white America? Not only had black faces infested the White House but good people could find nothing on which to impeach them, to drive them from their exalted positions. That both grated and rattled the man who sat listening to Wagner and contemplating recent events.

And somewhere, somehow, it might be starting to unravel. He could feel it. Oh, he yet had hope but not the certitude that existed before this pandemic and the seemingly endless missteps of Trump. What had seemed like the culmination of decades of money spent, careful plotting, and unceasing efforts to reframe the American experiment into an autocratic utopia was starting to come unglued. Charles suddenly realized he was grinding his teeth given his internal anguish.

No matter the odds, Charles had comfort in the righteousness of his beliefs. My god, even the founding fathers realized that democracy was a myth. They were all men of property and position. They could not stand the rabble any more than he could. They saw leadership as the rightful exercise of privilege and property and position, that only the noblest and most successful were anointed for such a sacred role. That was apparent to him. Why could not his son see that? He was bright enough. Where had he gone wrong? Surely, it had to be Mary's fault, with her soft Catholicism and sappy spiritual tendencies. What rot.

If only he had started to cultivate his second son sooner, prepare and harden him. He could not shake this failing of his, a mistake made early on. He unthinkingly accepted the precedent that the first born should inherit all, an ill-considered homage to the principle of primogeniture. Junior clearly was weak, he should have recognized reality and jettisoned that thought immediately. Isn't that what Trump's father had done? Fred Trump had cast aside the eldest, also a Junior, when he failed to measure up. He seamlessly went to the next in line, the Donald. That worked fine. Ironically, Fred Junior drank himself to an early death, much like his own eldest did with the help of various pills. Junior was simply weak. The parallels suddenly struck Charles as did the differences. At the end of the day, Christopher was not Donald.

Suddenly, Charles gave out an anguished cry, loud enough for the outer door to open and Martina, his maid, to silently appear and ask, "Do you need anything, sir?"

He looked at her uncomprehendingly for a moment. "Oh, it is you." He blinked several times. "No, no, I am fine." She turned to leave but he stopped her. "Come and sit. I need someone to talk to."

"Yes, of course." She sat on the edge of a chair, ready to exit as quickly as feasible.

"Do you have children?" He wanted to refer to her by name but realized he had never bothered to learn it. She was just "the girl."

"Yes, sir, a boy and a girl."

"That is too bad. I was going to warn you that they break your heart. Hitler never had children. He was a smart man, stayed married to a cause, to a vision. Principles remain true but offspring? With them you can never tell. They take the best from you and then spit in your face."

When he said nothing further, just stared at her, she felt a need to speak. "I wouldn't know, sir."

"Let me tell you a story. When Hitler rose to power he was helped by the *Sturmabteilung,* or the assault division. They were better known as the SA or the brown shirts. He could not have risen to power without them. But you know what he did when he made it?"

"No, sir."

"He killed their leaders, including his good friend Ernst Rohm and disbanded the rest. He didn't need them anymore and the army distrusted them. He realized he needed the Wehrmacht more. Ever the practical man was the Fuehrer. You cannot exercise power if you are weakened by compassion or sentiment."

"I suppose so, sir."

"What should any man do when he is betrayed, when he finds that those whom he gave birth to no longer are useful. Worse, what should he do when they defy him?"

"I would not know, sir."

"The answer is obvious, my dear. You cut them out as if they were a cancer on the body. That is what you do, you cut out the rotten parts so that they do not infect what is pure and good.

But here is the secret, and not many know this. So, listen carefully, my dear. You start with the tissue adjacent to the cancerous part. You eliminate that first and work your way toward the festering puss. You know why, of course."

"No, sir."

"Very simple, my dear. If you don't get it all, it will survive and spread. It is the tissue that is not obviously diseased that just may be the most dangerous. Do you know what I am talking about?" Martina merely shook her head but said nothing, now too afraid to speak. "Oh yes, there are parts of the body that look healthy, seem pure, but nevertheless carry the disease. So, you go after that first. You must seek out and discover and excise what looks innocent, but isn't, from the body." He looked at her to the point where she desperately wanted to leave but could not. "And what should I think about you, my dear."

"Sir, I do not understand."

"Really, you do not. I wonder. I wonder. Just be careful, understand?"

"I am, sir. I do my work, that is all."

"I wish I could believe that." Charles stared at the frightened woman with an unnerving intensity.

"Just my work." She managed in a trembling voice.

He stared at her for a long time. "You can go."

After she left, Charles leaned back in his chair. Whom could he trust? No one. There was something about her, just like Beverly. He shook that thought out of his head. Why focus on detail when there were bigger disasters afoot. Trump was dissolving in his own incompetence and delusional thinking. All that work and promise going for naught.

Well, he thought. Perhaps this was 1944 all over again. The allies were rolling toward Paris so why wasn't it burning? The end all but assured. He felt so alone, so angry. Yes, he suddenly thought. It finally was time for his *Gotterdamerung*. That would sate the pain.

CHAPTER 27

COUP DE COEUR

Mary Kelly fussed with her computer. "I can never get this Zoom thing right."

Suddenly, the others could see Kat Crawford appear next to her mother and reach down to make some adjustments. "Now you can see everyone, Mother."

"All I can say is that it was a lot easier when I was a girl."

"Mother," Kat laughed, "when you were a girl we could not even imagine having this conversation, the seeing one another part at least."

Mary got straight to the point she wanted to address. "Now, son, I am led to believe that dear Amar wished you and Jules to be married. That woman was way too good for you, Amar that is, and I miss her terribly. Point is, I just wanted you to know I think this a splendid idea though why such a beautiful and successful girl like Jules would want to be stuck with you is a mystery to me."

"A mystery to most of us, Mother, but I'm gratified you think so highly of me." Chris said with a touch of sarcasm. "However,

Jules had not committed to anything when she left, she was still playing hard to get."

Jules spoke up, "Chris, guess what, you are in luck. Your mother threatened me with bodily harm if I didn't agree to marry you. So, I'm in. I guess I could do worse."

"I did nothing of the kind," Mary protested.

"Really? Sounds exactly like you, Mother." Chris broke into a broad smile.

Mary Kelly wagged a finger at the screen. "Christopher Crawford! Don't make me walk across the ocean. You will be one sorry young man if you do."

"Oh my god, I haven't heard that threat since . . . our last chat."

"So, that is settled," Kay said in a way that suggested she had something to add. "Then I have an idea."

"Oh Lord, spare us. My sister has an idea."

"Don't you play with me either, dear brother. I'll come over to your place and beat the crap out of you, right after Mother finishes with you, that is."

Mary sighed. "Oh, dear Lord, spare me. My children are in middle age and they still act like teenagers. But what is your idea, my dear."

At this Kay looked discomforted. "Well, it is like this . . . umm . . ."

Chris chuckled. "Oh, for Christ's sake, spit it out, sis. Usually I can't get you to shut up."

"Christopher, such language, and be nicer to your sister." Mary was getting irritated with her twins.

Kay spoke up with more confidence now. "Jamie and I are getting married . . . again. Karen knows, I told her for obvious reasons, but I want the rest of you to know."

"He's taking you back?" Chris tried to look surprised but his glee at the news was noticeable. "What is wrong with that man. Did he suffer a head wound when he was in her majesty's service? Is it PTSD?"

"I'll ignore my brother, which is easy enough since I've had a lifetime of experience doing just that. Jamie and I have been working together a lot recently, with the pandemic and all. I just realized how much I missed him, and the girls, I've not been a good mother. I suppose it is time to reorder things in life, get things right."

"And I have a thought." Karen chimed in, perhaps trying a bit too hard to mask any embarrassment that she and Kay once were lovers, if only for a while as Kay searched for her identity. "We can have a double wedding in Oxford, perhaps at Christmas. It is lovely during the season. We can get one of the old cathedrals in case anyone is up for tradition. They are underused these days."

The conversation continued with various suggestions on the matter of weddings before there was a lull and Peter Favulli broke in. "Okay, I hate to interject a somber note, but we need to talk about security now. That's the real purpose here."

"Of course," Kat said. "It's just hard to move away from good news, there's so much bad."

"Weddings are good news? Could have fooled me." Chris offered and moved on before anyone could respond to him. "Peter, you'll want to hear the latest, I assume."

"Well, we know about the vandalism and threats to your people, Chris," Peter said. "Has there been more?"

"Well, more death threats, yes. But no more break-ins. I do have worse news. The girls, I mean Azita and Deena, along with Cate, Meena, Connie, and Usha are off to Afghanistan. Josh and I are beside ourselves with worry. But once these women make up their minds, you cannot stop them. Ever try to prevent women from doing what they want? Cannot be done. Freaking impossible. What happened to the old days when women listened to men?"

Kat guffawed. "Those days only existed in men's fantasies."

Chris groaned. "And no one listens to me. I said no like a dozen times. They just smiled. I thought I was in charge. Hah!"

Kat laughed out loud. "We let you think you were in charge."

Josh spoke up, "Let me back up Chris's despair here. I'm having nightmares about Cate and the others Rachel loved so much. What gives me some comfort is that, unlike Azita and Deena, they might not be targets, and that this is a quick trip. Maybe all will be okay. But I will be in agony every moment they are gone."

Kay added, "Listen, I love Azita and Deena as if they were my own, but I understand them, what is driving them. I don't know the others as well, but I can guess what's up. You get to a point where you face risk or give into it. You must decide between security and conscience. It happens to all of us who put ourselves out there for something that matters. They looked at the possibility that the program they have devoted so much in might falter unless they make an appearance. They are frantic to let those on the ground know it is alive and well and, most of all, that they are willing to risk all for this dream. After all, healing Muslim girls is popular nowhere in this region, some places worse than others. Everyone involved is taking a risk. How could they ask something of others they were not willing to face themselves? I have nightmares as well, but I understand."

Karen cleared her throat, signaling to others on the zoom call that she wanted to speak. "Chris may want to fire me, but you must realize that I helped them prepare for this trip . . . with logistics and expenses. Really, do you think they could have done it so quickly on their own? We talked over the risks, getting in and out as quickly as possible, not taking silly chances. Over the coming months, they will get to other sites, but we want to get Azita back asap to have her baby." Karen took a deep breath. "So, boss, should I clear out my desk?"

Chris looked a bit defeated. "You're not going to get fired that easily, but I do have plans to make you suffer. Make no mistake about that." He managed a small smile, but his insides churned with anxiety.

"No forced meals at The Hare, anything but that." Karen tried for lightness.

"Worse, I'll force you to listen to my uni lectures."

Peter broke in again. "Back to business. They are not the only one in immediate danger. Let me lay this out for you. My sources, while not great, give me some insights into what

Charles Senior is thinking. He is imploding, I believe, just as Trump might be as both see their dreams possibly going down in flames. From snatches of things he has shared with certain people, he wants to take down his enemies."

"His *Gotterdammerung*, his twilight of the gods," Chris muttered distractedly.

Peter continued after a momentary pause. "Everyone on this call is an enemy of his, by the way. And he has said things that make it look as if he will start with those on the outside of the immediate family and then move toward the center. In his twisted mind, that makes family members suffer more."

"Sounds exactly like him," Kat interjected.

"Oddly enough, the ones in Afghanistan now might have removed themselves from harm's way. We don't think his reach goes that far but surely it does to England. Be careful. Get more security. From now to the election, no unnecessary trips, though the pandemic has kept us all at home. Got me."

"Got it," Chris responded, "but how vulnerable are you guys? Should you come over here, bring my family with you."

Peter answered. "That's no guarantee, obviously. Besides, your people are as stubborn as you are. I do worry about Julianna, in particular. She is so public and has attacked him and his cause through the media. He must loathe her. And with the marriage, holy shit."

"That makes me want to marry Chris even more," Jules stated with conviction.

"And all this time I thought it was my body."

"Enough jokes. The next few days may be critical. What really worries me is that a woman on the inside, his maid, and a source of intelligence, has disappeared. Another information source is convinced he is suspicious of everyone, classic late stage paranoia. Everyone is in danger."

* * *

Ali, Deena, and Azita were led to the site of the bombing, accompanied by four members of a security force which Shahed had insisted accompany them. The remainder of the group, including Cate, Meena, Connie, and Usha remained back at the hotel where they met with various staff who had been recruiting young girls for further education and training as part of the new program. This was proving a shot in the arm for the program. The girls had been despairing that anything would come of their ambitions to better themselves. But now they were spending hours talking about science and the law and educational programs with these eminent figures. It was what they needed. The promises seemed real again.

Ferhana and Bahiri guided them to the site where the bomb had exploded. There was little evidence remaining of the blast. Azita felt weak, nevertheless. It was here that she lost her husband and being here brought back the reality of it all. She felt her belly which now revealed her late-stage pregnancy. As if sensing something, the fetus kicked. Ahmad's legacy was still there, growing inside, a comfort in an otherwise raging set of emotions.

"As you can see, we are making great progress," Bahiri said. "And we have been able to keep our services going as if nothing happened. You would think that people might stay away, but that is not the case. The community has rallied about us. They are outraged that the memory of Pamir and Madeena Masoud has been sullied by such violence. The people are tired of the killing. We sense a change, hope for a change."

"So much progress in rebuilding." Deena was taken aback. "I never would have guessed. You are miracle workers."

It was Ferhana who responded, "Hardly miracle workers. I will tell you who they are, the ones that do miracles. It is those local teachers and community leaders who have been reaching out to young girls, getting them interested in the broader world. Yes, we have brought computers and technology to this place. But it must be people, those they trust, to get past the suspicions of the girls and their parents and open new possibilities for them. If you had stayed away much longer, we may have lost momentum. This would have been another set of promises not kept. These are people who have been disappointed too many times. But now, now you have seen how bright their eyes are. One thing is true. If you always have had access to education and the outside world, such things are commonplace. But if all this is just now being offered to you, it becomes everything."

Azita felt tears streaming down her face. "Can I sit down for a moment?"

"Of course," Ferhana said, as they all sat in the courtyard where there were benches for those waiting to be treated. "Are you feeling ill? Bahiri, go get some cold water."

"Please don't concern yourself for me. I am fine, a little emotional I think. I seldom see myself as an emotional woman, but with the pregnancy, the hormones perhaps get the better of me."

"Understandable, my poor husband can tell you some stories," Ferhana said with a smile.

"I think I have been feeling sorry for myself. Self-pity is like a disease. It can take over your body and dominate your mind. But seeing this, meeting the girls, has been a miracle drug. It is so easy to forget what you are about back in Oxford. I love that place, but it is not reality. This is reality. You are right, Ferhana, if we had not forced the issue, insisted on coming, all might have been lost, perhaps not forever but . . . a setback for sure."

"Perhaps we should return to the hotel," Deena suggested.

"First, I want to take you to a place important to me. And one other thing, we must go back to our home in the north. Archie and Agnes have been asking us to visit. We must now go, Deena. That is where I first became a doctor, not in medical school but there, in the camp with Papa, Kay, and Amar. And that is where you first started building schools and bringing girls to educate them, build up their hopes and give them a vision."

"Oh, my sister, Ali will not be happy with you. That is also the place where two attempts have been made on our lives. She will surely say you are tempting fate."

"So, I will go alone if that is your wish."

Deena threw her head back and laughed. "As if I would ever let you be killed without me. We will arrange to fly north as soon as we can."

As Azita led the group away from the clinic, two local men who had been loitering nearby talked with animation. They smiled with satisfaction as they looked after the retreating group, something they heard had pleased them.

Within ten minutes, Azita and the others arrived at a square and marketplace of seemingly ancient provenance. Azita spoke excitedly, "This market has been here for generations. It is also a public meeting place, one where I spent much time as a young girl before I became obsessed with my Papa's world and medicine. I loved to listen to the gossip and think about the concerns and interests of others. I suppose that is where I first realized that I had this insatiable curiosity."

Deena rolled her eyes. "Oh, my sister, the only thing I noticed about you as a young girl is that you were insufferable, and never around when there were chores to be done."

"That, too, but I discovered that I wanted to know more about the world beyond what we could see every day. And that is what we must find in the girls we want to help. They must be curious above all else. Back up north, when the dangers of coming to school for girls was great, some would risk all to get to a classroom, as simple as it was. They thirsted to have their minds opened. Those are the ones we want." Azita suddenly changed direction and led them to a wall on which notices were posted. "And here is where, as a girl of eleven, I was beaten senseless by the Taliban for reading a poster. Sometimes people would post things that were not found in the newspapers."

"Were you reading something forbidden?" Ferhana asked.

"All I recall was that the poster involved the Taliban blowing up the Buddhist statues at Bamiyan. I remember being appalled. In any case, my sweet brother saved my life that day. Odd, the simple act of reading was considered a crime or perhaps I showed my disapproval of what the rulers had done. Whatever, I had sinned in their eyes."

The small group stared at the wall, lost in thought. Suddenly, a man approached. Azita noticed him first. He clearly was heading for them. Did he represent danger? Should she raise some alarm. In a moment, she decided against that. She would presume good, not evil. "You are Azita Masoud. Word has spread that you are here." As the security men leveled pointed their rifles at him, he threw his arms wide to reveal no weapon. "I mean no harm."

"I am Azita Masoud," she responded in a level voice and gestured to the guards to lower their weapons.

"Good. Many years ago, as a much younger man, I was here in this square. Allah forgive me but I was one of those that beat you that day. I am glad you are here. Allah has granted my wish. I have wanted to apologize to you for many years." The man looked on the verge of tears. "Can you forgive an older and wiser man?"

Azita looked into his kind eyes and said softly, "Of course. But how did you remember? There must have been so many young girls that you . . . beat."

He winced at her words. "But none that became so famous. You are a legend here, as is your sister, and your parents. The Masoud family is talked about with reverence. I now have daughters. They are in school, learning much. You are much loved."

"Not by all, we think," Deena added. "We still fear for our lives."

"Small streams of hatred yet run through the country but they are not like the rivers of old. And they become smaller every day. I have hope, much hope, for our land and people."

Azita looked at the man whose face was lined with age well beyond his actual years. "So do I, my brother, so do I." She smiled at him kindly. "I know that Allah will welcome you into paradise. I forgive you and He, after all, is the merciful one."

Tears formed in the man's eyes. "Thank you, my sister. Thank you."

* * *

The next day, Jules left a downtown Chicago office building on LaSalle Street. She saw Peter Favulli waiting for her. "Oh god, you are like my shadow."

"Get used to it, my dear, I am dedicated to seeing you get to your wedding. But you are not making it easy, I must say. What the hell are you doing running all over town?"

"Peter, I am a network celebrity with a job to do. I cannot do it by hiding in my closet."

Peter sighed with exasperation. "You are such a pain in the ass. Does Chris know what he is getting?"

Jules chuckled. "If he does not after all we have been through together, he really is as dumb as he looks."

At that, Peter laughed. "Okay, the two of you are well matched. And I must say that sometimes protecting you makes me feel like Kevin Costner with Whitney Houston. But I can't remember the name of that movie."

"Neither can I but I'm sure of one thing. You are no Kevin Costner."

"Well, my dear, you are no Whitney Houston." Peter chuckled at his own witticism. "By the way, where are you going?"

"Another appointment, just a block away. What's the worry, it is midday in downtown Chicago with all kinds of witnesses around. Nothing is going to happen, trust me."

But Peter did worry. He had lost touch with his two inside contacts. He tried reaching out to them over the past twenty-four hours with no response. Probably nothing but terrible scenarios kept floating through his head. At that moment, Peter noticed two men crossing the street. Instinct told him to pay attention though he was not exactly sure why. They were dressed in casual clothes designed to blend in with the crowd. Their expression conveyed nothing of interest and while their pace of movement was quick, it was not frantic by any means. One was on his cell phone and the other simply walking in their direction. What alarmed him?

"Jules, get behind me."

"What?" She had been lost in her thoughts.

It was the eyes of the man not on the phone. They were fixed on Jules. Of course, she was a media star. People stopped her for autographs or to gush over her looks and style of dress all the time. It was mostly a nuisance. That was common enough. But Peter knew these were no fans. One look at their grim faces was enough to tell him they were on a mission though they seemed intent on obscuring that fact. As they reached Peter's side of the street, the two men angled their direction slightly to head straight toward them. The one on the phone ended his call, shoving it in his pocket and reaching inside his coat. The other slid a hand inside his light jacket, which struck Peter as out of place on this warm August day.

"Jules! Down!" Peter shouted as he reached for his weapon and pushed his way in front of her. He knew it was hopeless. He was not as agile as he once was. Besides, in thirty years with the agency, he had never been in a real gunfight. Oh, he had drawn his firearm several times but never in the heat of the moment. He could hear Jules say something, but it was lost in the moment for him. His weapon was out when he felt something slam his chest, pushing him back into Jules who screamed. Another object missed his head by a fraction. Then his body slumped toward the ground despite his will to stand erect. He managed to fire once while thinking that now he was in trouble. The agency really frowned on firing one's weapon in public places. One of the shooters grunted and fell to the sidewalk. Had he shot him, had someone else? There were screams and more shots, but he could not quite comprehend what was happening. As his world stopped spinning, one of the men was now on the ground, blood spurting from his neck while the other was jumping into a car that had pulled up to the curb.

"Chris, where are you?" It was the voice of Julianna Jackson, known to many fans across the land, as the girl who had risen from near poverty on the west side of Chicago to national media stardom. It was the voice of the woman who had finally agreed to marry the man she had loved since her childhood.

The words seemed far away to Peter. But he realized Jules was next to him, his head was resting on her leg. As a crowd gathered, most looking on with horror or indecision, Peter managed the obvious, "Call 911," but his own voice sounded distant and artificial. Had he really said those words? *How silly*, he said to himself, *the 911 center must have received a dozen calls already*. He struggled to his knees to see blood pouring from her chest. Instinct and adrenalin took over. He crawled into position and began to press on the one wound he could see in Jules, trying desperately to stanch the blood. But he felt so weak, so weak.

A female kneeled at his side. "I'm a nurse. I'll take over."

"No," he managed to say, "I can do it." But one of his arms literally shook with pain and he could barely focus. As he sank to the cement himself, he kept repeating, "Jules, stay with us! Jules, stay with us!" His head began to swim but he struggled to hear her voice. Nothing.

The nurse beside him was shouting orders.

"She needs compressions! We're losing her!" And then counting. "1 . . . 2 . . . 3 . . . 4 . . ."

Why are they counting? He wondered. "And I need someone to press this man's wound, now! We can't let him bleed out."

Whose wounds? Peter thought. Then it hit him she was talking about him. But that was not his concern in the moment. No, he was overwhelmed with guilt. *And the Irish thought they had a monopoly on Catholic guilt.* He was supposed to protect these people for his good friend, and he had failed. Josh had trusted him. What could he possibly say to him? But it was all fading away from him, the sounds and even the guilt. This sleep would be a blessing, yes, a blessing.

* * *

Deena, Azita, and Ferhana had taken a helicopter up to the medical and educational camp in the Panjshir Valley where Pamir Masoud once used his medical skills for healing and Madeena Masoud first began educating young girls not of her own family. Now, Dr. Archibald Singletary, his wife Agnes, and some of their children, also medical personnel kept things going. The focus now was less on healing, since there was no war, and more on education since this was something new in this remote part of the world. Even the Covid virus appeared to have avoided this place. Ferhana had insisted on coming since it had been a rather long time since she had seen Archie and Agnes. She liked the older couple, thought of them as surrogate parents in a way. Ali was still sputtering about the dangers they faced as the copter took off to head north. She now thought of Azita and Deena as her own children, or maybe younger siblings, and the fact that they insisted on putting themselves in harm's way drove her to distraction.

It had been a while since they had visited the camp. They were astounded at the changes in the place. Everything appeared calmer, cleaner, and more peaceful. Soldiers and guns were not omnipresent. While there were a steady stream of medical issues to be addressed, a great deal of the work now centered on preventative and community development issues, hygiene, inoculations, progressive parenting, education, basic infrastructure, public health, and inspiring the next generation to better themselves, both boys and girls. As Archie kept repeating, hope is the best vaccination against so many ills. A daughter-in-law of Archie and Agnes had taken charge of the new technologies that were being used to broaden the horizons of the younger children. At one point, Deena, overcome with emotion and enthusiasm, spontaneously embraced the woman before apologizing profusely, then realized that the gesture was most welcome.

Ferhana spent several hours comparing notes with Agnes about the respective challenges they faced in reaching some of the more suspicious and traditional parents. Nothing came with ease, they lamented, but progress had been undeniable. They could see it in so many ways, including how receptive families were to their programming. It had not always been so. Archie had moments when he worried for his family in the beginning. However, it was hard to dismiss his infectious good will and kind personality. No one could deny these traits.

Deena was thrilled with the education program. She spent much time talking with the brightest girls and imagining which could make the leap to the outside world. Education in Kabul and then perhaps England or America. The cultural leap was the greatest challenge of all, but she was certain it could be done. After all, their father had done it, growing up in a remote village not far from this site and making it to Oxford to get his medical degree. It was a bigger leap for girls but that was what they were all about. She saw several who were excellent candidates.

At one point, she realized that she had to get to the family village, where her father had been raised as a child. They had built a school there, one of their more remote sites and she wondered if it was doing well, though Archie and Agnes assured her of that fact. She had to see for herself. Bad memories lingered, of course, it was there that she had been shot by the son of the very man she had killed after their parents had been assassinated so many years ago. Two assassination attempts in that place. Could there be a third?

Deena reflected on the first attempt which she recalled more vividly. After her parents were assassinated, Azita and she had fled into the hills to save their own lives only to be hunted down by the Taliban as Chris frantically searched for them. At one point, shortly after Chris had tracked them down, they were cornered by an extremist fighter who intended to complete the job that had started with the murder of their parents. Deena remembered she had a pistol hidden in her clothes. As the terrorist paused to savor his imminent satisfaction, she drew it out and, without hesitation, shot the man dead. In a tribal world, such things are never forgotten. Vengeance is essential, a duty. The bombing of the clinic bore tragic testimony to that. The second attempt occurred as they visited the home in which their father had been raised. It had been much improved since then but retained so many memories. As they left the building, shots rang out. They never did know if the bullets were intended for Deena or Azita.

This would be a quick visit, however. It would be fine, she told herself. Lightening may strike twice in the same place, but certainly not three times. She half heartedly tried to argue that Azita stay in the main camp, why endanger both of them. But she knew there were no arguments that would work. The younger sibling merely smiled. *You think I will let you be a martyr on your own. Hah!*

The visit had been everything they had imagined. Their family home, the site of the tragic attack and assassination of Pamir and Madeena remained a community memorial and public place. It was a shrine to their most famous resident, the boy who some three generations ago went off to become a doctor in England and then returned to heal his people. And now it also contained artifacts of his two daughters who, with a similar sense of purpose, had gone on to change the world. Both women were brought to tears which they tried without success to hide. The school was even bigger and more complex than they had recalled. On closer examination, they realized it had been enlarged to meet an expanding demand. Once it became known they were there, students flocked to see and touch them from the whole area, including teachers and parents who only knew them by reputation.

Finally, the excitement settled down. As Azita was considering whether it was time to depart, a young man approached. "Oh please, in Allah's name, can you come to look at my mother? She has been struck with some illness and you are a great healer."

"I have no medicines," she protested. But the youth protested with such sincerity that Azita felt that she must at least look. "Where is she?"

"In that home beyond the school where the village begins to rise into the hills."

As she followed the youth, Deena called out, "Where are you going?"

"This boy wants me to look at his mother who is ill. If it is serious, perhaps we can take her back to the clinic with us."

"Do you want security to go with you?" Deena called out.

"Deena, don't be a silly goose. I'll be right back."

Deena, anxious to leave before the sun disappeared, was a bit irritated but understood what motivated her younger sister. For a moment, she looked as the two figures disappeared around the school. That worried her, suddenly, but she pushed aside her fears. Just a touch of paranoia, she told herself.

* * *

Azita was beginning to sense a similar dread. The house looked empty, abandoned, with no sign of life. Why didn't she accept her sister's suggestion of security? She turned to confront the young man to see a pistol in his hand. Her heart froze for an instant.

"Keep walking into the hills. If you scream, I will kill you here. I just want to talk."

They went on in silence weaving higher among the rocks until she realized their destination. It was the same cave and place where they had fled to escape the Taliban the morning of her parent's assassination. When they arrived, she tensed, expecting a bullet to strike her each moment that passed. It was clear he wanted way more than a few words, he wanted revenge. She wondered what she might think about in these final moments. At first, it was a blur of jumbled images before the kaleidoscope settled on Amar, Kay, Chris, and her sister. Oddly, an image of

Ali crowded in on her. She had not realized just how much she had come to love this colleague and mentor. She had been so fortunate to know and love such people. The faces stopped with an image of Ahmad. She wondered if talk of an afterlife was more than talk. Would she soon be joined with him? She tensed for the pain of a bullet, but none came, only words.

"You know this place?"

Azita turned to face the words. "I know this place."

"You know who I am?"

"Were you the one that planted that bomb that killed my husband and my friends? Am I correct?"

"Yes, I did Allah's will. But that is not important. I am also the son of the man you killed here and whose brother died at your hands in that village back there."

Azita felt total calm. She considered correcting him, telling this earnest young man that he was wrong. It was her sister that shot his father, and that she had no choice since the boy's father was about to murder them. And it was a member of the security detail who killed his brother, another young man driven by hate to attack in a moment of religious insanity. But she would not say these things. That would send him back to kill her sister. Better to let him believe his revenge was complete. "You cannot believe that Allah wants all this senseless killing to continue."

"It is His will. I am certain."

Her voice was preternaturally calm. "My son, Allah did not tell us to hate. Everywhere I have been, among Christians and Jews and Hindus and Muslims, there are these so-called holy men who sit in their madrassas or temples or churches and teach their followers to hate. But they are misguided. They are simply wrong."

"Silence," the young man yelled.

Azita continued calmly. "You know, there was once a man called the Mahatma, the *great soul*, who helped his country achieve independence from England. Many of his followers wanted an armed struggle to reach their goal but he always said no. He told them that God was a Hindu, and a Muslim, and a Christian, and a Jew, and a Buddhist. He taught them simple lessons, that an eye for an eye would leave the whole world blind. Do you know what that means, what he was saying?"

"Shut up. Just shut up." His eyes filled with tears but Azita could not tell whether they were from rage or guilt or fear or uncertainty. "Now just say your final prayer before I send you to hell!" He was screaming now; spittle flew from his mouth.

"You will also be killing this innocent baby inside me. You must realize that. Would Allah wish that, to kill an unborn that the divine has created?"

The youth simply screamed in return. "No innocent baby! A spawn of the devil! This is Allah's will! You are an infidel, damned in the eyes of the almighty!"

Azita closed her eyes. She had no words to turn aside such hate. She was resigned, oddly at peace. "I will say a final prayer now, one for your soul, my dear brother. I will forgive you and ask Allah to also forgive you. That is our greatest gift and blessing . . . forgiveness. Please accept it."

As she held her breath, a huge bang deafened her momentarily. The recoil echoed down the hillside where, for the first time, she heard voices calling her name. But they were too distant, of no help to her. She kept her eyes pressed tight, waiting to feel something. But there was nothing. That confused her. When she opened her eyes, he was not where he had been. More confusion. Then she saw, the young man lay before her with a gaping wound visible in his chest. His eyes were open as if in surprise. She looked around expecting to see her villagers, a rescue party. All she saw was a single older man with the grizzled dress and features of a mountain fighter. His menacing weapon was not pointed at her but at the now dead youth. The voices of the search party will still distant though more frantic given the obvious sound of gunfire.

"You killed him?" Azita mumbled.

He looked at her for some moments. The voices calling her name edged a bit closer. "Yes. It had to be done."

She managed the words with great difficulty. "I don't understand. I don't . . ."

The grizzled man barked, obviously with emotion. "He was my brother's boy, just a baby when you killed his father very near here."

Azita again rejected the desire to tell him that it was not her but that seemed irrelevant in the moment. Suddenly, she was confused. Did he want to kill her for himself? But that did not make sense. Besides, a look into his eyes did not reveal a man bent on vengeance. They suggested a haunted soul more stricken with weariness and grief than rage. "Why did you kill him, your nephew?"

"It must end, all this madness. It must end. It must." With that, he slung his weapon over his shoulder and began walking up the mountainside. Just before disappearing over the rise above her he turned. "I listened to your last words to that tortured boy. They touched my heart. I wish they could have reached him." And then he was gone.

Azita collapsed to the ground and wept. She was not sure why. Perhaps for relief or sadness over another senseless death or perhaps, just perhaps, she sensed a new beginning in a land that had been troubled so long.

The voices calling her name were closer. She tried calling out, but nothing came from her throat.

* * *

Back in the camp, Azita went into labor and delivered a baby girl. The trauma of events had thrown off her planning though she had calculated that she was taking a chance on this trip. It had not mattered. She had taken pride in planning to work right to the moment of birth, much like the women of her native country had done since time immemorial. Her sister thought the idea nonsense and never let an opportunity pass to remind her of her folly.

Azita looked at the reddish baby in her arms. "It is right that she be born here, near the ancestral home and among our people. It is right."

"So," Deena asked excitedly as she looked down upon the newborn, "have you decided on a name?"

Azita smiled. "I was going to name her Hope, but I decided on names that mean the same . . . to me at least. She will be Madeena Amar Zubair. And she will be a great teacher one day."

CHAPTER 28

REDEMPTION

After a frantic trip to Chicago, Josh walked into the hospital room. He looked at his friend lying in the bed for some moments. He thought he was prepared, but the sight of the tubes and medical paraphernalia still surprised him. *You are never ready,* he concluded. Reality often had a harsh presence that defied anticipation. He willed himself past that moment while putting on his game face. Then he noticed Laura, Peter's wife, sitting on the other side of the bed. She had been a looker in her youth but now was a matronly-looking woman who seemed out of central casting for the role of Italian grandmother. Peter never noticed the change in her appearance over time. She remained the Italian ingenue he first met over five decades ago. Josh had always liked Laura though he never got to know her well until later in life. He walked around the hospital bed to give her a big hug.

"I got here as fast as I could. Can you forgive me, Laura?"

"What's to forgive, you big Mick. You didn't shoot him. I certainly have been tempted to do the very same thing lots of times over the years. How did you get in by the way? I thought it was family only."

"I told them I was his brother."

Laura guffawed. "And they bought that, you two look nothing alike."

"Yeah, I know. I don't really think they bought it, but they know the story. Big news in Chicago, even with the daily slaughter. Besides, no one wants to see an Irishman lose his temper in public."

Her eyes teared up a bit. "Josh, I am so glad you are here. He is closer to you than to his own brothers."

"Thus, my guilt. He wouldn't be here if it were not for me." Josh looked down at the bed. "Is he better?"

"Much. He still sleeps quite a bit, but the doctors are now hopeful. It was close. Turns out a nurse was there, did the right things until help could arrive. But they could not save that poor girl."

"Yes, I know." Josh could not say more as his voice caught.

Laura sighed. "That is what he will need you for as he recovers. He will be wracked with guilt. He has asked about her, but they have put him off. He knows, I am sure. Maybe you can . . ."

"Of course."

"Oh, you should know that rich woman, Katerina, and her mother are in the waiting room."

Josh didn't register for a moment. "Oh, you mean Kat. I never hear anyone use her formal name. I'll go find them in a bit. I want to speak to this lug first when he wakes."

There was a rustling sound from the bed, Laura and Josh turned in Peter's direction. "I'm awake. Guy can't get any rest around this joint with all this racket." He opened his eyes a crack. "Oh damn."

"What's wrong, buddy?" Josh leaned toward him. "Are you in pain?"

"You bet."

"Where?" Josh asked with genuine concern.

"Well," Peter managed to get out with some effort, "I've got this huge pain in the ass leaning over my bed. But at least I know I'm not dead since this isn't heaven."

"Don't follow." Josh smiled.

"You always were slow for a Mick. No way you would ever be found in heaven. So, if you're here then I'm not there."

"True enough, true enough."

Peter shut his eyes tight. "Jules is dead. I screwed up."

"Well," Josh stammered, looking for the right words.

"Don't fuck with me, I'm not an idiot."

"Sorry, they couldn't save her but, damnit, you didn't fail."

"If she had only listened. If she had only listened." Tears formed in his eyes. "Tell Chris I did my best."

"He knows."

Peter's eyes closed. "I think I'll nap a bit. You go see the others, Josh, and take Laura with you. She's driving herself to distraction, probably frantic that she can't find my life insurance policy."

"Oh," Laura exhaled. "You are such an insufferable man."

Josh laughed and took Laura's arm, leading her from the room. As they exited the door, Josh looked back. "You must be the only Wop I know with a sense of humor."

The words "fuck you" drifted back to him as Laura whispered, "Thank you for coming, Josh. You are the world to him."

Moments later, they found Kat sitting in a waiting room. Several unknown men sat around and nodded as he entered. Josh recognized some as Peter's associates from the agency. Kat ended a call as they entered. "How is he?"

"Well, he swore at me as I left the room moments ago so, I would guess, much better," Josh deadpanned.

Kat smiled. "I can see why you two are best friends, yet another mystery is explained to me."

"Which is?"

"Why you and my brother have become so close so fast. He's charming but not easy to get to and you've done it."

"And the explanation?" Josh was curious.

"Oh, simple, really. You both are twisted beyond recognition."

Mary Kelly spoke up, "I am so glad Mr. Favulli is recovering. After losing Richard and Julianna, and what almost happened to Azita, I could not bear more loss. I'm not young anymore."

Josh sat down next to Mary. "You do know that Chris and Kay wanted to be here in the worst way. They loved Jules, as you did. But Chris felt he had to fly to Afghanistan, wants to bring his first grandchild back. He was torn with worry about his daughters and Kay stayed behind with all the threats to his staff. As this election approaches, it's as if the world is falling apart."

Mary Kelly looked at Josh with clear eyes. "My children do not have to be here to demonstrate their love. I know where their heart is. I know as only a mother can. I had many shortcomings as a mother in their early years, but the dear Lord somehow gave me a second chance with them. They are my life."

"And your legacy," Josh murmured and wondered to himself if his words were overly insipid.

"Ah, you are a charmer like my Christopher. You are good for my son as was Richard and Julianna. They became my children as well. Now I have lost my eldest boy, his wife, and my daughter-in-law, and those two precious jewels. A parent is never supposed to bury her children, even those simply embraced with her heart."

Josh smiled. "Mary, you have a pure Celtic heart. People say the Irish are cold, but no one loves as we do."

"You are a wise man." Mary's eyes looked distant, as if she were thinking about some impossible conundrum. "Look after my children still with us, will you promise me that." Before Josh could respond, she rose and walked to the door.

"Mother," Kat called out, "where are you going?"

"Just to the rest room, my dear. I hope an old lady has your permission to answer a call of nature." Mary gave Kat a stern look as her daughter rolled her eyes with exasperation.

* * *

Later, Mary Kelly peaked out of the restroom. As she suspected, a man sat nearby whom she recognized as someone Kat sent to keep an eye on her. It was like being a prisoner. She breathed a sigh of relief when he answered his phone and turned away. She slipped out the door and quickly walked in the opposite direction, surprising herself at how well she could yet move when motivated. By the time her absence was noticed, and an alarm raised, she was in a taxi headed for the bakery where she hoped her estranged husband would be on this Sunday morning.

"Driver, park here." She looked at the front of the store. There were still a couple of tables and some chairs out front but not as many as were there during the peak summer months. Her heart sank as they were all empty. As she waited in the cab, trying to decide what to do next, there was some commotion at the front door, several customers exited including a tall, distinguished gentleman dressed in an expensive suit as if he was going to a Fortune 500 board meeting. Even with his mask, there was no mistaking his identity. Mary smiled, paid the driver, and got out. She knew that there would be no further need for his services.

She walked directly toward Charles Senior as he sat in an available chair and took a big bite out of his bulkie. It was his ritual and rituals were not to be ignored. They gave a sense of structure, even permanence, to lives often dominated by the ephemeral. He stopped mid chew, looked at the approaching woman as his bodyguards shifted to attention. But with a wave of his arm, he indicated that they could relax as he gained control of his momentary irritation. He refused to reveal such a human emotion to this woman. He managed to twist his face into a visage of disingenuous interest. "How nice of you to join me, Mary. I'm a bit surprised, though, with all the . . . unpleasantness going on in the city these days."

Mary stared at him. “I must say, you hid it well, Charles.”

“Hid what, my dear?”

“The fact that you have no soul, when you courted me all those decades ago, well courted my money at least. You went to mass with me every Sunday, prayed as I did, and said all the right things. I never saw inside you. You did have a gift, I must say. I thought I was rather good at reading people. All those other suitors I ignored for you. Most of them probably cared for me and I picked the one that only cared for my riches. How blind of me.”

Charles smiled with ingratiating insouciance. “You realize, I hope, that you were never much of a bargain for me. You proved way too independent and had all this sentimental empathy for others. Where did that come from? So useless, so useless. We could have been a great team, but you believed all that religious crap about compassion and forgiveness. That was not your worst crime, though.”

“Enlighten me on my faults, Charles. I am fascinated.”

“Simple. You turned my children against me. Now, that was unforgivable.”

Mary gave out a big, humorless laugh. “I did not do that. You still don’t get it, do you? You did that all on your own. I only wish I could take the credit. I was a drunk when they figured out what you were. You never had a chance.”

“Well, my dear, all will be decided very soon, won’t it . . . the fate of my children, of the country, of the world.”

“Still smug, aren’t you, Charles? You have never lost that arrogance, what I once thought was drive and ambition. Now I see it for what it is—narcissism and self-delusion. You are the mirror image of your hero Trump."

"He is a fool. I am far superior to him. No matter what happens to him on election day, we will prevail."

"And right there is proof of your arrogance," Mary announced triumphantly. "That evil man also believes he is God and thus blessed with omnipotence."

Charles issued a laugh that emerged as a cackle. "Oh, Mary, I forgot how clever you could be. You were cleverer than the other girls and, of course, richer. However, my dear, do not be lulled into confidence by Trump's recent struggles. No way will our future be decided by the people. Democracy is so quaint, such a dated concept. But you will see soon enough. Everyone will see. My regret is that my children might not be there to see it." His face eased into a fixed grimace.

Mary stood still. If she had any doubts, they were erased. He was moving in on her children, starting from the outside and inexorably moving closer to what he saw as the heart of his problem, the issues of his own seed. "Well, Charles, my guess is that they will see your candidate fail, your cause fail, and you fail."

Charles cackled one more time. "I would not bet on that, my dear."

Mary repositioned her handbag so that she might open it. "Answer me one thing, Charles."

"Of course my dear." He seemed to be enjoying their verbal duel.

"Did you go after Richard and Julianna Jackson just because they were the wrong color, was that why they had to die."

The smile faded from his expression but only by a fraction. "Please Mary, I never."

"Don't lie to me, Charles. At long last, don't lie to me." She opened her handbag. "By the way, I have a gift for you."

"A gift, Mary? How decent of you." His eyes, however, narrowed imperceptibly.

"Of course. Have you forgotten my promise already, the one I made at our last meeting?" Mary looked at his ingratiating smile for another moment. Then she reached into her bag and pulled out a small, silver handgun. It looked so fancy that onlookers might have confused it with an ornamental gift of some sort. The bodyguards did not react immediately, they had relaxed assuming the old woman harmless. The moment unfolding before them proved a total surprise.

"Mary, what?" For the first time, Charles registered what was about to happen.

"Yes, Charles, a one-way ticket to hell, reserved especially for you." With those words, she fired one shot directly into her husband's forehead. Charles looked surprised. That puzzled Mary. She had been fully transparent about her expressed intentions if he ever harmed another of her loved ones. Unfortunately, for him, he never, not for a moment, believed her threats. *For once in your life, you should have taken me seriously, you poor fool.*

Charles opened his mouth as if to say something. Nothing emerged, though. He staggered one way then another. Then sounds did materialize. "Not done yet . . . Barbarossa," these words came out with a kind of strangled desperation. "Barbarossa!" Then nothing more as his lips continued to move.

Mary noticed little blood was issuing forth from the rather insignificant-looking wound in the center of his forehead. She wondered if the one shot would be enough. Should she fire another? Though intending to do so, her trigger finger was frozen. After what seemed like an eternity, Charles reached weakly in her direction before slumping to the ground. That look of shock remained on his face. His eyes were open, lifeless, looking up at the blue sky. *You are looking in the wrong direction, my dear, you are headed to that other place,* she whispered to herself.

"Son of a bitch," one of the men who had been guarding Charles uttered in surprise.

She put her gun back in her purse and looked at the two men who were now aiming large handguns at her. "Well, aren't you going to earn your keep for today? Shoot me."

They looked at one another and then down at their boss. One bent over to take his pulse. "Gone," was all he said to the other man who seemed to be in charge.

"I had to do it, you know. Otherwise my son would have felt obligated and taking a life would have left him too scarred. He is so sensitive, and I could not have that on my conscience." Mary then spoke with considerable insistence, "Just shoot. Get it over with so you can make your escape. I prefer that over prison."

To her surprise, the man whom Mary took to be the leader looked more uncertain than anything else. Mary thought she could see his finger tighten on the trigger. Odd how one's perceptions are heightened in moments of intensity. Then, his finger appeared to pause, and he lowered his weapon. "Shit, I'm not risking anything for this sack of shit." With that, he sat down and picked up the half-eaten bulkie. "These always looked good to me, but the bastard never offered one to us." With that, he began to munch on the Polish delicacy. Looking at Mary with casual disinterest, he said, "Would you join me? These are surprisingly good."

"No, thank you," Mary responded while collecting herself.

The man paused from his breakfast. "By the way, do you know what *Barbarossa* means?"

Mary looked at him impassively. "I have absolutely no idea. Do you?"

"Not a fucking clue." The man took another bite.

She had wondered what she might feel at this moment but was surprised when she felt nothing . . . perhaps a sense of finality. How odd that she should feel so tranquil right after committing a mortal sin. She had intended to say a perfect act of contrition right away, to demonstrate her contrition to God before she herself died, though she doubted God could be so easily fooled. The first line, however, had escaped her. Now she would have to request a priest for confession after they put her in jail, perhaps the Cardinal. She never noticed when one of the men guarding her husband deftly placed a weapon in the right hand of Charles. Mary now heard sirens. Feeling weak suddenly, she primly sat to wait for the authorities. Of course, there are sirens in the windy city all the time. Maybe she would have to wait her turn to be arrested.

* * *

At the hospital, Kat was frantic, having now convinced herself that her mother had somehow been kidnapped. Her thoughts were dominated by a fear that Charles had struck again, even as breaking news announced that an eminent Chicago heiress was missing.

"Mother, where are you?" Kat asked of no one.

"Any thought on where she might have gone?" a burly Chicago detective asked.

For once, her incisive mind went blank. "Look for my goddamn father, her husband," was all she could say.

As her frustration continued to mount, Josh walked up and put an arm around her shoulder. "Take a deep breath. I know where she is."

"What, where?" She shouted.

Rather than answer, he showed her his phone. It read *Breaking News: Heiress slays estranged husband on Chicago Street.* Josh held her tight as Kat's legs went limp, helping her to a nearby chair. She buried her head in Josh's neck as she sobbed, repeating *oh mother* over and over.

CHAPTER 29

DECISION DAY APPROACHES

Early November seldom provides memorable weather in England. As Chris, Kay, and Josh began a leisurely walk from Baliol College, cutting through the green space adjacent to Trinity College and around the Bodleian Library, they noticed the steel grey sky and wondered if they should have brought umbrellas. Their route would eventually take them close to Brasenose College before they would find the thoroughfare that would take them to the Hairy Hare.

Kay broke their initial silence. "Darn, I would have thought that the public health people would have shut down that place by now. I keep hoping."

"You mean The Hare?" Chris feigned shock.

"No, I mean Baliol College."

"Hah, hah! No way, The Hare is a venerated institution, almost as revered as some of these decrepit institutions we are walking past at this very moment."

"Right," Kay responded in her best sarcastic tone. "However, it is nice to have everyone back. This whole thing has been a nightmare. I keep thinking I'll awake and find it is all a dream. That happened to me the other night, sort of. I was having a terrible dream and realized what it was. I forced myself awake to escape the nightmare. I immediately realized that reality was worse and tried to get back to sleep. That sucked."

"The worst is almost over." Josh ventured. "We just have that nasty election to endure. I cannot believe it is finally here. I would get these money appeals starting with something like *'only forty more days to the election so send us all your money.'* My reaction . . . still another freaking forty days. That is an eternity. This election has been going on since I made it to puberty. The more I think on it, if the founding fathers had realized how screwed up their system would become, they would have chosen a parliamentary form of governance. More efficient and far less torturous. The winning side gets to pick the PM. And when the winners can't govern, they can announce an election and it is over in five weeks. How sane is that?"

"Ever think how odd things have turned out?" Chris murmured distractedly.

Kay smiled knowingly. "Now, Josh, you listen up. You must realize that when my brother says something like that, it is a sign that he's having a fascinating dialogue inside his head, fascinating to him that is. If you stay with us, you will need to remind him that he is with other people when you see this happening. Not that you need to listen to his nonsense, but it keeps him going. He gets cranky when ignored, like most children."

Chris feigned a wounded look. "I remember when my sister had no sense of humor, that was just yesterday in fact. Now she has fooled herself into thinking she is as witty as me. By the way, what I was thinking is fascinating. The founding fathers probably rejected a parliamentary system since it was tainted with the monarchy at the time. Couldn't have that, no way. In their frantic search for checks and balances they instituted an independently elected President which, in other systems, is largely a ceremonial head of state. Here, the queen serves that function. In any case, our wise founders had their doubts about the office but felt they needed a chief executive with limited powers. Nothing that could become a king. But over time, the damn position has assumed almost monarchical powers, something that those guys in Philadelphia would have hated. And that is exactly what this American election is all about. Will we take the final steps to an authoritarian presidency? Trump and the Republicans have wet dreams over that prospect."

They walked some more as Chris's observation was digested. Then Kay spoke, "Damn, I hate to admit this in public, and I will deny it if either of you clowns repeat it, but my brother does sound smart. He had me fooled as a kid on that until I saw his report cards. I always beat his ass in the classroom, that was my first clue that his so-called brilliance was all smoke and mirrors."

Josh issued a brief guffaw. "Sorry, my recorder is going." Then his visage went serious. "You two squabble all the time but let me say something. What the two of you have is precious, irreplaceable. Never forget that."

"I suppose, Josh." Kay said quietly. "No need to remind me of that."

"No indeed," Chris sensed the mood and sought a different trajectory, "because I remind my sister of how lucky she is to have me every single day."

They all chuckled as Josh said almost to himself. "Hmm, I wonder if Rachel thought I was smart."

"Believe me, Josh, your sister and I had many woman-to-woman talks before the tragedy. We often shared the burden's we bore in being stuck with such loser brothers. Despite all, she loved and respected you more than you can ever imagine. And that you can record."

"Thank you," he responded. "Did you think of Ricky as a brother?"

"Absolutely." Chris and Kay said simultaneously, and then smiled wanly at one another.

Chris continued, "I came to think of Jules as a sister, which wasn't easy given our early history."

"Pervert," Kay muttered with a smile.

"Hey, I admitted it wasn't easy. I think Jules and I both were uneasy about following through on Amar's last request. I fear we had become too close to be lovers anymore. I'm not sure what we would have done if . . ." He could not finish. "Hell, they were like family to me . . . Jules and Ricky. I'm relieved their folks are gone. I could not have born the guilt of telling them I killed their children. Sometimes the cost of all this is unbearable."

"No one is listening to your guilt trips anymore." Kay put an arm through her brother's and pulled him a little closer, leaning up to peck his cheek. "I keep thinking you are a jerk and then you do something to show that you are human, with real feelings and all."

Chris leaned over and kissed the top of her head. "Thanks, but I never make that mistake with you." All three laughed in the moment. "By the way, Josh, what's the latest with Peter?"

"Peter is well on his recovery at home. I can tell that all is back to normal since I could hear Laura yelling at him in the background. She wanted Peter to tell me that he was nothing more than a royal pain in the butt, and that she wanted to ship him back to the hospital or, even better, back to England. Now, there is a successful marriage . . . really!"

"Chris," Kay suddenly said with seriousness, "I have a warning for you."

"What?" He could not tell if she was serious. "I thought we were relatively safe now with Father dead, at least here in England."

"This is far more serious than any threat of death, more painful for you, at least."

"What, damn it!"

Kay could not suppress a smile. "Here it is . . . Zita and Deena are plotting to hook you up with Ali. Mark my words, when we get to The Hare, there will be an empty chair for you next to her."

"Oh my god." He rolled his eyes. "Is she in on it?"

"Heaven's no. That woman is sensible and has standards. They know she would flat out reject you."

"Not after I share my news." Chris smiled. "Then I'll look like a total stud."

"What news?" Kay looked at her brother suspiciously. "Usually, that kind of suggestive statement is merely a prelude to some joke of his, something only he finds funny. You know, something about how women can't keep their hands off him. Now, that is fall-down hilarious."

"This is deadly serious and will force you to be nice to me for a change."

"There is no such news." Kay issued with confidence.

"Just listen. Kat told me she has been made privy to Father's will. You won't believe it, but that idiot never changed it. For sure, I thought Father would have left all his treasure to his right-wing causes. Apparently, he thought he had plenty of time left. He never gave up on me becoming his heir apparent until recently, perhaps after our last session at Oak Beach. He surely would have gotten to disinheriting me right after the election or when he had finished his coup for taking over the country. On the other hand, he likely thought I'd be dead by then so disinheriting me would be moot."

Kay laughed. "Oh, sweet karma. Did he leave all to you, that primogeniture thing? Guess I'll have to get used to kissing your derriere now."

"Bet your sweet bippy you will, but a mere curtsy will suffice. I don't want you anywhere near my derriere." Chris was smiling at the thought. "Now do you want to repeat that admission of how brilliant I am for the record?"

"I didn't . . ." Kay managed but finished her thought by giving her brother the finger.

"I'll take that as a yes." Chris smirked. "Now, there were provisions to some of his causes but basically the bulk is to be distributed as follows. Some 10 percent each to you and Kat, nothing for Mother whom he always thought wealthy in her own right, and the remainder to his favorite surviving son . . . that's me if you are confused. This must be an old document since it is still written as if the bulk would go to Chuck with me next if he was deceased. How long has he been gone now, at least two decades?"

"That would make you a billionaire. Who woulda thunk?" Kay gave her brother a sarcastic curtsy.

"Not really. Well, on paper yes, but I told Kat to work out something that shifted everything into the family foundation. Zita and Deena won't have to scrimp on expenses going forward, that's for sure, nor will Karen have to watch her budget so closely. And we'll have plenty to work with as we try to alter the political landscape. However, in the short term, don't tell Ali about my giving this fortune away. I want her to think she's missing out on a king's ransom by rejecting me flat out."

"This is delicious. Father's fortune going to the work he so despised and to providing opportunity to the very people he saw as subhuman." Kay skipped a couple of steps in her excitement. "And throw my share in the pot. Jamie and I won't need it."

"Jamie and you?" Chris expressed surprise though knowing the answer.

"Don't act dumb, you nimrod. You know very well that we're getting back together."

Chis assumed his smug posture. "Of course I do. But I want an admission from you that you were an idiot to leave him in the first place, just so Josh can have it on that recording he's making."

"Asshole," Kay smiled. "Josh, I take back everything nice I said about siblings."

* * *

As they entered The Hairy Hare, Chris looked hard at the well-proportioned barmaid. "Damn," he said to no one in particular, "I think that's the original barmaid's granddaughter. I have been coming here too long."

As they entered their private back room, Chris smiled as Deena steered him to a seat next to Ali. He did not resist, though he leaned over to his colleague as soon as Deena was out of earshot. "You do know that there is a plot afoot to pair us up?"

"I do," she responded in a low voice, "those two co-conspirators think I must be unhappy as a spinster or that I've been pining away for you at night."

"You have, haven't you?"

Ali guffawed as she noticed Azita and Deena looking at her with interest. She whispered to Chris. "They are convinced that you are helpless and that you need a woman to survive."

"You nailed it," Chris replied in an equally low voice. "They know me for sure but why stick you with that onerous task?"

He expected her to deny their hypothesis, but she merely smiled in return which caused Chris to blush. Instead, Karen Fisher's loud voice brought the murmur to a halt. "Chris, you've been in touch with Chicago and Josh has been there helping his childhood friend recover. What's the latest from the other side of the pond?"

Chris began. "The best news is that Mother is completely cleared. No charges are pending. Self-defense apparently. Also, Father's plots began to unravel when that thug Peter shot survived and spilled the beans to get a lighter sentence for gunning down Jules in the middle of the day."

Josh looked puzzled. "Really, what kind of planning was that? So not subtle, way too obvious. I think your father was losing it at that point, or he figured he would be immune from any prosecution after the election. Trump would pardon all those supporting his takeover."

"We'll know soon enough if we still have a democracy and the rule of law. Tomorrow is decision day." Kay's words caused a short pause.

Then Chris continued. "What shocked me is that the guys providing security for Father flipped on him in several ways. They slipped a gun into his hand and told police he threatened Mother with it. Turns out they hated him as well."

"The police bought that?" Carlotta asked.

"Not really. Other witnesses gave conflicting accounts. But they wanted to wrap this up, and charging a rich, matronly woman for putting an end to his miserable life didn't seem like a winner to the cops. Besides, the authorities were coming around to agreeing that Father was dirty, likely a serial killer, so this was some rough justice in the end."

Josh spoke up, "Some of you know that there were two people working for Charles Senior who disappeared shortly before, what do we call it, the incident. They were feeding Peter information and he was frantic that he had gotten them killed. He had lost at least one CI like that while with the agency."

"Much as we have always suspected Father did to my sister-in-law, Beverly," Kay said mostly to herself.

"Happy ending in this case, however. We tracked the woman down to her home in Guatemala. She surmised that Father had guessed her role and had fled in fear . . . from one frying pan into another. It was in her best interests to get out of that troubled country as well, so we are bringing her here. And my father's driver was just laying low, also fearing Father's wrath. Kat is offering him a good job in the family company. Thankfully, the innocent escaped."

Glasses were raised in a toast.

"And the election, is Trump toast?" Cate asked.

"If you believe the polls but I can't forget 2016." Chris seemed glum. "Nor is it clear whether Trump and his followers will follow the rules of a democracy."

No one else responded immediately until Josh started in a thoughtful manner. "I haven't lived in the States since I was some twenty years old. That's a long time. As all of you know by now, I escaped during another era of crisis. The 1960s went from a time of great hope, Camelot, to great despair. The Vietnam War tore us apart, our cities were ravaged by riots, there were acts of domestic terrorism almost weekly. It looked and felt as if things were falling apart. On a cold and snowy November evening, when I tried to decide whether to stay or go, I was thinking mostly about myself. But I was also looking at the collective future of what then was my country and I was equally as confused. Part of me said that nothing would change. You must remember that racial discrimination had remained a dominant feature of American life since the inception of the Republic. It was there at our founding, we fought a savage civil war over it that cost 600,000 lives, and we still had the remnants of racial apartheid in the 1960s. Was there any freaking reason to believe we would, as a society, ever change?" He paused and looked around the table. They were listening. "But now I wonder sometimes, if people like me had stayed, perhaps things could have changed as we came into power. History is not destiny, nor is character fixed. We can make things better if we have the courage of conviction . . ."

"Do you still believe that?" Meena asked.

"For most of my adult life, no. My moments of early optimism were illusory, and I never regretted my decision to emigrate. I thank god I'm a Canadian citizen."

Chris spoke. "I have to ask. If you were a young man now, would you leave the country? Assume you cannot know the outcome of the election, or whether the Trumpsters can somehow retain control by legal or illegal means. Given that ignorance, would you stay and fight or leave?"

Josh smiled. "I'm reminded of a moral test the Harvard scholar John Rawls suggested. Everyone should choose their moral compass, and make their life decisions, based on not knowing where chance would situate them. What would you choose if you didn't already know your place?"

"Clever," Chris said, "but evasive."

Josh looked at Chris. "I think, I think I might do what I did that last time."

"Leave?" Chris wanted to make sure he understood.

"Not that. Once again I would flip a coin to decide."

"So," Karen announced in a way that commanded attention, "have you two cowards stopped running?"

Chris and Josh looked at one another before the former responded, "I'm guessing we have, figuratively at least. By that I mean I'm not going to look at the world out there as something over which to despair but as an opportunity to make things better. We can look at the 40 percent or whatever it is, that apparently adore the most corrupt, incompetent, and evil man to be elected to high office and decide to abandon America because it has so many losers. That is so very tempting, by the way."

"No shit," Cate exclaimed, "yet I expect a but is coming."

Chris spoke as Josh appeared to be thinking intently. "I keep thinking of Zita and Deena here. They never backed down, no matter what and now look at what they are accomplishing."

"Not so much yet," Deena said quietly, "but just wait."

Few noticed as Ali reached to place her hand on Chris's. He leaned closer to her to whisper, *I have news to share about my Father's will that will make even me look good.*

Chris did not pull his hand away as Ali whispered in return, *you might not need that much help.*

No one noticed the exchange as Josh spoke up. "Perhaps I've been wrong my whole life. Zita and Deena got it!"

"Got what?" Deena asked.

"No need for any damn coin flips this time around. No matter how the American election turns out, we all need to stay and fight. There is a world to save, a future for which the struggle is worth it. Even Charles Senior got that right. It has always been about the future and evolution. But now we are not talking about growing a new appendage to give us a better shot at survival. We are talking about which ideas will prevail, which vision of the good life and which perspectives on human relations can advance us. Yes, that is it. It always has been."

As the crowd digested Josh's words, Chris cleared his throat as a way of commanding attention. "I want to assure all that no speech is coming. I would need a couple more tankards of Guinness before doing that. But I want to say that Josh is spot-on. Well, perhaps I'll add a point or two."

A groan went up. "Oh, no, a damn speech is coming." Kay lowered her head.

Chris continued undaunted, "Despite my sister's obvious eagerness to hear more wisdom from me, just a simple and quick point. It might not be apparent but all we have done has had a future orientation. That is something we can build on. The service delivery models we develop, the political arguments we formulate, the educational opportunities we develop are all about the next generation. And think about that. What gives us a sliver of hope is that the youth of America, and elsewhere, are not like their parents. Race is not a big divider among them, like it was for us. They see government more as a positive thing. From now on, all that we do should focus on the future, on having an intergenerational impact. So much is about timing and this may be the time."

"Yes!" Azita blurted out and then looked embarrassed.

"And second," Chris quickly added, "when we were young, the major existential threat was a visible enemy, the Communists. That was an us-versus-them scenario and served to cloud over a lot of our internal issues. We could not focus on our own sins if we were obsessed with preserving that flawed system against something much worse. I sense a difference now."

"How so?" Cate asked.

"I can answer that," Deena interrupted. "Just think. Climate change and global pandemics are universal threats, at least on our planet. Kids today see that collaboration, not competition, is the basis for survival going forward. I'm convinced of that. And that has always been the central question, hasn't it? I can remember talking about this with Madeena, our mother, when I finally responded to her efforts to educate me. More than once, she took my hand and looked me in the eyes. *Which vision is to dominate, a primal competition to see which tribe will dominate, or which SOB within each tribe will rule over the others? Will we always fight over how to divvy up the pie or will we choose cooperation and collaboration, a vision of working together, all of us, to thrive and advance.*"

"You were damn lucky," Karen spoke up. "All my mother said to me was that she would tan my backside if I went and got the preggies."

Deena laughed. "Azita and I were fortunate indeed though it took many years to get what those words meant. Sometimes

I kick myself for being so slow. However, I'm betting that kids today have a better sense of which path to follow. It won't take them as long to get it. They just need a bit of direction. After all, when our long-ago ancestors faced the mastodon, it was tribal cooperation that permitted survival."

"Perhaps we'll know more this week about where we are headed . . . with the American election, I mean." Kay offered.

Azita nodded thoughtfully before breaking the ensuing silence with a question. "Were those your two points or do you have another?"

"Oh, no," Karen groaned. "Why did you remind him."

"Thank you, my dear. I did almost forget something which would have been unfortunate since this involves you and Deena. While everyone around this table has taught me something, I'll just stick to what you two have taught me." He paused to collect a thought. "Basically, it is this—love isn't easy. I so loved you that there were times that I tried to keep you here in Oxford, away from potential harm. I confused love with selfishness. That was wrong of me. Keeping you locked up in this wonderful intellectual prison we call a university would have been the equivalent of ripping you away from your fate. That is like a death . . . like slaying one's soul. Can you forgive me?"

"There is nothing to forgive, nothing at all," Deena whispered but her voice caught, and she could say no more.

After a moment, Chris brightened. "Oh, I just thought of another point."

At that, a shower of pretzels descended upon him.

As the attack on Chris abated, Azita spoke as if talking mostly to herself. "Thank you all for bringing a bit of laughter to me. I need that today. Another woman I admire has been arrested, this time by the Saudi police. Her crime is what we do, advocating for Muslim women."

"Who?" Ali asked.

"Ms. Loujain Al-Hathloul, I read about in on the way over. There have been so may, Mena Mangale, and Gulalai Ismail, and Malala Yousafzai, and Nasrin Sotoudeh, and so many others. Do these men really think they can stop us?" Azita's words were more statement than question, spoken in a harsh tone. Then her face and her words softened. "Sometimes, when I get down or think of evil in the world, I recall the words of *the Mahatma* that mother shared with me not long before she passed. They bring me such comfort."

When I despair, I remember that all through history the way of truth and love have always won. There have been tyrants and murderers, and for a time, they can seem invincible, but in the end, they always fall. Think of it . . . always.

CHAPTER 30

HOPE

Cate Connelly and Meena Muhaison watched with pride as a young Afghan girl holding a bouquet of flowers walked down a cathedral aisle. She was preceding Professor Shahed "Ali" Al-Hussein and Doctor Kristen "Kay" Crawford. At the altar, two men waited for the women. Professor Christopher Crawford and Doctor Jamie Whitehead looked on with pride as the two women approached.

It was a special moment for Cate and Meena. It was the first public appearance of their newly adopted daughter, whom everyone at Toynbee Hall had agreed was a gifted child. She had been able to read and do numbers at three years of age. But her father had been killed in a tribal blood feud that had emigrated with the family from the land of her birth while her mother recently had succumbed to the ravages of the pandemic. Cate had been tutoring the prodigy when, rather impulsively one day, she asked the child if she might want to live with her and Meena. The return smile said it all.

It was just before Christmas. Everyone was gathered in an East End Anglican Church as Luke Geoghegan replaced his normal role as Warden of Toynbee Hall to assume his role as minister in the Church of England. He made sure that the double wedding ceremony contained sayings and sentiments drawn from each of the major faiths of the world.

Kat was embarrassed when tears ran down her cheeks as her brother said the words *I do* to Ali. More tears followed with a similar affirmation to Jamie moments later in their own affirmation of a love that had gone astray for a while. Karen looked on and smiled, knowing that this moment was right. Azita's heart burst with happiness as she cradled her new baby who eyes reminded her so much of Ahmad. Deena stood next to Ali as the maid of honor. Kat served the same role for her sister as Josh awaited next to Chris just in case, as the betting had predicted, he passed out during the ceremony. Karen had bet big that he would. Colonel Gupta, the now retired British officer who married Chris and Amar some two decades earlier in that remote military camp, returned to be Jamie's best man. All had come full circle.

Outside, snowflakes fell across London, gently placing a white blanket over the city. Inside, the warm ambiance of new beginnings and hope could be felt by all.

EPILOGUE

A few years later, Azita and Deena stood before a large group of Muslim girls who had been gathered from institutions of higher learning in the British Isles and elsewhere. Some were doing their studies on the continent, others in America. Chris had insisted on bringing them together so that they might share their experiences, participate in those intellectual opportunities that Oxford could provide, and bond over days of socializing and sightseeing. Chris thought it would also be a chance to visit one of the world's greatest universities and to get to know the England-based program staff on a more personal basis. For Chris, the prime purpose was to facilitate a form of bonding among the young women that could advantage them in the future. They had been selected from the less affluent families from across the Muslim world ranging from Indonesia to the Horn of Africa. This would be their network to rely upon in the future.

He hoped that, with enough of these events, they would begin to identify with each other rather than the provincial and artificial impositions imposed by national, religious, and cultural constraints. Mostly, he had let Shahed Al-Hussein and the Masoud sisters run this program as they saw fit as he continued to work on the intergenerational attitudes toward issues of global importance. He saw his role in this program as one limited to financing and occasionally opening doors at various educational institutions where doubts persisted about the credentials and abilities of these young women. Fortunately, the question of financing had become irrelevant when the full measure of his father's treasure fell into his hands. *Karma is great,* Chris thought.

He loved to tell reluctant university admissions officers the story of Azita when he first introduced her to an elite secondary school shortly after bringing her from the Panjshir Valley to England. The head of this august school was skeptical that this Muslim girl from nowhere who had, as far as he could see, no formal education, could ever compete in his school's rigorous curriculum. Chris suggested that he spend some time simply talking with the girl, perhaps that might change his opinion. The anticipated fifteen-minute conversation had stretched to almost an hour before Chris knocked on the door to see what was happening. Azita was at a blackboard correcting a mathematical puzzle which had stumped the headmaster. Azita was accepted on the spot. Chris savored that moment.

The timing of this gathering struck Chris as perfect. Professor Al-Hussein had just been elevated to the position of Don at St. John's College at Oxford. This had to be visible proof of what was possible. And that was what this program was all about—hope and opportunity. Had not Azita and Deena survived great odds, defied the Taliban, and even escaped death to pursue their dreams. Chris sometimes laughed at what he considered to be their stubbornness in the face of hostile and dangerous obstacles. He had conceived this idea of reaching out to neglected Muslim girls for the wrong reason, primarily to keep the two young women he so loved as his own children out of harm's way. He had intended to keep them within the university while others would recruit candidates for the program in the field. Then, Azita and Deena would work with the successful candidates in England once the recruits had been identified. But he soon found out the best laid plans of mice and men oft do go astray. They simply would not listen and wound up spending more time in places that, to say the least, seldom appreciated their vision of what emancipating Muslim girls meant. Confronting cultural norms can be a dangerous business.

The one fact he had never considered fully was that destiny, or whatever one wanted to call it, could not be denied. There is something within each of us that is special. The trick is to find it and then never let go. His greatest gifts to Azita and Deena were not in trying to protect them but in letting them find their own way. Once he realized his role, all became clear to him. He would let fate, or providence, or divine aspiration take care of the rest.

Chris suddenly realized that Deena had finished her introductory remarks and that Azita now was addressing these future Muslim female leaders, students of medicine, law, science, engineering, the humanities, and education. This was a vanguard from an untapped pool of talent too long shunned by the world. He fought back a tear as he struggled to focus on her words. He picked up her talk as she discussed the importance of mentors and role models. The young women in this room had an obligation to others, this would be their own legacy beyond any professional success they might enjoy. "My sister and I had several strong women in our lives. We had our biological mother, Madeena Masoud, who gave us life and taught us to love learning. We had our adoptive mother, Doctor Amar Singh, who inspired us with her wisdom and courage and sense of sacrifice. And we have our newest mentor, Professor Shahed Al-Hussein, who took a chance on this vision and turned it into the miracle it is today."

Azita turned and clapped to Ali who seemed embarrassed by the attention. "I did little but keep the two of you out of trouble from time to time." Those assembled laughed.

"There were other women, Doctor Kristen Crawford and Karen Fisher and Carlotta Ciganda and others whom we love dearly. There were even a couple of men I should credit, though that gender has few heroes in their midst." More appreciative chuckles. "My biological father, Doctor Pamir Masoud, was the kindest and most sensitive man I have ever known." Her voiced cracked a bit but she held it together. "And my adoptive father, Professor Christopher Crawford is the man from whom my sister and I learned the blessings of humor and the gift of compassion. And I should mention Professor Joshua Connelly, whom we recently lost. He had become a grandfatherly figure to all of us."

Chris now fully battled his emotions, but he managed to get out one of his humorous retorts. "Well, the bill for my contributions is in the mail."

"I am sure it is. And so is my payment in full." She smiled back at him.

"I know some of you better than others. I can recall several of you from a visit to the school in my family's home village several years ago. You were mere girls then, so anxious to pursue knowledge. Of course, I recall that day since it came so close to being my last . . . but no need to go into that. Now you are studying at such fine institutions as Durham, York, St Andrews in Scotland, Trinity in Dublin, and several in America. You are also here, where Deena and I were fortunate enough to study. Those of you from my original village have made the people there so proud. All of you, no matter where you come from, have . . ."

At that moment, the door opened with a bang and Sir Charles Howard, the Emeritus Don of Baliol College, entered with considerable urgency. Many years ago, he had green lighted this project and then defended it against jealous scholars always protective of their own interests. The elderly man walked directly toward Azita while summoning Deena and Ali to join him. Chris was puzzled, fully taken aback by his obvious intent to disrupt her talk which, Chris was rapidly coming to appreciate, was as smooth as any that he might give. When had she gotten so good at this? But more to the point, why was the Don being so rude?

"Ms. Masoud. Please forgive me. I have some urgent news that cannot wait. When they could not get in touch with any of you, they contacted me. I believe you, and your collaborators, should be informed before this is announced all over the world, which will happen in a few moments."

Azita looked flustered as Deena asked anxiously, "What? Something bad?"

"No, quite the contrary my dear," the man of eminence said in his baritone voice. He faced the audience and broke into a broad smile. "The world is about to hear that Doctor Azita Masoud, Professor Deena Masoud, along with University Don, Professor Shahed Al-Hussein, have just been awarded this year's Nobel Prize for Peace. This honor has been awarded, and I quote, *for their untiring work on behalf of Muslim women throughout the Mid-East, thus opening educational opportunities, and possibilities of achievements not previously available to them.* It goes on but the thing is . . . the three of you are Nobel Laureates." Now he beamed with full-out pleasure and pride. "I, for one, could not be prouder."

For a moment, there was silence. Then a few women in the audience realized what had just happened. They stood and began clapping. Then more and more joined in. In moments, a wave of shouting and applause swept through the auditorium as they surrounded the three women who responded with a mixture of astonishment, pride, and wonder. The acclaim soon became thunderous. Outside, bells began chiming across the Oxford University community.

Chris quietly slipped out the door. He did not want the world to see him crying unabashedly.

ABOUT THE AUTHOR

Thomas J. Corbett is emeritus senior scientist and a longtime affiliate of the Institute for Research on Poverty at the University of Wisconsin–Madison, where he served as associate and acting director for a decade before his retirement. He received a doctorate in social welfare from the University of Wisconsin and taught various social policy courses there for many years in the School of Social Work. During his long academic and policy career, he worked with governments at all levels including a stint in Washington, DC, where he helped develop President Clinton's welfare reform legislation. He has written scores of articles and reports on poverty, social policy, and human services issues and given hundreds of talks across the nation on these topics. In addition, Dr. Corbett has consulted with numerous local, state, and federal officials on various poverty, welfare, and human services issues both in the United States and Canada. Among many other things, he has testified before Congress, worked with the Wisconsin and other state legislatures on important social issues, and served on an expert panel for the National Academy of Sciences. His most recent fictional works include ***Casual Choices*** along with the first two volumes of a fictional trilogy: ***Palpable Passions*** and ***Ordinary Obsessions***. His sole-authored works include several non-fiction books: ***Confessions of a Clueless Rebel***, ***Confessions of a Wayward Academic***, and ***Confessions of an Accidental Scholar***. Earlier this year, he published a memoir of his Peace Corps group's service in India in the 1960s, titled ***It Seemed Like a Good Idea at the Time***. He has also co-authored several works and written too many book chapters to mention. His latest academic work, the 2nd edition of ***Evidence Based Policymaking*** was coauthored with Karen Bogenschneider has recently been released by Routledge Press. Now retired, the author resides in Madison, Wisconsin. You can find more information at www.booksbytomcorbett.com

CPSIA information can be obtained
at www.ICGtesting.com
Printed in the USA
BVHW080013300321
603653BV00001B/20

9 781948 000796